FROST BURN

By: K.T. Munson & Nichelle Rae

Cover art by Michal Krasnodebski.
Map art by White Noise Graphics.
Edited by Tanya Egan Gibson.

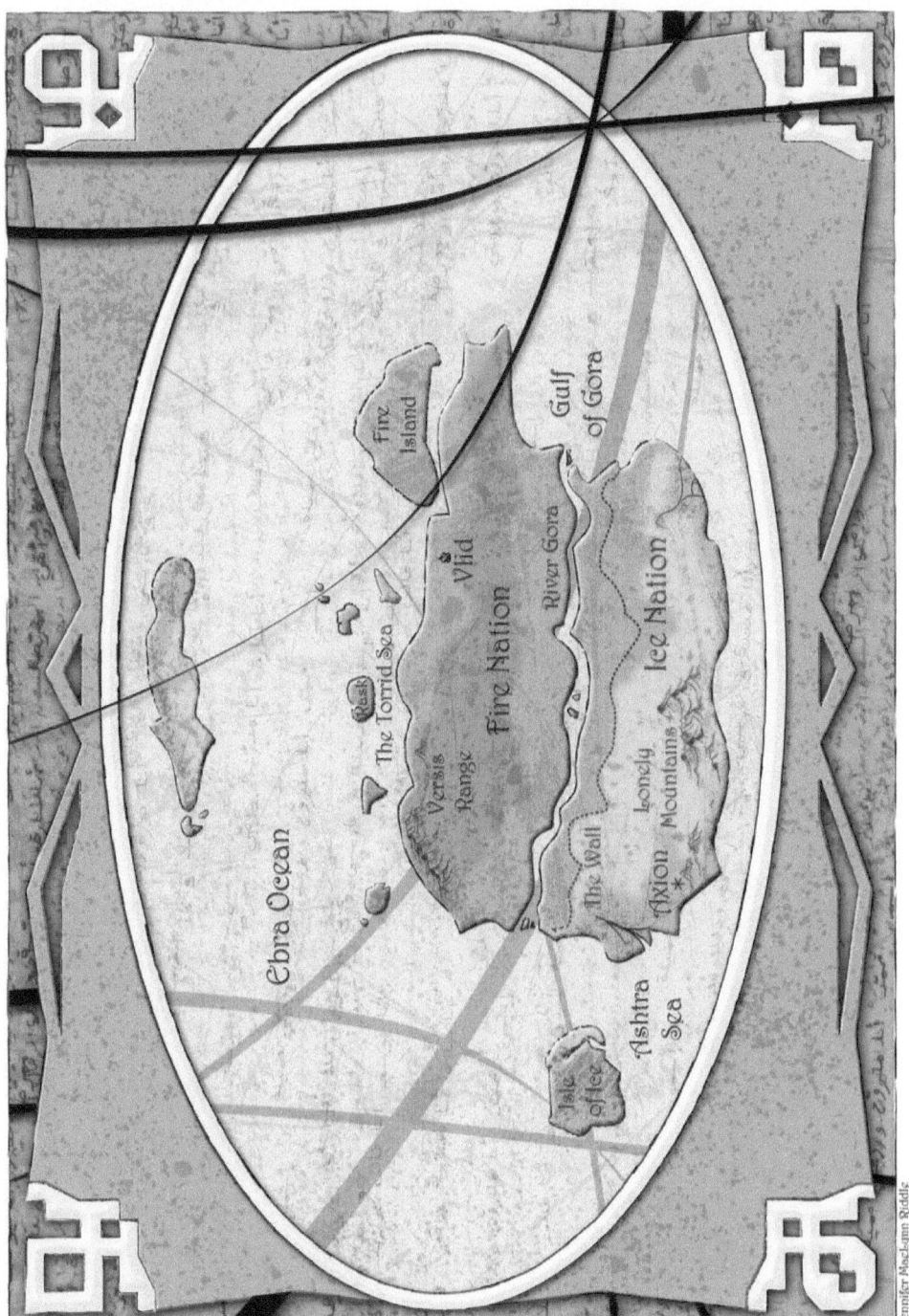

Fire Island

Gulf
of Gora

Vlid

Fire Nation

River Gora

Ice Nation

The Torrid Sea

Resk

Versis
Range

Lonely
Axion Mountains

The Wall

Ebra Ocean

Ashtra
Sea

Isle
of Hex

Part 1

"How do you fight a storm…" - Queen Darha

Frost: Chapter One

—————— o ——————

Aradel lurked across the edge of the lake with her weapon held tightly in her fist. Her quarries stalked her closely, but she was careful to stay well hidden behind the snowdrifts. She couldn't see them, but she knew they were there. The wind had been bad these last few weeks and provided perfect cover. Her bare feet made no sound on the snow keeping her movements secret.

The soft glow of the cloud-hidden sun made the ground shine even brighter. Without the snow, she imagined this place would look like a dead wasteland. The snow is what gave it life. The only time it appeared more beautiful was under the glow of the moon.

Glancing hastily over the top of a snowdrift, she saw nothing. Scanning the trees, she wondered if it was worth the risk. She finally slipped around the edge of the bank, her pale blue gown and simple short cape not restricting her movement as she took cover with her back against a neighboring tree. She peered around the side, but still saw no one watching her. Her dark blue eyes narrowed as she looked for any movement in the pale snow. Then something shifted.

Focusing on it, she lifted her arm, her weapon primed and ready. She saw the top of his hat, and crept carefully across the short clearing toward the lake. The rest would not be far from him, and if she struck him, they would likely flee. Aradel's anticipation grew as she rounded the snowdrift.

"Ah-ha!" Her inner child called out.

Her excitement turned into confusion when all she saw was a lonely hat without its owner.

"Now!" someone called.

She shrieked as snowballs pelted her from all directions. Hearty laughter filled the forest as she covered her head. Focusing on that deep laughter, she threw her snowball wildly in that direction. Kirill's laughter was quickly cut off and Aradel glanced up.

Snow fell off Kirill's face as he blinked in surprise.

She pointed at him. "Ha!"

"Get her!" he yelled, and the children stampeded toward her.

She yelped and skipped out of their reach, lifting her skirts as she went. Kirill laughed as the children hurried after her. She heard their feet

1

crunching in the hard snow, but their little legs couldn't keep up with her. Reaching the end of the lake, she turned to face them, and lifted her arms, letting her powers flow through her.

A wave of snow lifted, and the children screeched, falling over themselves in surprise. Aradel let the snow swirl until an army of snow creatures formed. The children watched, with their little mouths dropping open in wonder. Miniature polar bears, no bigger than her palm, suddenly marched forward. The children tripped over themselves to get up, all yelling at the same time.

"My army will defeat you!" she cried.

Kirill stepped onto the lake. "Your snow is no match for my ice!" he called back, and ice bubbles formed around all her little creatures.

Lifting her arms, the polar bears took to the sky, leaving their ice globes behind. The children gasped. The bears then began to dance, leaving little trails of snow behind them that rained down on the children. The children, awed at her creations, watched them overhead.

Finally, they cried one by one, "Aradel wins!"

"There, you see," Aradel called. Her face hurt from how much she was smiling. "They have named their victor."

"You were their favorite anyway," Kirill called back, his voice attempting to mock a hurt ego. "I could never have won."

She let her bears go and they dropped on top of the children, who howled with excitement. They rolled around in the snow left behind as she made her way around the ice bubbles. When she reached them, they jumped to their feet and pulled at her clothes, begging for more tricks. She laughed, patting them as she made her way to Kirill. He had his arms crossed and his nose in the air.

"It was very clever with the hat," she conceded. "You very nearly won this time."

"Next time you won't be so lucky!" he declared, still sounding aloof.

"Children, it is very nearly time to go back," Aradel announced. Hearing their groans of dissatisfaction, she added, "But before we do, I believe Kirill needs a hug!"

His expression of annoyance quickly turned to horror as he put an arm out, "Now wait a minute."

They all abandoned her and streaked right toward him. He took a startled step back just before fourteen little bodies toppled him over. Snow fluffed up around them and Aradel had to cover her mouth to keep from laughing out loud. If she laughed, Kirill would never let her hear the end of it.

He slowly disentangled himself from them, though they fought him fiercely. Aradel waited until he was nearly out before she called out, "Time to go!"

With sounds of protest, they slowly got off him and joined her. Kirill stood and dusted the snow off his clothes, shooting her a look that made it clear he didn't appreciate her little trick. She kept the smile from her lips until she turned away from him, and began leading the children back toward the palace.

When they reached the edge of the lake, Aradel gazed down the road. It was made of stone for ease of travel, but a continual layer of ice under it held it level and in place. Seeing something disconcerting, she put her arms out and stopped the children. A few of them peered around her skirts.

"What is it, Lady Aradel?" one girl asked.

"Kirill?" she called, having completely forgotten their fun.

"Yes, Lady Aradel?" he mocked with a snide grin. "Who are they?" she asked, trying to tuck the children completely behind her.

He followed her gaze and his grin vanished. "Outlanders," he said, as the people drew closer. "Take the children back."

She ignored him, wondering why so many of them were coming this way. Kirill stepped onto the road, drawing their attention. They appeared to be beaten and battered, exhausted to their very bones.

Aradel's eyebrows rose in surprise. She turned toward the children. "Come along," she said, hurrying them in a row down the road toward the palace. Thank the stars they weren't far from the castle.

"What is your business here?" she heard Kirill ask, his commander-of-the-guard voice kicking in.

Aradel peered over her shoulder at them. Kirill was blocking the strangers' way. Her eyes scanned their faces, and she gasped in shock and horror as her gaze fell on one. She pushed past Kirill toward the crowd which parted for her. The people likely recognized her necklace, which marked her as a member of the elite, those few chosen as possible successors to Queen Vesna.

She stopped before an old woman. When the woman lifted her head, Aradel could barely manage to keep herself from gasping again. Her entire cheek was covered in fractured skin, looking like ice after someone stomped on and cracked it.

Aradel touched the woman's face letting her powers fill the wound. The fractured skin mended, but it was likely that she would have that faded blue mark of healing for the rest of her life. Once it got into the skin, nothing could make it vanish.

"What happened?" Aradel whispered, and the old woman's eyes filled with tears.

"The spring," she said, her voice heavy with emotion. "The spring came early."

Aradel contemplated Kirill's expression, who had come forward, and he appeared to be as shocked as she was. She glanced behind at the children huddled together for comfort. The spring meant everyone had to go back behind The Wall, the magnificent, magical ice structure at the northern border of the Frost Nation. The Wall kept the warmth of the spring and summer out of their land and kept the frost people safe from danger of the heat. Beyond The Wall were the farmlands and it was harvest season. Something was wrong if the Outlanders would abandon their fields so early.

Aradel turned back to the old woman. "Where is Lord Drykus?"

"Dead," a man to her right said. "The heat was too great."

"He died so we could come to tell the Queen," another woman called out.

"An honorable man," a young man added.

Aradel wrapped her fingers around the old woman's hand and turned to the crowd. "The Queen must be told," she declared.

Fire: Chapter Two

o

Darha stood on a small grassy hill overlooking the white crests of the rushing river. They were miles past the edge of the banks where the water usually halted. She had long before pulled up the hood of her gray wool cloak, but it wasn't just because of the cold wind blowing; it was to hide her trembling. Her people couldn't see how distraught she was. If they knew, they would panic. Lucky for Queen Darha, her older brother Coor and sister-in-law Thea were holding it together as they executed their specific duties.

Coor was on the river's edge with the Derser Rects, the planetary religious sect of the Fire Nation, as they took samples of the ground, water, and even the air along the flooded river. Coor was overseeing them with calm diligence, which greatly comforted her. Darha glanced over to her left and saw Thea, who was overseeing the evacuations of the southern regions. Thea was already gazing her with deep concern. Darha couldn't hide anything from Thea. She was too perceptive, and knew Darha too well. They'd grown up together, after all. Seeing Thea, in her fitted black leather armor, with her red cloak flying in the wind, and the brown craggy rocks of the landscape rising behind her, Darha felt a little calmer. Coor and Thea were pictures of strength, strength the Queen did not have right now. Not in the face of this.

Darha's red gown and heavy cloak blew to the side, and the cold wind hit her legs in such a way that she instantly felt them go stiff. Her skin got so painfully hard that she clenched her teeth, but hid it as best she could. She would not let her people see her suffering.

Composing herself, Darha rotated her wrist to try to work the stiffness out of it, but she knew the attempt was futile. Being outdoors during a storm was a huge risk these days, since the storms were getting colder, and one was brewing now. Cold weather was dangerous, and possibly even fatal, to the people of the Fire Nation.

Observing the line of evacuees making their way out of the southern regions, she noticed the cold was making everyone a little stiff. Some were having trouble walking, and a few small children were being carried. Darha desperately wanted to use her fire to warm her skin, but if her people couldn't warm the stiffness out of their skin, she wasn't about to warm the stiffness out of her own. Most of them were not magic users.

Darha only had herself to blame for suffering in this cool weather anyway. Coor and Thea had tried to talk her out of coming for fear of her safety, and Darha had nearly let them, but she had wanted to see this for herself.

Now, she wished she'd stayed home.

An enormously loud hiss filled the valley. The Queen's head snapped to the right where the sound originated. A new pillar of steam rose up just a half a mile away. Rising floodwater of the River Gora had been cooling a few long-standing lava pools along the south and west coasts of the Fire Nation. Now, houses along the river were being flooded as well.

Darha looked back at the river and saw Coor coming up the hill toward her. With every step he took, she felt a little more strength. His armor was gold and red, colors that marked him as a General, and his cloak was black. His well-trimmed, honey blonde beard and moustache nearly concealed his frown and stiff upper lip, but Coor's emotions tended to travel up into his hazel eyes anyway. He was worried.

Darha gazed up at her brother desperately. "Do they know anything yet?"

Coor shook his head and rested his hand on her shoulder. "No, not yet."

"Do they have a clue?" she begged.

He rested his other hand on her shoulder as if to hold her together. "All we can do right now is get these people to safety, then head back to the palace and wait for the results."

Panic rose in her chest. She glanced away from Coor to hide it, but her brother knew her better than that. "Darha, you have to calm down. You can't let your people see you like this."

"I know. I know," she said, and then met his eyes again. "But I'm scared."

Coor nodded. "I know you are."

Darha shook her head. "How do you fight this?"

Coor sighed helplessly.

"How do you stop nature that's bent on killing your entire nation? How do you fight a storm, Coor?" she cried, giving into the panic for a moment.

"Hey, hey," Coor said, gripping her shoulders more firmly and lowering himself to her eye level. "We will figure it out."

"Coor! Darha!" Both turned in the direction of Thea's voice. She made her way up the grassy hill until she was in front of them. "The team that went to the East is returning."

All three of them headed down the hill to meet the approaching mounted scouts that were coming up along the edge of the river. Darha was in no shape to deal with this. If they were coming back this soon, the news was almost certainly going to be devastating.

The front man of the six-man team dismounted his horse and gave a bow to the Queen. "What of the Eastern Bridge?" Thea asked.

The look in his eyes told Darha all she needed to know. He shook his head sadly. "It's gone."

"Damn," Thea said softly, bowing her head.

Two bridges crossed the River Gora leading to the hostile Frost Nation to the south. The two nations had had bad blood between them for hundreds of years, but they needed the trade the Frost Nation offered—oil and wood to keep lamps and hearths lit, and livestock fences mended. In return, the Fire Nation provided them with the metal tools they needed for their livelihood. One of those bridges was now lost.

Darha's heart was racing because the scouts that had been sent to check on the Western Bridge hadn't returned yet. If that bridge was gone as well, both nations would slowly suffocate. That is, if they didn't flood first.

Thea faced Darha, and her heart clenched at seeing the sadness in Thea's usually strong, confidant eyes. "Your majesty, why don't you head back to the palace? There's nothing more you can do here, and it's getting stormy."

Darha couldn't deny she wanted to go home, but as all royalty had to consider, how would it be perceived if she left before the other scout team even returned? Would it be frowned upon by the public? Would they panic? Or would they accept the excuse that it was for or own safety?

"Coor, go with her," Thea said, taking the public opinion into consideration, too. If the prince left as well, the public would more readily understand that there was no need for the royal family to stay. "I'll wait for the western team and continue to oversee the evacuations."

Coor gave an appreciative nod and then leaned in and kissed his wife's lips. "Be safe."

Thea nodded and touched Darha's shoulder as Coor guided her toward the royal carriage. Darha followed with no complaint. She wanted to go home. She felt bad about wanting to go home, but she did.

She climbed into the carriage and leaned heavily against the interior wall, letting herself get lost in her own thoughts and fears. The fact that nature itself was on the offensive had had her losing sleep for months.

It started with the increase in volcanic eruptions on the north coast and the islands. Storm had increased as well. The Fire Nation usually only saw two to three hurricanes a year; this year they'd seen seven. The palace and the capital, Vlid, weren't as affected since they were located farther inland, but the people on the north, east, and west coastlines, which were mainly made up of farming families, had been devastated more than once this year. Food production was at its lowest since Darha's great-grandmother had reigned. Now, the River Gora had swelled inland four miles. Nature was in an unprecedented uproar, and it felt like her nation was unraveling at the seams.

Why did this have to happen during her reign? She could handle men, and the rebel antics of the magic haters just fine, but nature? How did you stop nature from killing you?

Frost: Chapter Three

———————— o ————————

As they walked along the main thoroughfare through town, Kirill watched Aradel closely. She was speaking with the elder woman whose face she had mended, and had also drawn a young girl to her side. The young girl's hand had a little crack on it that Aradel had done her best to heal. . Yet it shouldn't have been warm enough to crack skin, not for a few more months. If Aradel was worried about this, she hid it well—a talent she had had since she was a child.

As a member of the Frost Nation's army, it was his job to protect the queen and her potential successors, Aradel being one of them. Who would have thought the ragged little girl from the Dregs would become a candidate for queen?

He still remembered when she arrived at the winter palace. Her bright hair was dirty, and in ragged little braids. She had a timid but defiant expression on her face, and he had admired her even then. Now she was a sister to him, and the closest of his friends. Their differences in status and rank had been bridged years ago by her amazing magical gifts. Aradel had traded in her two braids for one very adult one. It was hard to think she had ever been a child because her bearing had always been the same.

The children around him held tight to his clothes where they could, fearful of what was taking place. Kirill felt strange without his armor, which he'd taken off for their outing. The citizens of Axion gazed at him and the injured and worn crowd of Outlanders. People peered out the windows of their stone homes, which had only curtains to keep the snow out, but allowed the cold in.

A few people called to Aradel, recognizing her as they would any of the other elite candidates. Most of the elite had taken up duties that the Frost Nation's aging Queen could no longer fulfill. Their Queendom had always been ruled by women, the strongest amongst them, to protect their great nation.

Kirill crossed his arms in annoyance as he watched Aradel mingle with the people, trying his best to feel less vulnerable without his armor. The children fanned out behind him like ducklings following their mother. He had to take care not to walk too quickly.

Aradel glanced back finally, her eyes taking in his expression, and the children's state, before continuing toward the palace. If they had been anywhere but in the middle of Axion, he surely would have frozen the end of her skirts to the ground as revenge for the amused smile on her face during their outing.

"Who are they?" one of the children whispered, tugging on his clothes and pointing to the crowd walking with Aradel ahead of him.

"Outlanders," he answered, looking down at the towheaded boy. "They live beyond The Wall for parts of the year."

"That's scary," a raven-haired girl said, tightening the hold she had on her friend.

"They get to see the world beyond The Wall," Kirill added, glancing around at their exhausted faces. "Normally it is safe for a few more months before the spring comes."

"Did the Fire Nation do it?" one of the girls asked, her little mouth open in fear.

"I thought the fracturing happened when it was hot outside," a boy cut in before Kirill could answer. Kirill didn't have an answer anyway, so he just continued forward, only half listening.

"It does," a black-haired boy with sharp features said matter-of-factly. "During the second war, the Fire Nation attacked using temperature against us. They warmed the area around our army and killed them slowly in their sleep. Only the strongest survived!"

The children peered at the Outlanders, many of whom did not have magic. Lord Drykus, a non-magic user, had likely died for the old woman and the girl. Kirill's eyes narrowed on the girl as Aradel said something to her. He could sense the magic in her since she had not learned to dampen her aura yet.

Another person called to Aradel, and he half wished it was any other day, because the streets would be far less crowded. They needed to get to the Queen. Today was the day of reverence, though, on which each family paid homage to the moon. They would make trips throughout the day to their Moon Temple, but then tomorrow work would start again. It was considered shameful to conduct business on Moonday.

When they finally reached the gates, which were open and hardly guarded, Aradel didn't even hesitate and marched straight up to them. The upper sections of the palace could only be accessed by creating a bridge of ice. Their enemies in the Fire Nation couldn't build ice bridges. Besides that, everything in the realm of the palace could protect itself by the Queen's will with snow and ice.

10

"Make arrangements for the citizens of Axion to take them in," Aradel commanded, as an army of servants met her at the palace. "These two shall remain under my protection," she added, indicating the elder woman and the child. The servants rushed off to obey. Aradel's word was one that would be followed.

One of the teachers hurried forward, worry etched across her face, until she spotted the children surrounding Kirill. Many of them hesitated to let him go with so many strangers around. He looked like an angry grizzly bear with a flock of ducklings on his back as he made his way through the crowd of Outlanders.

"Children!" she called, opening her arms. "We had better get you home."

They made their way around each side of him and through the crowd of people, gravitating to the woman's familiar face—all but one little girl, who stopped and stared up at him. Her blue eyes seemed unfazed by his frown. She smiled bashfully, admiring him in an awestruck sort of way. "I wanted you to win," she said before quickly turning and running off to join the rest of the children.

When he glanced up, Aradel was kneeling in front of the girl with the blue scars on her hand. The old woman was listening carefully as they spoke. When the little girl nodded, Aradel waved Kirill over. Uneasy about what was happening, he quickly moved to join her.

"The Queen is expecting us," she said when Kirill drew close enough.

He nodded, only giving the old woman and the girl a sparing glance before following Aradel into the palace. They walked up the steps to a great open area in which stood a forest made of ice. Kirill could see the two guests gape at it in wonder. Although the palace was open to everyone, few Outlanders ventured this far south. A moon butterfly flapped its wings softly as it settled on a bush. The girl paused a moment to gaze at it, and Kirill wondered if she had ever seen one at night when they gathered to drink from the moonbeams.

They reached the end of the courtyard where two guards opened the large double doors, allowing access to the Queen. One raised his eyebrow at Kirill's state of dress, but said nothing. He wouldn't dare or he would surely catch Kirill's wrath. Kirill grinned menacingly in his direction to reinforce that worry.

Up a short flight of steps was a throne of ice. It had sharp edges resembling inverted icicles at the back. Queen Vesna sat there now, expectantly. Her face betrayed her age and her exhaustion. She was still powerful, but she was old. In the coming years, another would take her place. Kirill contemplated the moon pearls draped around her throat as they glowed softly. The moon pearls acted as a crown, and enhanced the natural power of the Queen who wore them. A line of young women stood at the foot of the throne, all of them prospects to take Queen Vesna's place when the time came.

"Your Highness," Kirill, Aradel, and the two Outlanders said and all bowed to her.

"What brings you all from Lord Drykus's providence?" the Queen asked. She must have seen them coming from far off.

"Lord Drykus is dead," the old woman said. The girl tucked her chin to her own chest. "Spring has come early."

"A natural spring?" one of the candidates at the foot of the throne asked, her sharp features betraying her hatred for the Fire Nation.

"We cannot be sure," the old woman answered, but her face showed worry and doubt.

"Aradel, take our guests to the kitchen. They have had a hard journey," Queen Vesna declared. "The rest of you shall tend to the others as I consider what has happened, and the best course of action to take in the face of the early heat."

"As the Queen commands," they recited, Kirill's voice deep in comparison to the rest, and everyone went off as instructed.

"Not you, Kirill." The Queen stood from her throne as they dispersed, and came down the steps toward him.

"What do you command of me?" he asked, offering his arm to the aging Queen.

"Carrier Owls arrived this morning," Queen Vesna informed him, taking his arm. "Our traders to the north have sent word that Queen Darha was seen along the river bank. I need you to be my eyes, see what the purpose is in her being there."

"Do you worry they are behind this?" Kirill asked, his voice pitched low for fear of being overheard.

"I worry there will be war in my lifetime," Queen Vesna replied, her face filled with wisdom. "If I do not find the truth behind it, word of her presence will spread and poison already distrustful hearts due to the warmth in the Outlands."

"You don't think they are behind it?" Kirill asked, surprised. Even he wondered if the Fire Nation had a hand in this. Now he wondered further about Queen Darha's presence among the River Gora.

"I think if we are going to lose hundreds of our people to another war, I want to be sure," Queen Vesna said. "I will not allow blame to be placed, when it could just be a simple coincidence she's seen on the river bank in this heat. Go and find me proof." The Queen stopped and released his arm before turning down a hall.

He bowed. "As the Queen commands."

Fire: Chapter Four

Thea ran her long dark brown braid through her fist, pulling it over her shoulder as she gazed up at the graying sky with concern. Seeing the cloud movement and smelling the air, she realized this storm was moving quickly. It would be about thirteen minutes before the rain fell, and the last of the lower region evacuees were still an hour away from Vlid, where the safe houses were being prepared. They were going to need to use the leather tarps to stay safe in the rain.

"Lady Thea," someone called, getting her attention. A person branched out from the line of evacuees on the road, two more following, and came toward where she stood on the water's edge. Thea recognized the robes of the regional leaders. A decorative collar of woven elaborate gold designs encircled the front of the chest and neck before going over the shoulders and down the back of each red robe. Below the designs, the fronts of the robes were plain.

"Lord Guyus," Thea said, nodding. "Lady Orn. Lady Waik." They were the three regional leaders of the southern provinces that were being evacuated now. "I hope you had your people prepare tarps."

Lord Guyus nodded. "These days, we rarely overlook any precaution."

"Can't blame you for that."

"All of the magic wielders are bringing up the rear as well, so you know."

Thea eyed him, impressed. "Smart. Well done."

That meant she could worry less about the evacuees, since the fire wielders could keep themselves warm in cold rain. Having the non-magic users leave first, they were likely to beat the rain to the safe houses, and the tarps wouldn't be necessary. Those things could be heavy and clumsy in any situation, especially a windy one, never mind during an emergency evacuation in a storm.

Guyus, who was in his mid-twenties, was the youngest regional leader in the Fire Nation. He was tall but youthful looking, almost childlike, with short dark copper red hair that was longer in the front than the back. He had a defined jaw structure that made him handsome, but he was no silly fool. He led his region with kindness and strength, and his people liked him. Orn was a lady in her mid-forties with long, thin blonde hair and no lack of lovely silver streaks that fanned against her shoulders. Since her mid-twenties, she had been elected each year as regional leader. Waik was in her late thirties with straight, short, steel black hair mixed with white. She was the sternest of the regional leaders, less enjoyed by the people and more just respected. She wasn't unkind—just not overly kind.

"Lady Thea," Guyus said, drawing her attention again. His voice dropped from the light tone of a politician, to a deeply worried one that was matched by the worry in his light brown eyes. "Do you know what's happening?"

Thea sighed and shook her head then nodded toward the Derser Rects. "Hopefully they're going to figure it out."

It was a couple of minutes before the Dersers finished packing up their equipment and started toward her. "We have everything we need," the temple leader, Dorsh, declared.

Thea nodded. "Thank you, Rector," she said, addressing him by his formal title. "Please get yourself and your team home safely, so you can figure out why the world is collapsing around us." Dorsh nodded once, and the Derser Rects headed for the evacuation line and climbed into a waiting carriage.

To her left, Thea saw the western scouts returning from the bridge. Her heart started racing. "Excuse me," she said to the regional leaders, staying as professional as she could as she hurried to meet the scouts without running. She didn't want to worry the remaining evacuees. The regional leaders unexpectedly followed her. Thea didn't have the time or the mindset to tell them to stay put, so she let them come. People were desperate for answers, so it was understandable.

"Fitzu," she called to the front man as he dismounted. He was tall and handsome, with wide shoulders. He had short, spiky, raven black hair and a well-trimmed black goatee that matched his leather scouting armor. His dark gray eyes were serious as Thea approached him. "Tell me you've got good news."

Fitzu sighed. "The bridge is still intact." Thea's pulse quickened. "But not for long." Her heart sank. "When this storm ends, it will be gone."

Thea let out a heavy breath. She looked out over the wild River Gora, a river so wide that the Frost Nation to the south couldn't even be seen with the naked eye as more than a faint purple line along the horizon. That bridge had to be saved, and the Frost Nation probably didn't even have a clue it was in danger. They were completely useless, like they always had been.

Thea pinched her bottom lip and looked down at the ground. It was only seven minutes before the rain would come. Both nations had built the two bridges together 500 years ago, after the war to make sure they could still trade, even if hostilely. It had taken fire magic to molten stone and manipulate the lava to make the bridge, and ice and snow magic to cool it properly so it would harden and keep its shape without cracking.

A desperate idea came to her as she glanced up. She had to do something. "Your wisdom of evacuating the magic users last may have just saved our nation," she said to the regional leaders. Their brows dropped in confusion. "Rally them," Thea said. "All of them. The rain is coming in six minutes. Tell them to start blazing their cores, and get them horses wherever you can find some, and have them follow me." All three nodded and left to follow orders without question.

"What's in your head, Thea?" Fitzu asked in a warning tone.

"Saving that bridge," she replied and began to blaze her own core, heating up her skin so hot that an orange aura of fire magic lightly haloed her body and the cold rain couldn't hurt her. The water would evaporate with a hiss and a puff of steam as soon as it touched her.

"Thea," Fitzu said doubtfully, as his skin started to glow. "It's a thirty-minute ride up the riverbank. That only leaves three and a half hours of constant magic use to try to save this bridge before our magic quits and we have to rest. After that, without our magic to blaze our cores, the cold rain will kill us all. I don't fancy being turned into stone."

Thea gave him an impatient, angry glare. "I'm well aware of how our people's magic works, Fitzu." She took a step toward him. "But I couldn't live with myself if we didn't at least try. As much as I hate it, and hate the Frost Nation, we need that bridge to trade with them."

Fitzu shrugged. "Do you see me glowing orange?" He asked flatly, indicating he already knew he wouldn't be able to talk Thea out of trying to save that bridge. Thea smirked at him and gave him a nod. Her men knew her so well.

The rain had already started by the time all two hundred and fifty magic users were rallied, on horseback and heading west along the river bank. Guyus, Orn, and Waik were even riding along, their titles and ranks forgotten, niceties and protocols abandoned; everyone was just a person trying to save his or her nation right now.

A half hour later, Thea and the party arrived at the bridge. The sight was shocking, devastating. Thea pulled on her horse's reigns so tightly that she nearly caused him to rear up. The water was almost level with the bridge, and raging waves were already crashing along its sides, and exploding over the top of the stone.

One look and Thea realized she wasn't going to be able to just thicken the top so it didn't flood. She would have to strengthen the very foundation which was already missing huge pieces and swaying.

"What do we do, Thea?" Fitzu called over the crashing waves and pouring rain. He was cloaked in his own halo of steam, like everyone else, as the rain water sizzled off their burning skin.

Thea clenched her teeth and dismounted. "Everyone! To me!" she cried over the roaring river. She pulled at the throat of her red cloak, taking it off, and threw it over her horse's neck, out of the way.

The entire party dismounted and went to stand in front of her. "The foundation is breaking," Thea began. "The bridge will wash away if we don't strengthen it. Flooding we can deal with because at least there will still be a bridge to cross. Without the freezing magic of the Frost Nation, I want you to use the water as a cooling agent after you heat the stone. Yes! I realize the water is wild, but therein lays the challenge. Make that water evaporate so it stays out of your way while you heat the stone. Lessen your heat gradually to allow the water to cool and harden it, layer by layer. Normally, the frost people have conscious, intimate knowledge of how to cool the stone with their magic, but apparently, they're taking a sick day today." Thea rolled her eyes as the crowd shook their heads and glanced around at each other.

"I'm going to be honest," Thea continued. "It might not work." Eyes darkened and shoulders in the crowd drooped. "But we have to try anyway." Resolve came back into the fire wielders as they nodded in agreement. "Keep a constant report of your progress, or lack of progress, to your respective leaders and commanders. Leaders and commanders, keep me informed in turn. If this becomes too difficult, I'll make the call to quit, and we'll all head for home with our magic reserves able to keep us safe from the rain. We'll figure things out then. For now, we have to save this bridge!"

Cheers and roars rang out as every fire wielder in the southern region took to the bridge. Thea spread them out, putting them in twenty-foot sections that she thought they could handle. They wouldn't make it across the entire length of the bridge at this rate, but if the Frost Nation's side washed away, maybe that would wake them up to the issue, and they could possibly fix the rest of the bridge later. It was better than losing the entire thing. Taking boats across the River Gora, especially when it was flooded, was no picnic.

Waves and water pelted the fire wielders and constantly threatened to wash them into the river. To a fire nation native, that cold water would be deadly in two minutes flat. Their hair and clothes were soaked as they worked, but because their cores were still ablaze, the water that clung to their skin stayed warm, and couldn't turn them to stone. They worked more diligently then any oxen in the farmlands during plow season. Thea was working on her own twenty-foot section and despite—or perhaps because of—the danger they faced, she felt her heart swell with pride for her people.

An hour passed, and Thea couldn't believe the reports that came in—the reconstruction was actually going well. The consensus on the solution seemed to be to melt the already existing stone foundation completely, and then press the molten stone downward six inches and let the water cool it. It shortened the bridge, making it more susceptible to flooding, but thickened and strengthened the foundation. The bridge felt slightly wonky and out of sorts as different sections shrank a little, but it was a small, temporary price to pay to save this bridge.

Thea was nearly finished with her section when a chill ran up her spine. It was the kind of chill only a warrior would recognize—it happened when something was wrong but you weren't quite sure what. She looked around her immediate area, not sure exactly what she was searching for, but she was certain she would know it when she saw it.

All the sudden, every single horse they'd ridden here decided to bolt. In the same instant, every single bird in the area took to the sky. Thea watched with wide eyes as the sky to the north was filled, nearly black, with the silhouettes of birds in flight. She wasn't sure what that meant, but she knew it couldn't be good.

Seconds later, the ground started trembling.

Suddenly, the bridge shook so violently, Thea was thrown onto her back. At the same time, a wave came up over the side and crashed down on top of her. Thea was pitched over the edge, but somehow managed to hold on to the side with one hand. Dangling helplessly, she was shaken so hard by the vibrations she couldn't even see straight. Screams and splashes came to her ears as her people were pitched into the water and swept away to places only the Sun God would know.

Above the screams and rumbling that filled the entire world, one sound stood out, the cracking of stone. Thea's eyes went wide hearing the bridge breaking apart, and felt it start to sway amidst the shaking of the land. Another wave came down on her, threatening to push her into the river.

Though she'd never faced anything like this before—knew nothing about what she was supposed to do—she did know one thing. She wasn't going to die like this.

Clenching her teeth, she brought her dangling hand up, and gripped the side of the bridge with both hands. Though the shaking made it difficult, she held onto the edge so tightly she felt her own fingers break. Ignoring the pain, she began to pull herself up. Just as she got one leg up on to the bridge, another massive wave came down on her. Thea ducked down, clutching the edge with her hands and between her legs to keep from going over again. She let the next few waves crash over her, nearly drowning, since she could barely take in a breath between them. Her entire body rattled with the rest of the land, and the inside of her skull ached from its violence.

She heard the loud cracking of the stone again. Looking up, she saw the bridge breaking apart before her eyes. Thea gasped and scrambled to her feet, running as fast as she could toward the mainland. A loud groan came from behind her. Chancing a peek back, she saw another massive wave lift a large section of the bridge. Thea fell to the ground as it broke apart, but regained her footing as the section was completely washed away. Bodies went down with it, the bodies of her people.

The stone Thea stood on began to crack and fracture right under her feet. She turned to continue toward the mainland, when she heard a scream to her right. Lord Guyus was clinging onto the edge of what remained of the bridge. Thea ran to him, the cracks still expanding under her. She grabbed his arm, put it behind her neck, and gripped the back of his robes in a fist, pulling him up.

"Come on!" she screamed when he took a moment to find his feet. His ankle was broken, she realized. Keeping hold of him, he hopped while she practically dragged him toward the mainland.

Seconds before another wave came up, Thea jumped off the bridge, landing hard on her side, just as the rest of it was washed away. Only after that final explosion of sound and water did the trembling slowly start to cease.

Lying on the ground, Thea waited patiently and impatiently at the same time for the shaking to stop. She took a quick inventory of her health. The worst of her injuries were her hands. They were a disaster. She had several broken fingers, her tendons were stretched, some probably torn, and the skin was covered with cuts and bruises.

Before the quake had even fully ceased, Thea was on her feet searching frantically for survivors. Anyone she found, she piled up next to Guyus. Of two hundred and fifty beings, only thirty-three remained; of those, only six were in good enough shape to help her search for other survivors. Fitzu was among the survivors, though he had a nasty head injury. Orn was alive, though terribly injured as well. Waik was lost, as were seventeen members of Thea's scout team, leaving only eight.

"Come here," Fitzu said, once all the survivors were found. He took Thea's hands and fired up her bones with his magic, fixing and reshaping them properly, and healing her skin. He met her eyes a little playfully, but Thea could see the incredible pain he was in. "Can't have you unable to shoot a bow." Thea reached up to heal Fitzu's forehead, but he jerked away. "Don't. I'm fine. Save your magic to make us a shelter; you might be the only one who can at this point. We have to get out of the rain right *now*."

Thea nodded and jogged toward the nearest rocks formations. Firing up her magic, she melted the rock, reshaping it into a cave large enough, and deep enough, to fit everyone left, including the injured. The six people in decent shape helped move the wounded into the cave so that they could get out of the rain before their magical energy was depleted. Once everyone was inside, there was nothing to do but rest and wait for their magic to replenish, or for the rain to stop.

Frost: Chapter Five

———————— o ————————

A harsh wind snaked through the trees as Kirill's elk picked its way across the landscape, approaching the great wall. Underneath were passageways for the Frost Nation to navigate during times of war. It was what kept the Frost Nation safe. No warmth passed through this manmade barrier of snow, ice, and magic.

This particular post was an unmanned outpost where a key was required to gain entry. If anyone tried to rush The Wall, or break down the doors, a collapse would be triggered. The under passage would flood with ice and snow that would take days to dig out, buying the Frost Nation time to muster a response to any threat that might occur. It had been created during the Cold War, long before the Second War, the war to end all wars.

Kirill dismounted the elk. "Don't go far."

The elk shook its head and meandered off. Kirill watched it for a few moments before adjusting the pack over his shoulder and facing the structure. He pulled the necklace over his head that held the key. The key in hand was made of the same material at the doors. If anyone from the Fire Nation touched it, the key would turn to water. As he inserted it into the lock, the ice almost seemed to ripple, but it was just a trick of light. Magic sung to magic and the door opened, swinging in and away from him. He stepped through, his boots crunching on long forgotten snow, and the doors closed silently behind him, sealing him inside. The ice hummed with a soft blue glow, lighting his way.

The Wall was a hundred feet thick and over five hundred feet tall, spanning from east to west along the entire northern coast of their nation. It was their border, which had existed for thousands of years to protect them from the heat. Aradel told him once that there had been a time when they'd feared the spring, a time before The Wall. It was difficult to imagine, as he walked beneath its mass.

Since he was a child, he and Aradel would look out the highest part of the palace and wonder what it was like beyond The Wall. It was only as adults that they realized it wasn't safe. Aradel had only been in the Outlands once, in the dead of winter, but even then the heat had affected her. Her power was too great, and it weakened her against the warmth. The stronger the magic user, the more susceptible to the opposite temperature source he or she was. Aradel was very powerful with her frost magic, thus very weak against heat. A hot day could kill her in an hour.

Kirill was a very powerful magic user, but not of full blood, because his mother did not have any magical abilities. That meant Kirill could resist heat better. It was that combination of high heat resistance and powerful frost magic that made him invaluable to Queen Vesna.

The door at the opposite end opened, and he stepped out into growing warmth. Wrapping himself in a cocoon of cold, Kirill moved toward the River Gora. It wasn't long before he had to stop and take a drink of water to replenish his powers. Members of the Frost Nation relied upon water to create their ice and snow magic. Without it they would perish, which is why most didn't venture beyond The Wall. The heat was too much.

The day was warming considerably. It did feel as though spring had come early. Yet it was odd to have such a thing come so early. The more he thought about it, the more suspicious he grew that the Fire Nation was somehow mixed up in it. They were always as greedy as the fire, wanting to consume anything and everything around them.

He hurried along through the tree line, getting closer to the merchant town of Secille. During the winter months, many of the merchants traveled beyond The Wall for ease of trade. It was the oldest town with ancient homes that had withstood the ages. During the summer months, they moved behind The Wall to New Secille. Most people stayed behind the safety of The Wall, but those ambitious types, or desperate types, occupied it for as many months as they could.

When he reached the edge of the river, he found a spruce tree, one of the tallest and oldest. Kirill dropped his pack before taking hold of the first branch. Hand over hand he made his way up to the top. Taking the telescope off his belt, he opened it up with a quick snap of his wrist. When he held it up to his eye, his eyes widened.

The bridge was half submersed in water. Violent waves were crashing around it, and some even erupted over the sides. He saw members of the Fire Nation lining the bridge using fire on it. Kirill couldn't believe they were trying to destroy it. The fools would suffer just as much as the Frost Nation if they succeeded. He started to count them, but abandoned his tally when he saw a woman, who seemed to be in charge, applying her abilities as well. His gaze narrowed, and he leaned forward watching her closely. He realized that she wasn't destroying it, she adding a layer of molten stone to the outside foundation.

Before he could contemplate that further, a bird squawked, and flew up by his telescope. Kirill nearly lost his hold of the branch as he jerked away from it. Suddenly, all the birds took the sky, an inky black cloud of feathers, and Kirill stared in awe.

Suddenly the tree he was in started to sway violently. Kirill gave a startled cry and wrapped both arms tightly around the branch. The telescope slipped from his fingers, but he hardly cared about its departure as he desperately held on with both his arms and legs. His stomach rose to his throat from the violence of the shaking, and everything was a blur.

Surveying the area below, he saw the ground begin to crack. He cried out as the tree he was clinging to was ripped from his arms and he began to fall. He let his power fly and landed roughly in a tall mound of snow. Most of the snow gave way, and he half struck the ground. His body arched in response to the pain and he rolled onto his side.

He barely had a moment before the great tree that he had used as a lookout, tore free from the ground. It groaned and cracked loudly. Kirill gasped and rolled away as it dropped down toward him. He barely had enough time to reinforce the shield of ice around him before the boughs smacked against him laying him flat into the ground. His shield took the brunt of the hit, but his aching back told him he hadn't escaped unfazed. The pain distracted him and a smaller set of needles raked against his face, forming three scratches as he pushed his way free of the branches. Blood dripped down his cheek as he tried to walk despite the shaking.

"By all the stars!" he cried as he stumbled toward the shore like a newborn lamb.

Kirill heard cries rising from the village. His people were suffering, people who needed him, and yet the unruly ground continued to tremble. He glanced toward the bridge and discovered it had been lost to the river. He stumbled again, ending up on his knees with his back protesting every move.

Finally, the trembling slowed and Kirill got to his feet. He looked to the sky and saw the birds circling, clearly unwilling to land. He was unsure if that was a good sign or not.

When he looked down again, he saw the ground splitting right across his path. He stumbled back and nearly fell again as dirt gave away at the edges like water through a sieve. He created a short ice bridge over it and hurried across, and found the old village in chaos.

People were screaming for help, many of them trapped below the rubble of a once-standing building. He saw a little girl clutching a raggedy doll and crying for her mother. Her dusty face was streaked with tears.

He began ordering non-magic users toward The Wall, while ordering magic users to search for survivors in the collapsed building. Another gentler quake made many cry out, but something told Kirill that the worst was over. Reaching the rubble of the building, he pushed a rock out of the way by rising ice spikes to lift it, and helped two miraculously uninjured people to their feet.

As they thanked him, Kirill saw the woman do a double take and her wide eyes rested on The Wall. "Look!" she cried, pointing.

Kirill turned. A massive crack had formed in the ice; a crevasse of nothing was before him. He stared in horror as people in the square moved slowly toward The Wall. Terror clutched their features because they could already feel the cold escaping. That meant the heat was seeping into the Frost Nation!

Sparing only a few glances, Kirill moved farther into the village to help others. He vowed that if the Fire Nation was behind this, he would make them pay dearly.

Fire: Chapter Six

――――――――― o ―――――――――

The din of the rain falling outside of the cave hadn't let up at all in two hours. Thea and Fitzu tended the wounded as best they could, but they lost three more people while waiting for their magic to replenish or the rain to stop. Fitzu was the only magic user among them with any healing ability, but it was very minimal, and some of the injuries were fatal.

Thea sat on a rock in the farthest corner from the entrance of the cave with her elbows resting on her knees, and her head bowed low between her shoulders. She'd never had a brush with death like that—not like that. Men and weapons and magic she could deal with, and had dealt with, but how did you fight nature that was trying to kill you? It was too big, and there was no weapon or magic that could kill it or even harm it. She was beginning to see what Darha was so afraid of, and was beginning to feel afraid too. She couldn't admit that here, though. She had to be strong for her men and the survivors right now. She could curl up with Coor later when they were alone and no one else would see her fall apart. Her husband was the only person to whom she ever showed her vulnerability. Even Darha had never seen Thea fall apart.

Coor was always strong for Thea when she needed him to be, and Thea was strong for him when he was vulnerable, like the time Darha was eleven and became so deathly ill they didn't know if she would make it. Coor, seventeen at the time, trembled and cried in Thea's arms for six days until Darha's condition improved. Thea had held Coor together then, and Coor had held Thea together numerous times since.

Thea sighed thinking about her husband. He was more than she ever deserved in this life. She'd been nothing but a wretch from the streets, orphaned and abandoned first by her father, and then her mother, by the time she was eight years old. Thea had scrounged and scratched out a living on the streets for two years before the King and Queen stumbled upon her and took her in as their own. Coor was twelve at the time; Darha was six and heir to the throne of the Fire Nation. Thea wondered for years what any of them wanted with her, but they treated her like family from the moment she arrived. Over time, she came to love them with a fierceness she didn't think a person could be capable of.

When she learned that Coor had similar strong feelings for her, her entire world clicked into place. Everything made sense, right down to her parents abandoning her. Thanks to Coor, she could forgive them. Thea knew without any doubt, that if it hadn't been for that event, she would never have known Coor or Darha, and none of her wonderful life since then would have happened.

"Thea!"

Thea's head came up and she stared wide-eyed toward the opening to the cave.

"Thea!" It came again in the distance.

Panting, Thea was on her feet running toward the opening. "Coor!" She screamed.

"Thea!" He was closer.

"Coor!"

Before she even reached the entrance to the cave, Coor came whisking in. Seeing Thea, he threw his leather hood back and, with one step, closed the distance between them and gathered her up in his arms. He kissed her neck, and cheek, and head multiple times without putting an inch of distance between them. He was covered from head to toe in leather pants, gloves, and a parka. The rainwater remaining on the leather made Thea shiver, but she didn't care.

"You're okay," he breathed into her hair, kissing the side of her head. "You're okay." Coor put his hands on her cheeks and slightly pulled away so he could kiss her lips.

Thea let him kiss her for a long moment, but as badly as she wanted to stay in his arms, she gently pulled away from him. "We've got wounded."

Coor nodded once. "I've got healers." He went to the entrance of the cave and waved some people inside. A group of four healers came in, all of them outfitted in the same leather protection gear, including Kimbro, the most powerful healer in the Fire Nation.

Kimbro took his hood off and dipped his head in respect as he quickly passed Thea to tend the wounded. "Lady Thea."

"Kimbro," Thea said relieved. "Thank you for coming."

He didn't respond, as he was already kneeling next to Lord Guyus, speaking gently to him and tending to his ankle. Kimbro was always like that. He didn't mean to be rude or absentminded, but when it came to wounds and illness, he was intensely focused. He was nearly forty and very short, only coming up to Thea's shoulders, and very thin. He had short, light brown hair and enormous light gray eyes that almost seemed too large for his face until he smiled. His smile was so wide and broad that it balanced out his large eyes.

Thea faced Coor again. "Darha? The palace? Is everything all right?"

Coor shook his head. "That quake set off a reaction of massive tidal waves in the north that came seven miles inland and flooded all the northern islands." Thea's eyes went wide, and Coor shook his head. "The Fire Island is wiped out. We watched everything, the reserve palace and every home, crumble into oblivion from the watch towers."

"What?" Thea gasped.

"Your magic? Is it replenished?"

Thea shook her head. "Not for another couple of hours."

"All right." Coor put his hood back on and headed out into the rain again.

Thea turned back watching the healers work. She listened as life began to echo off the walls of the cave as people were healed and energized. Thea could not believe the relief that came over her with those sounds of life.

Lord Guyus approached her with his head bowed low and tears streaming down his youthful cheeks. "Thank you," he choked out, and then cleared his throat to try and compose himself. "Thank you," he said a little stronger, "for saving my life, Lady Thea."

Thea gently touched his shoulder. "Of course, Lord Guyus. I was glad I was able to." Lord Guyus nodded once and then left to comfort one of the wounded until a healer could reach her.

Fitzu approached Thea, looking well with the gash in his forehead completely mended. Thea had seen her share of injuries and knew that only Kimbro could have healed a wound that wide without even leaving a scar. "I'll wait here with the survivors until the rain stops or our magic replenishes. You get to the Queen."

Thea nodded. Just then, Coor came back into the cave holding piles of leather tarps and leather protective gear in his arms.

"My Prince," Fitzu said, stepping forward immediately, "allow me to assist you." Fitzu started taking the pile of leather out of Coor's hands before he even responded.

Coor glanced at Thea and gave her a small shake of his head, which made Thea chuckle quietly. Fitzu was always formal and proper with Coor, even when Coor told him not to be. Fitzu would even kneel before him, right in the middle of a pub, before every casual social occasion. When it had gotten to the point of bothering Coor, he'd asked Thea about it. Fitzu was her second in command in the scout division, so Thea asked him. Fitzu said he never wanted to forget he was beneath the royal family's authority, no matter how good of friends he became with Coor—and they were very good friends.

"Thanks, Fitzu." Coor took one thin stack of leather off the top of the pile. "Please pass the personal protective garments out to the strongest of those among you. Have them bear the leather tarps that will cover the rest of them so you all can get back to Vlid."

Fitzu bowed once. "As you command," he said and went to carry out the task.

Coor handed Thea the leather parka and gloves he'd taken off the pile. "We've got to get to the palace."

Thea nodded and unfolded the parka, throwing it around her shoulders. This was one of the reasons the scouts' armor was leather—in the case of rain, which used to be a rare occurrence, they would be safe if they were caught in it. Thea didn't need more than the parka and gloves to cover her skin because her armor was leather already. She put the gloves on, pulled the hood over her head, put her arms through the long bell sleeves, and clipped the front secure.

Before heading out, she faced the cave. "Fitzu," she called. He looked back at her amid passing out the leather protective gear. Thea grinned. "I don't have to tell you what to do here, do I?"

Fitzu rolled his eyes. "Get our people home safe."

"And don't be stupid," she added.

Fitzu shook his head, "Goodbye Thea," he said in a flat tone of dismissal.

Thea grinned as she and Coor headed out into the rain together. She was glad Fitzu didn't treat her with the same formality he did Coor because she would probably have dismissed him from the scouts long ago, despite his skill. She could not spend long treks over the land with him talking to her like that. The rocks were no place for formality, especially for extended amounts of time. She wasn't royalty, though she was considered a member of the royal family, and because of that he didn't have to treat her with any kind of formality, except maybe as a ranking officer; but he didn't even do that, for which she was glad.

Coor led Thea over to the horses that had brought the rescue party. Before even mounting, Coor grabbed Thea's shoulders out of nowhere, pulled her against him, and kissed her mouth firmly and deeply right in the rain. Thea sunk into his embrace until his arms around her were pretty much the only thing holding her up.

After a few minutes, Coor finally pulled away. Both were breathing a little heavily. He pressed his lips to her forehead, lingering for another moment before his intense hazel eyes met hers under the leather hood. "You know that I love you, right?"

Thea smiled. "I know." She placed her hands on his cheeks and kissed the hollow of his throat before pressing her cheek to his chest. "I love you too."

Coor wrapped his arms around her and kissed the top of her hood. Eventually he sighed and reluctantly pulled away. "Come on." He kissed her lips quickly. "We have to get back to Darha."

They mounted two of the six horses and started in a full gallop across the land. It was a very long and wet two-hour ride before they reached the outskirts of the capital, Vlid. They didn't talk much, too focused on getting back to their fragile young sister and Queen to have much else on their mind. Thea's magic replenished and the rain had slowed to a misty drizzle by the time the thirty-foot brown stone wall of First Gate rose up before her eyes. They passed under the raised portcullis, and then her tunnel vision ended.

Blazing her core, Thea threw back her leather hood and looked around with unconcealed horror at the overrun lower ring of First Gate. The safe houses were so overcrowded that leather tarps had been erected outside each one, and people were sitting under them wrapped in blankets and next to pit fires. Worse, some of the safe houses were in ruin and nothing more than a pile of debris on the ground now. Tarps were the only shelter many people had. The stone statues of the deceased that had become victim to the cold were arranged in lines to Thea's left, out of the way of the chaotic streets. People's eyes were wide and fearful, yet hollow and hopeless at the same time. People that Thea recognized as healers, or medical professionals, were running all over the place in a hurry to tend to hundreds of wounded, either wrapped in leather or blazing their cores if they were magic users. Lifesaving healing and procedures were being done under the few erected medical tarps, but many of them were being done right in the middle of the brown stone streets under randomly erected and heavily worn spare tarps.

Thea picked up her horse's pace to ride up next to Coor. "These aren't just the southern region evacuees," she said.

Coor shook his head. "Many are likely refugees from the north that were affected by the tidal waves."

Thea shook her head. "Come on." She pulled out ahead of Coor, and both of them went as fast as they could through the clogged streets toward the palace. They still had four gates to go through, so it was another thirty minutes before they were dismounting at the foot of the steps. They went up the wide, smooth brown stone staircase to the twenty-foot gold double doors. Two guards stationed there each pulled one open, bowing low at the waist as Thea and Coor headed inside.

Spectacular red and gold marble floors greeted their feet as they entered the throne room. The gold of the floor flashed like metal in the firelight as it swirled around the red, looking as if it had gently been stirred in liquid form then suddenly frozen solid. A long red carpet with gold tassels sewn along the edges began a few steps in, a thin pathway that led up to the Queen's throne. As if people needed directions. The single elaborate golden throne with puffy red cushions sat on a wide circle platform with two steps around the entire edge of it so the Queen could leave in any direction. Two small gold pillars rose on either side of the platform, each holding a steady, constant flame.

As Thea and Coor walked the carpet, five enormous golden columns, twenty feet thick and fifty feet high, stood like sentries guarding the throne room on both sides. Golden decorative arches connected the columns at the top, which supported the red and gold marble balcony above. The room was lit by thousands of decoratively placed oil lamps and in four chandeliers, forty-feet each in diameter, hanging from the ceiling. Three large decorative red tapestries with the Fire Nation crest sewn down the length of them adorned the back walls just under the grand window.

Up near the roof, and coming halfway down the back wall, was a gold-paned window. The gold metal work depicted an abstract outline of the sun with S-shaped rays going in every direction. It was the most magnificent window Thea had ever seen. It faced the southeast, so the sun would always shine on the throne. Now, however, gray clouds were the only thing visible out the window.

A group of about seventy-five people surrounded the platform on which Darha's throne sat. All of them were tense, appearing eager to get their concerns out, but only one person was speaking, her words quick and her tone nervous. Darha sat listening intently. She was never more at home than when she sat on that throne dealing with political issues and trying to help her people. Coor and Thea were not like her in that respect. They were warriors. Darha had a gentle, peaceful, and fragile heart that always wanted to please people. She looked calm now, but anyone who knew her like Thea did, knew she was more rigid and wide-eyed then she'd ever been in her life.

Thea caught Darha's eye as she and Coor approached the platform. "A moment," Darha declared, and the crowd in front of her instantly fell silent. Darha stood from her throne, hitched up the front of her red gown, and went down the two steps quickly. The crowd parted as she made her way toward Thea, her waist-length honey blonde hair flashing in the firelight like the gold in the marble. "You're alive," she gasped and threw her arms around Thea.

Thea smiled and hugged her little sister back. Darha was a half a foot shorter than Thea, so she had to bend a little to fully embrace her. "Did you really think the world shaking to pieces would kill me?"

Thea had meant for that to be a joke to lighten the mood, but she saw restrained tears in Darha's light gray eyes when she pulled away. Darha took the sleeve of her gown in her hand and dabbed them dry. "I need you both to head north. I already dispatched nearly the entire army in that direction."

"What do you want us to do there?" Coor asked.

Darha glanced at him and shrugged weakly. "I think all that's left to do at this point is to search for survivors. Bring them here."

Coor nodded and leaned down to kiss his sister's cheek. Thea gave her a weak smile and touched her shoulder, and then both of them headed back out of the throne room to aid the north.

———————————— o ————————————

Aradel was in the throne room with the other candidates when she felt the first trembling of the planet. The Queen had been addressing their people and answering some of their questions about the stream of Outlanders coming from beyond The Wall; everyone had seen them. Queen Vesna believed every voice and concern should be heard in order to calm them into making sensible decisions. The Queen seemed to give particular attention to the voices that involved the Fire Nation, and the rumors that were already spreading about their possible involvement with the early arrival of spring.

The shaking rose like a tide. Aradel stumbled and gave a cry of terror, joining the other voices in the room. The shaking increased and people fell to the ground. Pillars cracked, and bits of ice dust rained down on everyone that was gathered in the throne room.

Aradel's heart raced with fear and worry. The palace had not been built to withstand such quakes. The first place she looked was to the decorative ceiling behind the throne. She built up her magic in her chest, preparing to seal any cracks in the ice that might occur. But when nothing in the ice palace came crashing down, she scanned the room looking for anyone wounded.

Just as quickly as it had started, it stopped. "What was that?" a woman exclaimed.

"A quake," Queen Vesna responded as she stood. People helped each other to their feet.

Aradel could still feel vibrations under her feet as she stood. Her eyes scanned the room again as she helped up one of the other candidates. Suddenly a second quake hit, throwing Aradel onto her back. This time, she heard the ceiling crack with a noisy snap.

"The ceiling!" Aradel yelled, as cracks ran along the ice like spider webs above her.

She got to her feet and raised her arms, using her magic to reinforce the crumbling ceiling. One of the candidates joined her.

"Protect the Queen!" the candidate shouted.

The Queen had fallen from her throne. On her knees, she gazed up at the chandelier as it swung up and struck the ceiling, shattering to pieces. The sharp ice splinters rained down on the throne room. A woman ducked and screamed, holding her arms above her head to protect herself from the falling shards. Before they could reach her, Queen Vesna held her arm out, and the moon pearls around her throat began to glow brighter. Just as swiftly as Aradel could take a breath, the dangerous falling ice turned into snow, and floated gently around the woman in a harmless heap. The Queen did not need to be protected.

Aradel fell hard to her knees but continued to reinforce the ceiling even as a jolt of pain went through her. The other candidates joined her in her efforts until the shaking finally subsided. Aradel hurried to Queen Vesna, helping her stand.

"This is more powerful than anything I've ever seen," the Queen exclaimed, taking hold of Aradel's arm.

"We have had quakes before that have cracked the ceiling," Aradel said, remembering that it had been reinforced after the last powerful quake two hundred years ago.

"That chandelier survived them all, yet now it breaks?" Queen Vesna said with worry in her eyes before addressing everyone else. "Is anyone injured?"

"Not here," one of the candidates called. She had gone to aid the crowd when Aradel had gone to the Queen.

"Thank you, my Queen," the woman in the snow heap said as she hugged a child to her chest.

"Go back to your homes," Queen Vesna called loudly enough so everyone could hear her. "Help those you can, but make sure your families are well. We shall continue these discussions at a later date. Special mass will be held at the Moon Temple until this disaster is behind us."

Even though Queen Vesna stood tall, she was using Aradel to support some of her weight. Aradel stayed next to her, waiting until the last person had left before turning to the candidates. They instantly swarmed toward her, but the Queen waved them off. "Attend to the town. Go and help those you can."

"Is it them?" a girl asked, and Aradel didn't have to ask who she meant.

"I do not know," Queen Vesna said. "But I don't believe they have this kind of power."

The girl nodded but seemed unconvinced by the Queen's words as she left. Aradel watched her go. As soon as they were alone, the queen let out a sigh and leaned heavily against Aradel, who bore her weight. She had felt the Queen straining earlier and now understood how much of a toll the planet's trembling had taken.

"Are you hurt?" Aradel asked, instantly inspecting her.

"It's these old legs," she said, but she began moving with Aradel's help. "Not as young as they once were."

"Your power is unchanged," she countered, making a valid point.

"That is true," Queen Vesna said, fingering the pearls around her throat.

"Do you really mean what you said? About the Fire Nation?" Aradel asked, because she doubted even they were strong enough to cause this.

"I do," she replied. "I would not be surprised if they were as devastated as us."

"What will we do?" Aradel asked as they reached the doors.

Queen Vesna stopped as her personal attendant opened the door for her. She touched Aradel's face. "You were always the strongest of my girls. Quick to act and plan, but you always defer to me. One day I won't be here, and then you must make your own decisions."

"That won't be anytime soon," Aradel insisted, but she felt a pit form in her stomach at the thought.

"Then tell me," Vesna said, dropping her hand to Aradel's shoulder, "what would you do?"

"I'd defer to you," Aradel responded with a smile. "You are the Queen."

"If I told you to command our outer regions to start building and fixing our boats, and send a message to the Fire Nation to meet, would you agree?" Queen Vesna asked, her face the picture of a wise matriarch.

Aradel considered her words before responding. "I would, but I would also increase our defenses at The Wall."

"Hmm," she muttered before patting Aradel's cheek. "Smart girl. Write the letters and send the owls posthaste."

Aradel watched as the older woman left. The Queen moved carefully, but she walked on her own. When she rounded the corner, and the attendant moved after her, Aradel stayed until the doors closed. Turning, she made her way across the throne room toward the scribes' quarters, glancing up at the now-empty ceiling a final time.

Since the Cold Wars, they had held a tenuous peace with the Fire Nation. They were less refined than her people, but they weren't much different. They needed things that only the Frost Nation could provide, and her people needed the tools that the Fire Nation manufactured. Perhaps because her own family had been so terrible, she believed they couldn't be any worse than that. All she had known was other people's hatred for the Fire Nation, but that meant little to her.

Queen Vesna's decision to treat them with kindness might be perceived as weakness. Few shared her indifference toward them. Even Kirill didn't much care for the Fire Nation, and had said so many times. As she walked through the palace, her attention turned to Kirill. Whatever the Queen had sent him to do had taken him far away, and she hoped he had weathered the quake all right.

On her way to the scribes' quarters, she paused at the tower of the messengers. Glancing up at the spiraling staircase, she walked up, forcing herself not to hurry in case anyone was tending to the birds. She did not want to lose face by looking like a rushing child instead of a candidate for Queen.

She reached the top of the tower and smiled at the sight of so many sleeping owls. They were nocturnal and most preferred to hunt mice and other birds, so at night the tower was nearly empty of them.

When Aradel was first taken from her family to become a candidate for queen, she would come here often. She went directly now over to a nesting mother. Bending down, she peered into their little nest and saw the family sleeping. One owlet cocked an eye at her, chattered softly, before returning to sleep.

It was here that she had first met Kirill, still a page for the Knights then. He'd stumbled upon her crying in a corner after one of the girls had pulled on her braids. All the girls' words had stung then since she was still recovering from what her parents had done. Kirill had told her then that he was becoming a Knight so that all the girls in the world would be safe and never cry again. Whenever she missed him, she always found herself here, remembering all the adventures they had as children. Yet with each passing day, those memories became more and more distant.

She went to the tower window and surveyed Axion. There was a great split across their road, and the ground had become uneven. Houses were caved in, and trees had been tipped over by their roots. She could see people working hard to move rocks and help the injured in the streets.

In a flurry of skirts, Aradel hurried back down the tower, throwing protocol aside. The faster she sent those letters, the faster she could join in helping the citizens of Axion.

Fire: Chapter Eight

———————— o ————————

Darha tilted her head to the side and looked curiously at the strange creature. She knew what it was; she was just having a hard time believing it was here. It was an emissary owl…from the Frost Nation. It sat on the scribe room windowsill, watching Darha with wide and almost engaging eyes. It was probably wondering why Darha hadn't taken the letter off its neck yet.

Darha regarded the scribe who had fetched her. "Is this…I mean…?" Darha didn't know what to say. She wanted to ask if it was a joke or a prank, but her people wouldn't do this for any reason, least of all during a national emergency. The scribe shrugged his shoulders helplessly. Darha looked back at the owl. It tilted its head as Darha had done a moment ago. Darha frowned. "Fetch me the letter, please."

"I tried your majesty, but it bit me."

"It bit you?" she asked with furrowed brows.

The teenage boy nodded. "I believe, if history serves, only specially trained owls do that, my Queen. Those owls bite anyone outside of royalty who tries to take the parchment. Some of our message hawks do the same."

Darha observed the pretty white owl again. She sighed. "Okay," she said and stepped toward it. She reached her hand out carefully, expecting to be bitten. The owl calmly held her eyes with his. Darha pinched the corner of the letter, and the strap holding it to its neck instantly came loose. The owl flew off.

Darha quickly unfolded the parchment and read.

In Greeting, Queen Darha,
I write to you on behalf of my Queen Vesna of the Frost Nation. She has been made aware of the natural turmoil that is affecting both of our nations and requests a peaceful meet with you on the Frost Nation's shores. We request your presence in three days' time. Since the bridges have washed away, we will expect your arrival by boat on the bank of the former Western Bridge. Please respond accordingly if you are willing.
Regards,
Servant of Queen Vesna
Aradel

Darha folded up the parchment as panic started to rise up in her chest. This was huge. This was enormous, and she was terrified. She didn't know what to do. Dealing with the Frost Nation on these matters?

Hiding her fear, she faced the scribe. "Have one of my men fetch Coor and Thea from the northern disaster area immediately."

The scribe bowed low. "As you command." He turned and left in a hurry.

Darha slowly paced the scribe room, flicking the letter back and forth between her fingers. Meet the Frost Nation on their shores? Coor wouldn't be okay with that, but if they needed to meet with Queen Vesna, Thea would insist on a heavy Fire Nation presence. Either way, Darha had a feeling they were going to this meeting.

Darha made her way quickly to the throne room. Upon her entrance, the regional representatives waiting for her bowed low at the waist. "Ladies. Gentlemen," Darha said shakily. She wasn't sure if she should be making a call like this without Coor's input. He was so much better at being royalty than she was; he always had been. He was wise, and brave, and responsible. Darha was a newborn kitten compared to the lion of a leader that her older brother was. However, the tradition had always been that women in the royal family sat on the throne before men. "I need all of the forgers in every one of your regions to start repair on all the ancient boats in the archive building."

Everyone looked around at each other, confused, and Darha nearly panicked. She felt dizzy and short of breath. She stiffly sat down on her throne, lest her legs give way. She tried to comfort herself with the thought that even if Coor refused to allow the meeting with the Frost Nation, the boats she was ordering repaired could still be used for trade, since the bridges were out. She awaited challenges and questions from the regional leaders, but none came. They all just started giving orders and instructions to their entourages and then dispersed to carry them out.

Five hours passed before Coor and Thea could return, since it was a two-and-a-half-hour ride to and from the disaster area in the north. Night had long fallen, and Darha was alone now, sitting on her throne, slumped slightly to one side of it with exhaustion. She hadn't slept all night. She just kept tending to the concerns and emergencies of her people. A new death report. Not enough tarps. Flooding beginning on the southeast coast. Another storm brewing. Her largest concern now, however, was that some of their natural springs were turning a strange grayish brown color and the water tasted and smelled odd. Some pools farther north were already undrinkable. Darha had a feeling she already knew what was wrong, but samples of the water were sent to the Derser Rects for analysis.

Coor and Thea whisked into the throne room covered from head to toe in leather, rainwater dripping off them. "What happened?" Coor called.

Darha gazed up at him, her eyes red and half-closed with exhaustion, and handed him the letter from the Frost Nation. She didn't say a word as he opened it and read. His eyes went wide, then he handed the letter to Thea, who snatched it from him.

"What the …?" she said, looking at Coor with wide eyes.

"Have you responded to them?" Coor asked.

Darha shook her head. "I was waiting for you. But I did order the ancient boats to be repaired."

Coor sighed and regarded Thea. "What do you think?"

With Coor and Thea discussing this, Darha instantly felt a four-ton weight lift off her. They were both smarter and braver than she could ever hope to be. For an instant, she hated being saddled with the title of Queen. Even though she was adopted, Thea was more suited for it than Darha was. Why did Darha have to be Queen now? She could run a peaceful, prosperous land, but this disaster? She didn't even know where to begin to deal with it.

Thea sighed. "If they're reaching out to us like this, they've got to be suffering as well. I think we should meet with them and see what they have to say, but not without a very heavy Fire Nation presence."

Darha smiled a little. She knew her sister so well.

Coor nodded once. "I'll send the letter. Thea, would you please get my sister to bed?"

Thea nodded. "Absolutely."

Thea reached for Darha and helped her stand. Leaning heavily on Thea, Darha let her lead her to the bedroom chambers. Coor would take over the royal duties while she was indisposed. Darha didn't even recall her head resting on the pillow before she was asleep.

———

Three days passed quickly, and before Darha even knew it, they were piling into the boats at the edge of the River Gora and shoving off their shores to the Frost Nation. The boats were little more than decorated rowboats that barely fit fifteen people. The patchwork done to them was good enough, but it had made the boats rickety and ugly looking. It didn't matter, though. Darha was not really concerned with impressing the frost people.

It was hot, finally—granted much hotter than usual, but it was wonderful. *And here we are*, Darha thought bitterly, *about to go into the cold*. Darha had had it with cold, but this meeting was already underway.

Her heart was racing. She'd never, ever personally dealt with the Frost Nation. The traders and merchants were the only ones that ever did. She wondered what they were like. She knew they were cold and emotionless. They had passion and compassion for nothing, not even their own people. She wondered if they looked different. Did they have white skin or hair? Or perhaps blue? What kind of clothes did they wear? Darha imagined them covered from face to foot in animal fur to keep themselves warm in their frigid world.

Darha, Coor and Thea were all dressed in their formal wear. Darha had put on her largest, puffiest red gown, which sparkled subtly in the sunlight. She also wore a large heavy gold cloak, trimmed at the collar and ends in red dyed fur. Not to mention the red fur gloves that went up past her elbows, and thick red fur-trimmed leather boots. Darha left her long, honey blonde hair cascading down her back, hoping it would make her appear friendlier and unthreatening.

Darha glanced to her right. Thea was next to her at the front of the lead boat. Darha rarely ever saw her in anything but black, but today she was in gold armor with red trim and a red cloak. Her long brown hair was back in its usual tight braid, and she wore a red and gold helmet that resembled flames sweeping back away from her face. She was down on one knee with one arm resting across the top of her raised thigh. Her very light gray eyes were fixed ahead in grim determination. Thea was beautiful. Darha had always thought so. Now, however, in her gold and red armor, her dark hair and fierce eyes, Thea was stunning. Darha noticed the way Coor's eyes lit up when Thea had walked into the throne room this morning. She wasn't sure Coor had ever seen Thea in her formal armor. There had never really been occasion for her to wear it.

Coor's armor wasn't much different from what he usually wore, except that instead of gold armor with red trim, he wore gold armor with black trim. The red and gold of his usual armor made him look distinguished, while the gold and black made him look dangerous. The black cloak he wore was bigger and heavier than usual, and so was his personal arsenal. Darha wondered how in the world he had fit that many weapons on his person. But Darha knew better than to underestimate her older brother when it came to his knowledge of warfare.

The River Gora was so wide it took six hours for the party of fifteen boats to row across it. Fog got heavier along the way, concealing the river from their view. The temperature did drop steadily, but it was still warm enough to be very comfortable for Darha and her Fire Nation soldiers. Where was the cold she expected? The freezing temperatures?

Through the mist, as they reached the other shore, an enormous structure filled Darha's vision. Her eyes widened. It looked like a mountain! But no. As they drifted closer, Darha realized it was white; it was a massive wall of ice! It completely filled the horizon so the edges couldn't even be seen. Darha glanced at Thea in a panic. Were the frost people giants or something? Thea's eyes were also wide as she slowly stood up, staring at the massive ice structure. Coor stepped up behind Thea with the same expression of awe and disbelief.

"Coor," Thea said, her eyes on the structure, "I'm so sorry I made fun of you for bringing so many weapons."

Coor nodded. "I'm sorry I teased you for suggesting such a large host come with us."

Darha took a deep breath and blew it out slowly as the shore came into view through the mist. Darha could do this. This was what she was good at, the only thing she was good at—diplomatic resolutions and keeping peace. She wasn't sure the Frost Nation would be so willing to keep peace, but that's what Thea and Coor and the two hundred and twenty-five soldiers at her back were for.

Coor and Thea took their places on either side of Darha as shadows on the shore started to become visible. Darha swallowed a couple of times and commanded herself to relax and put on her mask—the mask her mother taught her that made her seem fearless and dispassionate, even if she was trembling inside. It was a placid, expressionless façade a Queen wore when dealing with enemies. Darha had mastered it when she was young, but it was always a game to her then. She wasn't playing a game any longer.

Darha expected a grand host of frost people to fill the shores, but only sixteen silhouettes developed in the mist. Darha's brows dropped in confusion, her mask cracking. As they neared the shore, she saw what had to be Queen Vesna. A very small, squat old woman with gray and silver hair tied up in a neat bun at the crown of her head, sat in an unimpressive chair, surrounded by a bunch of young girls. They seemed cold—in a way that had nothing do with the temperature. All of them did, that is, but one.

Darha's attention was drawn to the girl to the far left of the Queen who stood proper and still, watching the boats with a childlike curiosity.

She had long, thick silvery blonde hair pulled back in a single braid down the length of her back. She wore a thin, blue sparkling gown that bared her shoulders. Her feet, too, were bare. The man by her side made Darha cringe a little. He had long, golden blonde hair and dark, fierce eyes that made him appear angry. They reminded Darha of how Thea's eyes had looked this morning. His uniform was very light and like that of the Knights of the Fire Nation, so Darha assumed he was a Knight. The only things out of place were the thick gloves on his hands, which seemed odd among his lighter attire. Darha's teeth clenched in discomfort; they were completely normal looking, except that they were dressed like it was 90 degrees out, when it was closer to 50.

As they reached the shore, Thea and Coor hopped out and started to drag it onto the land. The blonde man approached Darha without a word. His eyes were unfriendly. He wouldn't attack her—he wouldn't dare with her army at her back! — but still she felt afraid. She felt the tension rise in the men behind her as he stepped up to the boat, stooped down, and held out his hand to her. Oh. He was being polite. Begrudgingly polite, because she could see in his eyes he wanted to be as far away from Darha as he could get.

Darha reached up to take his hand, but before she could, Thea spun around and gave the Knight a hard shove backward. "Get away from her!" Coor was instantly next to his wife, his hands grabbing for the hilt of his sword. Darha felt her soldiers' tension rise, and saw the Frost Knight's eyes become fiercer, and realized a war was about to start.

"No!" Darha cried, throwing propriety out the window for a moment. "Stop! Stop! Stand down, Thea! Coor, stop!" She looked behind her at the army. "Stand down!"

Panic of a war starting amid these massive natural disasters made Darha's voice sound different, strangled and high-pitched. She could not deal with a war—and Thea was warrior enough to singlehandedly start one on her own.

Darha brought her hands up to her face in a gesture that looked like impatience so she could press her gloved hands into her eyes to absorb the fearful tears that burned in them. She couldn't cry, not here, not now. She took a deep breath and composed herself, making sure her tears were at bay, before she turned her attention back to the Frost Knight.

"My apologies, Sir Knight," she said and held her hand out to him.

The Knight regarded them warily, first Thea and then Coor, before stepping toward the boat again. The Knight grasped her hand, but as soon as she touched him, Darha cried out in pain and snatched her hand away.

She suddenly heard the metallic ring of weapons behind her and saw magic ignite all around her.

"Stop!" Darha commanded in a voice she didn't even recognize. It was firm, less frail and desperate. It echoed over the river behind her and off the ice wall in front of her. No tears came this time; all of her being was focused on preventing war. Shockingly, all movement ceased, even from the Frost Nation. She looked up at Thea and Coor with a confidence and authority she never imposed on them. "He was just cold, and it hurt my skin," Darha said slowly.

Thea and Coor pressed their lips together and glanced at each other. Thea nodded at the men in the boats behind her. They all returned their weapons and extinguished their magic.

"That is my fault, Queen Darha," Queen Vesna interjected. Darha looked at her and saw the deep, genuine regret and a bit of fear in her eyes. "Our people don't do very well with the heat, and it is very hot for us out here, so I'm keeping us cold." Darha saw her touch a set of glowing pearls around her throat. "We thought Sir Kirill's gloves would be thick enough to protect you."

Darha gazed in hidden astonishment at the old Queen. She was taking responsibility for the mistake and being kind and apologetic about it. Not only that, but she had taken measures to protect Darha from the Knight's coldness. Kindness? From the Frost Queen?

Recovering from her amazement, Darha nodded once. "Everything is well, Queen Vesna." She held her hand out to Coor, who took it and helped her out of the boat. She looked at her brother. "Keep the boats off the shore. They are not to set foot on land and become a threat here." Darha did not like talking to her brother like that, but she was so desperate to prevent war that she couldn't bring herself to be affected by it right now. Coor didn't argue; he just nodded once and quietly gave orders to the men remaining in the boat from which she had disembarked.

Darha approached the Queen with Coor and Thea at her side. She saw the older woman struggling to get up out of her chair out of respect. Another amazing thing. "No no," Darha said quickly, holding her hands up. "Please don't stand. It's quite all right."

Vesna smiled, the wrinkles in her cheeks deepening in a charming, grandmotherly way. "Sweet girl. Thank you," she said as she sat back down. "Can I offer you a seat, Queen Darha?"

Darha smiled and shook her head. "No, thank you, madam. It was a long boat ride and my legs wouldn't mind a stretch for a moment."

Vesna nodded as the blonde girl and the Knight that she had called Kirill—who pulled off his thick gloves and put them in his belt—approached her side. They weren't giants or monsters; their appearance was hardly different from her people. They were all paler and had elegant features, and many had the strange silvery hair, but they were similar.

"I imagine we are not alone in our difficulties as of late," Queen Vesna said, her voice that of a caring grandmother, and Darha felt herself relax a little. This woman appeared to be reasonable.

"No," Darha answered, making her voice sound strong, though she felt weak.

"I believe this widespread disaster is affecting both of our nations," Queen Vesna said, the glow of the pearls reflecting off her face as she gestured behind her. "I wanted to take the initiative and offer you a gesture of peace."

Behind her were several large cubes of ice. They were still frozen despite the warmth of the day, but she imagined that wouldn't last. Darha felt like crying again; this water was exactly what they needed.

"Thank you," Darha responded, keeping her face carefully neutral.

"Sir Kirill will stay with the ice until you have put it in the boats and carried it off." Her eyes swept over the river. "Although it seems you have more men than boats."

Darha felt her face burn at the remark. She had brought two hundred and twenty-five men, and here this old woman sat with fifteen young women and one Knight. There was something to be said for caution and something perhaps better for restraint. At least she had kept them off the shore, a sign that she wasn't completely useless.

"A precaution," she countered carefully.

Vesna turned her ancient eyes to Thea. "Your idea, I presume, but assure you it is unwarranted. We were both hurt by this tragedy, and though my people want someone besides the planet to blame, this meeting is to show that we do not blame you."

Darha knew her people, too, felt the need to blame someone. But blaming the Frost Nation hadn't been logical from the beginning. The Frost Nation had no power over volcanoes, or storms, or the ocean which had washed away the Fire Island. Darha glanced at Thea, who still had deep suspicion in her eyes. She glared at the old woman, and Darha worried she intended to say something that would ruin this moment.

"Who is 'we'?" Thea asked, staring at the young women behind the chair.

"These are my queen elects," Queen Vesna said with a general wave of her hand. "They are here to see the terrifying Queen of the Fire Nation in the flesh." She chuckled and Darha nearly choked at the unexpected comment. "I believe they are disappointed that you don't have hair made of fire and a dress made of lava."

The sudden turn of conversation had thrown Darha completely off. What in the world was this little old woman doing? Regarding her curiously, Darha shifted from one leg to the other as she considered what could be gained by this line of conversation. Darha wanted to ask Coor and Thea, but she dared not look at them and make it appear she was unable to making her own decisions. If she remembered correctly, the Queen's elects were the most powerful women in the Frost Nation. Realizing that, Darha considered that perhaps her two hundred and twenty-five men at her back were not such an exaggerated precaution.

"I am sorry to be a disappointment," Darha responded.

"On the contrary," Queen Vesna replied with a simple smile, while the rest of the women stayed still and stony-faced. "You are exactly what I expected, and I believe we shall foster in a new age of peace because of this trying time."

At the word "peace" Darha felt relief flood through her. She observed the women. All of them seemed to regard her with suspicion, save the one. Her gaze was simple curiosity, like a child inspecting a new toy, but she alone among the fifteen girls seemed to lack any sense of reservation. The Queen of the Frost Nation waited, and Darha glanced back, observing the small army she had brought, her brother and sister, and then faced the old queen.

"Peace is all we desire," Darha answered. The elderly Queen nodded. "Please tell me what you know of the quake."

"Very little," Queen Vesna replied, holding up a hand, in which one of the girls placed a parchment. "My temple has been researching past occurrences of earlier springs that are joined by quakes, and so far, we have found nothing. What have you discovered?"

Carefully phrasing her response, Darha said, "The Derser Rects, our planetary religious sect, took samples of the soil, water, and air along the flooded river and different parts in the Fire Nation. They have been analyzing them for days. They have also been studying weather and ocean current charts and volcanic activity in the north for the past one hundred years."

"We can provide samples of our own for comparison," Queen Vesna replied. "Send a messenger hawk with what samples your Derser

Rects require and we shall provide them. For now, our focus should remain on finding a solution."

"Yes," Darha said, although she felt a little lost under the confidence of this long-lived queen. "I shall send the message as soon as possible."

"We have moved our merchants closer to The Wall for now, but they are still available to provide fresh water from our mountains if you desire. I imagine your water has already begun to turn sulfuric due to the enhanced volcanic activity in your northern islands."

Darha swallowed heavily holding back tears again. "Yes."

Vesna nodded deeply. "We lost many trees when the quake happened, but the wood is being processed for your consumption, and the making of boats has been commissioned so we may cross the River Gora to continue trade. When they are ready, the merchants intend to use them in place of the bridges." Darha felt a bolt of pride go through her because she had also thought of repairing the boats to be used for trade. "Expect them to be operational in the coming days."

"That will be good," Darha responded. She glanced behind her toward the river. "We will give these boats to our merchants as well."

"Wonderful," Queen Vesna said with a soft friendly smile. "If there is nothing else, I believe this meeting is concluded."

"Yes," Darha said. She gave a small curtsy to the elderly Queen and then turned and headed back to the boats.

"Queen Darha," Vesna called, making Darha turn. The old woman began to push herself up into a standing position, swatting away any hands offered to aid her. She met Darha's eyes kindly and dipped her head in a gesture of respect. "It has been an unexpected pleasure."

Darha dipped her head in response. "Likewise."

They climbed back into the boat, and Darha watched the gifts of ice get loaded into several of them. When they shoved off, Darha kept her eyes on the shore until it vanished in the fog. She glanced up at Thea, who continued to stare to the south long after the mist had swallowed any view of the Frost Nation. Darha looked at Coor, who was staring warily between his wife and the shoreline.

"That went better than expected," Darha said steadily, even with excitement bubbling in her chest. They could commence trade, she hadn't made a total fool of herself at this incredibly important meeting, and Queen Vesna was not a monster.

"Yes," Thea said, but her voice wasn't filled with excitement; it was full of hard suspicion. "Yes, it did."

Part 2

"Any chance is worth the risk." - Lady Aradel

Frost: Chapter Nine

—————————— o ——————————

Aradel stared at the brown ground at her feet, an arrow shape that spread from the fracture in The Wall. The heat from beyond their protective barrier was spreading and melting snow and ice alike. They were fortunate that, for now, the damage seemed contained here. She didn't want to imagine the devastation creeping further inland, yet she had a bad feeling it would. All this area was melting, and land that had been eternally frozen, was thawing. Flooding would soon become an issue at the break, and before long, further beyond The Wall.

Since they had met with the Fire Nation, a peace of some sort had been formed. Aradel had remained at The Wall while Kirill had returned to the mountains to begin moving sleds of snow and ice to reinforce it. Yet even Aradel's magic, and the snow, did not seem to be enough to heal their wounded barrier. Very few of their people were still in the Outlands, most having taken shelter within their boards to keep themselves safe from the heat.

She watched as men lifted the ice and snow onto The Wall, and lowered it into the crevice. When the ice was nearly settled in its spot, Aradel lifted her arms and magically filled the gaps around it. The frustrating thing about this task was that it required old snow and ice from the Lonely Mountains, the same mixture that had been used when The Wall had first been built, hundreds of years ago. As she watched the blue and silver of her magic interlace with the block of snow and ice, she wondered if using the old ice would be enough. The details of how the ancient Wall had been constructed, after all, had been lost with time. She lowered her arms, and another small portion of the wall became whole.

Queen Vesna believed the Fire Nation intended to keep their word about wanting peace, but she was not foolish enough to leave such a noticeable fissure in The Wall untended. The western outpost was now a full garrison, and would remain that way until The Wall was fixed. Something nagged at Aradel, though, telling her that the work here was only a temporary fix, because the heat was getting in no matter what she did.

Hearing a gentle bell ring behind her, she turned to see a team of wolves pulling a large sled filled with old ice for repairs. A second set of wolves, and then a third, quickly appeared at the tree line following the first. The fine wooden parts of the sleds were made by their people, but for the metal of the skis they had to trade goods—a reminder of how important the Fire Nation was to them. Without the Fire Nation, their farmers in the Outlands wouldn't have tools to farm either. Those without magic would be cast into the elements with no weapons to defend themselves—no swords, no arrows. Without the Fire Nation, they could not cut wood, nor have metal ships, and they would have no harpoons for whaling; without which they would lack oil for light. Although they mostly used wax candles, oil was always burned in the temples, and it was also a product they sold to the Fire Nation. It hurt her to realize how reliant they were on the Fire Nation for their metal, but the frost people had no way to harness heat without worry of injury. Even those who were less affected by heat would not last long standing by pits of fire to melt the metal down.

With a call from the driver, the wolves slowed down, though many strained to reach her. Wading into the pack of fur, she petted their heads as they licked her fingers and threw their bodies against her legs. Unlike the wolves of the Outlands, the mountain wolves stood as tall as her hip, and were beasts that could compete with bears.

She looked up to the old man driving the sled, who had made many trips that day. "Yorten," she said with a smile, "your pups are getting faster."

"You are too kind Lady Aradel," the old man said as the other two sleds stopped as well. "I'd like to introduce you to my youngest son, Tallus."

"A pleasure, Tallus," she said with a polite curtsy as he bowed to her.

"Lady Aradel," he replied, and she was surprised to discover he had a voice nearly as deep as Kirill's. She missed her dear friend. She had seen less and less of him in the past days and worried that this trend would continue.

"How many sons do you have? Are there not two already working on The Wall?" she asked, gesturing behind her to the ant-like men lowering another block of ice down into the crack.

"Just the three," Yorten admitted with a proud laugh. "But I have two daughters at home."

"I do not envy you," she replied with a soft laugh. "Given how much trouble Kirill and I caused growing up, I can only assume five children must have been a handful."

Before Yorten could respond, Tallus replied, "There is a reason my father's hair has turned gray prematurely."

Aradel laughed loudly before she could help herself. She was momentarily embarrassed by her outburst, but she had found his joke quite clever. She stifled herself a little too late, but was pleased to see Tallus and Yorten grinning widely.

Tallus was handsome to be sure. It was impossible not to notice. Yet she had seen his brothers. Their bright blond hair was like their father's, while Tallus had dark brown hair. It was rare in the Frost Nation, but not unheard of, and she was having a difficult time keeping her eyes off it. Not only was his hair dark, but stranger still, it curled. How unbelievably rare.

Straightening her spine, she decided it was time she returned to her post. "We had better return to work," she said with an amused smile. "There is a wall to fix."

Yorten, his son, and the third man whistled to the wolves. They strained against their lines, the rope going taut as they pulled the sleighs forward. Snow swirled behind them in the sudden movement, and Aradel felt her hair dance in the breeze they produced. When Tallus passed her bringing up the rear, their eyes met. With a gentle smile, she picked her way along the line of snow and headed back toward The Wall.

The heat was spreading like a sickness, and she had to suppress it. As the next block of ice was lowered into place, she raised her arms to secure it. She had hardly started when a second massive block suddenly slid off the edge of the ice scaffold. The men above her cry out as it crashed against the side of the fissure, sending an avalanche of snow and ice hurdling down from the top of The Wall. She let out a startled cry as she split the falling block of ice in two and then tried to secure the first block that was in the wall before stopping the coming avalanche. She quickly secured the first block, but the snow and ice still rushed toward her. "Cut the lines!" she heard someone yell. The wolves howled, and she hoped they were being cut free from the sleds to get to safety.

Thinking of Queen Vesna during the quake, Aradel focused her power on the falling ice and snow. The ice turned to snow instantly, but the snow continued to fall. Suddenly she felt an arm wrap around her waist and she was pulled to the ground. She barely had time to snap an ice shield up before she and whoever had grabbed her were buried in snow. The pile on her blocked out all light and sound.

Taking in a sharp breath, she opened her eyes. They immediately shot over to whoever was buried under the snow with her. The edge of her ice shield hummed with a soft blue light allowing her to see, and she was surprised to see Tallus raise his head. He gazed around in surprise at the bubble of space surrounding them.

"Amazing," he whispered and turned toward her. He looked like he wanted to say more, but their noses nearly touched, and he froze. Aradel felt her breath catch. Never had she been so close to a man other than Kirill.

"Thank you," Aradel said after a moment, trying to seem unmoved. "But you can let me go now."

"Oh," he replied, blinking before glancing down at her waist. "Oh!" he added as though suddenly coming to his senses and pulled his arm off her waist like his skin had suddenly caught fire. She couldn't see his face very well, but she imagined he was just as embarrassed as she was.

She swallowed her embarrassment and focused. This was not a time to lose her calm or her head. She soothed herself as she started to expand her ice shield out through the snow. She sat up, and soon the shield was tall enough for her to stand in. Getting to her feet, she smoothed out her dress. It slowly became brighter, and the soft magical glow of her shield was replaced with blue tinted sunlight when it reached the surface of the pile of snow they were under. She was conscious of Tallus watching her, and of the sense of awe he had at her power. Glancing over at him, she expecting him to be a little afraid of her, but instead he was looking around in complete wonderment.

When the top of the snow fell back away from her shield, she dispersed it and could hear shouting. She turned back to Tallus as he stared at her with the same unflinching astonishment, and held out her hand to him.

"Come with me," she said boldly before she knew what she was saying.

He didn't hesitate to step forward and take her hand. She pulled him along as she waved a hand in front of her. The ice and snow in front of her shifted, forming steps. As she stepped on the bottom one, her magic molded into an escape route, and she pulled Tallus behind her.

"Lady Aradel!" She heard her name called repeatedly.

When they emerged out of the top, she observed the pile of snow surrounding her and called out, "We are here!"

She waved an arm, and Tallus called, "I'm fine, Papa!"

Yorten waved back, appearing relieved. He was surrounded by two packs of terrified wolves.

Aradel beheld The Wall. There was very little damage. It would only put them behind a few hours. Relief flooded through her as she faced Tallus. She glanced down at their hands, embarrassed, before daring to look back up at him.

"You are amazing," he exclaimed as though he didn't notice their joined hands. She felt her cheeks turn red. "I've never seen anything like that."

"Thank you," she said, pushing stray hairs behind her ear as she tried to figure out how to get her hand back.

His stare finally shifted, and then he pulled his hand away. "My apologies, Lady Aradel."

"Aradel," she corrected, glancing up at him a moment. "Someone who tries to save my life does not require a formality such as Lady. You may call me Aradel."

"It seemed like you didn't need much help," he pointed out with a shrug and took a step forward. He instantly sunk up to his armpits in the snow pile.

Aradel covered her mouth to keep from laughing and even had to press her lips together. He had forgotten that she was keeping the snow locked in place and needed to stay close to her side.

He looked up at her, his face filled with surprise. "Don't you dare laugh," he said, but his voice betrayed his own amusement.

She shook her head, but her body quivered with silent laughter. She had to put both hands over her mouth to try to contain it, but he started laughing himself. Her own laughter quickly joined his as she reached down and helped him up. She made steps in front of them so they could walk back down the mound to ground level. Reaching it, she suddenly felt a touch of warmth brush against her cheek cracking it a little, and her eyes widened.

"What's wrong?" Tallus asked.

"Nothing," she answered and quickly reinstated her shield of cold on her skin. She studied the crack in The Wall and realized then that the quake had done more than break their wall.

Aradel suddenly grasped the gravity of the situation. The Wall had been damaged, but worse, the curtain of magical cold that extended up beyond The Wall had been damaged as well. It wasn't that heat was just getting in through the crevice, it was getting through because of a tear in the fabric of the magic. With a shallow breath, she suddenly knew that spring was coming to more than just the Outlands, and this was its entry point.

Fire: Chapter Ten

———————— o ————————

"Coor, do you understand how hard I had to bite my tongue?" Thea said.

"I know, sweetheart," he replied, sounding exhausted as he threw more debris to the side. Coor knew these rants of Thea's well enough, and understood he just had to let them rip. He wouldn't be able to say anything to calm her down anyway.

"I mean, that Frost Queen!" Thea bent down tossing more debris to the side. "Sure, she only had fifteen girls with her, but those were the fifteen most powerful girls in their entire freezing nation! They probably could have wiped out our entire force!"

"Yes, sweetie. I know."

"And don't get me started on that Frost Knight. What was he thinking, stepping up to our Queen like that? Our history with them could hardly warrant such bold behavior. Sun God almighty! My only regret is that I didn't knock him on his ass!"

"I know, honey."

"Coor?"

"Yes, baby?"

"Coor?"

"I know, sweetie."

"Coor!" Thea yelled, finally getting his full attention. She placed her hands on her hips. "Were you even listening to me?"

Coor sighed and came toward her. "Truthfully, not really." Thea glared at him. "Listen, the meeting went well. Unexpectedly well. Let's just be glad for that. Darha doesn't need a war with the Frost Nation on top of this mess," he said, indicating the ruined shoreline of the east coast.

Thea deflated immediately and started picking away at the debris of a ruined house again. "I suppose so, but I still don't like them or trust them by any means."

Coor bent down, getting back to work as well. "Who would?"

"Darha would," Thea said flatly.

Coor gave a gentle chuckle. "That's true."

They dug through the debris for a few more minutes, Coor moving a very large five-foot section of clay, grunting as he pulled it aside and over. Suddenly, a stressed-sounding meow came from below.

"There it is," Thea said as she ducked into the small basement crawl space of the destroyed home. "Stupid cat. Hold my legs, Coor." Coor took her legs and gently started to lower her down into the hole. He could just hear Thea's voice echoing out, "If you bite me or scratch me, I will snap your neck, and we'll tell Emma we found you dead."

Coor laughed soundlessly. Thea would never let him live it down if she heard him laughing at her. Thea pretended to be completely hard and callous, but it was mostly a show she put on for everyone else. Coor knew her soft side; he'd seen her vulnerability, and she only showed it to him. Growing up, that had confused him, but as an adult he realized how special those sensitive moments with Thea were. She was beautiful when she was tough and beautiful when she wasn't. But what made it special was that she saved that vulnerable soft side just for him.

"I got it," Thea called, and Coor pulled her out of the crawl space, now holding a small black kitten. It was soaking wet and trembling, but it was very much alive and screaming bloody murder. "Hey, hey!" Thea said as it began to crawl up her neck. She sighed heavily, rolled her eyes, and gathered it in her hands firmly. Thea looked like she might snap its neck, but instead she ripped off a piece of her red cloak and wrapped the kitten up in it.

Coor smiled at her. "Softy."

Thea gave him a warning look. "Don't tell anybody."

Coor brought the corners of his mouth down and shook his head slowly. "Never."

"If anyone asks," she said standing up, "this was your idea."

Coor stood and nodded once. "Naturally."

Thea smirked playfully and then headed back to a wide-eyed, curly haired, red-headed little girl waiting beside her mother on the beach. Her father had been killed in the hurricane that had slammed into the east coast while they were meeting with the Frost Nation. Darha had gotten word when they returned and immediately dispatched Coor and Thea in that direction, which meant no sleep for them last night. Darha also sent a messenger to the army that was still up north trying to clean up from the tidal wave disaster to come east to search for survivors. But because traveling to and from the Frost Nation took so much time, there was nothing left to do by the time everyone arrived except attempt to clean up.

"Midnight!" the tearful girl exclaimed as Thea approached with the cat. Thea handed the bundle down to her, and after a quick snuggle, the girl handed it to her mother and then slammed her face into the front of Thea's legs, hugging her and crying. "Thank you, Lady Thea. Thank you."

53

Her big brown eyes moved up to Coor, but she didn't let go of Thea. "Thank you, my Prince."

Coor got down on one knee and smiled at her. "You're welcome, Emma."

She pulled away from Thea and watched Coor nervously, wringing her hands and biting her lip. She wanted to hug him, but she wasn't sure if she was allowed to hug the Prince. Coor's heart melted and he gently took the little girl's hand and pulled her against him. He even went so far as to pick her up in his arms, and she rested her head on his shoulder.

Coor's heart ached. He'd wanted a child his whole life, and he and Thea were trying; they'd been trying since they were married, but it just wasn't happening. He knew it broke Thea's heart as well. Thea may not have wanted a child as badly as Coor did, but she wanted to make him happy.

Coor glanced in the direction of his wife. She had moved away closer to the sea and was staring out over the disaster area and the ocean in almost a daze.

"You take care of Midnight, okay?" Coor said to Emma.

Emma lifted her head off his shoulder and nodded, her red curls bouncing with the gesture. He kissed her cheek quickly, set her back down on her feet, and went to Thea's side. By the expression on her face, Coor knew this was going to be one of those special, vulnerable moments he rarely got to see from his wife.

"What is happening out here, Coor?" she said in a pleading tone.

Coor sighed and rested his hand on her lower back. "I don't know, sweetheart."

Without another word, Thea leaned against him. Coor wrapped her up tightly in his arms as she began to quietly sob on his chest. To anyone watching, it probably looked like they were just hugging and looking out over the water, and that's how Thea and Coor both wanted it. Thea would never approve of the army, or anyone else, seeing her cry because it showed weakness. And Coor wanted these moments with her just for himself because this was a part of her no one else got to see.

"All hail the Queen!" one of the heralds from the army called.

Coor heard Thea suck in a breath. She quickly wiped her eyes before they both turned and saw the royal carriage on the disastrous beach. It was halted at the edge of the small hill where the grass met the sand, and Darha was just stepping out. Coor could see her shaking from ten yards away.

"What is she *doing* here?" Thea asked, and both went quickly toward her.

"Darha?" Coor asked as they approached.

"I, um." Darha allowed tears to fall down her cheeks. "I wanted to"— she swallowed heavily — "to see it."

Coor sighed and panned the beach. "Unfortunately, there's not much left to see."

Darha nodded and sniffed. "How many survivors?"

That was just like Darha, to ask how many lived instead of how many died. Thea and Coor glanced at each other before Coor looked back at his sister. "Of the 31,000 people who lived in the disaster area, 1,033 survived."

It appeared that all the air rushed out of Darha at once, like she was physically punched in the chest, and she nearly collapsed. Thea took hold of her, keeping her on her feet. Darha's eyes closed, and two large tears dripped down her cheeks. Coor couldn't even bring himself to correct her on not letting the people see her like this. Perhaps they needed to. Maybe they needed to see that the Queen was affected by what was happening to the nation and that she cared about them.

Darha met Thea's eyes desperately. "Please, escort me to some of the people. I need to see them. I want to speak to some of them."

"Are you sure?" Thea asked.

Darha nodded as another tear dripped down her cheek. Darha wiped her face with her sleeve as Thea took her first to Emma and her mother and her kitten. Coor heard the mother whisper some quick instructions on how to address the Queen properly.

"No, no." Darha said gently, holding her hands up. "She doesn't need to do any of that." Darha got down on a knee in front of Emma right in the sand. "Hello there," she said with a forced smile.

"Hello, your majesty," Emma said shyly and did a quick curtsy even though she was in pants.

The effort made Darha grin more genuinely through her tears. "That is a very pretty kitten you have."

The girl held the cat up under its arms in front of Darha's face. "This is Midnight."

Darha gently petted the kitten. "Hello, Midnight," she said in a stuffy voice and sniffed.

Emma held Midnight to her chest again. "Prince Coor and Lady Thea rescued him from my broken house."

"They did?" Darha said with some brightness. "I'm glad for that."

"Me too," Emma said. "My daddy died here and he gave me Midnight."

Coor saw his little sister swallow heavily. She bowed her head and tried to compose herself for a moment before looking back up at Emma. "I am so sorry, honey." Darha said, resting her hand on Emma's cheek.

Darha stood up and met with a few other stranded families, giving them what little comfort she could offer them. It wasn't very long, though, before Coor could see her becoming overwhelmed. He clenched his teeth and resisted the urge to pick her up, throw her into the carriage, and bring her home to keep her safe and away from all this pain and suffering. But it wasn't his place to do so. Thankfully, Darha soon headed back toward the carriage on her own with instructions that everyone should head to Vlid for shelter and supplies.

Darha paused next to the carriage and faced Coor and Thea. "Thea, I need you to come back to the palace with me, and Fitzu, and the rest of your scout team. Coor will you please stay with the army and escort these people to Vlid."

Coor nodded. "Of course."

Thea appeared confused. "I only have eight men left in my unit."

Darha nodded. "I know. I need them. I need the most powerful magic users."

"Why? What's wrong?" Thea asked.

Darha wiped her sleeve over her face again and bowed her head before meeting Thea's eyes. "The Derser Rects analyzed the water sample I sent them from the northern springs." She swallowed heavily and nodded. "It's sulfuric." Both Thea and Coor deflated, bowing their heads in defeat. "So severely sulfuric that people shouldn't even be breathing in the vapors from the natural springs."

Coor ran his hand through his hair. Sulfuric water was the result of volcanic gasses near a natural spring, above and often beneath the surface. When sulfur content reached high levels due to higher volcanic activity, the water became poisonous to drink. It was the only real concern of nature the Fire Nation ever had, due to the large chain of volcanic islands in the north. There were eruptions every now and then, but that was normal. As a precaution, however, the Derser Rects did routine checks, twice a year, on the sulfur levels of all the natural springs. Thea and her scout unit always accompanied them on these routine checks for protection from animals or the magic hating tribes in the Versis Mountains. The sulfuric levels in the Fire Nation's entire history had never been high enough to affect their drinking water. Worse still, severely sulfuric water meant acid rain. With the increase of hot days evaporating more water, and the increase in the rain storms and hurricanes, this was the worst thing that could happen to the Fire Nation at this point. It didn't *get* any worse than acid rain.

"But," Darha said sniffing, "the Frost Nation has sent boats over. From the watch towers, it looks like there are over thirty of them filled with snow and ice for us to melt down into drinking water."

Coor could see Thea didn't even have the fight left to make a snide remark about the Frost Nation. She just shook her head and hopped into the royal carriage. "Let's go." Darha watched Coor and gave him a forced, sad smile before climbing into the carriage with Thea.

Coor stepped up, rested his hands on the sill, and looked in at his wife and sister. "Be careful."

Thea glanced at him and then practically leapt across the carriage to press her lips to his out the window. She kissed him deeply before gazing into his eyes. "I love you."

Coor gently caressed her cheek with his knuckles. "I love you, too. Get some rest on the way home."

Thea nodded, gently running her thumb over his lips. "You too."

They kissed one more time, and the carriage driver pulled off. Thea watched Coor out the window until she was over the hill and out of sight. Coor then shook his head and faced the disaster area before him. He and his wife were long overdue for some alone time to fall apart together. Both felt their strength waning in the face of their nation's massive losses.

Frost: Chapter Eleven

———— o ————

The ice and snow crunched under the hunter's boot as he moved across the frozen wasteland. Behind him were two more men with long metal spears. The spears had a thick, coiled spring that, once inserted into the ice, shot the harpoon deep into the water then through the whale. Usually the body of the whale surfacing partially broke apart the ice, which allowed ease of harvesting.

Occasionally, a hunter went swimming in the blissfully frigid waters. They wore little else but a simple leather tunic and pants made from seal skin. Most hunters didn't mind swimming in the waters, but few liked to stay wet. These outfits shed water and kept them reasonably dry. The quake the day before had broken parts of the oceanic ice, but most of it had remained unmoved, so in the early morning they had resumed their hunt.

The hunters were part of a group that migrated with the whales during certain parts of the year from the western coast of the Frost Nation to the colder waters of the south. When winter began again, they would migrate back north toward the Isle of Ice. There were also small pods of whales that came from the gulf, but those were smaller with less to offer.

In a way, the hunters had become like family to the whales. If a young whale got separated, they would herd it back to the rest of the pod. If they got themselves stuck in ice or beached, the hunters would work together to get them back where they belonged. They tried to only take the old and the injured, but since the quake, word had spread that more from the whales would be needed. Food that had been plentiful in the farmlands was wilting because many people were afraid of the early spring and weren't tending the farms or harvesting what had grown this season.

One of the men suddenly called out and waved an arm to the others. It meant there was a whale and he was moving toward it. Before the other hunters could respond, the man was thrown backwards as the body of a whale broke the surface of the ice. The hunter gave a cry as the ice shook once more and another massive body burst through not far off. He dug his spear into the ice to keep himself steady as it shook under him.

He heard a great snap as the surface broke yet again behind him. He turned in time to see another hunter vanish beneath the ice. The first hunter ran toward his comrade. Should the ice turn over, he would drown.

The hunters may not fear the cold, but they needed air as much as any man.

"Help me!" his comrade called as the ice started to settle around him. He was flailing, desperately trying to stay above the ice that was closing in around him, which was as thick as an old tree trunk.

The first hunter fell to his knees beside his fallen friend and held the ice open with his bare hands as it tried to crash closed. He reached in and took hold of his drowning partner's arm, but yelled in pain and yanked his arm out of the water. To his horror, he saw his skin was suddenly covered in pale blue cracks.

It was impossible, but the sea was boiling!

The ice melted around him as he helplessly watched other man sink below the water, his skin cracking and breaking as the dark depth of the sea swallowed him. The injured hunter quickly backed away from the hole and rushed toward the rest of the hunters, holding his fractured hand to his chest.

"We need to go," he yelled.

There was another great crack behind them, and they stopped to look back. Another whale had broken the surface. As they stood in awe, four more whales floated to the surface, breaking through the ice. The injured hunter glanced back at the others. Not far in the distance, they noticed great chunks of ice melting before their eyes.

"We need to get back to Axion," he said before turning back to contemplate the dead whales and melting ice. "Something is wrong."

————

Kirill folded his arms as the newly mended throne room filled with angry voices. People had been flooding in since word of the dead whales had spread. Whales were sacred animals that were revered and used sparingly. They were more than cattle or sheep; they were beloved and admired creatures.

"What is being done about the Fire Nation?" one older man demanded, his face filled with hatred.

Although Kirill shared his dislike of the Fire Nation, he didn't want a war. War meant death, and they needed metal and stone from the Fire Nation. He instinctively glanced at Aradel, who stared forward with a straight and unyielding face.

"There is no proof they were involved," Queen Vesna insisted, but she looked tired. Her injury during the quake had set her back. She tired easily lately, and soon the moon pearls would glow for the next queen.

Kirill could not help but wonder if that next queen would be Aradel. He didn't put much faith in the moon pearls choosing someone of low birth, but he knew Queen Vesna had come from a normal family that was neither rich nor poor. Why should Aradel be any different? Unlike him, and many of the candidates, she seemed indifferent to the Fire Nation.

"What about the sulfur in our north-western springs?" another called.

"There have been reports of many volcanic eruptions," the Queen replied over all the voices. "Our great priests of the temple have found records in which our water supplies in the Outland have turned sulfuric in the past. This is not uncommon. We have retracted all our people from those areas and harvested what little we could before the sulfuric groundwater ruined the plants. We do not expect it to spread, but most of our people are in Secille, close to the safety of The Wall."

"Is it true?" a woman's voice broke through the crowd, "that The Wall is melting?"

"Only a section that was disrupted by the quake," Queen Vesna replied calmly as people started muttering. "We have no other reports of The Wall melting, and we have men working to keep that area contained."

"Damage to The Wall I can believe," the same older man interjected. "Even the sudden sulfuric waters. But I cannot believe we have any record of massive whale deaths!"

"That is true," Queen Vesna replied, and the murmurs around the room grew to a buzz. Kirill frowned in annoyance. These people were on the edge of panic.

"It must be the work of the Fire Nation," the older man concluded, and the sound in the room grew again.

The Queen appeared exhausted, so Kirill called, "Silence! The Queen speaks!"

Silence fell again, and the Queen straightened and turned to her people, taking in each one. Kirill could see her eyes scanning the room.

"They need the oil for light as badly as we do," Queen Vesna reminded them. "They have done everything we have asked and more. I do not believe they are working to destroy us. I believe they are as much victims as we are."

At this, silence resonated and only her words seemed to fill the room. Queen Vesna was a spiritual leader for the people as much as their actual leader. She had ruled for over three decades, and many had become fiercely loyal to her. She had never voiced hatred for the Fire Nation, but she had never spoken for its people with compassion before. Many people were confused as to where their loyalties should lie.

Kirill doubted Queen Vesna's ability to rule any longer, but the moon pearls still glowed softly for her. Until they faded, their winter world would bow to her decision. All of nature and its animals would do nothing to stop her will. The people had their doubts and worries, but Kirill knew that, so long as the Queen kept them safe and nothing showed a direct attack by the Fire Nation, they would continue to follow her.

Aradel stepped forward. "That concludes today's audience with the Queen. Please return on the morrow to have your voices heard."

People left, many speaking in whispers until at last they were alone. The candidates waited to be ordered away or given a task. Instead, the Queen continued to stare at the closed door. They waited.

"Has there been any word from Queen Darha?"

"None," Kirill replied, as he had overseen the message.

"We are sure they received it?" Queen Vesna demanded. He did not take her doubt personally. She was tired, and every detail must be considered.

"The owl returned without the samples." Kirill confirmed.

She nodded her head but continued to stare at the door as her fingers tapped on the icy throne. Kirill stared at Aradel, who was watching him closely. When their eyes met, she turned toward the Queen with wide eyes and nodded. He looked at her with confusion before she moved her hands subtly in an upward motion, indicating he should say something else.

"It will take time for news to return," Kirill reminded her, sending Aradel an annoyed look. He moved closer to the Queen. "You should rest before dinner."

Queen Vesna stopped her tapping and glanced up at him. Then she regarded the candidates with suspicion. None of them reacted to her stare; they all just waited. Without protest, she put up an arm. "Very well."

The women swarmed to help her to her feet, then all but carried her out of the door in a flurry of blue dresses. Only Aradel didn't follow as she came to stand next to Kirill. His arms were still crossed because of his frustration, but he turned to look at her.

Aradel swallowed before resting her head against his shoulder. It was in these moments that he remembered he was an entire head taller than her, and twice her width. He could snap her in half, but he had not her power or intuition. Were she to become queen, she would be the first from an impoverished family, and one of the most powerful Queens in history.

"She weakens a little every day," Aradel whispered sounding frail.

He uncrossed his arms and put one around her shoulders. He drew her close because she sounded so lost and confused. His frustration at not being able to stop what was happening, didn't match Aradel's emotions. That frustration dissipated, though, as he held her small shoulders and fell easily into his role as her surrogate older brother.

"It is the stress," Kirill said, confirming that he had seen the same in the Queen. "If we can figure out what is going on, perhaps that will help her."

"By the moon, I hope so!" Aradel declared. "May the Fire Nation find something soon."

Kirill pursed his lips. "I was surprised they didn't have scales and breathe fire!"

"Kirill!" Aradel admonished him for his crude remark and pushed at his side.

His laughter filled the great throne room as Aradel stalked out. Kirill watched her go and was pleased he could make her forget her worry, even for just a moment.

He sighed though when she was out of earshot. If things continued as they were, the pressure would bury them all. Something told him that when they did hear from the Fire Nation, the news would not be good.

Fire: Chapter Twelve

— o —

Darha heard another host of galloping hooves, and whatever feeble strength she had left collapsed inside her. She pressed her hands to her ears and curled up into a tighter ball in the back seat of the royal carriage. It was well into the wee hours of the morning, and Darha was supposed to be asleep. Thea had tried to convince her to go back to the palace to rest, but Darha couldn't bring herself to leave, so she lay down in the carriage. As she heard muffled talking, Darha squeezed her eyes closed and started crying silently. She couldn't take anymore bad news. The devastation on the east coast the other morning had sapped everything out of her, so many families, children, just dead or homeless. But the day had just begun.

After that, reports had come in for two days of livestock dying by the hundreds all over the Fire Nation, from either lack of food over the past six months or, farther north, drinking the poisonous sulfuric water. In the evening, as the sun was going down, reports came in of fish, another source of food, all turning up dead in the ocean. Some larger game fish like tuna and bass had washed up on shore on the north coast, with birds buffeting on their corpses. When the fishermen set out to investigate, there was so much dead floating sea life that they could barely see the water anymore. Large fish like sharks and whales, huge whales fifty feet long, were floating on the surface, half eaten by scavengers. Food was now getting scarce. Samples of the dead animals and sea life had gone to the Derser Rects yesterday.

After leaving the beach on the east coast, Darha, Thea, and a dozen fire wielders had headed to meet the Frost Nation boats that were coming in over the River Gora, only to find the river had swelled in another half mile. The water now filled the streets of the southern region villages, and it was as high as lower level windows of the houses. Darha had looked around when they arrived yesterday and felt a shiver run through her entire body. It was so cold and quiet and still. After the sun fell, the windows of the houses were as black and lifeless as the night sky. The only light was the cold moon reflecting off the still water filling the streets. The only sound was it gently lapping against houses.

For the past two days Thea, her scouts, and a few other fire wielders had been melting down the snow and ice the Frost Nation had sent for drinking water. Thea had staggered the melting process in two-hour increments so their magic wouldn't all run out at once. For two hours, half would melt the snow and ice, while the other half delivered the water to Vlid. When they returned, they would switch. The delivering of the water allowed those fire wielders to replenish their magic so there was no gap in the melting. Vlid was suffering badly, mostly for water. The city was overrun up to Third Gate with refugees from across the entire nation. Half of their food and water supply was gone; the other half was dwindling quickly. Darha feared reserves would be tapped into soon, especially with the reports of dying fish and livestock.

Along with the snow and ice, the Frost Nation had sent what very well could have been every ounce of oil they had. Eighty barrels had been unloaded to keep fires and lights going in Vlid. The latest death report said that one hundred and five people, mostly children, had been turned to stone because of the cold and lack of firelight during the nighttime hours. With that knowledge, Darha had that oil rushed to Vlid by the army and even ordered the oil be taken out of the four chandeliers in the throne room and distributed to the people.

Darha had watched the Frost Nation traders help unload the barrels and other goods. A heavy, uncomfortable silence had fallen over the usually bustling activity of a large trade like this. It was almost somber. No one said a word to another, aside from quick, empty directions. The Frost Nation traders regarded her with both hatred and sympathy. They still clearly had their reservations about Darha and her people—the two dozen armed guards that stayed in the boats were proof of that—but they also saw the suffering of her nation. They were now aware of just how far the River Gora had swelled inland. They could see for themselves the dark, dead, quietness of the flooded village in which they were doing business.

The building stones Darha had prepared for the Frost Nation were packed up in their boats to be used for rebuilding dwellings or constructing safe houses. Darha had nothing more to offer them because seven forges of the Fire Nation were either flooded along the River Gora or permanently damaged from the massive quake several days ago. She felt guiltier as two hours passed and the Frost Nation was still unloading the goods Queen Vesna had sent. Darha had started to cry then, and before she could wipe the tears from her cheeks, one of the armed Frost Nation soldiers waiting in the boats had caught her. He met her eyes and pressed his lips together in a sympathetic smile and nodded once. Darha nodded in response. She wished that soldier would have come over and talked to her, maybe eased the tension of the trade, but he didn't. Should she have she gone over to talk to him? Neither one did, and the Frost Nation shoved off toward their shore without a word of parting.

Now, lying down in the royal carriage with her hands pressed to her ears while the melting of snow and ice continued, Darha was crying heavily. Even though she knew none of this was her fault, her heart was heavy with the sick feeling that she was failing her people somehow. As Queen, she should be able to protect them, and all she was doing was nipping at the heels of whatever was wrong with the planet and trying to clean up its mess.

"Darha?" she heard softly through her hands. Darha opened her eyes and saw Thea's face through the window of the carriage. Thea quickly pulled the door open and climbed in. Closing the door, she shifted the curtains so no one could see inside. "Hey, hey," Thea said gently and reached for her. Darha started shaking with sobs as Thea lifted her upper body and pulled her into an embrace. "Shh, shh," Thea said rubbing Darha's hair. She cried on Thea's shoulder for a good ten minutes.

To take her mind off her nation falling to pieces, she thought about Thea and how strong she was. Thea hadn't slept in two days and she was holding it together. The woman barely even complained. The extent of her complaining was a soft sigh now and again and a rub, or scratch of her forehead before she was back to work doing what needed to be done. Why couldn't Darha be more like that? The Fire Nation needed a Queen like Thea in these disasters, not Darha.

"I don't want to be Queen anymore," Darha moaned quietly.

"Shh, shh," Thea said soothingly as she continued to rub her hair. "Listen to me," she said gently. "This fight isn't over yet."

"How is it not?"

Thea gently lifted Darha off her shoulder. "The Derser Rects have finished their analysis." Her heart started racing as Thea pinched a loose strand of Darha's hair and tucked it behind her ear. "They know what's wrong. And if we know what's wrong..."

"We might be able to fix it," Darha said.

A faint smile came to Thea's lips, and she closed her eyes and nodded.

"Leave your orders, and let's go."

"I already have," Thea replied.

Darha suddenly felt stronger then she had in months. It was like coming back from the dead. Her heart was beating so fast she felt it in her ears. She practically leapt over Thea's lap and threw aside the curtain, shooting halfway out the carriage window. "Driver! Get us back to the palace!"

———

The driver pulled up to the Temple in eastern Vlid that was miraculously unharmed by the quake. Crowds of refugees naturally took it as a sign of the Sun God's provenance and surrounded the entire building, completely flooding the steps. Some people were on their knees or their faces, praying or screaming at the Sun God, asking why he'd abandoned them. One woman was weeping over a dead child who had turned to stone. Hundreds of people sought shelter on the top tier of the Temple just outside the main doors, which had a narrow lip of roof overhead that could protect them from the rain should more come.

Darha and Thea stepped out of the carriage, and an entourage of personal assistance and soldiers, who would escort Darha to the research area in the basement level of the Temple, quickly came forward. At the same time, the terrified civilians rushed to gather around the Queen, reaching for her between the escorts, begging for help. Darha cowered against Thea as the entourage closed ranks around her, keeping the panicked people at bay. Darha had never felt so helpless in her entire life than she did at this moment, seeing the terrified and desperate faces of her people, her nation. Darha could have collapsed easily and given up right then and there if Thea had not suddenly put her arm firmly around Darha's waist and held her tightly to her side. Darha looked up at her exhausted sister and drew strength from the fierceness she could still muster in her eyes, as she carefully watched the crowd to make sure no one breached the protective detail around them.

They made it up the gray, wide stone steps, fighting the crowd the entire way, and stepped through the two silver double doors. Walking through these doors was almost like stepping into the palace throne room but, to Darha, it was even better. The main sanctuary was a vastly wide, round room. It didn't appear to be very much, with empty gray stone walls and floor. Silver, decoratively forged pews filled the room, bowing out in a half circle around the altar at the front where the Dersers preached once a week. There really wasn't very much to it at first glance, but once you got out from underneath the balcony above, the sanctuary didn't seem so plain anymore.

The ceiling was cone shaped and massively tall, but the stunning thing, was the multiple stained glass windows arranged in the roof so that they spiraled upwards into the very tip, looking like the shell of a snail from down below. Each window was a different depiction of artwork, whether it was the face of an ancient hero, or a single rose blossom or flower sitting on a plain background, or one with no definitive picture at all, just multicolored designs or shapes. At the very top, just inside the tip of the cone, was a stained-glass depiction of the sun. Patrons always made a point of gazing up at the ceiling whenever they entered the Temple, no matter how many times they had seen it in their lives, because a sight like that never got old.

The Temple was overrun with wounded refugees. Not a single pew or square inch of floor was empty. Exhausted healers and medical experts, and a few of the capable wounded, looked up when she entered. They followed her with their eyes for a few moments as she was led to the left side of the sanctuary and through another, smaller set of silver doors. Past them was a wide stone staircase that spiraled down to the basement where natural research took place.

Darha had always hated it down here. It smelled funny and there were a lot of restrictions in a lot of areas. You couldn't touch anything in some rooms for fear of contaminating the work. Today, however, she strolled down the white, smooth limestone hallway with hope and joy. There was no place she'd rather be at the moment.

The soldiers led her to the right side and, at the end of the hall, more people and soldiers waited. Coor was already there, standing outside the door with his arms crossed, talking to one of the Dersers. When he saw Darha and her party coming down the hall, he excused himself and went quickly to meet them.

"Hey," he said and kissed Darha's cheek. He leaned in to kiss Thea's lips, but paused and looked at her face in concern. "You haven't slept," he said rather than asked.

"Like I had time," Thea responded and leaned in to kiss her husband's lips quickly. "Let's go," Thea said, gesturing impatiently toward the room. "We have to figure out if this mess is fixable."

Everyone filed into the oval-shaped, brown, stone room. Darha liked this room the most out of the entire basement. It wasn't so white and sterile feeling. There was actual warmth to the stone. Long silver tables were set up in a 'U' shape where some officials were already gathered, along with prominent figures like Fitzu and Kimbro, the regional leaders, and the four province overlords from the north, south, east and west. Everyone in there bowed low at the waist as Darha entered.

67

"Ladies. Gentlemen," Darha said, acknowledging their sign of respect in the strongest voice she could muster. She held tightly to the image of fierceness she'd seen in Thea's eyes just outside the Temple, and it doubled her determination. If Thea could still be strong after no sleep for two days, Darha could be strong now.

Coor pulled out Darha's chair in the center of the head table, and she sat down. Thea took a seat to Darha's left, and Coor sat on her right. All the regional leaders and overlords took a seat after that, looking toward the front where Dorsh, the head researcher of the Derser Rects, stood amongst a lot of paperwork and charts. He appeared nervous, or perhaps scared. He was a short man in his early forties, with thinning orange hair. He was skinny throughout his whole body, save for the small pot belly which seemed a little out of place on his thin frame. He had large, sensitive brown eyes that reminded Darha of a nervous deer.

"My Queen," he said, his voice shaking. "Prince Coor. Lady Thea. These disasters have proven quite a challenge to diagnose." He swallowed heavily. "And I'm afraid the diagnosis is…" He paused, and Darha's heart leapt up into her throat. "Catastrophic."

Nervous glances and murmurs went around the room. Darha herself even shot one at Coor and Thea. Coor returned the glance, but Thea's light gray eyes just narrowed on Dorsh, and Darha wondered for a second if Thea was afraid of anything, anything at all.

"Get on with the explanation," Thea said firmly.

Dorsh hastily bowed once. "Of course, Lady Thea." He turned toward the wall behind him and pulled down what looked like map of the planet, including the Frost Nation to the south, only with a new dark line surrounding both nations that cut through some of the land as well as the sea, in an irregular shape around the two nations.

Dorsh faced the ensemble again. "As we all know, the planet the Gods gave us runs on its own self-sustaining cycles. The Sun heats the world and water. Water evaporates, which later turns into rain. The rain cools the planet again. Cycles like that occur all around us all the time, whether we notice them or not. It's the Gods at work." Dorsh's brows furrowed in fear. "What we have learned recently thanks to the samples, particularly the samples the Frost Nation sent us, is that there is another cycle we were not aware of happening under us."

"Under us?" Fitzu asked.

Dorsh nodded. "We do not have all the details yet—we may not have all the details in two lifetimes—but what we know so far is that under the ground of the planet, there is another cycle that destroys and renews the very land of our planet."

"What is this new cycle's process?" Thea asked.

"Very deep underground, below even the sea level in some places, the current land is being melted into the lava that erupts from our volcanos. Now, if that were happening without some land renewal someplace, we would have run out of land eons ago. If the planet is melting its own land, where is more land coming from?" Dorsh pointed to the black line on the map. "Thanks to high levels of sulfur we found in the Frost Nation's ocean, where no aboveground volcanic activity is seen, we have made the conclusion that there are underwater volcanos, and they all run along this black line on the map around both of our nations."

Darha glanced over at Coor and Thea again. "What does this cycle beneath the planet have to do with these disasters on the surface?"

"It's given us a point of origin."

Darha's eyes went a little wide, "Which is?"

Dorsh pointed to Rask, a large island in the northern volcanic island chains. Darha's heart sped up because that was the only island on the entire planet that held a mega-volcano. That volcano had been dormant since before the dawn of time, which was a good thing—since it was the only volcano with the power to destroy the planet with one eruption.

Darha leaned forward in her chair and pressed the tip of her finger a little too hard into the table top. "Are you telling me the volcano on Rask is active?"

Dorsh swallowed heavily and nodded, "Yes."

Loud chatter erupted suddenly as panic went around the entire room. Darha was lost in her own silent thoughts for a moment, thinking the world was about to end, when she noticed Dorsh trying to calm the mass and say something.

"Be silent!" Darha yelled without looking away from Dorsh. The room went silent immediately. "What are you saying, Rector?"

Dorsh brushed his hand across his sweaty forehead. "There might be a way to stop it." Murmurs erupted again as Dorsh met Darha's eyes desperately. "There is a chance that the volcano can be cooled." Curious noises went around this time, and Dorsh swallowed heavily, clearly having a hard time getting the next words out. "With the help of the Frost Nation."

Angry sounds erupted in the room. Fists went flying into the air and accusing fingers pointed at the head Derser. Dorsh looked afraid as some soldiers threatened to kill him, others called him a traitor, many called for his execution. Darha's teeth clenched as she stared at the top of the table. She didn't know what to do. Anger was not an emotion with which she was well acquainted.

"Did you not hear the Queen!" Thea suddenly yelled and jumped up from her chair. The noised in the room dimmed. "Be silent! Or I will execute every one of you myself!"

Darha's eyes shifted up to Dorsh's. He held his hands out to her pleadingly. "It's the only hope we have, your majesty," he said in a small voice.

Darha took in a deep breath and looked back down at the table top. "Everyone out," she called sharply. Soft murmurs went around the room. "Everyone out except the four regional overlords, Kimbro, Fitzu, Coor, and Thea. You all stay. We will discuss these matters without the risk of further outbursts."

Darha didn't take her eyes off the tabletop as the soldiers and regional leaders all filed out. Coor followed and closed the door behind them. The silence wrapped around Darha's throat, choking her. Thea lifted a chair and put it on the other side of the table, then slid herself over the top of it, landing on the opposite side, and sat down again, this time facing Darha. Kimbro, Fitzu, and the overlords all gathered closer around the Queen as well.

Darha looked at Dorsh again. "Rector, are you sure about this?"

Dorsh nodded. "Yes, your majesty. The recent disasters are all linked to the heating of the Rask Island volcano."

"How?"

Dorsh pointed to Rask Island on the map. "As you can see, this black line we have drawn around our planet, lines up with all visible volcanos on the surface. It only stands to reason that there are also volcanos under the water along this line." He faced Darha again. "Or there could be fissures, or cracks of some kind. We aren't completely sure without further studies. They don't have to be the cone-shaped volcanos we are accustomed to seeing on the surface, but"—he returned to the map— "either way, as the surface volcanos act as vents for the immense pressure and heat under the land, so do these underwater anomalies." He looked back at the small crowd. "The amount of sulfur in our ocean, and the Frost Nation's ocean, and our natural springs, could only come from massive volcanic activity that only the mega-volcano on Rask could be responsible for. One of the regular volcanos in the north, even the largest one, Tamon, could not be responsible for as much devastation as Rask has put out already." Dorsh dragged his pointer along the black line of the map. "The activity of Rask has caused a chain reaction along this entire black line, affecting everything in its wake." He turned his attention to Darha again. "The sulfur output from Rask, even in just six months of activity without a full eruption, would cause a massive amount of sulfur, not only in our water, but in the air. The excess sulfuric gases in the air are causing the hotter days we've experienced, thus causing the excess storms, and putting the weather patterns out of whack."

"What about the quakes?" Thea asked.

"That is why, Lady Thea, we believe these underwater vents are actually cracks, or fissures, rather than traditional cone-shaped volcanos. We believe the masses of land on either side of these fissures are moving...floating, if you will...on top of the lava under the ground. Because they are not stable, they are crashing into each other, causing the quakes."

"The tidal waves?" Coor asked.

Dorsh nodded. "Those are the result of the quakes under the ocean. When the land moves suddenly in a quake, it displaces those tons and tons of water in the ocean. That water has to go somewhere, so it comes inland, where there is room for it."

Darha let out a short breath. "And cooling the Rask volcano will stop these disasters?"

Dorsh shifted uncomfortably. "We don't believe it will stop them, but it will greatly minimize them. It will certainly reduce the risk we are at now with Rask active. If Rask is cooled, it will end the superheating of the fissures and volcanos along the black line. They may still run hot, but won't be deadly. And if we can stop the rising of sulfuric gas in our sky from the excess volcanic activity, our planet won't heat up any further and weather patterns will eventually return to normal. Also, if we can stop this volcanic chain of reactions, it will end the rise of sulfuric effects in our drinking water."

Darha sighed heavily and sat back in her seat, placing her hands on her lap. Everyone remaining in the room regarded each other silently. Thea sat back in her chair as well, and crossed her arms as she looked from Coor to Darha.

Darha rubbed her forehead with her fingertips. She saw no other option. She scanned the faces of the gathered people and shrugged a shoulder. "So, we will inform the Frost Nation that they need to save our planet."

"Now hold on a moment, your majesty," Askari, the Northern regional overlord said, holding up his hands. The north had suffered the

71

most in these disasters, since it had started with the volcanic activity there. Unable to understand why he would be objecting, she stared at him in astonishment. "Your majesty, we have our own problems to attend to. The Frost Nation is an extra unneeded burden we should not concern ourselves with."

"Let them burn for all we should care," Porva, the Eastern overlady said with a careless shrug.

Coor and Thea stayed frustratingly silent. "Did you not hear the presentation?" Darha said slowly, trying to stay calm. "Rask needs to be cooled. And we have an entire nation of ice and snow magic wielders just a six-hour boat ride south of us."

"Let them deal with this in their way, and we will deal with it in our own," Askari sneered.

Recalling the kindness of Queen Vesna during their meeting, and the huge abundance of gifts she had sent to aid the Fire Nation, Darha felt herself get very angry deep inside, where she never let anger reach her.

She glared at Askari so hard that from the corner of her eye she saw Thea's eyes widen. "If you think for one moment that I will spare any aid to my nation, including from the Frost Nation, you have seriously underestimated me as your Queen." Askari's eyes went wide. "I love this nation, and I will spare nothing, *nothing*, to save her. Least of all my pride over some ancient grievances with a nation that has done nothing but help us abundantly since communication about these disasters began. Do I make myself perfectly clear?"

Askari sat back in his seat. "Y-yes. Of course, your majesty. I apologize. I didn't mean to offend."

Darha continued to glare at him. "Do not challenge my decisions again about the Frost Nation. Do you understand me?"

Askari dipped his head down low until his chin touched his chest. "Yes, your majesty."

Darha glanced at Thea, only to find her faced turned to the side, eyes squeezed closed, lips pressed together, and her shoulders shaking with silent hysterical laughter. Darha tried not to smile since business wasn't concluded yet, and pursed her lips instead. "I will write the letter to Queen Vesna myself and arrange a meet in three days' time to discuss a course of action. I will only take a small host with me this time. Thea, Coor, I want you to stay here and continue disaster aid with the army and the melting of ice and snow for drinking water." Darha loved her brother and sister, but based on the last encounter with the Frost Nation, she didn't dare take them on this run. "Are there any questions or concerns?" Everyone stayed silent. "Good." Darha stood.

Without a word, and without her entourage, or her brother and sister, Darha swept out of the room feeling fearful, yet exhilarated from that meeting. They knew what was wrong. They might be able to fix it. But still, that was a big "might." If they couldn't cool Rask, the world would end. *End!* Everyone would die.

Her emotions were a mess. She wasn't completely sure what the proper thing to feel was. All she knew was that she and Queen Vesna needed to meet. After that, things would be decided and action would be taken. She could not wait to get to the southern shore.

Frost: Chapter Thirteen

Aradel stared straight ahead as the soldiers constructed the makeshift tents. When they were done, two large tents would face each other—one to host her people, and the other for the Fire Nation. Most of the candidates were with Queen Vesna, but Aradel had needed some time to herself, so she had come to watch Kirill order people around. He was always very good at ordering people around.

Aradel stopped watching the activity of the men working and walked across the softening landscape to the edge of the river. The River Gora had been so far from her, and now she had been there twice in a short time. She felt the warmth press in around her as she kept her shield carefully secure. The world was deteriorating so quickly Aradel worried that not even their wall could protect them. From the serious tone of the letter, it seemed that whatever the Fire Nation had found out did not bode well.

She heard the soft ringing of a bell. With a smile, she turned back toward the activity and waved at Yorten and his son, Tallus. Memories of their last encounter flooded her mind, but she kept her emotions in check. There were more important matters to attend to. Aradel looked back over the river as both started to unload the ice and stack it around the Queen's tent. Queen Vesna would keep them cool until the Fire Nation could take it. The good thing about ice and snow is that they had it in abundance. Although the Fire Nation had little they could trade, the stone they did have had repaired many homes.

"Lady Aradel." Tallus's voice broke into her thoughts, and she turned around again, unable to hide her surprise that he had approached her. "It is good to see you again."

She felt her cheeks warm softly at his attention. Careful not to stumble over her words she replied, "And you. In these trying times it is good to see a familiar face."

"Yes," he replied still grinning. "I just wanted to thank you again."

"Your continual thanks aren't necessary," Aradel replied, facing him completely. "You and your father have worked tirelessly. Has there been any progress at The Wall?"

The Queen elects had each been assigned weeks at the wall, and hers had already passed. It would be some time before Aradel would be up again to help with the repair. Queen Vesna had been talking about going to their mountain palace. Deep within the Lonely Mountains, the power to repair The Wall was waiting for them. If the moon pearls could harness the power of the ancient Ice Crystal, the tear in the magical fabric of The Wall could be fixed.

Tallus's grin fell a little. "It is higher, but continues to slowly melt. It will take some time for it to return to its former glory."

Aradel nodded, guarding her emotions, and gazed back over the river. A light fog kissed the surface of the water, but she could still see when the first boat broke the horizon. It seemed that fewer boats, with fewer people were coming toward them than had last time. She glanced back at Tallus and found that he, too, was watching the boats.

"I had better go back," he muttered and started away.

"Tallus," she said and faced him. He paused, looking back at her expectantly. For some reason, she felt comfortable around him even though she had known him such a short time. There was something unassuming about him that put her at ease. "Please be careful," she finally added.

He nodded, "I always am."

When Tallus returned to the sled, Yorten waved. Aradel waved as well, and then remembered the Fire Nation was at her back. She peered over her shoulder and figured the boats were far enough out that she likely hadn't been seen. Hurrying to the tents, she kept her head up and her face serene.

She found Kirill in the tent set up for the Fire Nation, throwing wood into two fire blazers in anticipation of their arrival. He appeared deep in thought, putting the pieces in one by one. Kirill was one of the highest ranked in their army; he didn't need to do it himself. Yet Aradel knew that when he was worried he felt the need to do something with his hands.

"Kirill," Aradel called, stepping close.

He looked up as though coming out of a daze. His expression was serious. "What is it?"

"They are nearly here," Aradel told him and then glanced toward the Queen's tent. "I'm worried."

Kirill stopped stacking wood, clapped the wood dust off his hands, and put a hand on her shoulder as he always did when trying to comfort her. He had done it as a boy and he did it now as a man. It was good that if everything else was changing in her life, Kirill would remain as he was.

He bent down to look her in the eye. "We can handle the Fire Nation."

"I'm not worried about them," Aradel explained, remembering that, despite what had happened, hatred toward the Fire Nation remained. "I'm worried about the news they bring."

He pointed at a group of soldiers and bellowed, "Finish stacking this."

They hopped to it, fearful of Kirill's wrath if they moved too slowly. It still amused her that so many people feared him when she felt safest at his side.

They left the warmth of the Fire Nation tent and went into the other. Under the Queen's tent, which had a thicker canopy to keep the sun off, there was one large chair. A light fabric infused with wax for protection from possible rain connected the two tents above. Behind the frost tent was a private tent for the Queen.

Kirill stopped in front of the throne and whispered, "We will figure something out. I know you are worried about Queen Vesna, but the moon pearls still glow brightly for her."

"You're right," Aradel conceded.

"Of course I am," Kirill replied.

"Commander Kirill!" a guard called, rushing toward them. "The Fire Nation is preparing to land."

"Shall we go and greet them?" Kirill asked, and she managed a meek smile.

"I shall tell the Queen," Aradel said and swept from the main area to the small break in fabric behind the throne.

Queen Vesna lifted her head as Aradel entered. There was tension on her face that the old Queen couldn't hide. The pain of her hurt knee had kept her awake and been a strain during their travels. Were it not so vital that the Queen be present, she likely would not have traveled at all. "They are here," Aradel announced, and instantly all the elects were on their feet getting the Queen into place. Queen Vesna no longer argued and tried to do things on her own.

She had placed a ring of ice around her knee to keep it stiff and cold. That had helped tremendously, but it had not fully fixed the problem. They exited the private tent and set the Queen in front of her chair in the main tent. Not a moment passed before Kirill walked around the corner. His face was grim and serious as the Queen of the Fire Nation, and a small entourage, followed close behind. The Queen was, however, without the two warriors that Aradel had seen at their first meeting—the woman who had shoved Kirill, and the man by that woman's side. Given the last encounter, that was probably wise.

Queen Vesna remained standing. Though she seemed unsteady, she did not fall as she smiled and called gently, "Greetings Queen Darha."

"Hello Queen Vesna," the Fire Nation Queen responded kindly, but noticing the pinched expression on her face, Aradel could tell she was worried. "How have you been?"

"I do not believe we have time for niceties," Queen Vesna responded as she took a step toward the table set up under the canopy between the two tents. "We have eagerly been waiting your arrival and your news for two days. You can understand my impatience."

"I can," Queen Darha replied, waving a small man with strange orange colored hair forward. "This is Dorsh, the head researcher of our Derser Rects. He has made use of all the samples and believes he understands what is happening and perhaps has a solution."

The man had a rolled parchment clenched to his chest. He hurried forward and unrolled it on the table. Both Queens stepped closer and Dorsh licked his lips nervously. He glanced over at his Queen, who nodded.

"Our problem is here," he said, pointing to a large island to the north of the Fire Nation. "On Rask, there is a volcano that we classify as a mega volcano. It has the power to end our world, and it is now active. If it erupts, we won't survive it."

A heavy silence fell over the Frost Nation as everyone, including Queen Vesna, looked at the little man in horror. Aradel glanced back at Kirill. His face was impassive, but his eyes did shift over to hers. There was a glint of worry in them, which set Aradel's heart racing with anxiety that she was determined to hide.

"How can a volcano all the way up there affect us down here?" Queen Vesna asked in disbelief and pointed at the southern pole area where the whales had died.

"See this black line?" Dorsh asked, less nervous as he went into full lecture mode. Aradel had seen it happen to her teachers. For teachers, there was nothing as natural as lecturing.

"Yes," Queen Vesna replied, staring at the dark black line.

"That is where our records indicate a possible chain of fissures is located. Based on the high sulfuric content and high temperatures in your ocean water, we believe this line continues down along your west coast and continues around the southern part of your nation before reconnecting with the line here in the northeast," he explained, tapping the eastern side of the map.

"Fissures?" Queen Vesna asked. Clearly she was as unfamiliar with this word as Aradel was.

"They are almost like our surface volcanos, releasing heat and sulfuric gases in massive amounts. Only they are likely not cone-shaped structures, but rather cracks in the sea bed. The land on either side of these fissures seems to be colliding into each other under the water as well, which is causing the quakes and the massive tidal waves." Aradel leaned forward to inspect the map and the dreaded black line.

"But a quake didn't kill those whales," Queen Vesna pointed out.

"In a way, it did," he replied before pointing at the Fire Nation's western coast. "We are having the same problem with finding dead sea life, and it has been attributed to underwater activity. We believe the same substance that comes out of our volcanos is spilling out into the ocean floor from these fissures. When the fissures along this line first erupted and opened, resulting in that devastating quake, there was likely a concentrated blast of hot water and gas that preceded the lava. This is what killed your whales."

"Are they still in danger?" Queen Vesna demanded, concerned.

"We can't be sure, but it seems that only the initial underwater eruption is deadly." Dorsh shrugged. "After that, the sea life likely adapts or migrates elsewhere."

"What is causing it?" she asked, point blank.

The man licked his lips again nervously. "The mega volcano. So long as it's active, the quakes and resulting damage will continue. Rask's activity is causing the activity among all the volcanos and fissures along this black line. The excess gas being released into our sky from this activity is what's causing the warmer days and heat that is harming your people. These gases are essentially trapping the sunlight's heat and keeping it from escaping into our sky. That's why the River Gora is flooding too. As your snow and ice melts, it causes the river to swell."

"And your solution?" she asked, her voice commanding.

Queen Darha stepped forward and interjected before the little balding man could respond. "We want to cool it down."

Queen Vesna blinked a few times, and Aradel realized what the Fire Nation Queen was saying. Silence marched on as the reality of the situation settled in. Aradel glanced between Queen Vesna, and the tired faces of the Fire Nation people. They looked far more worn out, like threadbare rugs that were fraying at the edges. They were certainly getting the brunt of these massive natural events. Queen Darha particularly looked worn. Aradel couldn't imagine the devastation she was facing farther north in her land. Yet somehow, she seemed determined to remain poised and dignified, although Aradel could see that the Fire Queen would rather collapse.

"What do you need from us?" Queen Vesna asked finally, her question directed at Queen Darha.

"Dorsh believes that if we get a large enough piece of ice and place it into the volcano, it may work, or at least buy us time," Queen Darha managed to reply.

"May?" Queen Vesna asked, studying the map. "I can't send a member of my nation to certain death on a maybe."

"My Queen," Aradel interrupted before she knew what she was saying. "I volunteer." All eyes swiveled to her, but she remained unfazed. Her face was set in determination as she met the eyes of her Queen, whose word was the only one that mattered.

Queen Vesna blinked at her in surprise. "Why?"

"Any chance is worth the risk," Aradel reminded her, thinking of The Wall, and her people who only survived because of it.

Queen Vesna pressed her lips together reluctantly. "You're right," she agreed, before turning back to Queen Darha. "We will break off a piece of our Isle of Ice here and transport it through the ocean. Your people can escort until the climate becomes too much for the Frost Nation, where upon they will return here and the Fire Nation will have command of the mission. We will transport barrels and barrels of water for Aradel's consumption, enough to last the entire trip there and back, so she can use her magic to keep the iceberg cold, and keep a constant ice shield around herself to protect against the heat."

"My Queen," Kirill said suddenly, stepping forward as Aradel resolved herself to the quest. "Lady Aradel is needed here. I am the best choice to go on this quest. I can both defend myself, and am powerful enough to keep the iceberg cold. I will also consume less water because of my higher heat resistance through the Fire Nation's warmer climate."

"Kirill," Aradel breathed, shaking her head as her heart started to race.

"I'll not make a decision now," Queen Vesna insisted before looking up at the Fire Nation's Queen. "Do you consent to this plan?"

"I will spare as many men as I can," Queen Darha agreed.

"We'll have boats made to aid in pushing the great iceberg," she responded, leaning on the table to take the pressure off her bad leg.

"Twelve at least. You shall need enough men to man all twelve boats and three scout boats."

"Why would we need scout boats?" Queen Darha asked, her perfect eyebrow raised in confusion.

"Icebergs seem reasonable from the top, but most of their mass is underwater," Queen Vesna explained. "You'll need to check water depths to make sure it can pass through without causing damage or getting stuck."

"I understand," she replied. "We will send you a message when all arrangements have been made."

"We shall do the same," Queen Vesna parroted before waving a hand to the side. "Please take this box of food as a gift. If I understand correctly, it is something you don't have."

"What are they?" Queen Darha asked as the box was set on the table.

"We call them Winter Berries," she explained as the Fire Queen peered inside it. "The children call them Blueberries for their dark color. They were taken from my personal garden."

"Thank you," Queen Darha managed as a range of emotions passed over her face.

"You are welcome," Queen Vesna replied, straightening her back. "Though I warn you, they are tart." Queen Vesna smiled at the young queen in a grandmotherly way.

It was one of the Queen's many abilities. She could put just about anyone at ease, while also telling them exactly what to do. Queen Darha was no exception, and she seemed genuinely warmed by their encounter before parting.

Aradel kept her eyes fixed on the Fire Nation as they made their way back toward the River Gora. "Queen Darha," Aradel called and went after the young northern Queen, recalling the exhaustion and slight despair in her eyes.

Queen Darha turned around, as did her small entourage. They all gathered close to their Queen's side and reached for their weapons. Queen Darha's hand went up, however, stopping any movement. Aradel watched them impassively as she approached. Being this close to her, Aradel realized the Fire Nation Queen was quite short. Her head was tilted up considerably so she could look at Aradel's face.

Aradel gave a small but graceful curtsy. "My name is Aradel, honorable candidate to Queen Vesna. I just wanted to say that you should not lose hope, Queen Darha."

Another wave of emotions went over the small Queen's face. She pressed her lips together and nodded once in respect. "Aradel, thank you for the encouragement." The whisper of tears erupted in her silver eyes, and she looked like she wanted to say more. Instead, she swallowed them down and nodded again before continuing toward their boats.

Aradel watched her for a moment before turning to go back to her Queen, and found Kirill staring after her. He appeared displeased, but Aradel didn't care.

"What do you think you are doing?" she hissed quietly at him as she approached.

"What am *I* doing? What do you think *you're* doing?" he countered.

"Don't change the subject," Aradel said, tapping into her Queen-elect's reserve of authority.

Kirill knew that look and sighed. "Saving your ass," he replied with a slight smile. He was trying to be jovial as they started back for the tents.

"You don't need to protect me," Aradel insisted. Even though she was angry, it still meant a lot that he would try to protect her.

"That is a bonus," he admitted, crossing his arms, "but I am the best choice. If something or someone attacks them, you don't know how to use a blade. You are powerful, but that is exactly why you should stay here. Our nation needs you to fix our wall."

Before she could respond, they reached the tents and Kirill swept inside, ending the debate. Aradel's breaths came in short angry bursts, as her eyes darted back and forth over the river as the Fire Nation boats faded into the mist.

The problem was that he was absolutely correct. Aradel was powerful, but she couldn't use a blade, and she could hardly manage a bow. As she turned to go inside the tent, she knew that he was right and that the Queen was going to see that as well.

Fire: Chapter Fourteen

o

Thea noticed Darha had been edgy and abrupt since the meeting in the Temple basement. It was not like her, but Thea had to admit the change was a little nice. Darha seemed more in control and in command, like a Queen should be. The only problem was that she wasn't used to being assertive, and it was coming off as unkindness and impatience. It was strange that over the past week, Thea had needed to remind Darha on a few occasions to be gentle. She would immediately deflate and apologize, but it wasn't long before she became a whirlwind again. It was humorous, and strangely tended to lighten Thea's heart a bit.

Thea was in her and Coor's bedroom chambers, sitting in the chair at her vanity desk, gazing into the mirror. It was hot tonight, so she was in a thin white nightgown with her hair down. Tomorrow they were to travel on the River Gora again, this time to its western mouth. They were meeting the Frost Knight called Kirill, supposedly toting along a massive iceberg like a child holds a snowball. Thea knew it might be possible for the Frost Nation, but she'd believe it when she saw it.

Darha had been in constant communication with the Frost Queen over the past week and a half via the messenger birds. Apparently, the journey up the west coast was going to take about a month, and Thea wasn't looking forward to it. It was going to be cold, and wet, and miserable, and she might end up slitting that Frost Knight's throat if he got mouthy with her. Then the job would never get done.

In truth, however, she knew that the Frost Knight was the only hope the planet had to survive, and she wasn't about to jeopardize that. None of which meant she had to like him; she just had to go with him.

Thea sighed as the heaviness in her heart set in over the fact that Coor was not going with her. It would be the first time they'd be apart for a month since they'd known each other. The two of them only had to discuss it once, though, as they both knew that Darha could not run a dying nation without Coor. He wasn't a magic user anyway, so he wouldn't have been able to blaze his core and keep himself warm near an iceberg. Thea was probably the most powerful magic user in the Fire Nation, just under Darha, and she knew how to handle herself in battle, so it made sense she would go.

The others chosen included Fitzu and her remaining scouts because they were one of the most powerful groups of magic users in the Fire Nation. They were also able to defend themselves with weaponry. Thea felt a small amount of comfort knowing she'd have Fitzu with her. He was like a brother to her, and they usually had a jovial time together on any mission. He would lighten the burden for sure.

Kimbro was going as well. Pretty much everyone, including Darha, had wanted him to stay and tend the wounded and ill in Vlid. But Kimbro politely, yet adamantly insisted he go with the iceberg party, saying, "This host is our only hope to save the planet. If something happens to them, we are all going to die. They need me much more than the regular populace right now." After a persuasive argument on his behalf, Thea and Darha conceded to let him come. That also brought a measure of comfort to Thea. She wasn't as close to Kimbro as she was Fitzu, but there was nothing wrong with the most powerful healer in the Fire Nation coming along.

Dorsh was coming. He had to come. He believed there was a specific spot inside the volcano where the Frost Knight could place the iceberg that would cool it more efficiently. He'd said something that Thea didn't understand about where the mantle and the crust met, or something to that effect—basically the hottest, most active spot in the volcano. Dorsh wasn't a magic user, so he would need to be protected and kept warm on the ocean.

A handful of about two hundred and fifty soldiers were spared for this trip, handpicked by Coor since they were his men. All of them were magic wielders, and accustomed to weaponry and battle situations. That would put about twenty men in each of the boats that the Frost Nation was building to push the iceberg. Thea only hoped that would be enough, but not many more soldiers could be spared because they were needed in the capital for disaster response.

Thea sighed at her reflection, trying to brace herself for this quest. Just then the chamber door opened and Coor came in. Thea turned toward her husband as he closed the door. His hazel eyes were incredibly sad. Emotion welled up in them both, and Thea stood from her chair and went to him, while he came quickly toward her. Throwing their arms around each other, they held on tightly as Thea began to cry into Coor's neck, and he buried his face in hers.

"It's okay," Coor whispered. "It's going to be okay."

No words were said for a few minutes as Thea sobbed, and Coor petted her long hair. They knew they couldn't avoid this trip, or this separation, because more was at stake than anything had ever been before—the life of their planet. It didn't make the separation easier—in fact it might have even made it harder—but there was no choice.

After a few minutes, Thea managed to quiet down, but they still held onto each other for dear life, not daring to put any space between them. "Are you ready?" Coor finally said softly in her ear.

Thea shook her head. "No."

"Everything is going to be fine. You'll see."

Thea nodded. She just wanted to be held by her husband. She savored every second she had with him. She paid close attention to his thick arms wrapped tightly around her back. She relished in his chest rising and falling against her as he breathed, delighting in his warm breath against her ear. She was acutely conscious of his hand gently running down the length of her hair, and the short bristles of his beard on her neck and jaw. She enjoyed her husband right now as completely as she could, feeling every inch of his body touching hers.

They spent hours together embracing each other has husband and wife, neither one seeming to want to stop. In one night, they made up the month of lost time together in advance.

———

The morning came too quickly for Thea. She'd gotten a grand total of an hour and a half of sleep. She wasn't complaining, though. In fact, she felt much more ready for this trip then she had been before her and Coor's long, passionate night. They were in the royal carriage now, heading west to the mouth of the River Gora. No crowds were around, so Thea allowed herself to curl up beside Coor with her head resting on his chest. He rested his cheek on the top of her head, fully relaxed, with her in his arms.

Darha sat on the other side across from them, biting her fingernails and staring out the window at the passing landscape. Thea smiled at her then drew her leg back and kicked her hard in the shin.

Darha cried out in pain, reaching down to clutch the injury and glared at Thea with incredible rage. "What do you…" she started to yell.

Thea kept smiling at her. She knew Coor was smiling broadly as well. Seeing their smiles, one slowly crept over Darha's lips until finally soft genuine laughter came forth. Thea heard the gentle rumble of Coor's chuckle in turn, and that made Thea start to chuckle. Soon all three of them were roaring with laughter.

It was an old joke between Thea and Darha. When Thea had been first adopted by the King and Queen, and they had taken their first ride as a family in the royal carriage, Thea was incredibly uncomfortable. She was ten years old at the time and started to act up by taking Darha's doll away. Thea thought it was hysterical that six-year-old Darha couldn't get it back from her. She just cried and cried, which Thea thought would be the whole of it. She'd been with the family long enough at that point to know Darha never got angry.

It wasn't until Thea held the doll out the window and threatened to drop it that this changed. Darha's little hands balled up into fists, her brows drew together, and she kicked Thea as hard as she could in the shin. Thea gasped in pain and then, out of pure respect for the little warrior that had suddenly emerged, she gave Darha her doll back. After that, Darha had kissed Thea's shin and petted her cheek saying she was so sorry and that she hadn't meant to hurt her. She was just worried for Mrs. Fancy Fire. Thea and Darha had been inseparable ever since.

The carriage finally came to a slow stop at the edge of the river's mouth, where the Frost Nation was already waiting. They were to take Thea and her host south to the Frost Nation's shores, where they would meet the Knight who was taking the iceberg up the coast. Thea, Darha, and Coor got out of the carriage and headed down to the shore to the Frost Nation boats. Fitzu, Kimbro, Dorsh, and the soldiers all disembarked their transports and joined them. A few of the Frost Nation boatmen greeted them with nods, while most just looked on suspiciously. None of them smiled. Thea felt her guard immediately go up, and the dread for this venture sunk in again.

One admittedly handsome soldier stepped forward. His hair was such a light, silvery blonde that it nearly looked white. He wasn't dressed in more than a sleeveless light blue top and thin light blue pants. His feet were bare. Thea thought she saw a glimmer of blue all over his skin as he stepped forward, but it was so faint she couldn't be sure.

"My name is Idok," the soldier said. "I will be the lead escort in getting you to the Frost Nation shores. I do hope you've packed warm clothes because the wind over the ocean waters will be frigid for you, especially in close proximity to the large iceberg Sir Kirill is sailing up the coast."

Thea narrowed her eyes. "I think we know how to keep ourselves warm."

Idok paused, looking like he wanted to say something else, but instead sighed gently through his nose. "We will await your departure in the boats."

Thea turned toward her men, taking a few steps back to address them all. "As we discussed, Ko, Julor, Beret, Thanhill, and Firns, you are my captains for the next month on this venture. Your groups of fifty will represent units one through five. Units, you report to your captains, captains you report to Fitzu or me. Questions?"

"No Commander," they said in unison.

Thea shot her thumbs over her shoulders toward the boats behind her. "Let's go."

Her men made for the boats. Right behind them were the supply runners, who began to pack them with food, warm clothes, leather tents, tarps, and armor, along with other essentials for a long journey. The Frost Nation brought tons of water for the Fire Nation, and the Frost Knight to consume.

Thea watched the bustling activity with crossed arms and a grim face, dreading the venture more and more with every passing moment. She didn't want to go. But the reminder of the devastation Rask could cause hardened her resolve that this was about to happen, and that it *had* to happen.

When the boats were packed, and the Fire Nation was all on board, Thea sighed and glanced at Fitzu, who just gently touched her shoulder and gave her a sympathetic smile before heading down. Dorsh and Kimbro followed him, and Thea turned to face her husband and sister. Both of them were trying to smile with encouragement, but it was obviously forced on both their parts. Thea sighed softly as she stepped up to Darha, and the two of them embraced tightly.

"I love you, little sister."

"I love you too," Darha said. She slightly pulled away and stared into Thea's eyes. "It's going to be okay, Thea." She forced a smile even as tears filled her eyes. "You weren't meant for anything less than saving our planet." Thea threw her head back and laughed along with Darha.

Thea took her little sister's face in both hands, and firmly kissed her forehead. "I'll see you soon."

Darha nodded and took in a trembling breath. "Consider it a command from your Queen that you return safely."

Thea smiled and bowed at the waist, keeping her eyes locked on Darha's. "Yes, your majesty."

Darha gave a brief smile and then quickly turned to go back to the carriage before Thea could see her tears fall.

Thea gazed at her husband, and the difficult emotions kicked in. He met her eyes, and they threw their arms around each other. Thea was in no hurry to get to the boats, and no one dared rush her. She and Coor held on to each other for a good long while.

"Darha's right, you know," Coor whispered softly. "You weren't meant for anything less than this."

Thea couldn't speak and just nodded, still holding on to him tightly. Coor kissed her neck quickly a few times, her cheek, and then her lips. It was a long kiss, and still no one rushed her.

Coor eventually pulled away and cupped her face in his hands. "I love you."

A single tear that she couldn't hold back fell down her cheek, and Coor gently wiped it away with his thumb. "I love you, too," she replied in a shaky voice.

He kissed her quickly one last time and, as if bracing himself for a hard hit, he took in a deep breath before he finally took his hands off his wife's cheeks. Thea took in a deep breath as well, keeping her eyes locked with her husband's, as she tried to gather her will to walk away from him. Only after a heavy swallow, and some fierce resolve, was she able to turn and head to the boats.

She climbed onto the one with Fitzu, Kimbro, and Dorsh, and the Frost Nation sailors shoved off. Thea remained standing as they started over the water. She wasn't sure if she was going to be able to turn around. Bracing herself again, knowing she was going to regret it if she didn't, she peered over her shoulder at her husband and sister. Coor was standing next to Darha with his arm around her shoulders, and both of Darha's arms encircled his torso.

Thea watched them for a long time until the shore was swallowed by mist. She permitted the pain to sink in for only fifteen seconds, and then hardened herself as she turned to look out over the river. She shifted her focus to her mission and what needed to be done to save her people. With her jaw set, and brows drawn together, she sat down in the boat and allowed the journey to begin.

Frost: Chapter Fifteen

Kirill was a grown man, and grown men didn't pout or sulk. They brooded.

Aradel had been there earlier, upset with him for taking on this quest. Annoyed, he'd pushed her out the door and closed it behind her, as if they were still children, unable to settle things with words.

He shoved things into his travel bag now with more force than was necessary. He understood her fears, and shared some of them, but her worry wouldn't change his mind. He was a soldier, and one of the most powerful men in the Frost Nation. This mission was perfect for him and his skills. She was needed here, with their elderly Queen and broken wall.

He tossed the bag roughly to the ground, put his hands on his hips, and stared at the floor. Aradel was right to be worried; this was a dangerous mission. He had been too hard on her, and she hadn't deserved to be treated that way. There was only one place she could be now, and he needed to see her, and his mother, before he left.

With a heavy sigh, he stepped over his bag and left his room. He weaved through their winter palace with purpose. When he reached the owl's tower, he paused at the bottom. Taking the steps two at a time, he paused when he heard her voice. She was singing the only song he had ever heard her sing; something her sister had taught her.

"Are we going to the sea?
They say that the moon
is big and bright and free.
Magic can happen here
magic stronger still,
if we meet at midnight
at the Ashtra Sea."

Her voice resonated around the stone walls as he began a slower, more careful ascent. She had told him little of her life before they had found her. The Queen had found her performing tricks for money in Secille. She had spoken of her older sister a few times over the years, but what she hadn't said spoke volumes. Her sister had been sold, and had died soon after. That was when Aradel had come to Axion and, as far as he knew, had never gone back.

"Are you coming to the sea?
They say that the moon
is full and fancy free.
Home is behind us
the sea ahead..."

Her voice trailed off. Aradel was resting her head on her hands and leaning on the window sill that overlooked Axion. The cold winter breeze made the few loose strands of her hair swirl and dance. When he stepped into the tower, his boot made a noise, and she glanced toward him.

"Thinking about your sister?" Kirill asked as he stepped up beside her, and surveyed Axion.

"Your leaving reminds me of when she left," Aradel said, but her voice seemed far away, as though she were lost in her memories. "When she left, she never came back."

"I'm coming back," he told her, though he couldn't actually be sure.

"How can you possibly know that?" she asked, looking up at him with her face full of sorrow.

"Because I am too stubborn to die," Kirill pointed out, crossing his arms.

Aradel appeared surprised. She blinked up at him. Some of the owls shifted on their perches, and some opened an eye or two. Finally, Aradel straightened and crossed her arms as well. "Well, at least we both agree you're stubborn."

"I know you're worried," Kirill said, letting his arms fall to his sides. "You have every right to be, but I won't die so easily."

"There are so many things that can go wrong," Aradel told him as she reached up and smoothed some of her hair back, something she had done since she was young.

"And everything could go right," he reminded her.

"It's my fault you're going," Aradel whispered, meeting his gaze straight on. "I insisted we should try."

"And we should," Kirill told her, taking her shoulders in his hands. "It *is* worth the risk."

Aradel looked at him with a heavy expression on her face. The owls slept behind them, the cold wafting in to keep them cool. A few cooed and some chattered, but most remained asleep. He studied the lines of her face and realized she was losing some of the roundness to it. Kirill didn't remember her face being so severe.

89

"When I was the one taking the risk, it was worth it," Aradel said. "You are the closest thing I have to family."

"We are family," Kirill told her, showing a softer side that only she and his mother saw.

Aradel swallowed heavily and nodded. "I'll take care of your mother," she told him. She threw her arms around his waist and put her head against his chest.

Kirill blinked in surprise. Aradel was not one for displays of affection. The older she had gotten, the further she had pulled away from everyone and everything. He felt that most of the time he was only scratching the surface of who she was. He put his arms around her slowly, and she held on tight, as though he might disappear if she didn't hang on to him. For once he felt as though he was seeing all of Aradel.

"I know you will," he replied, patting her back and feeling almost uncomfortable.

Aradel sniffled, but there weren't any tears rolling down her cheeks. Kirill had not seen her cry since she was a child, one of the traits that made her such a powerful candidate to become Queen. Should the moon pearls decide Queen Vesna was no longer fit, he knew Aradel would be a sure pick.

"Let us go and see your mother," Aradel said, putting on a brave smile.

They were silent as they came down from the messenger's tower. Kirill thought to say something to break the silence, but felt he had said everything already. There wasn't anything else he could do to lessen the blow. He was leaving on a mission that might be a one-way trip. The thought did not warm him, but he felt a duty to his country to go in Aradel's stead.

By the time they reached the Temple of the Moon, he had resolved himself. He glanced at Aradel as she moved forward to greet the temple leader with a smile. She was using her polite smile, the one she used when she was upset, but unwilling to let anyone see it. He used to call it her "princess face," but she had reminded him she wasn't a princess.

"High Priestess Kerin," Aradel said, putting her hands in the priestess's open hands.

"Lady Aradel," High Priestess Kerin replied, exchanging kisses on their cheeks.

It was customary for women of rank to display a presumed intimacy in public. The old woman's hair was as white as the snow around them. She had a small mole above her lip on the left side. It made her look more distinguished. Kirill wasn't all that fond of her. Though he admired many of the projects she had kept alive after her predecessor had passed away, he disliked her for her stance on the mentally impaired. He thought they should be cared for by the temple, but High Priestess Kerin believed they should be the responsibility of their families.

"Sir Kirill," High Priestess Kerin said with a slight bow of her head. "The Queen has told me of your undertaking. You do the Moon Goddess proud, and I bless you on your duty."

The old woman lifted her hands out of the long sleeves she wore. She held her hands up and muttered to herself. Kirill felt his face twitch, but kept all his normal retorts to himself. He didn't feel like fighting with the crotchety old woman on his last day in Axion.

"It is my duty," Kirill replied stiffly.

"We are here to see Tristra," Aradel interrupted, knowing full well how Kirill felt about the woman. "How is she today?"

"I do not know," High Priestess Kerin replied with a wave. "You may see her, of course."

"Thank you," Aradel smiled as she maneuvered Kirill into the temple.

"That woman," Kirill grumbled the moment they were within the temple.

"That woman is our holy leader," Aradel reminded him, to which he simply grunted.

The wide steps of the temple were filled with people, but it was worse inside. They avoided the large area to the right. It was made of pale marble and decorated to match the eerie blue of the moon. Aradel thought it was beautiful, but Kirill found no peace there. All he saw was a silent goddess who had not blessed them with anything since moon pearls a millennium ago. If the world was in fact destabilizing, and it would lead to their destruction, why would the moon goddess remain silent?

Since he had learned of the disasters and death coming their way, he had gone to pray. Yet still the moon goddess remained silent, despite the hundreds that came within the temple walls daily. He had lost his faith, but he felt purpose in his duty. Faith suddenly didn't seem necessary, and it also meant avoiding High Priestess Kerin. Both of which he could live with.

He had not shared his doubts with Aradel. She didn't need to be influenced by his sudden change of heart. If Aradel did become Queen, Kirill knew she would need High Priestess Kerin's support. All of which made Kirill keep his tongue still on the subject.

The pale walls of the temple and high ceilings reminded him of the palace. They had been constructed in likeness of each other. Unlike the ceiling of the palace, the ceilings of the temple were solid, and covered in an ongoing picture. It depicted one of the most well-known stories about the Sun God and the Moon Goddess, one which, even though it was familiar, was told differently by every person. Over the eons, the true story had been lost.

"Kirill?" a voice called softly, and he turned to his right to see his mother in the hall.

"Mother," Kirill said, coming over to her.

Aradel fell behind, likely not sure if Tristra would remember her today. He took his mother in his arms and kissed her softly on the cheek. She put her hands on his arms and gave a cry of delight. He had not visited as often as he should because of his trip to Secille, and the meetings with the Fire Nation.

"What are you doing here?" his mother asked, appearing almost like her old self.

"I have to go away again," he told her.

"But you've only just returned," his mother said sadly before surveying the room. She glanced back at him before asking, "Who did you bring with you today?"

"You remember Aradel," Kirill said and felt his eyebrows furrow.

"You've gotten so big!" Tristra cried and threw her arms around Aradel.

"I'm sorry I haven't visited lately," Aradel commented.

"I'll say so. You've only just started your candidacy," his mother exclaimed. She took Aradel's face in her hands and added, "And yet you look so much like an adult!"

Aradel had been a candidate for nearly two years. His mother was lost in a world that was years before. That was when her memory problems began, and she often returned to that time. That was her happiest time, when Aradel had first begun her candidacy, and Kirill had been promoted to Commander. He understood his mother's need to cling to those happiest memories and let the others fade.

"Are you going again as well?" Tristra asked Aradel.

Before she could answer Kirill interjected, "Aradel is not coming this time, but she will visit you as much as she can."

"Then I won't be as lonely this time," Tristra said.

"Commander Kirill," a soldier called, standing off to the side. He appeared to be uncomfortable for interrupting, but Kirill knew he had taken too long already. He put a hand on his mother's arm and kissed her gently on the cheek.

She patted his face as he straightened. "You're such a good son," she muttered, but Kirill could already see she was losing her hold on reality.

"Good-bye, mother," he said and gave a final nod to Aradel.

Aradel linked her arms with his mother, who seemed to come back to reality then. Even Tristra knew that Aradel wasn't prone to affection, too afraid of getting hurt. His mother patted Aradel's arm and said something Kirill couldn't hear as he turned away. That is how he wanted to remember them. Should he never see them again, the last image of his mother and Aradel would be of that moment.

Kirill hurried down the stairs of the temple without sparing High Priestess Kerin a passing glance. He mounted the elk waiting for him, as the young soldier who was sent to retrieve him did the same on his own. As they rode from Axion, out into the wasteland of snow to the east, he allowed himself only one final glimpse of Axion. He then turned forward and never looked back again, wondering what adventures were waiting for him in the north.

Part 3

"You're going to need all the help you can get." - Kirill

Fire: Chapter Sixteen

———————— o ————————

Now was the time. As Ekil contemplated his deformities in the cracked mirror, he finally, for the first time, felt proud of them. For him, the melted scar tissue down the left side of his face and neck, and half of his body, had been a reminder of his shame, his defeat. Not anymore.

Unrest was stirring in both the Fire Nation and Frost Nation over their tense partnership to try and fix the planet. They were fools, since they were the cause of what the Gods were bringing down on them. The rutty magic users needed to be destroyed. Only then would the planet return to normal.

Queen Darha was making a monumental mistake getting into bed with the Frost Nation, and Ekil was going to reap the benefits of it. Never had he been in such a position, not even the first time he took on the royal family. Doing them in now was the least he could do to repay Queen Darha for the scars, which her mother, Queen Berselis, had branded him with decades ago.

Before, he had hidden them because of the shame. Now he felt they were a talisman, a beacon of what he'd nearly accomplished.

A soft knock came on his bathing room door, and Hirsa popped her head in. "The emissary from the Frost Nation is here," she announced softly. Ekil nodded once, and Hirsa silently backed out of the door and closed it.

Now was the time to finish what Ekil had started in his youth. Finally, the annihilation of the magic users was at hand. The Sun God's wrath was coming down on the abominations of the magic users, the famous oppressors. They were an affront to nature, an offense to what was normal and decent. Only the Gods should possess such power!

With a last long look at his scars, he pushed himself away from his sink and headed out the door. Rounding the corner and entering his dark living room, Ekil saw the long, slender silhouette of the Frost Nation native. "Tulya?"

The woman slowly turned around to face him, drawing back the hood of her dark cloak, and short blonde curls spilled forth framing her face. In the moonlight, Ekil could see one thick streak of white hair on the right side of her head.

"Ekil." Her dark blue-green eyes scanned the remains of his house, which was little more than rubble from the quake.

His cooking room had no roof and only three walls. Holes ranging in size from his fist, to his head, were everywhere and cracks ran ragged through the entire length of his house. Sections along the seam of the roof were missing, and small piles of clay and rock dust littered his floors and carpets. He wouldn't leave, though, mostly because there was nowhere else to go. All the homes in the Versis Mountains were in the same general condition or worse; most were gone completely.

"These are not ideal conditions to be meeting in," she pointed out. "Perhaps you should have come to the Frost Nation instead." She gazed out the window. "At least to escape this horrid place for a short time."

Ekil resisted the urge to roll his eyes. He needed to remember that this woman was his ally at the moment. "An escape would be welcome. My tall, rocky landscape just hides you better during travel than your white, wooded landscape would hide me."

Tulya met his eyes briefly before nodding once. "Fair enough." She took the edges of her cloak and spread it out to her sides gracefully before sitting down on the edge of his large cushioned chair. Her blue-green eyes peered at him. "What happened to your face?"

Ekil slowly ran the tip of his middle finger down his deformed cheek. "The result of the last time I attempted to clear the planet of its magical filth."

"Clearly a failed attempt," Tulya concluded.

Ekil quickly sat in the chair across from her. His hands gestured to match his words. "But I need you to understand how close I was."

The woman's eyes were patient, but fierce. Ekil had heard of her through his very few, but very exceptional, spies in the merchant ranks that dealt with the Frost Nation during trade when the bridges were intact. He'd kept his letter to her brief and cryptic, in case it was intercepted, but he'd proposed the idea of an alliance. If she wanted to know more, she should meet him here on this day and time.

"I'm listening," she said.

Ekil interlaced his fingers together and looked Tulya square in the eyes. "I got to the royal family."

Tulya's eyes widened maliciously. "Did you now?" she asked, sounding impressed at last.

"The current Queen, Queen Darha, was only an infant at the time." Ekil repressed a sigh of frustration as he recalled the memory. "I was in the throne room. My army filled it to such capacity, that they overflowed out the doors and down the steps of the palace." Gritting his teeth, he shook his head. "But in a strange burst of strength, something I'd never seen before, and have never seen since, or even heard of, Queen Berselis took out more than three quarters of my army in one magical hit. One"— he held up a finger— "just one burst of fire, and I was defeated and—" Ekil indicated his face— "scarred for life."

Tulya pursed her lips and nodded slowly. "So, I assume since you summoned me here, you'd like to try to overthrow the royal family again?"

"Families," he stressed. "The Frost Nation's too."

Tulya's eyes widened slightly before she looked at him with a bored, flat expression. "The Frost Nation? Take out the Frost Nation Queen?" Ekil nodded confidently. "Are you daft?" she asked, making him freeze in astonishment. "That's wonderful that you managed to get so close to the royal family so recently, but no one has challenged Frost Nation royalty in more than a hundred years. We don't dare. I don't know much about your Sun God, but our Moon Goddess blesses our royalty. We don't fancy challenging a Goddess! We live in relative peace in the east. We are segregated from the rest of the nation, but we hold our own."

Ekil leaned heavily over his knees. "From what I understand, your Queen is incredibly aged and was injured in the quake."

"That's true, but the Goddess's moon pearls haven't dimmed on her time yet."

Ekil held up a finger. "But they will. They *will*," he stressed.

"And then they will choose another Queen," Tulya said impatiently.

"But a younger Queen. A less experienced Queen, yes?"

Tulya paused and visibly relaxed. "Yes, a younger Queen. But the many candidates who could take the throne are each incredibly powerful."

"That doesn't matter," Ekil stressed.

"Doesn't it?"

"Tell me, Tulya," Ekil said smoothly, his confidence returning. "Of all the candidates, what is the favored candidate's position on my people?"

Tulya shrugged a shoulder. "She seems indifferent."

"Is she in favor of partnering with Queen Darha?"

"She certainly is. But it's likely because Queen Vesna is in favor of the partnership. The favored candidate even volunteered to go on the quest with your people herself, but Queen Vesna ultimately chose someone else."

Ekil smiled broadly, baring his teeth, then held out his hands to his sides. "Look around you, Tulya." He met her eyes. "What is happening now is a perfect opportunity for both of us to overthrow our nation's royalty."

Her brows drew together curiously. "How?"

Ekil counted off his fingers. "Unrest in both of our nations due to the partnership between them. Unrest in the populace means distrust or anger toward the royal families. The planet falling apart around us on top of that cultivates incredible fear. Combine fear and the distrust for royalty, and people are going to be searching for answers." Ekil held his hands out far to his sides. "We can be those answers." Tulya's eyes brightened with such malice that Ekil felt a jolt of excitement hit him in the chest. "Hatred for our opposite nations still festers in the hearts of both our people—fierce, murderous hatred. But people stay silent so as not to oppose the Queens. They won't speak out against them unless they know, beyond a shadow of a doubt, that they are supported."

Tulya nodded enthusiastically and slowly sat up in the chair. "If we question our leaders quietly about their decisions regarding the opposite nation, people will begin to turn from their loyalty."

"The embers of disloyalty are already burning," Ekil said with quiet excitement. "Two of the four regional overlords in my nation have already muttered about Queen Darha losing her mind, and perhaps being too young, or unfit to rule."

Tulya nodded enthusiastically again. "The same thing is happening in my nation. People are saying Queen Vesna might have a mental illness due to her old age and may be unfit to rule any longer."

"If we can fan those embers, our numbers will swell exponentially because even our hated magic users will join our cause."

Tulya smiled wickedly. "And it couldn't hurt to have some powerful magic users in our ranks until the Queens are dealt with."

"A revolutionary fire will be kindled," Ekil said, barely able to contain his joy. "And when the royal families are overthrown, we can execute the remaining magic users."

Tulya's excitement was growing quickly, until it suddenly seemed to hit a wall. She sighed heavily and sat back in her chair. "This is pointless. The Moon Goddess would never allow it. The pearls still glow for Queen Vesna."

"Tulya," Ekil said abruptly, "the planet is disintegrating around us. Everything! The drinking water, the quakes, the storms, the sea life, the volcanos, everything that is happening to our planet is a clear sign of their wrath. Don't you see that? If the Gods were still pleased with our nations, why would they be doing this to us?" Tulya's eyes brightened with realization. "I think these pearls of yours still glow because your Goddess is testing your faith, to see if you have the courage to remedy the magical abominations regardless." Ekil saw Tulya's jaw working furiously as she thought about that possibility. "If we want our planet to survive," he continued, "the Gods' wrath must be sated. The only way to do that is to destroy the magic users that offend them. If we take that mantle upon ourselves, the Sun God and the Moon Goddess will bless our efforts. They have clearly abandoned everyone else."

Tulya nodded, excitement returning to her eyes as she sat up. "All right. What do we do first?"

"Right now, we need to quietly fan the flames of distrust and disloyalty toward our royalty. At the same time, allow ourselves to slowly emerge as capable leaders. Not too quickly, though, because that would raise suspicion. When there is enough uproar, and we have enough numbers behind us, we will meet again and discuss a plan of action."

"Our plan of action will likely need to be on the move. My nation hardly sits still these days. A large group just crossed the River Gora to pick up your soldiers and take them to the west coast."

Ekil nodded once. "We have scouts watching Thea's progress to the west. Once conditions are favorable to meet, we will send word."

"Very well," Tulya said and stood gracefully from the chair, pulling her hood back over her head. "After our royalty is overthrown, we will have nothing to do with each other, correct?"

"Absolutely not," Ekil said firmly and stood.

"Good," Tulya responded with barely concealed venom. "I don't fancy dealing with you or your people ever again."

"Likewise."

Tulya nodded once and walked to his door. Pulling it open, she stepped out into the night, and disappeared without a glance back. Watching her leave, Ekil felt a spark of hope ignite. Now was the time.

Frost: Chapter Seventeen

o

The virgin snow crunched under the weight of the elk. A large group of men and women marched behind Kirill. Unlike him, they would be turning back once the heat in the north became too much for them and the Fire Nation took over the journey escorting the iceberg. There was a chance he might not be returning at all, so Kirill took in every sight with a new, appraising eye, and committed it to memory.

A trip that had once seemed so long was suddenly very short. Already they had reached the top of the hill that led down to the shoreline. Off in the distance, across the horizon, sat the Isle of Ice. He couldn't see them, but he knew there were men working to break off a large chunk of the isle. If they had cut into the ice far enough, Kirill knew he could do the rest.

When the march caught up to him, Kirill started down the hill toward the shore. At the bottom, was the young man he had sent ahead, loading the last of the water barrels into the boats that would take him to the isle. Once the iceberg was free and floating on its own, his men would move the barrels onto it. Kirill wasn't sure how much water he would need to consume during their trip, but he decided it was better to have too much than too little. If he had too little, the consequences could be deadly. For a magic user in the Frost Nation, water was more valuable than any weapon.

When the soldier turned back toward the approaching host, Kirill lifted a hand in greeting. The young man waved back enthusiastically and Kirill tried not to cringe. The young soldier, Kip, was like an excited wolf pup. He seemed to be a huge admirer of Kirill—to the point of annoyance. This was the main reason Kirill had sent him ahead with the extra elk, although he'd done it under the pretense of having Kip alert the other soldiers to Kirill's arrival.

"Commander Kirill," Kip called eagerly.

"Soldier," Kirill responded before slipping down from the elk.

"We are ready to take the last of the supplies across and begin our journey north," Kip replied, hurrying next to Kirill.

"What is the status of the chunk of our iceberg?" Kirill asked, tossing both packs onto his back as he walked down toward the boats.

Kip all but skipped next to him as he answered, "They are delayed because of its size."

"I'll help with that," he answered casually and tossed his two waterproof bags onto the flag ship. It was the largest of the twelve ships that would be pushing the iceberg north. The great ship had been started before the rest, and was nearly the last that they finished.

He took up the last of his packs, and put a hand on the elk. It turned back as one of the caretakers came to take him. Patting his side, Kirill whispered, "Goodbye, old friend."

Kirill walked away toward the shore without looking back, and tossed the last bag into the boat before hopping in himself. The men who had marched with him boarded their own boats. Kip jumped onto Kirill's with a grin that could have brought forth spring. Kirill moved to stand at the front with his arms crossed, gazing out across the Ashtra Sea. He could all but hear Aradel singing of it. Glancing back at the shoreline, his elk watched him with eyes that seemed to gaze straight into his soul. They had always been that way, but leaving this time hit Kirill harder.

Turning forward again, Kirill took a deep gulp of fresh, frosty air, and let it fill his body with cold. He knew that once he left the Ashtra Sea, and entered the Ebra Ocean, he would not feel cold on his skin for some time. His only solace was he would be able to ride the iceberg alone and not have to worry about interacting much with the Fire Nation.

It was a quiet ride to the Isle of Ice because of the seriousness of the situation. Everyone seemed somber and grim. Kirill could practically hear Kip trying to think of something to say, but thankfully that failed.

When they reached the edge of the isle, the boat pulled alongside a rope ladder that went high up into the icy peaks. He raised an eyebrow at it but made no comment.

He turned back to the men on this boat. "Move all the ships to a safe distance."

"As you command," they answered dutifully.

Kirill then started up the ladder. It wasn't the most effective way, but it would do. By the time he reached the top, there was ice forming on his slightly sweaty forehead. Two men were waiting to help him up over the edge. Once he was standing on the iceberg, he surveyed the world below, and across the sea to Axion. There was nothing but the white of snow and the shadows of trees.

"Commander," one of the men said, coming forward.

Kirill faced him. "What is your progress?" he asked, following him across the surface toward the crack they had started to form.

"We have been working almost non-stop since we've arrived, but many of our strongest are at The Wall," he answered, sounding nervous. "We'll need more time."

It was a long walk to the fracture they were making in the isle. The isle itself was huge, and although they would be taking a hefty chunk of it, Kirill wasn't certain it would be enough. It might have been easier to try to move the island.

An hour passed as they made their way across the great expanse of the iceberg. Kirill approached the crevasse and peered down. Many of the men and women still worked to drill down further. Kirill was impressed with the progress they had made, but he was there now. He wasn't the most powerful, nor the most graceful magic user, but if there was one thing Kirill was good at, it was blunt force. He walked along the crack and saw that most of the edges were done, but the center ran deep, and was defiant to their efforts. Kirill believed he could crack it though.

"Get everyone out of the crevasse," Kirill commanded and they pulled back in surprise. Upon seeing the shock on their faces, he added, "You've done well."

"As you command," they chorused and gathered their things. One by one they used the rope ladders and crawled out of the fracture. Most appeared exhausted and about ready to collapse. He had thought to have their help, but he couldn't see them doing much more than what they already had.

"Get to a safe distance," Kirill ordered them.

They all seemed relieved. He reached down and helped the last of the workers out of the crevasse, then turned to watch them go. He knew it would take some time for their exhausted bodies to clear a safe distance. Thankfully, there were only a few miles of ice and snow left to break. Kirill walked up and down the crevasse, trying to find the best place to attack. In the time they had worked, they had made excellent progress.

Taking one of the ropes left behind, Kirill rappelled himself down the wall. It would be best to work up close. He started magically drilling away at the stubborn center that refused the worker's efforts. A little here, and a little there, Kirill worked away the edges as time ticked by. He didn't concern himself with how long it was taking because that just allowed the workers and soldiers more time to get a safe distance away.

Finally, he could see there wasn't much ice left holding on. Putting his back against the wall, he put his arms out, his palms down, and started to gather his powers within him. Ice and snow exploded in all directions as he bore down into the weak spot for several minutes. He did it again, and a

101

fracture formed along the final tendons of snow and ice that held the iceberg to the island. He turned away as ice shards flew toward his face. Kirill stumbled against the wall as the slab of ice he stood on fell away.

He quickly took hold of the rope ladder, and was jarred violently as the freed iceberg hit the water. He slammed against the side of the wall, dangling from the rope, and scrambled to gain his footing. Swinging away from the side, he took his dagger from his belt and buried it into the opposite wall to try to steady himself. However, he watched in horror as his dagger stayed with the isle, when the iceberg floated away. Looking down at the sea beneath him as he swung back and forth like a pendulum, he held the rope tightly. He did not wish to go swimming.

With a heavy sigh of relief, he started to climb back up the rope. It took him some time.

Exhausted when he reached the top, he flopped over the edge, landing on his stomach. Taking another dagger from his hip, he buried it into the iceberg and held on as it continued to bob in the water, threatening to throw him from its surface. When it finally settled, he heard someone yelling and sat up. The boats had made their way back to the iceberg in the time it took him to climb the rope.

Kip was waving at him, and Kirill noticed he was soaked from head to toe. It was quiet a moment before Kirill started laughing, realizing that Kip had gone swimming. Kirill lay back down, unmoving, as the ships got into position to attach themselves behind the iceberg and begin their journey north.

He rolled onto his back and stared at the cloudy sky, listening to the water gently splash as the iceberg moved slowly through it. He had to admit, that was an interesting beginning to his journey. He only hoped that wouldn't be the last time he laughed. Traveling with the Fire Nation, though, it likely would be.

Though he heard men approach, he didn't move. He normally would have stood up and yelled orders to keep them all in line, but everyone knew exactly how important this was. He didn't feel as though he needed to tell them. He glanced to the side as the rope ladder leading down to the ships became taut. Sitting up finally, he peered over the edge and saw that one of the men was starting to climb it. With one leg bent, he placed his elbow on top of his knee while his hand hung loose. "Commander?" he heard Kip call from below and suppressed an amused smile.

Standing, he looked down at the men on the boats below. Now that it was in the water, most of the iceberg was below the surface. The ships were now just fifty feet below him, which made loading supplies easier

"Throw them up," Kirill called.

He moved back from the edge as grappling hooks were thrown from the ships, and sunk into the iceberg's edges. Kirill lifted them up one by one, and moved them further inland. He sunk each one into the hard and unyielding body of the iceberg, attaching it to the ships. Sometimes he placed them in the ground and sometimes in the peaks of ice that rose in sharp points above him. Two other men joined him, carrying barrels of water for his consumption. Barrel after barrel was moved aboard while Kirill secured rope after rope.

Finally, the task was done, and Kirill wiped ice from his brow. It was hours of hard work, made only a little easier by the other magic users loading his supplies. Kirill would need all the water he could get if he ever hoped to reach the northern island the Fire Nation spoke of.

"Let's go," Kirill told the two men who had been loading the water barrels.

They nodded and dropped over the side, scrambling down the ropes back to the boats. The magic users who had been working on the crevasse settled on top of it with Kirill before they joined the men in the boats below. They would be able to help increase the movement of the iceberg until Fire Nation joined them.

He glanced around at the faces of his people and felt very alone. Instead of waiting near the back with the others, Kirill walked along the length of the iceberg. He intended to watch the scout ships as they moved far out ahead of them to start checking water depth. As he walked, he wondered if the Fire Nation would have enough men, or if they would even fulfill their promises. He imagined they felt as determined to see this through as he did, but he couldn't trust them.

After a couple of hours of walking, he finally reached the front. It was not as flat, and Kirill had to climb up a small steep edge. Settling against it, he watched the scout ships. They were small and easy to maneuver around anything. Two checked the depth of the water on each side of the iceberg, and one in the center. Kirill sat down cross-legged, watching for any sign, and drank water to replenish his powers. He didn't spare a glance back at the shoreline, knowing that Axion was too far away to see and he had already said his goodbyes.

The chunk of ice, as big as a small island, began its slow and careful journey north. For now, they were still making good time, but

Kirill didn't know what was to come. All he knew, as he sailed away from his home, was that he was determined to survive this adventure. It didn't matter how much Fire Nation helped him or hindered him; he was determined to try to save his people. That seemed like enough of a reason to survive and return to Axion. Return to his mother and Aradel. Return to his position and nation, content and peaceful. Return to his home.

Fire: Chapter Eighteen

———————— o ————————

The six-hour boat ride to the southwest coast was dull and uncomfortably quiet. Even Fitzu, who Thea had counted on to lighten the burden on her heart, was silent and rigid. She really hoped he wouldn't be like this for the next month.

Up ahead, the boats that had pulled in front started hollering at the boats behind. Idok, the Frost Nation native guiding her boat, yelled back. "Aye! Three clicks out!"

Thea looked back in a questioning manner. "What does that mean?"

Idok met her eyes coolly. "The iceberg is three miles out from land."

Thea nodded and passed a glance to Fitzu, who stared back at her, too, before they watched out ahead of them again. Thea could already smell the ocean, and she wanted to retch. It smelled like rotten old fish, a smell she regrettably realized she would quickly have to get used to.

Not much time passed before the land of the Frost Nation, and their ridiculous wall, opened to the vast sea. As soon as they sailed out from behind that massive ice structure, a blast of arctic sea wind hit them. Thea grunted as her skin got stiff immediately. It was freezing out here! She heard all her men grunt as well from the pain of the cold.

Fitzu instantly began to dig through their supplies. He drew out a heavy black wool cloak and tossed it to Thea. She caught it and quickly threw it around her shoulders, putting her arms through the long bell sleeves, and fastened it all the way down to her knees. Long black gloves came next that went up past her elbows. Everyone in the other boats started putting on more layers as well. Thea's heart sank. This was going to be more miserable than she'd thought. Her only solace was that they were sailing north and would be in warmer waters and climate in about a week or so.

The boats continued over the ocean for a while, and Thea kept searching for this iceberg that was supposedly sailing along. The boats, however, just seemed to be heading toward a random ice island in the distance. She wondered if the iceberg was behind the island, waiting. Sailing closer, Thea suddenly saw twelve ships behind the island that she'd been looking at, and her eyes went wide. The island *was* the iceberg!

It had to be twelve miles wide! Ropes attached to the iceberg from the ships finally came into focus, and she realized what she was seeing.

"What the f..." Fitzu said in disbelief, his voice trailing off as he stepped up next to Thea, gapping at the island with wide eyes.

Thea quickly changed her expression, making it flat and grim once again. She wouldn't give the Frost Nation the satisfaction of seeing her impressed with them. She subtly jabbed her elbow into Fitzu's ribs and they faced each other. They'd known each other long enough that they could communicate without saying much.

Fitzu immediately changed his expression to match hers and gazed over the ocean. "This will be fun," he muttered before he went to the supplies and continued digging through them.

Another half hour passed before the escort boats headed toward the ships at the back. One boat sailed toward the front of the iceberg to drop off the Fire Nation soldiers that would be manning the scouting ships up front. Thea's, however, kept course, and Idok pulled her boat right alongside the iceberg.

"What's going on?" she asked.

Idok stared at her from the back as it settled along the "shore" of the ice island. "You are going to need basic directions for how to sail with an iceberg, are you not?"

Thea sighed heavily in annoyance and looked back at the expansive mountain of ice in front of her. A staircase had been formed up the side, leading from the surface of the ocean up high to the peaks. Grasping the side of the boat, she stepped one foot over the edge onto the icy platform. Luckily there was some snow, so she had some traction under her boots, and it wasn't likely she would fall. Stepping her other foot over the edge, she stood solid.

"Come on," she told Fitzu, who followed.

Soon they were both making their way toward the more level section above. Clutching her cloak tighter at her throat as she reached the top, she stared at the endless cold white that surrounded her. At that moment, she hated everything.

"Hey," a deep voice said.

Thea glanced up and saw the Frost Knight making his way down some crevasses and pillars and coming toward her. His eyes were dark and his expression lifeless. Thea clenched her teeth, seeing he was very lightly clothed while she was doing everything she could not to shiver in several layers. He didn't even have gloves on!

"My name is Kirill," he said, stepping up to her. He was tall, almost intimidatingly so. Thea only came up to his chin.

"I know who you are," she replied shortly.

Kirill pressed his lips together in annoyance. "And you are?"

She almost didn't want to tell him, but figured he might need her name over the next month. "Thea," she said abruptly.

He nodded once. "The basic signals you're going to need to know are, 'Shallow Port,' which means we're entering shallow water on the left side. 'Shallow Starboard,' which means..."

"Let me guess, shallow water on the right side," Thea said. "There's also 'shallow water ahead,' which means we need to adjust our course into deeper waters. Lastly, 'trouble a vast,' which means something is wrong. Am I right?" Kirill's jaw started working and Thea locked her eyes on his. "I have sailed before. We have an ocean and a river, just like you do."

Thea saw Kirill's lip twitch. "The iceberg is about four miles under the surface of the ocean, so depths—"

"So depths greater than four and a half miles, no less, are safe to pass through," Thea finished for him and glared. "I'm not a simpleton, you know. I can read your Queen's instructions that she sent." Thea wanted off this iceberg right now. She turned away to head back down the stairs to her boat so she could be brought to one of the ships pushing the back.

Behind her, Kirill sighed heavily through his nose. "More insolent than I imagined."

Thea's head spun around with wide eyes. "Excuse me?" She turned and stalked back toward him. "What did you just say to me?" Kirill didn't respond, his face remaining impassive as she stepped up to him. "Let's get one thing straight, you are not my commanding officer. I don't answer to you, you got that?"

Kirill glared down at her. "You may not answer to me, but you will listen to me if you want to survive this trip." His eyes traveled over her warmly bundled form with disgust. "You're clearly going to need all the help you can get."

Thea's heart raced with rage, and she held up a finger at him. "Keep talking, frost flake, and I'll pitch you right into the ocean," she warned.

His eyes narrowed and became dangerous as he brought his face down closer to hers. "The ocean won't kill *me*..."

Thea let that threat hang in the air for a second before she brought her fist back and punched him square in the jaw. His face and upper body snapped to the side, but he didn't fall. Thinking fast, Thea hooked her foot behind his knee and pulled forward, throwing him onto his back on the ice. Yanking a dagger from her side, she jumped on top of him, ignoring the pain of his cold, and rested it against his Adam's apple.

"Let's get another thing straight," she said in a low voice as his half-closed eyes moved to meet hers. "I'm not one of the submissive little pipsqueaks you're used to dealing with in your nation either."

Thea suddenly felt a cold, deliberate tap against the back of her leg. Looking down at her thigh, she realized the Frost Knight had produced a wickedly sharp ice dagger from his magic, and was holding it in a way that would sever her leg in a moment if he wished it. Thea felt her eyebrow go up, impressed that he'd been able to pull it on her. Looking back down at his face, though, and seeing his cool arrogance, Thea clenched her teeth and leaned down toward him.

"Let's see who blinks first," she hissed. Adding pressure to her blade against his throat, she felt him press the dagger tighter to her leg in return.

"For the Sun God's sake!" Thea heard Fitzu cry out.

Thea didn't dare move or respond, and kept her eyes locked with the Frost Knight's. She honestly wondered who would cut who first.

"Thea!" Fitzu cried.

She heard the crunching of snow coming toward her. Suddenly an arm was hooked under hers and the dagger was lifted off the Knight's throat as she was pulled away from him. Thea and the Knight didn't take their eyes off each other as Fitzu dragged her off and Kirill picked himself up.

"Thea! Hey! Look at me!" Fitzu ended up having to grab her chin and force her eyes off the Knight. The ends of his spiky black hair danced a little in the ocean breeze, and ice was beginning to form on the tips. Gripping her shoulders, he stooped a little to bring his dark gray eyes level with hers, a sight so familiar that it calmed her down a little. "You know that I respect you as my commanding officer, and I love you as my friend, but you need to stop! In case you haven't noticed"—he pointed back at the Knight— "this guy is the only one that can get the iceberg to the volcano."

Thea pressed her lips together and sighed heavily as she looked past Fitzu at Kirill. She really wanted to finish what she'd started, but she knew Fitzu was right. "Let's get to the volcano then," she said and started walking toward the stairs. She deliberately slammed her shoulder into the Frost Knight's as she passed him, and he jerked slightly.

Fitzu followed close behind, and they both made their way back down to the boat. Idok shoved off and started for the cluster of ships at the back of the iceberg. Thea crossed her arms as she gazed out at the other boats. Fitzu was immediately by her side, regarding her expectantly.

"This sucks, you know that?" she finally said without a glance at him.

Fitzu nodded and looked out toward the boats as well. "I know. But we don't have to deal with him. We keep to ourselves, and he can keep to himself."

Thea felt her muscles begin to unknot. "This sucks for more reasons than that frost flake though," she said as she let a shiver run up her spine that shook her entire body.

"Tell me about it," he said. "I think I left my nuts back on the River Gora!"

Thea threw her head back and laughed as Fitzu grinned broadly. There was the Fitzu she'd been hoping to see on this trip. Maybe this wouldn't be so horrible. She just had to stay away from that Frost Knight on the iceberg.

———————— o ————————

Already Kirill could feel the heat of the north trying to melt the edges of the iceberg. He glanced at the water barrels with a frown and wondered if they would be enough to get him there and back again. The mass of the iceberg, along with the water barrels, should have been enough to sustain him, but no one anticipated it being so warm so quickly. He had moved them to different strategic locations with most of them at the center.

With a brooding frown, he realized the Fire Nation must be relieved, and that annoyed him. That fire woman was hot headed and impulsive, she likely didn't think about what the warmth was doing to the iceberg. The lot of them had stuck to manning the boats and stayed far away from him. He was glad enough for the solitude, but he would have to mention his concerns about the oncoming water depths sooner or later.

Later, definitely later, Kirill decided, scanning the water.

Kirill was about to go back to his solitary brooding when fire streaked through the sky from the scout ships. The symbol that appeared, and the direction it appeared from, indicated shallow water on the port side. Kirill blinked, stunned, and then reacted. He ran as hard and fast as he could to the back of the iceberg, gently nudging the entire thing as he and the boats moved away from the port side.

He was nearly to the back when a second flare of fire streaked through the air on the starboard side. He could feel the far edges of the iceberg as it approached the narrow way ahead, but already there was sweat on his brow from the strain of keeping it together and shifting it even slightly. He was going to need to drink more water soon. If they kept hitting shallow water, he was going to have to do a lot of running too, which meant more water he'd need to drink. It was something to pass the time, he supposed.

"Hey, frost flake, you up there?" he heard the fire woman calling from the boats below.

"Don't call me that," he growled down when he reached the edge.

"We've started to redirect down here," she called up without responding to his comment.

Kirill felt the mass of snow and ice shifting in the water. "Both sides have issues," he called out. "I need more eyes as we maneuver through this—at least three people."

At first, he didn't hear anything, but when he glanced over the side he saw three bodies moving up the rope ladder. Settling back on his heels, he counted the seconds to see how long they took. Minutes passed before the first arm gripped the top rung of the ladder. Kirill instinctively stepped forward to offer a hand—but stopped when he saw the glare in her eerie, silver-colored eyes. Crossing his arms, he waited for her to pull herself over.

Once she was on the iceberg, she pulled the wool cloak she was wearing closer around her body before turning back to help another man up. It was the one before, Fitzu, who had brought the fire woman around during their last encounter. He didn't like thinking about how she'd caught him off guard long enough to get him on his back. Kirill kept his mouth shut until the three of them were over the edge.

"We need to split into two groups and watch the port and starboard sides," Kirill informed them. "Per your scouts, it gets narrow up ahead."

Without waiting, Kirill turned and started toward the starboard side, which was the side closest to the shore. The closer to shore, the warmer the water. He needed to be on that side to help maintain a higher level of cold. He didn't care who followed him; he just hoped it wasn't the fire woman.

He heard her say in a commanding voice, "Signal if we get too close to the edges."

When Kirill started around the first snowy spire, he heard the distinct crunch of boots on snow behind him. His frown nearly reached his jawline when he saw the fire woman following him, and he hurried to put as much distance between them as he could manage. He half ran and half jogged over to the starboard side. It took a good amount of time, but thankfully they hadn't reached the shallower waters quite yet.

Peering into the water below, Kirill took a deep swallow of water before wiping the sweat away with the back of his hand again. It didn't take long for the fire woman to join him with a perplexed expression on her face.

She glanced over the protruding edge to the water below, and then stepped back again, tightening the cloak around her shoulders. "Shouldn't we be further forward?" she asked.

"This is the widest part of the iceberg," Kirill grunted. "You can stand over there."

111

"Over where?" she asked through clenched teeth. The look on her face suggested she wanted to bite off his nose.

"Around the edge of the mound where it bows out," he replied, peering down to watch the water again.

She put her hands on her hips and peeked over the edge again. "What exactly am I looking for?" she asked.

Annoyed, he contemplated throwing her over the side. "Ice or snow falling off the edges. It means we've run aground. Look for cracks forming as well."

She shook her head and marched off in the direction he had indicated. When she went around the mound, that put them both on each side of where the ice was widest. It was the most likely place to lose big sections. Unfortunately, though she was out of sight, she wasn't out of mind because he could feel her heat and the way it was affecting the iceberg.

Kirill peered over the edge and again adjusted the massive iceberg slightly when he felt it rub against the ocean floor. He worried that Derser Rect didn't know what he was talking about. They were following the route he mapped out based on his ocean charts. If he was wrong about this path, they could lose parts of the iceberg. From what he had seen, Kirill knew they would need every inch of it for their plan to succeed.

The Frost Nation didn't know much about the Ebra Ocean because the little they saw of it became something else. The Gulf of Gora or the Ashtra Sea were fed by it, but very little of the ocean itself touched any of their borders. They never had a need to venture that far north either, so they had to rely on what the Derser Rect told them. Kirill didn't like it, but he had little choice about putting his trust in that nervous little man.

Kirill heard a small pop of fire in the distance.

"Port side needs some room," the fire woman called. "Fitzu's only got about a four-foot birth along the edge."

Kirill adjusted the iceberg ever so slightly again. It was quiet as he continued to watch the water below for any signs of snow or ice.

"How do you stand this cold?" she suddenly burst out, as though she had been holding it in.

He didn't answer her and continued to maneuver the iceberg slightly out of harm's way. He could feel the ships at the back helping nudge the iceberg in the right direction. At first, he was content to ignore her, but after a while he could practically make out the sound of her teeth chattering. Worse, Kirill could all but hear Aradel in his head telling him to play nice.

"How long can your magic keep you warm?" he finally asked.

Silence followed his question, and for a minute Kirill wasn't sure she would answer. It was probably the first nice question he had posed to her since they'd met. Aradel was making him soft, and he sniffed at the thought. His mother would likely laugh at him as Aradel gave him that stare she had mastered in her candidate training. He hated that stare.

"Four hours," she answered plainly.

Kirill sighed softly. "You'd better fire it up. This narrow section goes on for a while," he said, although he wasn't sure exactly how long. "If you need to return and get a replacement, I'll understand."

"I'll last," she replied curtly.

Kirill glared over his shoulder in her direction. "I'll last," he mocked under his breath, with an equally mocking look on his face. Leaning back a bit, he could just make out the edge of a soft orange glow that was coming off her. He shook his head and looked back down at the water. The woman could at least try to be gracious. After all, he was making an attempt. Aradel was wrong; these people couldn't be reasoned with.

He shifted the iceberg again slightly when the ice and snow beneath his feet began to give under the pressure of the ocean floor below.

Minutes passed in silence, until finally she asked, "Why exactly did you need me here?"

"I need a second set of eyes," he reiterated as though she were inept.

"But do you really?" she asked and then suddenly let out a yell. "The snow is giving way along the edge!"

Kirill shifted the iceberg again as another streak of fire burned through the air behind them—from Fitzu he assumed—alerting them that the same thing was happening on the port side. They had reached a narrower part of the Ebra Ocean, and Kirill was right to be worried. He fell to his knees, bringing himself closer to the ice, and pressed his hands into it. Focusing, he held as much of the iceberg together as he could, but some ice would inevitably have to be lost for them to fit through.

He closed his eyes to expand his focus, feeling every inch of the iceberg as though it was an appendage. He could feel the ice and snow falling away in the depths. He also felt the heat from the three citizens of the Fire Nation as they slowly heated the frozen ground beneath their feet.

Suddenly, he felt the heat of the fire woman quickly approaching. Before he could find out what she was doing, she jerked him away from the edge. They tumbled backwards, cleanly breaking Kirill's concentration, and the ice and snow that had been directly below him gave way to fall into the ocean.

Kirill cried out as her heat slightly fractured the skin on his back when he landed on top of her. Sitting up, he stared at the new jagged edge in horror, but could feel that the rest of the iceberg was steady and intact.

He immediately got to his feet and turned to the fire woman as she sat up. There was snow on her cheek, and as it melted, he could see an ugly gray splotch of stone left behind on her skin that slowly faded before his eyes.

"What did you do?" he demanded.

She hadn't even fully straightened before she blinked at him a few times in astonishment at his reaction. "I saved you!" she yelled.

"Impulsive, idiotic woman!" he yelled, pointing at the place that had fallen away. "I was holding it together."

"It was giving way, you fool!" she yelled back, coming toe to toe with him.

"I had it under control!" he snapped, unwilling to give even an inch.

"Fine!" she cried. "Next time you're in trouble don't come to me for any help!"

"Fine!" he yelled as she turned and started walking away.

"Fine!" she shot back over her shoulder before she went around a large spire.

Kirill let it go quiet for a moment before yelling angrily, "Are you still watching the starboard side?"

"Yes!" she screamed back, just as angry.

Kirill quickly healed the fractured skin on his back. That blasted woman was going to be the end of him. He had never been more frustrated by one individual in his entire life. Not even when he and Aradel had fought over things did he ever want to throw her off an iceberg. He seethed on that idea for a while.

Kirill blinked suddenly as he realized that the fire woman was more impulsive, and perhaps sharp tongued, but she reminded him of Aradel. He groaned inwardly at the thought. He had to be wrong, that of all the people he had met in his life, the fire woman reminded him of the person he knew best. There was no way that could be right; she was a fire banshee. He had to be wrong. He was simply missing home and the company of those he cared for.

Another hour or so passed with no word from the banshee and no signals from the scouts or the two Fire Nation natives watching the port side. Kirill could finally see where the water widened below them, and he knew he was done. He contemplated making the fire woman and her companions stay on the iceberg and freeze, but he was drained, emotionally and physically.

"Fire woman," he called over once they were through the narrowest part.

She stepped around the edge of the mound she'd been behind with her arms crossed, her expression flat, and her skin still glowing orange. His connection with the iceberg told him she was burning hotter than she had earlier.

"We're past the narrow. You can—" He didn't even finish his sentence before the woman turned to head back toward the boats, getting in one final glare before disappearing.

Kirill shook his head and turned toward the barrels of water closest to his location. He could feel the very edge of his powers reaching out to keep the iceberg cold, and he could already feel it waning. He needed water and solitude. No more fire banshees if he could help it.

Fire: Chapter Twenty

———————— o ————————

Darha was numb. Past being angry or frightened, she was just numb. She was exhausted emotionally and physically, utterly drained from trying to tend to the endless concerns of her people. It wasn't that her people were asking too much; it was that she couldn't help them like she wished she could. Nature was too unpredictable, it was too violent, and she was helpless. So when the screams erupted from Fifth Gate, just outside the palace, Darha barely even blinked.

"Majesty! Majesty!" a breathless guard from the watchtowers cried as he entered the throne room. "Something is...I can't..." He looked terrified and pale. "Tamon," was the only useful word he could get out.

Darha's eyes went wide. "Coor!" she bellowed as she jumped up from her throne and ran after the guard in the direction of the watchtowers.

She'd barely gotten his name out before Coor streaked across the throne room to follow her, abandoning his conversation with two of the regional overlords. Coor, with his much longer stride, caught up quickly, and the three of them ran down the winding halls of the palace. Darha had abandoned her elaborate red gowns of distinction as soon as Thea left, trading them in for more practical traveling garb, and her golden circlet upon her brow as a mark of distinction instead. The way she was running around these days, it only made sense.

Her heart pounded as they raced past the guard, who halted beside the stairwell that spiraled up in rectangles to the watchtowers. Tamon. Something couldn't be wrong with Tamon! It just couldn't be. Not now.

That's when the rumbling and shaking began. It was subtle at first, just barely throwing her and Coor off balance as they ran up the stairs. Then a massive BOOM filled the entire world, followed by a violent shake that threw Darha into the wall of the stairwell, and then back down the stairs. Her hip hit an edge hard, and then her back and head slammed into the stone steps as she rolled down, her neck bending in ways it was never supposed to bend, until she was stopped by the wall of a landing.

Dizzy and disoriented, she wasn't sure which way was up and which way was down, but she heard Coor yelling her name. He was crouching in front of her a second later, holding her face in his hands and talking a mile a minute. She couldn't make out a word he was saying, but catching the foggy glimpses, she'd never seen him look so terrified. She reached out to touch his face, hoping to figure out which one of the two she saw was the real one. He brushed her hair away from her forehead and examined her closely just as her fingers grazed his nose.

Another loud boom and massive quake threw Coor backwards into the stairs she'd just fallen down. He hit his back hard, and the pain in his face made Darha's eyes widen and forced some focus into them. "Coor!" she screamed and started to crawl over to him.

He pushed himself up as she reached his side. "I'm fine," he said and got his feet under him. He gathered her up quickly in his arms and hurried up the stairs again toward the watchtowers.

Darha held onto her brother for dear life, burying her face in his neck. Tamon had exploded. She didn't need to see it for herself to know what had happened.

Darha painfully turned her head as Coor entered the northern watchtower. Another violent shake threw him against the wall, but his back went into it, protecting Darha from the brunt of the force. As Coor tried to find his footing, suddenly massive streams of black-gray ash erupted through the small square windows of the tower. Darha's eyes went wide. It was as if the volcano was spitting its debris directly outside the windows, rather than from ten miles away and across part of the ocean. Coor threw himself and Darha onto the floor, covering her with his body. Amid this horror, Darha was glad he couldn't be burned by the hot ash.

The shaking didn't cease, and the sound of breaking stone and groan of metal around her was almost drowned out by the roar of Tamon's eruption. Suddenly, with hurricane force, the roof of the watchtower was torn off, and the debris surrounded them both. Darha's eyes opened wide, even against the dust, as the entire tower began to sway.

"We have to get out of here!" Coor yelled down at her over the sound of crumbling stone and clay, the screams, and the eruption.

Darha scrambled to her feet, and both raced back down the stairs with Coor very close on her heels. Cracks covered the walls and steps, and dust filled the air where ash didn't occupy. Darha and Coor held their hands over their mouths and noses, but started coughing uncontrollably.

They exited the stairway and stopped in their tracks, stunned, when they saw the left side of the hall was now open to the elements. The entire back half of the palace was reduced to rubble. Ash blew past the opening and completely filled the hallway. Darha was too stunned to even be afraid as she stared outside in horror. Black clouds had begun to fill the sky, blotting out the sun, slowly casting the city into darkness.

117

Heavy running steps could be heard coming down the right side of the hallway that was still mostly intact. A large host of black and gold clad soldiers, the Queen's personal guard, turned the corner and raced toward her. Coor went to them, shouting orders she couldn't hear, as she continued to stare at the ceaseless ash. Dead. People. So many dead people. She couldn't imagine it. She didn't want to.

"Darha!" Coor screamed.

Abruptly, her brother took her upper arm and pulled her down the hallway away from the opening. The guards, at least two dozen of them, got into formation around her with their weapons drawn. She didn't understand why; it wasn't like they could fight nature.

"Where are we going?" Darha asked, too softly, too stunned. Where could they possibly go now?

"What?" Coor shouted, looking down at her as they turned a corner into another ash-and dust-filled hallway.

"Where are we going?" she yelled, forcing her words past her hands.

"The Temple basement," he replied. "It's the only place we think you'll be safe."

Something rose up in Darha's chest that moment. She wasn't completely sure what it was, but it was hard and fearless, which in itself was a little scary. She yanked on Coor's arm to stop him and the guards in the hallway.

"What are you—" Coor began.

"What about the people?" Darha asked him.

She saw Coor's eyes go a little wide. "Let me get you safe first!"

"No!" Darha yelled, surprising herself. "We all need to get out of here."

"Darha," Coor cried, "the entire nation won't fit in the basement of the Temple!"

Darha took in a shaky, ash-and dust-thick breath, suddenly nervous to say this to him. But she knew it was the right thing. She knew! "We evacuate to the Frost Nation."

His eyes got wide then. "Darha, you can't—"

"Coor," she interrupted him. "Please. I need you to trust me. Please. I know Queen Vesna will help us. I know she will!"

Coor's eyes got sad but held hers. "I don't doubt you, Darha. I don't even doubt Queen Vesna." He sighed. "I doubt the willingness of our people, as a whole, to be taken in by their most hated enemies."

Darha's heart clenched as she wondered for an instant if their hatred for the Frost Nation could really trump their willingness to survive. That fearlessness still sat in her chest, though, as she studied her older brother. "That's what we do," she said, forcing conviction into her voice. "Anyone who really wants to stay behind here, may." Darha nearly flinched at her own words. They seemed so heartless and callous. She doubted herself for a moment, and nearly took the words back, but Coor's confident gaze didn't waver.

"All right," he said. "How do you want to do it?"

Darha paused, taking a few breaths as she wondered, and weighed, and measured their options with their resources, abilities and time. A million thoughts, and ideas, and scenarios raced through her head about how she could get her people across the River Gora to the Frost Nation. Boats. They needed lots of boats. Magic users. Any forgers left. Food. Water. And lava. That would take time to gather. Everything would take time to gather, but it was the only option she had.

Darha met Coor's eyes. "Are there any standing lava pools left?"

"Just the ones to the southeast."

Another rumble violently shook the entire palace. Coor grabbed Darha, pressing her tightly between his body and the wall, as another section of the palace somewhere was reduced to rubble. Darha panted as she looked up at her brother.

"Walk and talk," Coor stated as he took her upper arm again, guiding her as they ran down the hall. The soldiers closed in tightly around them once more.

"Send out a summons to all four corners of the nation," Darha declared, "to meet at the lava pools to the southeast. Magic users and forgers make haste. We are going to make boats out of whatever scraps of metal can be brought, and out of the stone in the lava pools."

"Stone boats won't float. Lava is useless."

"Not if we have skilled enough forgers and magic users. And I believe we do." Coor regarded his sister. "They can make the stone thin enough, with enough air bubbles, to allow them to float."

Coor looked ahead of him again as they rounded the corner into the throne room. "That will take days."

Darha realized he wasn't really arguing, just stating facts, reasoning it out, considering all the angles and possibilities available to them in this situation and making her aware of them. So, this was what it was like to work with her brother, rather than have him make all the decisions. It was sort of nice and oddly exhilarating.

119

"Have the army empty out the food and water reserves and bring them to the southeast lava pools. We will make camp there while the boats are being made."

Coor smiled down at her, the ash on his skin deepening the lines and creases in his face, and making the pride he was feeling even more evident. "All right," he said.

Darha smiled in return. If he was looking at her like that, this must not be as rotten of an idea as she feared. But still, her people would rebel and, at the very least, rage against seeking refuge from the Frost Nation.

Yet Darha was past caring about that. The Fire Nation was no longer safe for them, and she knew Queen Vesna would not only allow them entry, but provide for them as well.

Of that, she had no doubt.

———————— o ————————

Aradel held her hands up as Tristra spun silk around the outside of them. Beside her was a spinning wheel already loaded with a spool that was nearly empty. Tristra hummed gently as she spun it around and around Aradel's hands, preparing it. The lines in the old woman's face became more apparent the more Aradel stared at her. Her eyes dropped down to Tristra's fine clothes which indicated that she was wealthy.

Kirill's father had been one of the Providence leaders within the walls before becoming Queen Vesna's chief advisor. They had a beautiful villa on the outskirts of Axion, with an ice garden that rivaled the one in the palace. Aradel knew this because for part of her life she had lived there.

"It is so kind of you to take time out of your day, young miss," Tristra said, softly smiling at her in a motherly way.

Today was not a day when Tristra remembered who Aradel was. Yet despite her lack of memory, she was in an agreeable mood. Whatever time Tristra thought it was, she was very happy. Her humming was a good sign.

"You look happy, Lady Tristra," Aradel replied, hardly noticing as the older woman continued to twist the silk into submission

"I am," Tristra replied brightly. "We have just taken in a young girl who the Queen believes will become a candidate when she is old enough. She seemed very suspicious of us, but today I saw her smile for the first time."

Aradel remembered that moment. Kirill had fallen off his elk while riding it backwards, and Tristra had scolded him harshly, until she had seen his pants were torn. Both Kirill and his mother had laughed so hard Aradel couldn't help but smile at them. That was the first time she had smiled in years.

"That was kind of you to take her in when she was all alone," Aradel said, trying not to interrupt the memory as she began to spin the silk onto the spool. The spinning wheel's pedal click-clacked as her foot pushed down and the wheel spun, pulling the thread along Tristra's guiding finger, before wrapping it around the fist-sized spool.

"Yes, poor thing was all alone," Tristra replied with a heavy sigh. "We tried to find her family, but her parents' neighbors didn't know where they had gone, and her sister had died some time before that."

Aradel froze and then lifted her head slowly. When she was a child, the woman next door had said her sister, Mera, had died, but Aradel didn't know how. All she knew was that she had been sold, and then died later. For as long as Aradel could remember, she'd imagined her sister had died alone and miserable.

"How awful," Aradel managed. She swallowed hard before asking as dispassionately as possible, so as not to upset Trista. "How did her sister die?"

"Childbirth," Tristra replied with another heavy sigh as she looked absentmindedly at the wood wheel spinning.

Aradel's mind raced, and her blood ran colder. Childbirth? All these years, Tristra had known what had become of her older sister. All these years, Kirill's mother had known, but had never said anything. Suddenly Tristra shook a little and glanced around. The wheel came to a sudden halt.

"You should be more careful!" Tristra cried, pulling at the unspun silk.

Aradel blinked, realizing that she had let her hands fall and ice crystals had formed on the thread.

"You know how important it is to pay attention, Aradel," Trista continued. "You are as bad as Kirill today."

"I'm sorry," Aradel said halfheartedly.

"I know," Tristra replied, stopping to observe her. Tristra patted Aradel's cheek. "You look tired. Have you been getting enough sleep at the palace?"

"Yes," Aradel replied as Kirill's mother moved to another time. She began pulling at the thread again until she found the snare. "Tristra, you were telling me about my sister."

Tristra immediately started shaking her head. "I don't want to talk about that."

"But we just were." Aradel pressed, leaning forward hopefully.

Shaking her head more violently Tristra cried, "I don't want to!" Then she abruptly stood, letting everything on her lap fall onto the ground. It clattered loudly, which made Aradel stand as well, but she held her hands up so she didn't lose the silk. Before Aradel could get an actual word out, Tristra cried, "I'm tired and wish to retire to my room." Without hesitation, Tristra left a very stunned Aradel alone.

Others in the room glanced at her as she broke from her shock. Carefully, she set the unspun silk down on Tristra's chair, and then left the temple in a contemplative silence. Her legs were numb as she walked back toward the palace, knowing she was going to arrive early.

Mera had been like the light to Aradel. When they were children, Aradel had had silvery blond hair, but Mera's had been gold, like captured sunlight, and she had been like the sun. Their parents hadn't so much been cruel as they were selfish. They hadn't cared much for their own children, only what leverage their daughter could bring, and the price they could fetch from a wealthy merchant. Mera had been thirteen when she had been sold. The thought of her sister dying in some birth room, with the child of a man she didn't love, broke Aradel's heart.

"Aradel?" Queen Vesna's voice broke through her thoughts. "What are you doing here?"

Aradel looked up as the Queen sat among a group of young children. She had a book settled in her lap, and a bewildered expression on her face. On instinct, Aradel had sought out the only woman she thought would understand. Queen Vesna knew where she had come from, knew who and what her parents were, and knew that her sister had died. She knew everything and had never judged. That was who Queen Vesna was.

"I apologize." Aradel drew out her words as she tried to think of a reason to interrupt.

"Come," Queen Vesna said, gesturing to her. "Come and read for me."

She forgot her own worries as she scanned the faces of the children. She walked around them and sat beside Queen Vesna on a pillowed bench. All around them the ice garden remained pristine and untouched, despite the quakes. Aradel wished The Wall had remained unscathed as well. Queen Vesna pointed at a part of the book, and Aradel smiled down at the children as she began to read.

They listened with intent, and for a time, Aradel forgot about their failing wall. She forgot about Kirill and whether she would ever see him again. She forgot about Queen Vesna's failing health. She forgot about the mystery surrounding her sister's death, and all those old painful memories. All she thought about was the book in her hands, and the story for the children, so that they too might forget their worries.

It was a collection of short stories that counseled children against many things—lessons to be learned, and warnings to be heeded. Although the stories' themes usually involved the heat of the summer, and avoiding people from the Fire Nation, Aradel artfully skipped over those she

123

remembered being too harsh. Queen Vesna did nothing to stop her as the children listened intently.

"And because the little girl made the cake herself without the help of any of her friends, she ate it all by herself," she was reading when the ground began to shake.

Aradel stood quickly, but nearly fell backward over the bench when the quake became more intense. The children started to cry out. Queen Vesna stood as well and pointed along the path that led out of the palace.

"Children, hurry!" Queen Vesna called as Aradel linked her arm with her Queen's and hurried after them.

The quake slowed for a moment when they were nearly out of the palace, then a second, stronger quake hit. The children screamed as they hurried down the steps into the courtyard below. The second quake was far worse, and Queen Vesna half fell. Aradel held them both upright by clinging to a stone pillar. Ice crystals rained down on their heads as the pillars rubbed against the ceiling.

A cry came from behind them, and they both looked back to see a young girl on her stomach on the ground.

Queen Vesna pushed Aradel forward as she fell backward against a pillar. "Save her!" she cried, her voice rising above the rest of the sounds in the room.

A column by the front gave way, crashing to the ground and blocking their exit. Aradel's heart seized but, looking around, she realized the garden was empty. The rest of the children had made it to safety in time. For that Aradel was thankful. With a glance back at her Queen, Aradel hurried to the crying child. She half stumbled, half crawled to the girl, whose terrified wails could be heard above the rumbling.

"I'm here!" Aradel called, gathering her in her arms.

People from different parts of the palace were flooding into the garden to escape, only to realize the exit was blocked. Panic in the room rose as pillars and gigantic trees toppled all around them. Ice shattered and sprayed across the path that should have led to safety, but was blocked by the column. Aradel held the terrified child against her chest and watched as yet another column of stone fell, crushing one of the guards standing by. Aradel looked helplessly at Queen Vesna.

Suddenly the elder Queen lifted her arms, and the ancient garden of ice fell away to mounds of harmless snow in an instant. The pillars barely holding the ceiling up were suddenly reinforced with ice. Queen

Vesna practically glowed with the power of her magic. The moon pearls shone like a full moon at midnight.

Aradel turned toward the exit, where already many were trying to crawl over the pillar to escape. She held the child tightly to her chest as she ran toward it as fast as she could with the planet still shaking. Focusing her power on it, the pillar of pale blue ice and stone suddenly fell into pieces. With no ice to hold the column together, the stones separated and fell away, making room for an escape. Those who had been trying to crawl over it were startled, but the moment quickly passed as the quake intensified, and they began to push through the rubble in a panic.

Aradel fell backwards, landing hard on her backside and the child in her arms screamed. She grimaced as she struck the hard stone of the floor. She was just barely able to regain her footing and started to run to the exit. Glancing back, Aradel saw Queen Vesna holding her arms up desperately, straining to heal the fracturing ice. Despite her efforts, the ceiling began to crack.

Aradel faced forward again. "You!" she called to a nearby woman and thrust the child into her arms. "Get her to safety." The woman took the child before fleeing from the crumbling palace. Once the girl was safely out the door, Aradel turned back to her Queen. "Queen Vesna!" she yelled.

Aradel pushed through the last of the people trying to get to safety. She screamed Queen Vesna's name again as the stone started to give way above. Still, the woman made no move to leave. Aradel ran, instinctively reaching for her. She was just a few steps away, when the ceiling gave way, and they were buried under stone and ice.

Fire: Chapter Twenty-Two

o

Darha could hardly believe the ash from Tamon's explosion had reached them this far to the southeast. Three days since, and it was still falling heavily, a constant nuisance throughout the camp. People had to be designated to brush it off tent roofs and tables, lest they collapse under the weight. They were constantly laboring over the duty, taking shifts all day and night to make sure the ash didn't accumulate too high.

A dull grayness had settled around them on everything—the sky, the ground, everywhere that it could. This wasn't normal ash like from a fire. This ash was gritty and heavy. It coated everything, and rubbed like sand between their fingers. Fortunately, the ash fall had thinned considerably from the sheets that had come down in Vlid, but Darha still worried. Snow was simply cold water and could be dealt with because it melted in the heat of the Fire Nation. But this stuff was a snowstorm from a nightmare that never ended, and never melted. They had no means to protect themselves from it.

Darha stood outside her tent now with a scarf covering her nose and mouth. It used to be a pretty light pink color, but was now as dull and gray as the ash that surrounded her. With dust and dirt covering her face and clothing, she looked up at the pale ball in the sky that used to be their brilliant sun, and silently wondered why their Sun God had abandoned them like this. She even prayed, asking him why. When her prayers were met with silence, she went back inside her tent with a heavy heart.

Pulling her scarf off her face and letting it hang around her neck like a noose, Darha went around a large wooden table and sat heavily in the temporary throne behind it. Coor had put a system of boat building and forging into place that was working smoothly, which didn't leave Darha much to do in that regard. Her job was mainly to quell the people who constantly ranted about evacuating to the Frost Nation. Darha was tired of the looks, the snarls, and the shakes of heads. So often she wanted to scream at them that if they wanted to stay so badly, why didn't they? Or, if they were agreeing to come, why did they have to mutter and complain about it? It made her angry because it made absolutely no sense.

She sunk heavily into her throne, putting her elbow on the armrest so her hand propped up her head, and closed her eyes. She hadn't known it was possible to be this tired. She wasn't sure how she could even function.

Because Coor was constantly busy tending to things throughout the camp, Darha was left alone quite often, allowing her way too much time to contemplate things.

She thought about Thea, and felt a burning ache in her chest every time her sister crossed her mind. Was she okay? Was she going to be okay? She knew Coor was in emotional pain, that was practically manifesting itself into physical pain from her absence, but he continued doing what needed to be done like warriors did. He never quit and never gave up…and never talked about Thea being gone.

Opening her eyes, Darha stared at the red and gold decorative wall of her tent. His reaction suddenly struck her as odd. Darha felt like Coor needed to talk about her, and how he was missing her, and worried for her.

Her eyes shifted to the entryway of her tent. "Jamsun," she called to her guard.

Moving the flap aside he poked his head in. "Majesty?"

"Will you please send for my brother?"

The older guard nodded. "Right away." With that, he disappeared.

Darha sighed heavily and continued to stare at the wall of her tent. It was big enough to fit more than ten people in here comfortably. She tried to repress the guilt of taking up that much space. It seemed pointless, but that was the role she played, Queen. And Queens needed protection and solitude to make sure they could still run things and conduct business. She closed her eyes again, and shook her head at the absurdity of it.

Hearing Coor outside her tent, her eyes shifted to the entryway as he entered. His skin and clothing was dull and gray and filthy from constant ash fall. He had a distinct smudge across his forehead where he had tried to wipe it away. Pulling down the grayish-red scarf from his face, he looked at her with concern. "What's wrong?"

Darha sat up a little and took hold of a chair beside her. "Sit down." Coor did. "How are you holding up?" she asked.

Coor sighed heavily and sat back. "I'm all right. The boat building is going better than expected. We've already got about twelve built, but it's going to be—"

"Coor," Darha interrupted gently. He looked at her, slightly puzzled. Darha shifted her eyes down to his hands on his lap. Leaning over her knees, with her elbows resting on her thighs, she took hold of one and met his eyes. "How are you holding up?"

Coor appeared confused for a moment, and then a wide range of emotions flashed across his face when he realized what she was asking. Darha could tell he wanted to dismiss the question, but seeing her concern, he softened. "I miss her," he admitted, his voice thick with emotion. He pressed his fingers into his eyes to hide the tears.

Darha didn't say anything and just held her brother's hand. She'd never seen him so distraught before. But for once, finally, she could be his rock as he always had been hers.

He lowered his hand and his red eyes met hers. "It feels like a piece of me is missing." Darha's eyes filled with tears at that. "And I want it back," he concluded, swallowing heavily. "I want my wife back, Darha."

Darha nodded. She gazed at the floor as a single tear slid down her cheek. A memory suddenly popped into her head, and she smiled up at him. "Do you remember when mom and dad brought her home that day?"

Coor huffed a short laugh, which allowed a tear to escape down his cheek that he quickly wiped away. "How could I forget?"

"She totally kicked Kohe's ass."

Coor threw his head back and laughed. Darha felt a weight lift off her heart with the sound of it. "Yeah, she did." Coor pinched the corners of his eyes again, trying to absorb the tears. "I remember mom trying to hurry Thea into the bathing room before she could get picked on."

Darha nodded. "But she wasn't quick enough, and we were already coming down the hall from study group."

Coor nodded. He lowered his hand and stared at the floor for a moment. Darha could see him lost in the happy memory of when he met the girl who had ended up being his soul mate. "Even at twelve years old I knew," Coor said, smiling. "I saw her and that fearless fire in her eyes when she punched Kohe hard enough to send him sprawling across the floor, and I knew."

Darha nodded. "And Kohe was a mini-giant."

"Taller than me!" Coor exclaimed with a grin, and Darha giggled. "You know I saw him years later, before he was killed, and his nose was still flat at the bridge." Darha threw her head back and laughed. Coor chuckled. "I would have hit him myself for putting his hands near Thea, but she beat me to it."

"What did he do again? I don't remember."

"He was a snob, offended by her ragged street appearance, and gave her a shove as we approached. Mom tried yelling at him, but Thea handled it."

Darha chuckled. "In the way only Thea can," she concluded with a smile.

Coor laughed. "Mom and I looked at each other when Kohe went sprawling. Both of us had our lips pressed together, hardly able contain our laughter before she finally got Thea into the bathing room."

Darha listened to him laugh, and let it die down before she squeezed his hand, making him look at her. "Thea will be back," she said confidently. "I know she will. She is too stubborn, and too in love with you, to let anything stop her from coming back home. You know it's true, too."

Coor smiled at her, "I know." He squeezed her hand in return and stood up. Cupping Darha's face in both hands, he pressed his lips firmly to her forehead. "Thanks," he said, looking down at her.

Darha smiled and nodded. "You're welcome."

Coor had just straightened when Jamsun threw back the flap of her tent. "Begging your pardon, your majesties," he said with wide eyes, "but you need to see this."

Darha's heart leapt up into her throat. What was wrong now? She got to her feet, and Coor took a step back to allow her to round the table first. Lifting the scarves up over their faces again, Darha and Coor stepped out into the world of falling ash. Everything around her was still gray and hazy, and she couldn't see much out of order. Everything seemed normal and quiet.

"Darha," Coor said softly.

She glanced up at him and saw his eyes were wide. Following his gaze, she found herself looking out at the River Gora nearby. It was fuzzy at first, but soon her eyes were as big as her brother's. They glanced at each other, and then both were hurrying toward the river's edge.

Boats, at least two hundred boats, a whole fleet of long rowboats, appeared on the horizon. It didn't take long for a crowd to gather behind the siblings. Whispers and murmurs broke out, some sounding confused, others afraid, a few angry. As the boats drew nearer, Darha started trembling with joy, relief, gratitude, and everything in between. It was the Frost Nation. They were in two hundred empty boats, and Darha knew they were here to rescue them.

Covering her mouth with one hand, Darha shamelessly started bawling her eyes out. Coor drew her close to him and she pressed her face into his chest, sobbing hysterically. She didn't even care who heard or saw her. Coor wrapped both his arms tightly around her and did his best to shield her as she cried. She couldn't believe it. Darha vowed to herself to hug Queen Vesna when they got to the southern shore, no matter how much her cold burned. As long as the old Queen could insulate herself from Darha's heat, she was determined to hug her.

The Frost Nation was pulling their boats ashore before Darha could calm herself. An incredibly handsome soldier stepped out and approached Darha with some haste. He was a little older, maybe Coor's age, with gentle, pale green eyes and straight, golden blonde hair that grazed the top of his shoulders and framed his features.

He had a small playful smile on his lips as he stood in front of her. "We understand you may be in need of some assistance, your majesty."

Darha recognized him. It took her a moment, but she quickly recalled him as the soldier who had noticed her crying during the Frost Nation's supply run weeks ago. Darha managed to laugh through her tears. "Yes. Yes, we do."

His smile broadened slightly, and he bowed a little at the waist. "My name is Cas and, per order of Queen Vesna, if you're willing, we've come to retrieve you to our shores, where you will be protected and provided for." Cas's eyes scanned the crowd behind Darha, and his smile faded.

Darha looked back and saw the hostile glares the rescue boats were getting. Darha couldn't believe it. She absolutely couldn't believe it. Getting angry, she slowly pulled the scarf off her face and turned to face them, deliberately stepping in front of Cas as if to protect him, and glared at her ungrateful nation. "How dare any of you gaze upon them like this," she said. "They came to rescue us. Rescue us!" she cried forcefully. "They didn't have to. They could have left us over here to rot, but they didn't. They chose to save us!" Darha felt her lip twitch. "But, by all means, if any of you want to stay here," her voice lowered to a growl, "be my guest."

Her people glanced around nervously at each other, some with a little shame, but not many.

She faced Cas again and the other Frost Nation soldiers. "Thank you for coming to our rescue."

Cas smiled again, but it was a little sad this time. "While Queen Vesna is welcoming you to our shores, hostilities are"—he glanced at the crowd behind her— "clearly still strong between our two nations, and you must be segregated, lest war break out."

Darha nodded once. "I understand."

"With the early spring, Hurra will be empty and available for your use. It is a small, but well-maintained town just across the river from here. There are houses, beds, food, medicine, and heat."

Darha nodded again. "It's more than we could have hoped for. Thank you."

Cas smiled warmly at her. "Shall we begin to evacuate you?"

Darha grinned in return, though nervously. "You realize it's going to take several trips?"

Cas nodded. "We were made aware of how many people were going to need to be evacuated. We are prepared."

Darha wiped one final tear from her cheek and felt the grit from the ash smear across her face. "Thank you," she said and then looked up at Coor. "Let's get our own boats into the water, too, and evacuate."

Coor faced the crowd. "Everyone start packing your things." Everyone started moving and talking at once. "Take only necessities!" He called over the noise. "Women, children, wounded, and elderly first. Provisions are on the other side of the river, so bring only necessities!" As the crowd disbursed, Coor stepped up to Cas. "Thank you," Coor said, his words heavy with sincerity. "Truly. Thank you."

Cas nodded once in reply. Coor and Darha then took off to tend to the preparations for evacuation and rescue.

Frost: Chapter Twenty-Three

———————— o ————————

Tulya watched as the boats departed the Frost Nation heading out on a misguided rescue attempt for the Fire Nation. Glancing up at the light ash that rained down around them, it pained her to think that only the magic users of the Frost Nation could protect themselves from hot embers that burned within it.

Selfish, self-fulfilling magic users. They cared little for those that weren't like them, and gave preferential treatment to those who had magic. Tulya looked back to the River Gora as the last of the boats were launched and lost to the fog. She was alone at the lookout, but not far off from those that supported her and Ekil's cause.

Tulya gazed down at her hand as frost formed on it. An instant later, it vanished. What they didn't know wouldn't hurt them, she thought as she closed her hand into a fist. If Ekil ever discovered she was a very weak magic user, he would likely kill her.

But the two factions needed to work together for now. Many members of the Fire Nation had joined their cause, even fire wielders. They'd finally realized that their Sun God didn't answer their prayers, and that the Fire Nation's Queen couldn't stop this devastation with her magic. To them, those lost and burdened souls, magic was to blame. All their weak minds wanted was something to blame, and all Tulya had to do was provide the focus for that blame. They had joined by the hundreds, desperate for the supplies Tulya and their group had offered. To her thousand members, Ekil had two thousand. Half of which now reported to Tulya. Well, mostly reported.

As she climbed down from the tree blind, Tulya considered their options. The Frost Nation could choose one of three villages to evacuate the Fire Nation to. The closest was Jipon, but Tulya doubted they would place the Fire Nation near a guardhouse that led under The Wall. That left Hurra and Demil. Hurra was closest, and, for the sake of efficiency, she imagined Queen Vesna would choose that one.

When she reached the bottom, she found Ekil's right hand man, Maris, waiting for her. He spat on the ground and smiled menacingly at her. "They all gone?" His hair was wiry and streaked with gray. It matched his pale eyes, which were the same color of the ash that fell around them.

She pushed her blond curls out of her face and turned toward him, trying not to glare. "Yes."

"Good," he replied.

He pushed off the tree he had been leaning on and started back toward their camp. Tulya pulled a sheer cloth over her head as she followed behind. She couldn't risk anyone recognizing her on the way back. Not to mention, it kept the ash out of her hair. She felt almost paranoid about being recognized, because nearly every citizen of the Frost Nation had fled behind The Wall. She couldn't risk being questioned.

"Did you come to escort me back?" she asked, wondering why exactly Maris had come.

He made a rude noise before answering. "You were taking too long. People were getting restless."

"We are about to cripple the magic users," Tulya said hotly. "Everyone is just ready to take the next step."

"Perhaps," Maris replied, "or perhaps they are restless because we've mingled Fire with Frost."

"They won't have to wait much longer," Tulya responded as she tried to conceal her excitement. "The Fire Nation's refugees will likely be brought to the village of Hurra."

Maris didn't reply, and Tulya was thankful for it. She had half expected an argument. Ekil, with his scars and ideas of grandeur, made her nervous. It did not surprise her that the man acting as his second did the same. Unlike Ekil's, Maris's scars were not visible, but she could still sense they were there, just below the surface.

Most didn't know Tulya's past, and she preferred it that way. Her father had had a soul as black as pitch, and a fist that hit like a mace. Unlike her parents, who were known to be magic haters and without magic, Tulya had repressed powers. She had repressed them right up until her father killed her mother—and Tulya had killed him in return. She had used the incident as leverage to get herself into a place of power, claiming they both had been murdered by a powerful magic user. No one had suspected she had any magic, and no one ever would. Not unless she wanted them to.

She wiped the ash away from her face and felt the grit of volcanic dust rub against her forehead. She was thankful that the ash no longer burned with the embers she knew had created it. Enough heat from them could betray her for what she was when her skin fractured.

Tulya pulled the scarf up further to cover her face as they went through the woods. Trees were overturned, their dead roots hanging as if desperately reaching for the dirt again to live. But they could not survive the way the planet had been ripped apart. Tulya's heart jumped at the thought. There was something raw and powerful about the way nature bowed to no man. Magic or not.

Tulya sensed the scout before she saw him. Peering up, she called him, "Gil."

The scout dropped down from a tree next to them. He was a boy of perhaps thirteen with greasy hair that hung in strings around his eyes. He had an expression on his face that reminded her of a child receiving a gift. She imagined many of their people were awaiting her return, and would have similar looks when she told them it was time.

"Don't do that!" Maris grumbled, spitting on the ground again.

"Are we going to kill them?" Gil asked, completely ignoring Maris.

"We are," Tulya responded as they went the last hundred feet to the camp. "We are going to kill them all."

Gil smiled and raced off, likely to tell the others. She watched him go before glancing at Maris. His gaze met hers steadily, but she sensed something beneath those eyes. Something was burrowing in her gut like a whisper of foreboding. Tulya lifted her head and entered the camp without giving him a second look.

When she passed by him, he whispered, "I know what you are."

She turned back to him in surprise. For a moment, she was speechless. Gritting her teeth, she narrowed her gaze into a glare.

"What do you mean?" she demanded, thankful that the trees were thicker here, which kept the ash at bay.

He leaned forward and smelled her head. She shifted away from him but didn't step back. A breath away from her ear, he whispered, "You have magic on you."

Carefully, she smirked and laughed at him. He shifted back but didn't join in. Tulya felt a cold sweat break out on her body as she put her hands around her stomach, as though he had told some great joke.

"Perhaps you smell the magic user I slept with to get the information that Queen Vesna was sending troops to get your people," Tulya replied with a shrug. "I'll likely be covered with his stench for a while."

He grunted as she left him there. It did her no good to try to make further excuses. Despite her calm façade, she worried her lie hadn't worked. Fortunately, it wasn't really a lie. She actually had slept with a magic user to gain the information.

When she emerged in the clearing, Maris wasn't following her, and below, her people were already starting to gather. The ash left a thin layer over everything like dust. In some places, it had been swept up and piled out of the way. Glancing toward The Wall, Tulya wondered how much further inland the ash went.

"Ready yourself," Tulya called, which quieted the crowd that was gathering with every word. "The Fire Nation's most powerful magic users are coming. They are going toward Hurra to seek refuge. It is a four-day walk, and we are going to head them off and cripple them while they are weak. Burn them with the fire they so love, and the Frost Nation magic users who are with them!"

The people below shouted, "To Hurra!"

"First Hurra," Tulya yelled, pulling a dagger from her hip and pointing it in the air, "and then Axion will fall!"

The forest erupted in joyful shouts. War was coming to the Frost Nation, and they would be victorious against the magic users. She let her arm fall to her side again as an aching pleasure filled her chest. The idea of finally overthrowing the magic users, and taking their place, excited her.

She sensed a movement to her left, and turned her lust-filled eyes toward the woods. Maris was watching her, and she knew he sensed her desire. The man could smell anything and everything, so she didn't try to hide it. Instead, she put the dagger back in its sheath and went to her tent. When she entered, he followed her in.

She turned back to yell at him, but he crushed his mouth against hers and lifted her up. Her bottom landed on the small makeshift desk she had put together. Things clattered to the ground, but she hardly heard them as she framed his face with her hands.

After a moment, she pushed at his chest and insisted, "You're being reckless and foolish."

"You've wanted this," he whispered, tugging her closer.

She smiled wickedly because he was right, but reason barely won out. Her voice was thick with desire as she spoke. "If anyone reports us to Ekil, he will know you're working with me. That you've joined me."

"It isn't betrayal, because now we're working together," Maris insisted before nibbling at her throat.

"I have a feeling Ekil won't see it that way," Tulya whispered softly as he continued down her neck. She looked toward the ceiling of her tent and rested her hand on the back of his neck. They risked much by being together as they were.

"He'd have to figure it out first, and Ekil is blind," Maris insisted against her skin.

Tulya pushed him off her, "But he isn't stupid," she said in a voice that was soft and verged on deadly. "He is brutal and harsh, and I won't give him a reason to suspect us. Now get out."

He frowned but took a step back, putting his hands up signifying surrender. Tulya slipped off the desk and landed on her feet. "After Hurra," Maris said, "we won't need Ekil anymore." Before Tulya could answer him, he left her tent.

She watched the flap swing back and forth until it finally stilled. Maris was right. If they were successful at Hurra, they wouldn't need Ekil anymore. She couldn't keep the smile from her lips at the thought. If they crippled the magic users, they could take Axion. The thought warmed her more than she could say, and she walked out into the chaos of a camp preparing for war.

Fire: Chapter Twenty-Four

— o —

As they neared the southern shore, Coor pulled the scarf down from his face and drew in a long heavy breath. Ash still fell around him, but it was small and scattered, allowing the first draw of clean air into his lungs in nearly a week since the eruption.

He glanced at his sister sitting closer to the front of the boat. She lowered the scarf from her face and took a deep breath, too. Coor had never seen his sister so filthy. Her exceptionally long, golden, honey-blonde hair had no luster. It was hidden under caked-on grime and soot and ash. Her entire appearance was one mute, dull, grayish brown color. Coor knew he didn't look any better. The fact that the royalty of the Fire Nation looked like mine workers was a little humorous, and Coor managed a small smirk, but the weight of all that they had lost kept it from lingering.

He and Darha had taken the very last boats across the River Gora. Cas was commanding their boat and he had been an absolute soldier. It had taken four days of nonstop, six-hour trips back and forth across the river to evacuate everyone from the Fire Nation. The Frost Nation rowers and soldiers had taken shifts to make sure the boats didn't stop running, but Cas accompanied every single trip, sleeping in the boat on the way back to retrieve more Fire Nation evacuees.

It was quiet as Cas came to crouch in the space between the two siblings. "Hurra is outside The Wall, so you will have the heat of the day to stay warm. Though with the crack in our wall getting bigger"—he sighed sadly— "you could likely survive just as well behind The Wall these days."

Darha turned to the southern native, giving him her full attention. "Are your people suffering badly?"

Cas shook his head. "It's not going well."

Coor heard something unsettling in Cas's voice and could tell, from her expression, that Darha did, too. "Is Queen Vesna well?" she asked. She reached for the Frost Nation soldier's hand in a gesture of comfort, but quickly retracted it before making contact—before they could burn each other.

Cas met Darha's eyes. "Another quake hit about the time your volcano erupted. Our palace was destroyed with Queen Vesna and Lady Aradel trapped inside."

"No," Darha gasped.

"Can we help?" Coor found himself asking. "Our magic users can melt the ice if necessary."

Cas gave him a small, appreciative smile. "Thank you, but we were able to retrieve them," he sighed. "Queen Vesna, however, was terribly injured."

Coor saw Darha's hand flutter up to her chest. "She isn't going to…" Darha asked, unable to finish the sentence.

Cas's response was a sigh and low bow of his head, as though the words could not be spoken aloud.

Coor watched terror erupt in his little sister's eyes as she turned to gaze out over the river. Concerned, Coor stood in a crouch and shifted his position to move closer to the front of the boat so he was across from her. "What is it?"

Darha met his eyes as she fiddled with the scarf at her throat. "I just…" She glanced away. "I trust Queen Vesna. I like her. She's helped us abundantly at every single turn without criticism, complaint or hatred. If she dies…" Darha swallowed heavily. Coor reached across and rested his hand on top of hers. "A new Queen will take her place. One who may be less inclined to be so kind and helpful toward our people."

Coor felt himself deflate. He ran his hand through his dusty, filthy hair. "I see."

Darha pressed her lips together in a thin line of worry, and an unsettling quiet fell over the boat. It was in this moment of silence that Coor heard the sounds. He snapped his head in the direction of the shore. The noise instantly drew Cas's attention too, and both men got to their feet and stared to the south. Coor knew those sounds. He'd been acquainted with them since he was six years old; they were the sounds of battle.

Coor felt his mental and emotional gears shift into soldier mode. He wanted to holler at the Frost Nation rowers to go faster, but it wasn't his place to order the Frost Nation to do anything. He had to tread carefully here; he wasn't home.

"Rowers! Double time!" Cas suddenly commanded, sparing Coor the turmoil of needing to move, but not being able to say anything. The Frost Nations rowers sped up so much that the breeze lifted Coor's hair off his forehead.

He looked at Cas. "Thank you."

Cas glanced at him and nodded. "You are under our Queen's protection. This should not be happening. Whatever it may be, it's our problem, too."

Every minute he had to stand there, listening, and unable to do anything, was excruciating. Hidden by distance and the thick mist, the shore wasn't in sight yet, but he could hear everything, just like he'd been able to on that day. They had come into his home then, the magic-haters.

He'd been six years old when his mother had shoved his infant sister into his arms and pushed them both into a nearby closet to hide them. Coor remembered crying. Not for himself, but because if his baby sister started crying, they would hear her and he wouldn't be able to protect her. As the moments ticked by and Darha just looked around, calm and alert, Coor had calmed himself down. It was as if Darha, even as an infant, had known something was wrong and that she'd needed to be quiet for him.

He'd heard the same battle sounds then, the clash of metal on metal, the stomping and running feet, but mostly the screams. The screams seemed to come through the door as if Coor was in an open arena. All of them sounded different. Some were high pitched, some were strangled, some gurgled with liquid, and others sounded like a deep moan. Some were a mix of all of these. All of them were composed of agony, anger, and fear.

Coor crouched in front of Darha now, resting his hands on both sides of her head. "When we reach the shore, stay welded to my side until soldiers arrive to escort you to safety. Do you understand me?" Darha nodded without a word. Coor firmly kissed her forehead and then stood and faced Cas. "Is there a place my sister can be safely escorted to?"

Cas's eyes were fierce and battle ready, which comforted Coor's soul. "There is a guard tower west of the town. It was just recently made a border guard to protect both our nations from each other's hostile attacks. There will be Frost Nation soldiers there to protect her."

"Will they allow my soldiers to accompany her without quarrel?"

"Yes. They maintain peace. It's what they were assigned to the towers for."

"General!" he heard called from one of the other boats. Rhett, one of his captains, stood with his hands cupped over his mouth. "Your orders, sir?"

"Prepare for battle," Coor hollered.

The command carried over the entire river until every soldier who had come across with this last lot of evacuees was armed. Most of Coor's soldiers had already crossed, for which he was thankful because they would be protecting the civilians who had also crossed, most of whom were women and children.

"Rhett!" Coor hollered.

"General."

"I want your unit to escort the Queen to safety. The Frost Nation commander, Cas, will have a location for you when we reach the shore."

"Understood."

"Soldiers!" Cas suddenly bellowed over the river in a booming voice Coor didn't expect from the soft, gentle looking southerner. "The Fire Nation is under the protection of our Queen. You will answer to Prince Coor and me for the duration of the battle. Whoever has attacked them, has defied our Queen, thus shall be considered traitors to the Frost Nation. Is that understood?"

"Aye, Commander!" The Frost Nation soldiers all said in unison.

The deep, rugged, and professional sound of it went into Coor's ears and settled down into his chest, warming and calming him. As the seconds dragged on, however, the boat quickly started to become a cage. Coor had to resist the urge to pace back and forth, lest he frighten his sister. He had to force his breathing to calm as the screams continued to reach his ears. Those were his people over there, dying! Their screams were reaching him, but he could not reach them! It took everything he had not to dive into the river. It was warm enough that he would likely survive.

Wait, he had to convince himself, wait.

The River Gora started to become cluttered with heavy debris. Coor watched as they passed even the tops of pine trees, as if they were sailing over the canopy of a forest. The Frost Nation rowers maneuvered the boats with impressive skill, not even slowing down as they avoided colliding with the debris. The flooding, Coor could see, had pushed the shoreline far back, as had happened at home, though the Frost Nation had more level and low-lying ground near the River Gora. Nearly half of the ground between the River Gora and the Frost Nation's wall was underwater.

Finally, the mist cleared enough that Coor could see the silhouettes of farmhouses, tents, and people, and he immediately began analyzing the situation. The Fire Nation soldiers had clearly been in formation, but the enemy had already managed to penetrate their center. They were split down the middle; half were up against the Frost Nation wall with the other half up against the River Gora. The enemy's main attack was concentrated in the center of the gap and was widening with every second.

Cas approached Coor. "We can envelop both their flanks from this position if we adjust the course of the boats—half to the west and half to the east."

Coor scanned the river at the boats. That strategy was risky enough with a large number of soldiers that Coor knew and trusted. If he had his whole force with him, he wouldn't hesitate with that tactic. As it was, most people in the boats were civilians. The only formidable force he had with him was Frost Nation soldiers, most of who were rowing. But he didn't know how the Frost Nation dealt with battle, and he couldn't risk that kind of maneuver with them on a first run. He had to admire Cas's bravery for suggesting it, though. It showed more trust than Coor was willing to put forth yet.

"No," Coor said without meeting the southern native's eyes. "We'll attack the west flank with the full force we have in the boats. If we can back them up enough, the ocean will be behind them in the east, the river to the north, and your ice wall to the south. We will box them in."

Coor could practically recite the concern Cas voiced next, since it would be apparent to any soldier. "What if they have reserves in the west?" he said. "We would be boxed in with enemy forces on our east and west fronts and the river to the north and The Wall to the south."

Coor sighed softly through his nose. "We'll deal with it if that becomes the case. We don't have enough soldiers in the boats to envelope their flanks."

Cas pressed his lips together when Coor shifted his eyes to his face. "Very well."

Coor felt a pang of guilt hit him in the chest as Cas sent the command over the river to the other boats and the boats adjusted course to the west. Cas knew Coor didn't fully trust him now. He shouldn't feel bad about that, but he did.

"I'm sorry," Coor ended up saying. Cas faced him. "It's just too soon." Coor didn't need to explain further. It was too soon to trust the Frost Nation, especially when his people's lives, women and children mostly, were at stake.

Cas's eyes softened slightly and he nodded. "I understand."

Coor smiled appreciatively though weakly and glanced back to the south. His heart started racing as the shoreline approached, and he drew the bow from his back. He thought about his wife, off somewhere on the ocean far to the west. He gathered a mental picture of Thea, looking back at him over her shoulder the day she left, and held that image of her until it burned like embers in his chest. She was the reason to survive. She was

141

the reason he would live through this battle—to see her again, to hold her again. Death came for all men eventually, but Coor refused to let it pay him a visit today.

"Not yet," he said softly to himself, like he did before every battle. He pulled an arrow out from the quiver behind him. "Not yet." He loaded the bow, taking aim.

As they were about to touch the shore, Coor drew the string to his cheek. "Fire!" He and the other hundred and fifty rangers in the boats, a mix of both Fire and Frost natives, let loose their arrows.

A small pile of enemies went down as the arrows hit their targets. It was a tiny impact on the overall battle, but enough to draw the enemy's attention to the fleet of boats. Coor pulled another arrow out as his boat touched the shore. "Fire!" he yelled. Coor and the rangers fired again. "Fire!" he called once more as he waited for Rhett's unit to get ashore. Just as the enemy started to regroup to try to deal with the new threat, Rhett's company was in front of him. "Fire at will!" Coor called before he put an arm around Darha's back and guided her to the side of the boat to disembark. Rhett took hold of her, helping her down.

Three stragglers branched off from the main battle and came toward them. Coor hopped onto shore, pulled out two arrows, loaded them both, and fired, killing all three. One of the arrows passed through the throat of a man in the lead, and plunged into the forehead of the one behind him.

Cas and his crew took up position behind Coor, between Darha and the battle, and started firing into the enemy at the center. As the rest of the boats landed, Coor's ground forces were quickly in position so they could cut off any further direct assault for the time being, allowing Darha to get to safety.

Coor took Rhett's shoulder. "There is a Frost Nation guard hut to the west. They are ordered to keep peace. Cas!" Coor called, "how far is it?"

"Esau!" Coor heard Cas holler. Looking back, he saw Cas take hold of an upper arm of a tall, broad-shouldered Frost Nation native with short, curly, pale blonde hair. "Escort the Queen of the Fire Nation to the western hut for protection. Make sure they know what's going on if they do not already. If they are aware of the situation, get their report. If trouble arises, take her and her escorts through The Wall."

"Aye, Commander."

Coor stared at Darha. Her eyes were wide like they usually were when she was afraid or worried, but something deep inside them had changed. Coor saw less fear in his baby sister's eyes than he'd ever seen before. "I'll be with you as soon as I can," Coor told her.

Darha nodded. She reached up for her brother's face and drew him down so she could kiss his cheek. "Be careful."

Before Coor could even respond, a blast of fire magic hit him in the back, knocking him forward onto the ground. He was paralyzed in shock for a moment, wondering why someone from his own nation, a magic user, was attacking him.

He spun around onto his back in time to see Cas and six other Frost Nation soldiers standing side by side in front of him. Their arms were held out across their bodies, and shields of ice were expanding from all their forearms, growing wider and longer until each shield joined together to form one thick solid wall of ice that touched the ground and went half a foot over their heads. Blasts of fire barraged the ice wall, nearly knocking Cas and his soldiers back, but they stood firm.

Coor was dumbfounded at what was taking place. He suspected the magic haters behind the attack, but he hadn't anticipated fire wielders, betrayers of his own!

"Coor!" someone yelled from behind.

Spinning onto his stomach to look behind him again, and his eyes went wide. Darha stood there, incredibly rigid and still. Her shoulders were up under her ears, her hands stiff with her fingers bent like claws, and her face twisted in a fierce snarl at the attackers. She looked more animal than human, and Coor knew exactly what was happening. He'd seen it once before, on that day, when his mother had summoned the Wild Fire to defeat the magic haters who had invaded his home. Coor's breath caught when he saw the heat vapors start to halo Darha's entire body.

He had enough time to suck in a breath and scream, "Soldiers down!" at the top of his lungs. It echoed off the Frost Nation's wall, landing on the anxious and confused young soldiers' ears. They had never seen the Wild Fire. "Soldiers down!" Coor screamed again. He reached up from the ground, gathering the back of Cas's tunic in a fist, and yanked him to the ground. He did see several soldiers drop, mostly older ones that had likely seen his mother's Wild Fire attack. Some were yanked to the ground who still didn't know what was going on. "Soldiers down!" The majority followed suit and dropped to the ground, including many Frost Nation soldiers.

Coor saw the light gray irises of his sister's eyes turn orange with fire magic before the fire expanded to outline her entire being. She was standing in a bonfire as tall as she was. Coor curled himself around Cas's

143

body, shielding him as completely as he could since Coor was more fire resistant than Cas was.

The fire magic expanded farther outward, and higher, until Darha thrust her arms forward. Then with the force of a hurricane, the fire storm blew toward the battlefield. It incinerated everything, friend and foe, in its path. Coor felt the heat of it on his back as it washed over him. He let out a drawn-out grunt of pain, and just did his best to try and protect Cas from it. He was going to have some fractured skin, though. All the Frost Nation soldiers would. He only hoped they wouldn't be too angry about it.

As soon as the Wild Fire ceased, Coor looked back at his sister. Her eyes dropped closed, and her knees began to sink to the ground. Coor scrambled to his feet and was able to catch her before she fell. Lifting her up in his arms, he turned to face what was left of the battlefield, which wasn't much. He looked down at Cas as the southerner pushed himself up from the ground. His hands and wrists were fractured badly, but everything else appeared intact.

Cas was about to say something when his gaze turned west. "Coor," he said. Coor saw the reserves of the enemy army coming down the shoreline. Coor and Cas glanced at each other. "Go," he said. "The eastern tower. She'll be safe there. Esau!" Cas called as the remains of the army closed ranks in front of Coor. The big southerner came forward. "Go with them. Same orders. Take them through The Wall if there's trouble in the east."

"Aye, Commander."

Coor's gaze lingered on Cas and he felt guilt slam into his chest again. He didn't want to leave the Frost Nation native in battle. Coor should be next to him. But with Darha in his arms in her condition, she had to be his priority.

"Rhett!" Coor called to his captain. Rhett spun to face him. "Put the Fire Nation under the authority of Commander Cas of the Frost Nation." Cas spun to meet Coor's eyes with slight surprise. Coor met the southerner's eyes straight on. "Obey him as you would me," he said quietly. Cas gave a gracious nod of his head before Coor turned to follow Esau east to the safe huts.

The small party had only made it a half a mile away when another small reserve army was spotted coming up the shore toward them from the east. Coor clutched Darha tighter to his chest. She was small and light enough to nestle comfortably in the crook of one of his arms. With his free hand, he pulled out his sword. He wasn't going down without a fight, even one he was going to lose.

o

Aradel and her small guard party left the outreaches of The Wall. She looked to the west in surprise as fire suddenly exploded in the air in a tall and vast column. Lifting herself up on the elk she tried to see more, but her view was lost to the hills and trees. Worry overtook her as she glanced at the guards around her.

"Hurry!" she called and urged the elk forward.

It had been difficult to leave Queen Vesna, but she had a duty to make sure the Fire Nation was settled, and their Queen was safe. Yet from the amount of fire she had seen, clearly something was wrong. She prayed she would arrive in time.

The heat prickled at her skin, and she had to wrap herself in cold. Of the guards with her, only one was a magic user. The rest would not need the comfort of the cold. She worried, however, for the men and women of their guard who had been posted to ensure the Fire Nation was seen safely across the river. Were it not for Queen Vesna's injury, Aradel would have been with them herself to provide support.

When they reached the top of the hill that overlooked the valley shore, she could see the battle. The clangs of swords and the cries of the injured reached her ears like whispers on the wind. Her elk shifted back and forth anxiously. Aradel noticed the battlefield closest to the river was completely scorched. The ground and the people who had been standing on it were nothing but burnt corpses. Such destruction had been wrought, and Aradel knew exactly how.

Glancing down the shoreline, she caught sight of a small group fleeing to the east. Among them was Prince Coor; his regal and imposing frame was easy to spot even from a distance. In his arms was a small bundle of clothing, and Aradel almost didn't recognize it was a person. Coming up from the east, cutting off Prince Coor's escape, was a small group of armed men and women.

Aradel's eyes widened. "Who are they?"

"Magic haters," Dain, the lead guard answered. "I did not realize their numbers had grown so large within our nation."

Turning from them, she looked back to the main battle. She had to join, for her powers and her position demanded it. Yet she had to close her eyes against the reality of that. Aradel had only wanted to use her powers to create and heal, not destroy. She had never taken a life, and the thought pained her. She felt her forehead furrow as she tried to remember the dancing bears she had created for the children. That memory seemed so far away now as she desperately grasped for it.

"Lady Aradel?" one of the guards asked.

She looked to him, trying to blink away the shock of the reality she faced. "What is it?"

"Your orders?" he asked, and then glanced at the other guards.

Aradel swallowed her fear and unwillingness. Kirill was out in the ocean trying to save their planet and their people. She could not be lost in what was past; she could only be the same force that Kirill had been. She had to move forward and change her role. No longer the creator and mender, she had to become the defender.

Glancing at the royal family of the Fire Nation, she pointed to them. "See that Queen Darha and her brother are escorted from the battle to safety," she commanded. "Then return and join the fray on the shore."

They nodded, and the lead guard recited, "As you command."

"Wait," Aradel called. "Hiron, you take a message back to The Wall and warn our people of the events taking place with the magic haters." Hiron nodded and turned his elk. In a gallop of hooves, he was lost to the trees.

Aradel turned to go down the hill when the lead guard, Dain, said, "Be careful, Lady Aradel."

She heard a child crying in the distance, and her heart broke. She turned a cold eye to Dain, "It is them who should be careful."

She turned her elk and rode him hard down the hill. Aradel left a trail of ice behind, as she leaned further forward on him. Already she could feel her rage building, and a cold fury overtook her. She was vengeance itself as she rode; vengeance that would be swift and ice cold.

She put her arms out, making a sword point of ice in front of her elk. She did not slow as she reached the shore, and broke through the ranks like a spear. Those who did not wear the silvery blue uniform of the Frost Nation's Guard, or the red and gold armor of the Fire Nation, were mowed down. She rode headlong into the battlefield, an icy plow that sliced through those who had chosen to stand against her people.

Reaching the western edge of the battle, she saw a second group running toward her. At their front was a woman in pale blue, with blond curly hair, and a streak of silver. Aradel recognized her, but couldn't place her. There was hatred there, and a daring challenge in her eyes.

She pointed a sword directly at Aradel. "To victory!" she cried, and a brief memory surfaced. The woman's father had been killed. Aradel remembered because it had happened around the time Aradel had arrived in Axion. Yet she couldn't remember the woman's name.

The elk suddenly lifted its hind legs and kicked a man square in the chest, nearly causing Aradel to fall off. She narrowly caught the elk's neck, and held on as it settled again. He huffed at the fallen man in triumph.

Aradel dismounted and put a hand on his neck. "Return home."

The elk stared at her with his deep, intelligent eyes, and seemed to hesitate. These creatures were smart, and they knew who took care of them. Aradel patted his neck before leaving, making sure he didn't have a choice.

She lifted her hands and focused her entire attention on the woman in the lead. The woman stopped then, as those of her army streamed around her to attack. The woman looked amused and overconfident. Perhaps it was time people knew exactly how destructive ice could be.

Aradel pushed her hands downward with her palms flat toward the ground, and ice began to form. It crept along the ground, spreading out under the feet of those running toward her. She waited only a moment before she lifted her hands up, and spikes of ice shot out of the ground, impaling every person in front of her.

She heard men rushing in behind her, and glanced back to see them dressed in the Frost Nation armor. It was the Guard. Aradel closed her fists and the ice spikes turned into snow, which was now pink with the blood of those she had maimed. She ignored it as she moved toward her quarry, their leader.

Aradel lifted a hand and swept it across her body. Every person between her and the woman was flung to the side as she manipulated the water in the air. She was nearly to her mark when a blast of fire magic suddenly hit her shoulder. Aradel yelled in pain and stumbled backwards as her hand went to her injury, and her ice shield snapped around her. . A second assault fizzled out against her shield.

"To Lady Aradel!" someone called, but it sounded far off. It was as though she wasn't in her body anymore. Everything was in a haze of silver and blue blobs huddled around her. She vaguely realized they were shielding her from every angle.

She inspected the burn on her shoulder. Cracks of blue were just starting to form under the singed skin. Her vision sharpened as she stood up straighter and looked at the smug expression of the woman across the

147

battlefield. It was clear that she had planned everything, and Aradel had fallen for it. She hadn't known that magic wielders had joined the cause of the magic haters. It was madness. Many of the magic haters surged around them, as those around her continued to defend her. Aradel tried to concentrate, but the pain she was in made it almost impossible.

The woman eventually fought her way through the scattered troops that surrounded Aradel. She brought her sword up for a fatal blow, and Aradel raised an arm to defend herself. The sword came down and glanced off her ice shield, leaving tendrils of frost on the blade.

"It won't last forever." The woman said, and hacked at Aradel again.

With the second strike her shield crumpled around her, and Aradel collapsed to a knee. The woman smiled, and Aradel knew she was seeing true evil. No one should appear so pleased with taking a life. Aradel lifted an arm again, but she couldn't muster her powers. She was not made for battle, she thought soberly; she was made for something else.

Just as hope began to leave her, when the woman raised her sword again, Aradel felt something smooth slide across her throat. Her eyes went wide as a silvery blue light shone under her chin. Her arms then dropped to her sides and her head fell back as a force of blue light erupted off her, throwing everyone within twenty feet backwards to the ground.

Time stood still for Aradel. That single moment seemed to stretch on for eternity. Looking to her right, she saw a ghostly version of Queen Vesna smiling with an affectionate and knowing grin. Aradel instantly knew what had happened, and pain filled her breast. Yet that familiar smile warmed her, too. It told Aradel everything was going to be all right. It told her that it didn't matter that Queen Vesna was gone, because if Aradel had the moon pearls, she would have a part of Vesna—the closest thing Aradel had had to a mother.

When time resumed, the moon pearls were at her throat, and their power hummed gently. It was an amplification of what Aradel already was, and much more. She could feel the ice world around her, and she knew it would bend to her. Suddenly her fears melted away, and she faced those around her.

The woman pushed herself up from the ground, and seeing the moon pearls, her faced paled. Aradel reached for her, but to her surprise, a very weak ice shield sprang up around her skin. Startled, Aradel hesitated. As the woman's shield dropped, she turned and quickly fled. The men and women with her appeared startled. Then Aradel watched as they all abandoned the battlefield to follow their leader.

Aradel turned around and, upon seeing the moon pearls, all the guards knelt before her, reaffirming their allegiance to a new Queen as was customary. Yet as she stared at the dead and dying, she did not want them to swear on a ground soaked with blood.

"Help the wounded," Aradel commanded. "Get them to Hurra." The guard quickly rose to their feet and did as commanded.

She could hardly breathe because she was so overcome with emotions, as she moved through those around her. . Seeing Commander Cas, as he shouted orders by the shoreline, she carefully picked her way through the bodies that littered the ground, feeling nothing but emptiness as her feet crunched on the scorched earth.

When Cas saw her, he appeared relieved. Then his eyes fell to the pearls at her throat. She resisted the urge to reach up and touch them; torn between tearing them off, and letting them sit proudly on her chest.

Cas stepped forward, kneeling before her with an arm across his chest. "My Queen," he affirmed.

"Rise," she said, thankful that a Knight only had to take the knee once before a new queen. When he was standing again she asked, "What happened here?"

He glanced around at the badly burned bodies, "Queen Darha happened."

"This power," Aradel said softly, "is so destructive."

"Her brother was injured," Cas informed her. "I think she lost control."

"Wild Fire," Aradel whispered so quietly that no one could hear her. She had heard of it, but never had she witnessed it. Only the most powerful of the Fire Nation could call upon it. Yet it was true to its name. It was hard to control, and its destruction was well recorded in their history books.

Cas waited patiently for her. When she looked up at him again, she said, "I have commanded that the wounded be taken to Hurra."

A man in gold and red approached them. He seemed to regard her briefly before turning to Cas, "We have started to gather every able-bodied man and woman to help move the wounded."

"We'll need to bury our dead," Aradel whispered as she examined the charred bodies.

"We burn ours anyway," the man said roughly.

"Rhett," Cas interjected, and seemed slightly offended by the man's tone. "This is Queen Aradel of the Frost Nation. You will address her with the distinction she deserves."

149

Rhett pressed his lips together and sighed softly. "My apologies, Queen Aradel," he said carefully with a bow. "I was not aware."

Aradel nodded her head and silently accepted his apology. She felt as though valuable time was being wasted on formalities. "We cannot help the dead, I suppose," she said. "We should focus on the living."

Rhett nodded, but said nothing. Cas on the other hand asked, "What about the magic haters?"

"Their leader fled and they with her," Aradel said. "I do not think they will bother us again, and we have more pressing concerns. If you do find anyone still resisting, take them as prisoners."

"I'm afraid they are more of a concern than you know," Rhett said. "I didn't see the leader of their group from the Fire Nation here."

"How is that a concern?" she asked, glancing round. "They may be one of the dead."

"If not, they may attack again," Rhett warned. "There were enough survivors to be an issue in the future."

"Then we should be ready for them," Aradel agreed. "We need to get to the safety of Hurra. Work together, and get every man, woman, and child safely to the town."

She turned to leave after issuing her order, but Cas called after her, "Lad—Queen Aradel."

"Yes?" she asked, turning back.

"Where are you going?" he asked quietly as he approached her.

"To make sure Queen Darha made it to the eastern guard post safely."

"Your people need you here," he whispered.

Aradel glanced around as people tried to help the wounded. She forgot that she was now responsible for them all. She couldn't leave them and take care of matters herself. She realized she was going to have to have someone to fetch the Fire Nation's Queen. She nearly laughed at the idea of her giving orders to anyone, but knew this wasn't the time or the place.

"Rhett," she finally said, "send a messenger to tell Queen Darha the outcome of this battle and that she is needed in Hurra."

Rhett looked surprised a moment before he nodded and took off to do as requested.

She glanced at Cas, who seemed pleased. Looking around the field, she frowned. "Let's get to work."

Fire: Chapter Twenty-Six

—————— o ——————

It took every ounce of willpower Thea had to not jump into the ocean and swim home when Tamon exploded. Coor and Darha were her first thoughts, her first fears, and her first longing. Even from the distance she was at, Thea could see the ash cloud rising up far to the northeast before the jagged peaks of the Verses Mountains blocked her view completely.

It took a lot of convincing, especially from Kimbro, to make Thea stay the course she was on now with this stupid iceberg. His greatest argument was, "You have to trust Coor to be okay." Thea had reluctantly accepted that, knowing she had to, whether she liked it or not. For two days after that, she'd been anxious and trembling, pacing the longboat impatiently, trying to calm herself. She wished with all her heart and might that she could be with her husband and sister again. She had already been on this ridiculous journey on the ocean for two weeks.

They had entered the wider expanse of Ebra Ocean early in the morning and were in much warmer water and climate. Before the sun was even up, the Frost Nation natives had disembarked the ships journeying with the iceberg to return home, as planned. That left the Fire Nation in charge of the boats and Thea in command of all of them, which did nothing to ease her stress. She felt like a trapped animal on the longboat, barely sleeping and hardly able to settle her mind with thoughts of home.

The warmer weather was great for her and her soldiers since they could strip down to one layer now, but from the few glances she'd caught of the Frost Knight, she could see he was having a difficult time keeping the entire island from melting in the warmer area. He was drinking a lot of water, and Thea unexpectedly found herself worrying about him, too. Not because she liked him, she told herself, but because if something happened to him, this whole freezing trip and time away from Coor and Darha and her people would have been a pointless waste. Over the course of the day, though, she couldn't deny her genuine concern for him any longer. Not a single native from his homeland remained, and that sounded lonely. Thea had Fitzu and was surrounded by people she knew cared for her, but the Frost Knight had no one, and he was the one carrying the brunt of this burden.

As the sun started going down, the Knight came to the back of the iceberg. Thea looked up and saw him wiping sweat from his brow and drinking water, yet again, from some of the barrels he'd placed there a few days ago. Thea couldn't imagine how much tremendous magical energy it was taking to hold this massive ice island together, in waters warm enough that a Fire Nation citizen might actually survive if he or she went for a swim.

She sighed heavily and cast a glance over at Fitzu and Kimbro, who both nodded. "Go," Fitzu said, indicating the rope ladder with a tilt of his head. "I'll handle things down here."

Thea nodded and made her way to the ladder attached to the bow of the longboat. She wasn't going up to the iceberg for the Knight, she told herself. She was going up there because she was climbing the walls down here. She took off her cloak and weapons and tossed them into the corner of the ship, leaving her in a fitted black, wool, long-sleeved shirt, black wool pants tucked into heavy black boots, and black wool gloves. In such close proximity to the iceberg, it was still too cold to put on any leather armor.

She stared up the ladder just as the Frost Knight went out of view completely. With another sigh, she began to climb. She reached the top a few minutes later and only had to take a few steps to reach the Frost Knight's exhausted form. He sat with his head bowed low between his shoulders, and his elbows resting on his knees.

"Hey," she said, feeling more concern for him than she'd expected. She went to him quickly and crouched by his side. "Are you all right?"

He wiped sweat from his brow once more and without even glancing at her responded, "I'm fine. This is just a lot of work."

Thea could see he was too exhausted to even try to be hostile toward her. "Well," she said as she scooped up two handfuls of snow and rested them on each side of his neck, "you knew it would be a struggle, right?" She removed her hands quickly before his cold could burn her.

Kirill looked up at her in utter confusion.

Thea knew what he was thinking and slightly shook her head. "Shut up," she said, without any real trace of scorn as she picked up more snow and rested it behind his neck.

The Frost Knight let out a short moan and dropped his head down between his shoulders as the snow began to melt and drip down the back of his collar. When it was gone, Thea scooped up another handful and rested it in the same place. It quickly got awkwardly quiet as that handful melted and Thea started glancing around, trying to find an excuse to escape. What had she been thinking coming up here? Things were too awkward between them.

Before any brilliant ideas came to her, the Knight spoke again. "How are you holding up?" he asked, meeting her eyes.

"Me?" she asked, genuinely confused. "I'm fine," she declared as if he were daft.

She felt the familiar flash of tension erupt between them, but for some reason, she didn't want to fight with him right now. Maybe she was just too exhausted as well, emotionally for sure, after having seen the eruption of Tamon.

Thea softened her expression and tone, and sighed. "I'm not the one holding together an island of ice, now am I?" she said, half-joking, as she picked up another two handfuls of snow and rested them on the back of his neck.

It was quiet a moment. "I saw that ash cloud, too, you know," he said suddenly, compassion in his voice.

Thea thinned out her lips and sighed softly. She didn't really want to talk to him about this. She didn't know him, and he didn't know her or anything about her people or their suffering. She debated how to respond as she reached down to pick up another two handfuls of snow.

"My husband is smart and brave. He's taking care of everyone and everything. My people will be okay," she said, letting some sadness and vulnerability seep into her voice as she absently scooped more snow into her hands. "He's going to be fine. He's going to be just fine." She figured if she said it out loud enough, Thea could convince herself it was true.

"You're married?" the Frost Knight asked out of the blue, jolting her out of her worried thoughts of Coor and Darha.

She stared at him. For a moment, she'd nearly forgotten where she was and to whom she was speaking. She looked back down at the snow she was collecting and nodded. "Yeah." Picking it up, she rested it on the sides of his neck under his jaw. The conversation seemed to die there, but not with any terrible awkwardness.

Examining the Frost Knight after that handful of snow melted, Thea realized he seemed a lot better. Not so sweaty and empty looking. She smiled and stood, slapping her hands together to get the snow off her gloves. "Well, don't you look all spiffy now?"

Kirill managed a small smile as he stood. It was an unexpected, nice thing to see. He actually had a very charming, gentle smile, which surprised Thea. "Thanks for the help."

153

Thea nodded and headed toward the rope ladder again with Kirill beside her. "No problem. If you need any more babying, just let me know," she said with a smile, and he actually managed a chuckle. It was a nice sound, too. It reminded Thea of Coor's chuckle, deep and soothing. Thinking of Coor made her sad, and she sighed again as she bent down to grab hold of the top rung of the ladder.

Before she even took hold, the iceberg jolted violently! It seemed to vanish from under her feet and she was over!

Suddenly, something like an iron bar hit her in the stomach and she was snatched out of the air and yanked in the opposite direction. She landed hard on her left side, which erupted in pain from the cold. Her entire back and stomach were also in pain. Trying to focus through that, as well as the jostling of the world, Thea realized the Knight had grabbed her. It was his cold causing the pain on her back and across her stomach where he was holding her. She caught a glimpse of his face behind her and saw the grimace in his own features, her heat likely fracturing his skin in turn, but he held her tightly against his stomach until the iceberg stopped jostling.

As soon as it calmed, both Thea and Kirill spun to their hands and knees, looking north in the direction of the scout ships. Sure enough, fire was erupting in the sky from all three with the symbol, indicating "trouble a vast."

Jumping to their feet, they made a run for it, heading as fast as they could north along the iceberg. Without missing a step, Thea sent a blast of her fire magic over the edge to the boats behind, signaling for Fitzu to get the soldiers up onto the ice.

Thea and Kirill hadn't even made it halfway to the north when it became terrifyingly obvious what was wrong. Stopping in their tracks, they looked up into the heights of the iceberg and saw that some of the peaks, one of them over six hundred feet high, had massive tentacles wrapped around them. Ocean water dripped from the enormous, fleshy appendages down the jagged ice peaks.

Thea's heart raced. She'd heard of this terror, but she'd never actually seen it with her own eyes. She doubted the kraken even existed, to be honest. The disturbance of the planet must have woken it from whatever slumber it had been in, sending it into waters it had never known before.

The tentacles began to tremble and the entire iceberg jolted again from the incredible power of the massive creature tugging on it. Thea and Kirill grabbed on to each other to keep their balance as the island sloshed around under them. Thea could only assume more tentacles were wrapped around different peaks out of view. When the island settled again, Thea and Kirill glanced at each other in wide-eyed horror. Then, as if by silent command, both continued running full speed north.

By the time they reached the northern edge and the ocean was in view, the sun had set and several more tentacles were stretching from the sea, wrapping around the tall peaks. There had to be thirteen visible tentacles, thousands of feet long or more, reaching from the depths of the ocean to those high reaches. Ocean water dripped like a steady rain where the appendages stretched overhead.

Thea watched the tentacles begin to tremble again. With a deafening crack, and a roar from the creature that sounded more like a loud moan from deep underneath the sea, the ice peaks gave way, breaking where they had been yanked. Kirill tackled Thea to the ground as the island jostled violently, shielding her from the flying ice shards. His cold burned, but Thea wasn't going to complain; she knew her heat was burning him as well.

Peeking over Kirill's arm, Thea saw a ripple of waves disturb the surface of the water, and her eyes went wide. Just beneath the surface she could see the kraken's head, or at least one massive eye—its left eye, which had to be five hundred feet long from one corner to the other. The eye took up nearly her entire view—which meant the kraken's head alone had to be about a mile long. Its tentacles? Six times that length, easily.

The Knight slowly pushed himself up until he was just hovering over her. He was already sweating and appeared to be exhausted. "That thing," he said, panting with his eyes closed, "is going to tear the iceberg apart." He swallowed heavily and opened his eyes. "I'm barely holding it together."

Seeing him so exhausted, knowing the effort he'd already put into traveling this far, and recalling the fact that everyone she loved and cared about would die if they didn't get this iceberg to Rask intact, Thea's resolved hardened in a way it never had before. The stakes had never been so high.

Thea clenched her teeth and shifted her dangerous gaze to the massive eye just under the surface of the ocean. As if it could physically feel the threat Thea now posed, the kraken eye shifted to her in turn, and the pupil constricted into a thin vertical line.

Thea slowly turned onto her side, pressing her palms deliberately into the snow, looking like a mountain lion about to pounce on its prey, and defiantly met the beast's gaze. "Come on," she growled.

With a roar that Thea was certain reached the ends of the ocean and reverberated back again, the monster started to pull itself out of the water. It seemed as though the entire ocean was rising up in front of her eyes. Then the water broke and the red and purple skinned creature breached.

Thea didn't think, she just scrambled to her feet and ran, leaping up onto one of the appendages that were giving the thing leverage to rise. She ran along its blubbery flesh, which was wide enough for four men to walk abreast, toward its face. She was instantly soaked from the sea water rushing down like waterfalls in every direction as the creature continued to rise, but it was warm enough to barely harm her. Even when her feet slid across its wet flesh, Thea didn't stop. This beast would not keep her from saving her homeland.

She reached its face just as its massive left eye fully breached the water. It instantly focused on her, but Thea already had her fire magic burning in her hands. With a scream, she stopped in her tracks and threw her hands out, sending a steady, wide column of fire into the creature's eyeball. It roared in agony and reared back as its eye closed. Its movement sent Thea sprawling, and the sound was so loud that it felt like she had been punched in the ears. Slapping both her hands over them, she felt a small amount of thick moisture. Looking at her palms, she saw a little blood.

Clenching her teeth, her heart pounding with determination to save her family, Thea got to her feet. Luckily, the kraken was big enough, and Thea was close enough, that even though its eye was closed, an accessible crack between the eyelids remained. Digging her fingernails into the fleshy material of its face with one hand, she sent a continuous blast of fire along the crack of its eyelids with the other.

The beast roared again, and this time Thea went deaf. It was eerily silent, save for a soft vibrating buzz that filled her ears and skull. The kraken lurched back, either as a reflex of pain, or in an attempt to throw Thea off. It was so big, though, and she was so small, that she was barely jostled. Continuing to send the current of fire along the crack, the horrific smell of burned flesh and burned fish invaded her nostrils so violently that she gagged and nearly retched. She quickly began breathing through her mouth to avoid as much of the smell as she could. Rancid brownish goo began running from the corner of the beast's eye, looking like a mix of blood and eyeball gunk. The substance tried to smother Thea's fire, but with a fierce growl, she increased the heat of her magic, making the gooey material boil as she continued to burn out its eyeball.

The beast writhed in agony, creating eighty-foot waves and sprays of ocean two hundred feet high. The tentacles finally came off the iceberg as it started slapping at its own face, trying to find and remove the flea that was causing it so much pain. Thea could see the iceberg jostling from the thrashing of the kraken, and the massive waves, but Kirill seemed to be doing well holding it together.

Finally, the creature seemed to weaken. It slowed its struggling and began to sink below the surface of the ocean. Thea was panting as the left eye started to sink into the water. With a brief sizzling sound, her fire went out, but she must have done enough damage because it didn't try to resurface.

When the ocean water reached Thea's bottom, she blazed her core and dove in. The water was kind of warm, but the swim was long. The creature had reared back at least a mile, a distance Thea hadn't felt while standing on its face. Realizing how far she had to swim, she wasn't quite sure she would make it. But she was sure going to try. She swam for about five minutes, during which time her hearing started to return, but her skin was getting stiff, making swimming difficult. She still had air in her lungs, though, so she kept going.

Suddenly, like a mirage in a desert, it looked like someone was walking toward her on top of the ocean. Thea paused, treading water for a moment as she watched. She blinked a few times, trying to clear her vision, but the figure just kept getting closer. When everything came into focus, Thea bowed her head, realizing it was the Frost Knight walking on a thin bridge of ice he was making with his magic. She stopped blazing her core and gratefully waited.

The water in front of her froze solid, and Thea looked up at Kirill as he stepped up to the edge. She raised her arm up as Kirill reached down, and they gripped each other's wrists. With one hand, he lifted her out of the ocean until her feet were planted firmly on the ice he had made. He must have taken down his ice shield because it didn't burn so much when he lifted her arm around his neck to help her walk. Then both of them slowly started back to the iceberg.

"I knew you were insane. I knew it," he grumbled before it could get awkward.

Thea looked up at him and ended up grinning broadly despite herself. "Don't pretend you aren't impressed."

With that, Kirill smiled broadly at her in return. "Don't let it go to your head."

157

Thea laughed genuinely for the first time since the eruption of Tamon. "Certainly not."

———————— o ————————

The morning after the kraken attack, everyone had made a slow trek back to the southern edge of the iceberg. They were all exhausted. Kirill, Thea, and all the Fire Nation soldiers had arrived just as the sun was coming up and found an upsetting scene, one that Kirill now frowned down at. One of the boats had been severely damaged from the massive sloshing ice island and resulting waves. Lines had been snapped on a few other boats, and some had gone adrift, though luckily not too badly so.

Thea had immediately began issuing orders and headed down to the ships that were left, while Kirill stood up above them all like a bump on an iceberg. Thankfully, they had been able to salvage most of the severely damaged ship before it sunk, but it wasn't usable in its current condition. The other ships that had been retrieved had broken oars, and another was leaking.

Kirill watched the bustling activity below and couldn't help the concern he felt watching Thea. The woman had just chased off a massive sea beast, nearly drowned, and hadn't slept. As the day waned on, she conducted her soldiers as professionally as ever. Several times, however, when she thought no one was looking, Kirill had caught her crouching down low on the ship deck, barely able to stand, and bowing her head in absolute fatigue. Kirill almost felt the need to go down and comfort her when he saw that, but she didn't seem like the kind of woman who would take kindly to it. As soon as someone would arrive, usually Fitzu, she was on her feet and alert, as if nothing were amiss.

Kirill had thought losing chunks of the iceberg to the north was bad, but this issue with the ships would slow them down quite a bit. The kraken attack had brought them to a dead halt, and they needed every ship to get them moving again. As much as he hated to admit it, he didn't have the power to do it by himself. He was lucky he had been able to keep the iceberg together with only a few lost chunks. If it hadn't been for Thea's quick—or rather, insane—reaction, he was sure they would have had two icebergs to deal with now instead of one.

Kirill glanced at the water barrels to his left. He hadn't told anyone that some of his barrels had been lost in the attack as well. He didn't think there would be any left for a return trip. It was likely a one-way journey for him. He thought of his mother and Aradel, realizing he might not see them again. But at least they would know he died trying to save them and their world.

"Hey, frost flake!" Thea called up.

He almost smiled at the name. He shook his head and sighed heavily before yelling down, "Don't call me that."

"We're going to head to the shore to repair this boat," she called.

Kirill glanced at the empty barrels again, and a thought came to him. Land meant the possibility of water. He could have the barrels refilled, and no one would ever be the wiser.

"Is there drinkable water?" Kirill called down, hopeful.

There was a long pause, and for a moment Kirill didn't think she was going to answer. He inched forward and peered over the edge and nearly jumped when Thea's face popped up over the side. He instantly came forward to help her up over the edge.

When she was on her feet, she looked him straight in the eyes. "What's wrong?"

"Nothing," Kirill lied. "I just thought we could take the opportunity to fill up empty barrels." Her eyes narrowed and he stared back, unfazed.

After a moment, she crossed her arms and gave him a flat bored expression. "You're a good liar, but unfortunately for you, I grew up on the streets surrounded by liars. Your privileged, pedigreed ass can't compete with the best scumbags in the Fire Nation, my dear," she said with a playful smile. "So I'll ask again—and how about the truth this time—what's wrong?"

He crossed his arms as well and leaned back on his heels. He hadn't expected her to call him out on his lie, but he should have known better. She was too street smart to fall for that.

He eventually sighed in defeat. "We lost some barrels." Kirill admitted. "There isn't just ship debris down there."

Her arms instantly uncrossed as she went to inspect his southern cluster of barrels. "How many?" she asked.

"There are enough left for now," Kirill insisted. That technically wasn't a lie because making it to Rask was all that mattered. And he had enough water to make it to Rask.

Thea raised both eyebrows as she faced him before tapping her fingers across one of the barrel's rims. "Are you sure?" she pressed, clearly not satisfied.

"I am sure."

She examined him silently for another moment before nodding once. "Good," she replied, walking back to the edge. "There isn't any drinkable water this far north because of the volcanos. But if you don't have enough"—she faced him— "tell me and I'll send men further inland to find some."

He hesitated. He needed the water, but there wasn't time to lose able-bodied men on a wild goose chase. He'd known that sulfur from volcanos could get into the ground water; he just hadn't realized it had come so far west. Thea stood waiting for him at the top of the rope ladder.

Kirill shook his head. "If I need more water, I'll just take it from the iceberg."

She seemed satisfied with that answer. After a final nod of her head, she started back down the rope. He watched her go before he grabbed the empty barrels and tossed them over the side.

"Are you crazy?" Thea yelled from her position halfway down the ladder.

He watched them bob on the surface of the ocean. "Use them to mend the boats!" he insisted before tossing over another. He smiled when he heard her grumbling.

They were more alike than either was willing to admit. They might not be friends, but he no longer hated and distrusted her. She was actually a remarkable woman.

Kirill turned and started walking to the east side of the iceberg. He wanted to be able to watch them reach the shoreline. He was nearly there when he felt something hit his arm. Startled, he looked up, and a piece of hail bounced off his forehead.

His eyes went wide. That couldn't be good.

Kirill jogged the last of the distance to the eastern side of the iceberg. In the boat heading toward shore for repairs, he saw the Fire Nation had already pulled out tarps, and were huddled under them. He was thankful they'd had the foresight to bring them.

He sat down, keeping the iceberg cold two miles off the coast, and watched as they landed and started to mend the ravaged boat. He pulled an apple from his pocket and bit into it. The nice thing about being on an iceberg was everything lasted longer. They still had apples and other foods that lasted longer than they should. The meat had been eaten quickly, so only the salted lamb and beef was left, but many fruit and vegetables remained. They hadn't started in on the tasteless reserves yet. Kirill shuddered at the thought of beans. The Fire Nation seemed to like the tasteless morsels, but he found them bland. They had a strange texture,

161

too. He glanced down at his apple with a smile. Thank the goddess for the food supplies he had brought from home. Their apples grew in colder temperatures along The Wall, and the cold of the iceberg preserved them.

He was about to take another bite when he saw something appear on the land's horizon. A small black shadow crested a hill in the distance just past where the Fire Nation was working. His eyes narrowed as he tried to make it out. Suddenly the black silhouettes expanded to the sides, and the horizon was slowly taken over by the slow-moving figures.

Realization dawned on him. His apple rolled from his fingers and off the iceberg. "By the goddess," he whispered, astonished.

He was slack jawed as he stood up. An army was heading their way, and Kirill didn't think they were friendly.

He lifted his arm to send a signal but then realized they didn't have one for "massive attacking army from the east." This was unfortunate because it would have come in handy right that second.

He had to warn them. He faced the iceberg and lifted his arms into the air, breaking off a few lengthy pieces. He shot them high into the air and, hoping they would understand, wrote only one word against the dark gray sky: "East."

He kept them aloft until the Fire Nation was on their feet and studying the horizon to the east. Kirill sighed in relief and let the ice pieces drop back down. He worried, though, that he hadn't warned them in time. Kirill bolted to the back of the iceberg, where the ships still waited. It took him far too long to get there. When he did, he had to take a minute to catch his breath. The men down below were talking and working slowly, unaware of what was happening at shore.

"They're under attack," Kirill finally managed to yell.

Some of the men looked up at him. "Where?" Fitzu called up,

"They're on the shore, and there's an army descending," he said, moving toward the ladder.

Fitzu put a hand up as though to hold him back. "You need to stay here. We will deal with it."

"No way," Kirill responded more loudly than he should have. "You are going to need me."

"The iceberg needs you," Fitzu replied as started giving the orders to head to the shore.

Kirill wanted to force them to take him. He was not one to be left out of a battle. Yet he knew the man was right. He couldn't leave the iceberg, for even a minute away would result in lost ice. They had lost enough as it was, and he couldn't risk losing more.

"Hurry!" he yelled before running back toward the eastern edge.

It was with agony that he knew Thea was sorely outnumbered on the shore. If Fitzu and the remaining troops got to her, they stood a chance, but she had only taken fifty men for the repairs. Kirill's fists clenched at the thought. They needed him but he couldn't leave their mission unattended. The iceberg mattered more than his desire to protect and defend.

Fire: Chapter Twenty-Eight

———————— o ————————

When Thea saw Kirill's "East" spelled in the sky, she spun around to see an army paused at the bottom of the nearest hill. "No," she gasped in astonishment, coming out from under the tarp where she'd sought shelter. Hail pegged her body with little sparks of pain where it touched her exposed skin, leaving gray stone spots in their wake. This could not be happening. "You can't be serious, Ekil!" she screamed in rage. She didn't have to see his face in the waiting mob to know he was there. "The planet is dying, and you're going to attack us like this!"

"When you magic users die," she heard his voice echo over the distance, "the Sun God will be satisfied and allow the planet to live!" Her eyes followed the sound until she found his scarred, aged face to the left of the army.

Her fists clenched. "You petty, ridiculous fool!"

He pointed his sword at her. "Time to meet your end, fire wielder," he replied calmly as his army slowly advanced.

She panted through clenched teeth as she turned to look out over the ocean. She saw Fitzu and her other two hundred soldiers already sailing for the shore to come to her aid. Time. She needed to buy some time to allow them to reach her. She only had fifty men on shore, while Ekil had an army of over a thousand.

She turned to face the coming mob again. Examining the land and the situation, Thea got an idea. She blazed her core so she could ignore the hail burns and stalked up to two huge rocky stone pillars. They stood to each side of her between her and Ekil's descending army. She held both of her hands out toward the rocks, palms up and fingers bent, and summoned her magic. She heated the rock up to a temperature that instantly began to melt it. Molten rock dripped to the ground like candle wax. When the pillars were flattened, she ran her hands horizontally across her body, which dragged the lava over the land in front of her. Raising both of her arms, she lifted the lava up, forming a tall wall between her and them. She pulled the heat out of the stone and released it into the air, allowing the lava to cool into solid rock once again.

That should hold them.

Thea was about to turn away when suddenly her creation began to melt once again. Her eyes grew wide as the wall became lava before her.

She didn't understand. She couldn't comprehend what was happening! The lava parted like stage curtains, and she instantly found the cause across the landscape.

"Askari," she gasped. He was the Northern Regional Overlord of the Fire Nation! A magic user!

Thea's eyes scanned over Ekil's army, and she was horrified to find numerous familiar faces among the mob—people she was friends with and had worked closely with for years. Porva the Eastern Overlady of the Fire Nation was also among them. Seeing some silver-and-blue clad strangers in the pack, she could suddenly feel her heartbeat in her ears. They were from the Frost Nation.

"Haven't you heard, Thea?" Ekil called as his army continued to close the distance over the landscape. "Even some of your fellow magic users have abandoned hope in the royal families and joined my cause."

Thea's mouth went dry.

"By the way," he continued, "you'd probably like to know that another, much larger pack of us is waiting for your precious Prince and senseless Queen on the Frost Nation shores." Thea's eyes went wide again. "Oh yes, they evacuated after Tamon's eruption." She could see his drippy, evil smug smile as he said the next words. "But they aren't counting on us showing up."

Rage exploded in her head and heart. She screamed at the top of her lungs and sent a column of fire as tall as she was toward them. She split it off in several directions at the last second and burned lava canals into the stone under their feet. She was fast enough that some didn't see that coming, and a few, mostly the Frost Nation natives who would be most susceptible to it, fell into the streams of lava she created beneath them. They screamed horribly before they were burned alive.

"I'm going to kill you!" she screamed.

Trembling from fear that Coor and Darha might be harmed, she raised her hands up, making the canals she had just created erupt like volcanos. Most jumped out of the way of the spewing lava, but some caught fire and burned. Clenching her teeth, she picked up the lava streams from the ground and manipulated them through the air like massive fiery whips. They licked and flicked at the air like the trashing tentacles of the kraken.

It was difficult to control, and sweat instantly started to drip down her temples, but she managed to catch a few dozen more on fire before another magic user took control of them. The lava whips hovered frozen in the air in several crazy directions. Scanning the army that was only fifty

165

yards away, she realized it was Porva. Thea was trying to move the whips and Porva was trying to turn them on Thea. Thea slammed her hands downward so the lava splashed to the ground, releasing both of their holds on it.

She was about to pick them up again, but the army was too close. She was dead. As were the soldiers on shore with her. As long as Kirill was alive to hold that iceberg together, though, Fitzu could finish escorting him north. Thea drew her sword with one hand, lit up her fire magic in the other, and glared at the army; she just had to kill enough of them to make sure they weren't a threat to Fitzu or Kirill.

Thea and her fifty soldiers bravely took a fighting stance in front of the approaching army; every one of them armed and lit up like she was. Not one of them even blanched. She was proud of her people. She was proud of the Fire Nation, and she was proud of her soldiers.

Abruptly, the hail balls that had accumulated on the ground all rose into the sky at once. The shocking sight of it made the oncoming army stop and stare in wonder. Thea and her soldiers couldn't help looking around at the unanticipated spectacle, too.

"No way," Thea whispered and spun to face the ocean. "Drecher," she said, not taking her eyes off the iceberg, "give me your long glass."

"Is that who I think it is?" she asked and handed Thea the telescope.

Thea immediately snapped it open and brought it up to her eye. She spotted Kirill on the southeastern edge of the iceberg. He was on his knees with his hands raised in front of him, and even in this little lens, she could see him trembling violently. His eyes were locked on the shore, and he was pissed.

Thea lowered the long glass and her jaw was hanging open. "Sure is."

Suddenly the hail, controlled by Kirill, reared back a few feet before it shot out toward the enemy army with the speed of hundreds of thousands of tiny arrows. Each little ball of ice became a deadly projectile. Thea saw tiny holes erupt all over the enemies' bodies. In an instant, the army looked like the targets of an archery range after clean up. Numerous holes littered their bodies, and every single person was down, if not dead.

The next moment, the hail that remained dropped and bounced lifelessly to the ground. Thea's breath caught, and she instantly returned her attention to the iceberg, looking through the long glass. She focused on Kirill just in time to see him collapse out of sight.

"No!" she cried. She dropped the long glass and ran to the edge of the ocean.

At the water's edge, she summoned more powerful magic than ever before in her life. She heated up a narrow path of the sea bed in front of her, stretching from the shore to the iceberg. Reaching miles and miles beneath water level, to the solid rock of the planet, she began to melt it. Sweat dripped down her back like rainwater as wisps of steam appeared over the surface, and a long, narrow, orange glowing strip of lava appeared beneath it. Thea raised her hands slowly, looking like she was singlehandedly lifting a two-ton boulder, and pulled the lava up from the depths of the sea. The glowing strip got brighter, and the ocean above it was moved to a rolling boil as the lava breached the surface. She released her magic and let the sea cool it into a rugged, sturdy path that extended two miles from the shore to the iceberg, and was miles and miles deep.

Thea dropped to her knees, nearly falling, but caught herself with one hand. The world was spinning, and she blinked a few times to still it. Fitzu and her soldiers began arriving on shore as she started to come to her senses.

"Thea!" Fitzu cried. He rested a hand on her shoulder and crouched by her side, gazing at her with deep concern.

Seeing Fitzu gave her strength. "Kirill collapsed," she managed. Fitzu's eyes went wide and he helped her to her feet. "Stay here with the men. Kill anything left of Ekil's army that remains, but if they retreat, let them go. We don't have time to fool with them."

Fitzu nodded. "Understood."

Thea ran out onto the path she had created. She barely felt the stone under her boots as she covered the two miles out toward the iceberg. It was the only option she had. She couldn't sail a ship alone, and she couldn't have Fitzu and her soldiers abandon the fifty on shore to sail her back, in case anything was left of Ekil's army.

It took her fifteen minutes to reach a ship that had been pushing the back of the iceberg. She grabbed one of the loose riggings that were dangling overboard, and hand over hand began to pull herself up toward the deck. She jumped on board and ran straight to the rope ladder that led to the top of the iceberg and started to climb. Her muscles screamed and trembled with exertion, and her brain demanded rest, but Thea carried on. She had to. Kirill was the only hope this iceberg and this planet had.

Halfway up the rope ladder, her true and genuine care for Kirill weighed heavily on her. She realized in that moment that her concern for him had somehow moved beyond his necessity to the success of the quest;

167

she genuinely liked him. He was very powerful and honorable, brave, and selfless. Sure, he was an arrogant ass sometimes, but Thea knew she could be, too. He'd somehow weaseled into her heart, and she had to admit to herself that she cared about him.

Reaching the top of the iceberg, she jogged to the farthest eastern side where she'd seen him collapse. Sure enough, she spotted his fallen form.

She ran to him and dropped to her knees. His eyes were closed, and he was completely still. "Kirill!" she cried and grabbed his cheeks with her bare hands on impulse. Her eyes went wide when he didn't burn her. "Kirill!" she cried again. Not only must his ice shield have been down, but his core temperature had to be way too high if his natural cold couldn't burn her.

Thea was breathless with panic. She put on the wool gloves she'd stuffed behind the waist of her pants, and immediately began to shovel snow on top of him. She started with his arms and head and chest, leaving his face just clear so he could breathe, then moved down to his legs. Her knees burned as the ice and snow seeped through her pants and started turning her skin to stone. She endured it, though, since she couldn't blaze her core for fear of bringing too much heat near him. Next, she ran and ripped off a few small pieces of the iceberg and laid them on and around his body.

When he had about a foot of snow and ice piled on top of him, Thea crawled away from him to keep her own heat at bay. On her hands and knees like a cat, she anxiously watched and waited for him to respond. Long tense moments passed. Thea started shaking.

Finally, Kirill took in a long deep breath and his eyes opened. He glanced around, confused, causing the snow to fall away from his head and his long, golden blonde hair to peek through. Thea let out a long breath and bowed her head in relief. He was alive. Looking back up at him, she realized he was too weak to move much. He lay in the pile of snow, staring at her in utter exhaustion.

Thea clenched her teeth. "You're an idiot, you know that?" she bellowed. "Did you forget that you were holding together a twenty-four-square mile ice island? You think you can take control of an entire hail storm on top of that?"

Kirill surprised her by smiling brightly. "Don't pretend you aren't impressed."

Thea froze, and then bowed her head again as laughter took her over. It was quiet at first, but soon full-blown laughter shook her entire body. She sat down, too tired to hold it back. Through her half-closed eyes, she saw Kirill sit up in the snow pile across from her, laughing as well.

When she was finally able to calm down, she looked at the Frost Knight fondly. "You saved my men's lives on that shore," she said. "Thank you."

Kirill nodded once. "You saved my life just now. Thank you."

Thea grinned and nodded in response. "How are you feeling?"

Kirill nodded and pulled some snow up on his lap to cover his legs. "Better. Not great, but better. A little while under some snow and ice and I should be fine."

Thea nodded and sighed heavily. "I hate to be the bringer of bad news, but there were Frost Nation soldiers in that army that attacked us."

Kirill's eyes widened. "What?"

Thea nodded. "I knew most of the army. The leader's name is Ekil, and that was his band of religious fanatics who hate magic users. I've had run-ins with them in the past, but they've never had any blue-and-silver-clad members before." Seeing the vein in Kirill's neck start to pulse, she pressed her lips together, regretting what she had to say next. "He said that another, bigger band of his tribe was planning an assault on Frost Nation soil."

The snow around Kirill fell away dully as he climbed to his feet. "What?"

Thea got to her feet as well, holding her hands up to try to calm him. "Don't worry. Ekil said their targets were my husband and my sister." She swallowed heavily. "My Queen, not yours. They evacuated to the Frost Nation when Tamon exploded."

Kirill sighed, rubbing his hand over his jaw, which had grown some golden stubble. He was clearly trying to stay calm as he gazed to the south toward his homeland. He eventually met Thea's eyes again. "Are you all right?"

Thea nodded. "I'm okay." She was lying, but she didn't want him to know that.

Kirill pressed his lips together sympathetically and took a step toward her. He even reached out his hand to rest on her shoulder. He was so close that he had to look down at her face. "Thea?"

Somehow, some way, she trusted this man. She trusted him, and she had no idea why. She burst into tears, and Kirill instantly pulled her against his chest in an embrace. He was still too warm to burn her, so she allowed herself to cry against him. She was torn between feeling

169

uncomfortable at letting a fellow soldier see her weakness—a man who was still pretty much a stranger to her—and being relieved at the opportunity to cry and be held by someone big and brawny who could keep her sane and hold her together. Kirill was powerful. She didn't have anything to be afraid of with him. She cried for a long time. The only other person she'd ever let see her like this was her husband.

"No," she ended up sobbing. She pulled away, tears still falling down her cheeks, and looked up at him with her brows furrowed. "I want to go home, Kirill. I know you do, too." She sniffed and swiped her sleeve over her soaked cheek before looking back up at him. "So let's get this done and go home."

Kirill nodded. "Let's go, then."

———————— o ————————

They stood on the western shoreline, where the Isle of Ice was just visible in the distance. Aradel wore her finest gown of silver and blue as she watched soldiers carry Queen Vesna's coffin of ice. She could just make out her shadowy figure inside, but Aradel knew she was gone. The closest thing she had to a mother had died silently in her sleep. She had seen her on the battlefield, but now the young girls sang her soul into the goddess's embrace.

The words were in the old tongue that had been mostly lost with time. It was the language used to communicate with their goddess, and only the priestesses learned it. The final rite of a soul was the first thing they learned. Let pure and innocent voices carry a wayward soul to the goddess, souls that did not want to leave this life, and those they loved. Though Queen Vesna was gone, she had not been unwilling to leave this mortal realm after her accident during the quake. It had been her time, and she knew it, because her soul had smiled when Aradel had been given the moon pearls.

Aradel glanced to her right at Prince Coor and Queen Darha. They were bundled up to the point that she wasn't sure they could see to the left or right. Normally the thought would have made her smile, but today was a sad day. It was the day she had to say goodbye. To move on, but never forget. To never forget Queen Vesna's vision for their future. It had been unparalleled, and Aradel intended to carry it on.

Queen Darha turned to her, looking both sad and hopeful as their eyes met. A mutual understanding seemed to pass between them before Darha nodded her head. Aradel did the same before facing forward. They both knew she would honor Queen Vesna's pledge of peace between their nations during these trying times.

The Knights waded into the ocean, and Aradel stepped forward, turning to the gathered crowd. She was no longer Aradel the candidate, or Aradel the outcast. She was Queen Aradel. She would do Vesna the honor of being worthy of the title that the moon pearls had bestowed upon her.

"Queen Vesna had the most courage of any woman I had ever known. She was brave in the face of adversary, and she was the embodiment of compassion. So, I ask on this day of mourning that you not dwell on the fact that she has left us, but instead think of how she lived.

Remember that moment when she affected your life with the gentle touch that only she could give. Remember her for the leader she was and the example she set. It is the example I hope to follow." Aradel did her best to hide the depth of her grief.

She turned back and nodded to the Knights as she called out the final parting with everyone joining in. They were one voice, and one heart, as Vesna drifted out into the Ashtra Sea. "May the Goddess watch over and protect this soul, and may we in turn be protected when our time comes. For the Goddess is kind and merciful." They watched as Vesna's coffin of ice floated away from the shore.

Aradel stood just a little ahead of the group, as was her place. She stood there to lead them, but she felt very much alone. She heard boots crunching in the snow, and turned when she felt someone come up beside her. She wasn't surprised to find Queen Darha —the only person who would understand what Aradel was going through as a young Queen— standing next to her.

"My mother died unexpectedly, too" Queen Darha said softly without turning her head.

"That must have been difficult," Aradel replied. She appreciated having the other woman there.

"I never thought I deserved it," she added, reaching black gloved fingers up to touch the decorative golden circle above her brow, "this crown."

That caught Aradel off guard as Queen Darha tucked her hand out of sight again. She hadn't expected such candor from her. "Perhaps that is what makes you such a good queen."

Aradel saw Darha blink in surprise. She seemed to consider that as her brows furrowed together. Then slowly she turned her head and smiled. "I never thought of it that way."

"I understand that feeling better than anyone. Feeling like you don't belong, like you'll never belong. That no matter how hard you work, you'll never be good enough," Aradel admitted before looking toward the floating coffin again. "She made me forget all of it. She made me feel like I belonged until I finally did."

"She was a remarkable woman," Queen Darha agreed, "and an even more remarkable queen."

"There will be none like her for some time." Aradel decided.

"I don't agree," Darha said, and their eyes met again. A feeling of being kindred spirits passed between them and they smiled. They would be facing this strange new world together as Queens and leaders of their nations, and hopefully as friends.

A cold breeze snaked across the water and flew against Aradel's face. She turned to it and took in the cold. She stopped, however, when Darha turned away from it, shivering. It was easy to forget that Queen Darha didn't belong there. It was still as cold as winter inside The Wall— except nearest to the crack, where the heat was still seeping in and spreading. Aradel glanced over her shoulder at Prince Coor. He eyed them with a brotherly protectiveness that made her miss Kirill.

"Queen Darha, perhaps it is time we went further north," Aradel said, gesturing for them to get started.

Queen Darha appeared to be relieved. "I agree," she said gratefully, then hurried over to her brother as though she couldn't get away from the cold fast enough. It made Aradel smile. Prince Coor put his arm protectively around her shoulders and held her close to his side to keep her as warm as he could, then loaded his sister into a sled. They hardly waited a second to get themselves settled before their assigned sled driver took off.

Despite their similar feelings and similar circumstances, the two still came from different worlds. Aradel's was ice cold, and too harsh for citizens of the Fire Nation, just as their home would be too harsh for her and her people to stay long.

Aradel would join them shortly in the north, but for now, she issued a few orders, discussed Queen Vesna's life, and helped others mourn her death. Slowly the crowd turned back to Axion.

As she watched them go, High Priestess Kerin came to stand next to her. "Queen Aradel," she said softly, "you have done well this day. Queen Vesna would be proud."

"High Priestess Kerin," Aradel replied, turning to her, "your compliment is of the highest honor."

"It is," she agreed with a nod. "And deserved."

Normally she would have joined hands with her to give an outward appearance of intimacy, but she was queen now. She was no longer bound by those rules. The Queen did not show favoritism to anyone without consequences. Not even to their holy leader.

"How is Tristra?" Aradel asked on impulse.

High Priestess Kerin hesitated only a moment before answering. "She is confused and misses her son."

"So do I," Aradel admitted. "You must excuse me. I have business to the north. We are working out plans to harvest certain resources before they are too badly damaged."

"I understand and would offer my services," High Priestess Kerin offered. "You will need a guide during this time."

"I have a small council," Aradel informed her. "However, I appreciate your offer. Any concerns I think you may be able to address, I shall not hesitate to seek you out. For now, I am pressed for time. I wish you a good journey back to Axion."

A darkness passed over her face before it was gone. She was a proud woman, and Aradel knew it. High Priestess Kerin had always acted as though she was above everyone, as if her very good opinion outweighed everybody else's. She was proud, and yet she was also compassionate. Once Aradel set boundaries, she knew High Priestess Kerin would respect them.

"May the Goddess protect you," was all the high priestess said before walking to her sled. Aradel watched it go before she turned toward her own sled, driven by Yorten.

Aradel nearly tripped when she saw Tallus smiling down at her. She hadn't expected to see him again for some time, and she realized that, even though they knew little about each other, she'd missed him.

"Queen Aradel," Tallus said, jumping down from the sled. He grinned at her in that same disarming way. It was good to see someone treat her exactly as before she had become queen.

"How have you been Tallus?" she asked carefully as he held out his hand to help her in.

"Busy keeping The Wall together," he said as she took it.

She couldn't look at him as she brought one foot up into the sled. She was all too aware of the feeling of his fingertips. The excited dogs pulled the sled forward a little and she stumbled. Tallus caught her around the waist to steady her, but oddly she only became acutely aware of the wolves whining, rather than his hands.

"What is wrong with you?" Yorten demanded of the pups before glancing back at them both.

"Are you all right?" Tallus asked, and she could hear his genuine concern.

He steadied her with ease, and she tried to keep herself from blushing. It was difficult for her hide her feelings around him. She knew he could likely see right through anything she tried to do to mask them.

"I'm fine." Aradel managed. "Thank you." She put a hand on the sleigh to steady herself, and he pulled his hands away from her side.

Before she got up into the sleigh again, the ground suddenly started shifting beneath her. She gasped. It had been some time since the last quake, and she'd thought they would have a greater reprieve. Her arms flailed, and she felt Tallus take hold of her hand and lock his arm around her waist again.

The dogs whined and Yorten yelled, "Get in!"

Tallus hoisted her up into the sled before getting in behind her. She half fell into the seat as it was pulled forward. Although the world still shook around them, the moving sled seemed to counteract it slightly, so it wasn't so disorienting. When she sat up, the wind pressed against her face, and she something before her eyes that made her heart drop. She didn't understand what was happening! Along the western shoreline, she could see something out past The Wall that stood as tall as it. Her eyes went wide. There had never been a mountain there before; there shouldn't be anything there taller than The Wall! She tightened her fingers around Tallus's as fear gripped her heart.

"What is it?" he asked as the quake subsided.

"By the Goddess," she whispered before looking at him. "It's a wave." And it would soon engulf their wall of snow and ice entirely; and they were heading straight toward it. She'd never seen such a swell, and she imagined it was like the one that had taken out the palace at the Fire Nation's island. Darha had told Queen Vesna about it on one of their visits. She'd warned them it might happen to them.

"Get us out of here," Tallus yelled to his father.

Before he could turn back, Aradel put a hand up and yelled, "No. Go faster, we have to get there."

"What are you doing?" Tallus asked.

She looked back at him as she gripped the front of the sled and stood. "Saving lives."

"You are Queen now! You must be protected!" Yorten yelled. "But I will not disobey your orders."

When they reached the temporary camp set up for Vesna's services, Queen Darha and her brother were already running to get back into a sled. Prince Coor himself took the reins of the wolves, ordering their terrified driver to stay at the camp.

Aradel's advisors rushed out toward her, calling for her to stop. But she knew what they would say, and she wasn't sure she wanted to hear it. "Slow down," Aradel commanded. Yorten slowed the sled to a near stop.

"You must come to safety," Lord Wiss called, reaching an arm toward her as though to beckon her down.

"Queen Aradel, it is not safe!" Lady Nanra called as she came within range.

Aradel hesitated for a split second, but she saw on Queen Darha's face a determined look as Coor snapped the reins and their sleigh sped off. That was the expression of a true queen. Terrified but resolute.

Scanning the faces of the men and women of her council, she yelled, "I am Queen, and my duty is to protect. Not run and hide." They seemed startled as she declared her intent.

Without looking back at them, put her hands on the front of the sleigh, and gazed over Yorten's shoulder toward the impending wave. They still called after her, begging her to stay, but Yorten snapped the reins without a word of command from her.

She looked up at Tallus standing next to her. "You should go before the sleigh gains speed."

His curly hair was pulled nearly straight by the wind, and his blue eyes danced with admiration. He curled his fingers around hers, and she didn't pull back. It felt completely natural to have the comfort of his hand on hers.

He smiled at her in the same unassuming fashion, but his eyes were serious as he spoke. "I will not let you face this alone."

She nodded her head because words could not express how much she appreciated it. That with him by her side, she felt more confident, more powerful. They stared into each other's eyes before they came alongside Queen Darha and Prince Coor's sled. When she looked to Queen Darha, she found the woman pale in the face of the approaching wave.

"What's your plan?" Queen Darha called as she stood and gripped the sled behind her brother.

"I am going to turn it into to snow. It should crash against The Wall but not break it apart," Aradel called back.

"Are you crazy?" Prince Coor called. "It's too big! There's no way you can do that!"

"I am and I can," she assured them as Tallus tightened his fingers around hers reassuringly. "I just need to get closer."

"I can help with that," Darha yelled. Her brother glanced back at her, confused.

Queen Darha closed her eyes, and the ground beneath their sleds started to shake again. For a moment Aradel thought it was another quake, but then a massive bubble of hot orange lava started to push its way up from the ground just inside of The Wall. Coor's mouth dropped open. Aradel tried not to laugh at his expression, as the hill stopped rising just a hairsbreadth short of the top of the Frost Nation's magnificent ice wall. Apparently, his sister had a few tricks up her sleeve that even he was not aware of. Queen Darha snatched her hands backward, and the burning lava cooled into a smooth, dark brown stone hill.

Aradel lifted her arms and cast snow over it so she could glide easily to the top. Then she cast ice magic, creating a bridge from the tall hill, to the top of The Wall. She intentionally only made the bridge wide enough for one sleigh.

"Go to your people!" Aradel called, looking over at the neighboring sled.

She saw that Queen Darha was going to argue, but before she could, Aradel threw up a wall of ice not far in front of Darha's sled, forcing Coor to yank the reins hard to the left, turning the wolves away from it before they crashed. She knew Darha would be angry, but then she would realize Aradel was right. They couldn't be anywhere near that massive pile of snow. It was deadly for them, and the further away they were the better.

She gave them only one sparing glance as her sleigh began the ascent up the hill. When they reached the top, and left the hill to dash across Aradel's bridge of ice, she saw that the wave was nearly to shore. It was starting to turn over itself, and would soon crash, likely taking their precious wall with it.

She looked at Tallus, and he returned her stare. She couldn't hide the fact that he meant something to her, but she didn't know how to express it either.

He seemed to sense her intent. Without a word, he lifted their joined hands and kissed the back of hers. His eyes were serious as he said, "Amaze me."

Aradel smiled. He let go of her hand just as Yorten turned the sleigh to run along the top of The Wall. With the moon peals glowing brightly, she faced the incoming wave, and lifted her arms. The wind pulled at her sleeves and dress, and her braided hair snapped against her back. Forgetting everything else, she focused her full intent upon the wave, and let her magic fly.

177

○

The group approaching was considerably smaller than the one that had left for the Frost Nation. In one way, Ekil was glad to see such a small group because it allowed him to feel less annoyed for his own diminished numbers. But this few returning meant they had to have failed. The royal families still lived.

Tulya was not among them. How interesting.

"Your numbers are quite diminished," he said to Maris.

"Yours don't look much better," a Frost woman answered as if he'd been speaking to her.

He slowly turned his head, regarding her as plainly as he could. "I hadn't counted on a Frost Knight taking control of a hail storm and turning my army into a target range."

"Yeah? Well we hadn't counted on your Queen creating a fire hurricane that took out over three quarters of our army in one shot."

Ekil's scars began to burn. He knew exactly what she was talking about because he'd been a victim of that same kind of magic, Wild Fire. The Wild Fire that Queen Berselis had summoned had won the day for the Fire Nation royalty—and had deformed him for life. Ekil absently ran his finger down his cheek; he hated magic users.

"Where is Tulya?" he asked Maris.

A dark expression came over his face. "She ran," he answered. "She used magic to protect herself, and then she ran."

"So she *was* a magic user," Ekil said.

He had guessed so the second she stepped into his living room during their first meeting. She'd had the faint, freshly fallen snow smell to her that all frost wielders had. He just hadn't been sure if it was her, or the guards that had escorted her. Either way, he'd figured she'd come in handy—a magic user that hated magic users. Besides, of late, Ekil wasn't beneath joining forces with magic wielders if they had the same aim and purpose. But what good was the woman if she failed? Not only had she failed at eliminating the Fire Nation royalty, but she was a coward.

"You suspected?" Maris asked, surprise in his voice.

"From the beginning," Ekil said.

"And you didn't tell me?" Maris demanded with subtle fury in his voice.

Ekil stared at him. "It wasn't necessary."

"The hell it wasn't!" Maris countered. "She never should have—"

"Shh," Ekil said, bringing his finger up to his lips. Maris fell silent instantly, swallowing back his words in a gulp of fear. "I said it wasn't necessary," Ekil replied slowly in a tone of finality.

"So where are we going?" Porva asked flatly from behind him. Ekil turned and lowered his gaze to where she sat on the ground against a rock. "There's nowhere to go now with the Fire Nation royalty still kicking. I know Prince Coor, and he will hunt every last one of us down until there is nothing left. In case you missed the part where your frost tramp failed to kill him, he's very resourceful, smart and clearly—given that he's still married to Thea—unreasonably stubborn."

Ekil reached down to grasp her chin in his fingers. She shied away just slightly in fear. Ekil could kill her. A big part of him wanted to; she was a magic user. But her time would come soon. For now, he would satisfy himself with another's blood.

"We live to fight another day, my dear," he replied almost seductively.

He straightened and gazed out over what he could see of his beloved Fire Nation. He would save it. He knew in his bones he would rule someday, someday soon. Then he would wipe the very memory of the magic users from the face of the planet.

"We live to fight another day," he said again. "But first we take care of all traitors."

———

Tulya felt like she was being hunted, and she was streetwise enough to know not to ignore a feeling like that. It was safer to travel at night where no one would recognize her as she slipped through the nearly deserted town of Seville, just outside The Wall. The moonlight mostly lit her way, but her feet knew the rest. She would have to stay here until she could think of somewhere better to hide. Luckily, she had a home here, and it meant sanctuary.

Eyes peered out at her as she slipped past houses with people in them who wouldn't leave The Outlands, despite the recent warmth. Tulya pulled the hood of her cloak tighter around her head and tried not to grimace in discomfort. This place was worse than sad because it was mostly abandoned. If they survived the disasters, she could start again here, though. She would have to find a way to darken her hair, but she could make a life, far enough away that Aradel and Ekil couldn't find her.

179

She turned down an alley, and was nearly to the end when she heard something. Whirling around, she searched, but there was nothing behind her. She took a few fearful steps backwards before quickly spinning and running the last bit of distance to the house.

The two-story stone building had horse stables around the side that had caved in from the quakes. There were cracks in the foundation, and a few of the walls, but it was whole enough. She pulled out an old key and shoved it into the lock as her hands shook. It finally clicked, and she nearly broke the key when she pushed the door open. Yanking it loose, she ran inside and slammed the door behind her. Breathing heavily, she locked it again and leaned her back against it. Her breathing eventually slowed, but the adrenaline would take longer to quiet.

Swallowing her fear as best she could, Tulya stepped into the room, and something punched into her gut.

She gasped from the pain she now felt there. Stumbling backwards slightly, her mind tried to catch up with what was happening. She managed to look up, and saw the scarred face of Ekil at the other end of his sword. He jerked the blade out, and she stumbled backward again before turning down the hall in a feeble escape attempt. Her hand went to her abdomen as her legs tried to carry her to safety.

"So, you thought you could run?" Ekil asked.

She staggered, knocking over a hallway table in an attempt to stay on her feet, but the blood loss was swift, and she fell against a bench. She tried to blink the haze from her eyes as he slowly came toward her. Her eyes went wide as she stumbled through the dark house again, trying to get away. Her legs quickly lost feeling. Unable to support her, she fell onto her stomach on the floor.

His footsteps were closing in on her, and he eventually crouched by her head. The bloody blade hung between his knees, as she desperately tried to pull herself away from him. Watching her futile attempt, she knew he was laughing inside.

"It's been a while since I've skinned a magic user. Near thirty years at least," he said while he let the tip of the blade twirl around on his thumb.

She forgot about anything but getting away and pulled herself along the floor again, and he laughed at her.

"Where are you going? We were just getting started."

She kept pulling herself along the floor, clutching at the walls to put any amount of space between her and him. His merciless grip suddenly clamped down on her ankle, and he dragged her from the hallway back to the front room. She dug her nails into the floor to try and stop him, but the smooth stone offered no grip.

The moonlight was bright in here, and she could see his scars better, as well as the terrifying smile on his lips. She realized this wasn't just about revenge; he was enjoying himself.

"Oh Goddess," she whispered.

"The Gods aren't here," he said, lifting a hand and allowing the silver moonlight to dance across his fingers. "I love the look of blood under the moon. It looks almost black."

Tulya felt a deep primal need well up inside of her, and with it came ice. It spread out from under her, coating the ground, and an ice shield snapped up around her body. Ekil turned his eyes down to look at her, and she was unnerved by his calmness.

He went over and crouched next to a pack on the floor she hadn't noticed before. "That won't do," he said. "We've only just begun."

The ice spread further out and around her as her fear rose. He lifted something out of the pack, a glass jar with a strange lid. There was some sort of liquid at the bottom, but it was hard to see in the moonlight. She kept the ice shield firmly around her, knowing it would only buy her a few more minutes. She needed to figure out a way to get on the offensive.

"Do you know what this is?" he asked, as though he was a professor teaching a class.

"No," she finally managed.

Ekil came toward her again. "It's a highly complex chemical compound which, if you aren't very careful, can melt your face off." Tulya started to tremble. "It originates, however, in volcanic gas." He tapped the jar with the tip of his fingernail. "Capture enough of the gas, eventually it condensates on the glass, and we can process it and store it"—he smiled menacingly— "for situations just like this." Tulya's breath sped up in terror. "I was going to use it on Queen Darha, but this as a much better idea."

Her eyes widened and she started to try to push herself away from him. "No," she whispered as tears blurred her vision.

"Oh yes," he said, opening the jar.

"Please," she whispered, pushing herself back.

"There is no room in this world for mercy," he said, walking toward her. "There is only room for the strong." Then he dumped the entire jar on her.

Her screams filled the night air, and those in the shadows cringed inside their homes, covering their ears. They didn't want to hear the destructive force of sulfuric acid as a woman died in agony.

———————— o ————————

Kirill had never thought he would be so happy to see a volcano. The island of Rask was basically one huge volcano that took up the entire horizon for at least forty miles. The summit itself had to be eight miles high! It was the thing he'd ever seen—and over the last several days, he had seen quite a few large volcanic islands which made up the Fire Nation's entire northern shore. But nothing could have prepared him for the sight before him now. This was the monster that threatened to end his world, and now he could see why.

Smoke and steam billowed out of the top of the cone, and Kirill found he was anxious to throw the iceberg down the shoot and cool this beast as quickly as possible. The worst part of watching Thea and her two companions climb it was that this terror was in his face the entire time, rumbling and threatening everyone he loved and cared for.

From the northern edge of the iceberg, he had watched Fitzu, Dorsh, and Thea work their way up the side of the volcano for the past two days. They were just now reaching the crater at the top. Once they figured out which part he should bring the iceberg to, Thea would send a signal, and then he would fly this massive pain in the ass over to the volcano. Once it was in and this was over, they would pat each other on the back and sail home. Soon, this would all be a very distant nightmare.

At least that's what Kirill told himself.

He looked through the telescope again and watched Thea as she hiked the mountain. She had her strength back after the battle a week earlier when he'd thought he had been done for. Saving Thea would have been worth it, though— as long as she had figured out a way to get the iceberg to the volcano.

Perhaps all of this wasn't a nightmare.

He didn't like to admit it, but she had been right to be angry with him for taking control of that hail storm. He'd definitely lost his composure when he thought she was in danger. It was weird, given how they had started out. They had once been at each other's throats, but now they were some sort of strange friends. At first, Kirill thought he'd been coming around because Thea reminded him of Aradel. But he realized it was because Thea was like him.

During the last week heading toward Rask, Thea had spent most of her time on the iceberg with him rather than down on the ships. Two nights ago, over the small campfire that was constantly between them, Thea had joked that she stayed up there in case he needed more babying while transporting the iceberg. Kirill had countered that he didn't mind because he needed to make sure the "kraken slayer" didn't do anything else insane that would get her killed. Laughter had become common between them and Kirill had grown to like her very much. She was powerful and stubborn and had a temper that rivaled his. He got her jokes and she got his. Had they been born on the same side of the river, he had no doubt they would have been an inseparable pair of troublemakers. She wasn't like Aradel, who was a sister to him; she was a friend, a comrade in arms, and his equal. It had only taken facing a mountain of obstacles with her for him to see it.

He didn't even think of the Fire Nation with any sort of hatred anymore. They weren't all that different, and if anyone had taught him that, it was Thea. The woman had weaseled her way close to him somehow. She was sneaky like that.

When they reached the top of the volcano, he lowered the telescope and crossed his arms. He could just barely make out Thea's wave. He waved back, though he doubted she could see him very well either. Thea helped Dorsh up over the lip of the crater, and they all started down into the volcano. He frowned and waited.

Soon, his finger started tapping on his arm as he stared straight ahead. Then all of his fingers drummed against his arm. He felt like pacing but kept his eyes firmly fixed on the gapping maw of the volcano. He soon felt his jaw working and his teeth clenching. Hours passed, and just when he thought he was going to explode with impatience, he saw a spark shoot through the air at the northern end of the volcano.

It was about time!

Kirill's arms instantly went out to his sides and he smiled, because this was the fun part. He lifted his arms, and the entire iceberg shuddered as his power flowed through it. He was well rested now, and the imminent conclusion of their trip left him exhilarated. He would be able to float back home if this worked. He wouldn't admit that to Thea, though. 'Floating' sounded too girly, and she would tease him if he said it aloud.

The iceberg began to rise. Water fell from it as he slowly and carefully lifted it into the air, and eased it forward. Up and up he went with his arms held wide, and his focus complete.

The air became thin as he floated miles into the sky, and he had to take in deeper, fuller breaths to get the correct amount of air in his lungs. As he moved closer, he could feel the heat of the volcano start to assault his ice shield, too. It was intense, and he hurried the iceberg along.

They planned to use the island like a giant wine cork, stopping the build-up of heat in its tracks. Hopefully it would be enough to end all the damage that was happening to their world.

Another flare shot through the air a few hundred feet in front of him, and he started to lower himself down. Soon, the open crater swallowed the iceberg. Kirill couldn't help scanning the area in awe as the rock walls rose up around him. As massive as the iceberg was, and as big a burden as it had been on him over the past five weeks, this stone beast consumed it whole.

When the opening above him narrowed slightly, officially making Kirill's palms sweat, he looked beneath him. At first, he only saw endless smoke, and his heart stopped. He wouldn't be able to see where he was going. No sooner had the worry crossed his mind than the entire smoke cloud swirled a little and was pressed against the far edges of the volcano. Kirill could now see the ground, which was just a little more than a mile from the bottom of the iceberg. Numerous, narrow canals of churning lava were beneath him, and the orange light was so bright, he had to close his eyes and turn away for a moment while they adjusted. When the stinging subsided, he peered down and could see the three dots of Dorsh, Fitzu, and Thea on the rocks below. From the expression of deep concentration on Fitzu's face, it was clear that he was the one parting the smoke.

Kirill focused on Thea as she directed him to a particularly violent pool of lava to the north. It sprayed up around the rocks like the Ashtra Sea upon the coast of the Frost Nation. Focusing his aim there, he began to float the ice island in that direction while still slowly easing it down. The bottom of the iceberg eventually started to hiss loudly as it touched down into the lava. Just as Kirill was about to allow himself a triumphant smile, the entire iceberg rocked.

Kirill nearly toppled over the front edge, but forced himself to fall backwards on his butt so he didn't go over. He kept his concentration despite the interruption, but then the iceberg dipped again, and rammed into the side of the mountain. Ice and snow rained down below him, and he heard Thea cursing. If she was cursing, then she was all right, so he wasn't too concerned about them below; he became concerned with what had stopped him.

He crawled over to the side and looked down at Thea. She had her hands out to her sides, standing near the outer edge of the pool where he was supposed to place the iceberg. "What's the holdup, frost flake?"

"I don't know," he yelled back. "I think—."

He was cut off as the iceberg was thrown backward toward the western wall. With a deafening crack, Kirill heard—and, through his magic, felt—the ice island that he had been holding together for the past month, suddenly break apart. One huge section disappeared from his awareness, while the section he was on crashed into the wall.

Before he could come to his senses about what could possibly be happening, the ice landed in a small lava pool. Steam exploded around him and burned his arms right through his ice shield. He yelled in pain and snatched them out of harm's way, stumbling to try to get to safety; but inside a volcano, there was no real safety for him. Kirill felt every degree of heat assaulting his cold shield that he desperately tried to keep around himself. Trying to focus through the heat, and the pain, and keeping his shield intact, Kirill made his way to a safer edge of the ice.

Before he could, the small section he walked on abruptly dropped. Snow, ice, and Kirill fell to the rocks below. His shoulder hit hard, jarring his entire body, breaking his concentration, and the heat instantly washed over him. He yelled in agony as his skin fractured along his neck, chest, and shoulders before he could snap a shield around himself again. The ice around his skin hissed, and all his injuries burned.

"Kirill!" Thea was yelling, with an edge of panic.

"Here," he moaned, pushing himself up. He needed to get out of there.

"What happened?" she asked, running up to him.

He didn't want her near his shield since he had to increase the cold to the point it would likely burn her even from five feet away. She bit her lip as he waved her off to keep her at a safe distance.

"I don't know," he panted, moving toward the now melting iceberg. "But I need to get out of here."

Fitzu came to stand beside Thea, looking concerned. Dorsh waited a few yards away near another lava pool.

Thea examined the remains. "Can you lift it again?"

"Yes," he said, hoisting himself up onto the ice to start climbing it. "But it moved and broke on its own, and I have no idea how." He began climbing. "I'm going to go to the top again and see if I can salvage the part that was somehow tossed out of here." He looked at Thea over his shoulder and saw her fearful gaze. "It's going to be okay," he said.

Thea nodded, appearing slightly relieved that this mission could still be successful, though much of the iceberg was gone.

Kirill continued to climb. Whatever had stopped him would be close by, though he couldn't imagine what it might have been. He needed to get back to the top. Maybe he could use the ocean water to refreeze the iceberg together. It would cost them another day, but it was better than costing them the planet.

He had just pulled himself up over the edge of the iceberg when he heard a yell from below him. It wasn't Fitzu or Thea. Quickly looking over the edge, Kirill saw Dorsh standing with a strange woman he'd never seen before. Her hand was on his shoulder.

Kirill's brows dropped. "What the…" What was a strange woman doing at the bottom of this volcano?

The woman was dressed in a long black silky gown that hugged her curves in a nearly inappropriate manner. The dress was strange, but well made, so she wasn't a homeless Fire Nation native. Her hair was a long mop of silvery blonde with broad black streaks that cascaded down her back; but it was her eyes that were most distinctive. As she looked up at Kirill with a cruel smile, he realized she had one orange eye and one blue eye that seemed to glow with magic.

Kirill looked over at Thea as she lifted her arms, taking up two long fiery whips from the nearby lava canals. Kirill had seen her do it before. What he didn't expect was for the mystery woman to raise a small lava wall in front of herself, absorbing the whips with which Thea attacked her.

Suddenly, it dawned on Kirill. This woman had to have moved the iceberg, and now she was manipulating lava. His eyes went wide. It couldn't be. That was impossible!

"My, my, my, look at what we have here," she said with a smile as sweet as poison.

"Let him go," Thea demanded.

She took one step toward the woman, and ice immediately began to spread across Dorsh's body. He barely had time to scream before he was turned completely to stone. The ice was so strong that frost even developed across his remains. Thea and Fitzu took a few steps back. None of them had expected that. Kirill nearly stopped breathing at what he saw.

The woman was both fire and ice.

"It isn't nice to trespass," she smiled wickedly as her hand began to burn orange and Dorsh's body shattered into a million pieces at her feet. "There's a penalty to pay."

Part 4

"A mistake we will not repeat." - Thea

———————— o ————————

"Rhett," Darha called among the hustle and bustle in Hurra.

Rhett handed off a handful of medicine to Hickson, whose son was suffering from an infected wound to his abdomen. "Majesty," Rhett replied as he quickly approached.

She handed him a pile of blankets. "Please deliver these to Forta's family. They are located on the second floor, seven houses west of here."

Rhett bowed. "Yes, your majesty."

"Jamsun," Darha said as she reached into the cart of bread the Frost Nation had provided. "Mark three blankets to Forta's family."

"Marked," Jamsun replied.

"Your majesty!" Myka called from down the street. "I have another four vials of medicine out with Breh and Gret to deliver!"

"Jamsun?' Darha called, looking around for him.

"Marked, your majesty."

"Majesty," Torla called, getting Darha's attention, "Hetta's infant is low on formula."

"Infant and child supplies are being doled out on the cross street from here," Darha called and pointed in the general direction.

"Understood."

"Darha," Coor called.

Darha grabbed three loaves of bread and handed them to Kulsa's teenage son for their family of six. "Three loaves to Kulsa's family," she informed Jamsun. She reached into the cart again for another loaf. "What is it, Coor?" She glanced up and saw him crouched down wrapping the wound of another teenage boy, Lim, before giving some bandages to him for his father, who was also injured.

He finally approached Darha. "They need help melting the snow Queen Aradel provided for drinking water. A few stubborn diehards ignored the schedule and have exhausted their magic. We're still desperate for water."

Darha nodded and handed a loaf of bread down to Juway before wiping her hands on a towel. "Jamsun, one loaf for Juway. Kemu," she called over her shoulder. The young corporal looked up from handing another struggling family another two loaves of bread. "Will you keep track of the rations?"

She nodded. "Of course, your majesty."

Darha nodded in thanks then both she and Coor started for the shore of the River Gora.

"I hate to put you to work," Coor said a little playfully.

"Please," Darha responded, trying not to let her exhaustion seep into her tone. "It's my responsibility."

They walked a few moments in silence before Coor asked, "What is the latest word from Queen Aradel?"

Darha sighed. "Cas last reported that she is heading far south to acquire something that will allow her to repair the magic of their wall. The heat is becoming severe for her people, so they are evacuating farther to the south."

It was quiet again before Coor asked, confused, "When did you meet with Cas? And where was I?"

Darha felt her cheeks flush crimson. "As soon as we arrived back in Hurra from Queen Vesna's service. You were busy with the wounded and the rations." Darha carefully glanced up at her brother and noticed the incredulous look on his face.

As soon as she glanced up at him, Coor's expression expanded into a mischievous smile. "Are you blushing?"

"What?" Darha cried as if offended. "Of course not! Why would I?"

Coor grinned. "I have no idea. Why would you?"

"I wouldn't! Would you—"

"Look at me," Coor said lightheartedly and walked backwards, studying Darha's face. Darha regarded him with a glare, hoping he would take her red cheeks for anger, or perhaps annoyance; she would take either one over the actual reason. But Coor threw his head back and laughed as he started walking forward again. She couldn't hide anything from her brother.

"Shut up," she said, shoving her shoulder into Coor's side, barely knocking him off balance.

They approached the shore a few minutes later where the mountain of snow rested in a hundred-foot heap along the River Gora. Already some of the snow was melting into the river and raising the levels slightly, but it would be days before all of it was gone. A dozen Fire Nation citizens were shoveling the snow into the hundreds of metal barrels waiting nearby. Only about twenty were full of water. Another hundred had some snow in them waiting to be melted. The other hundred or so were empty.

As they approached the soldiers that had exhausted their magic, they immediately stood and bowed, before looking at her with shame. "We apologize, your majesty," Naliah said mournfully.

Sokka sighed. "We lost track of time. The demands for water—"

"It's all right," Darha interrupted before either could go on. "There's plenty of work to be done that doesn't require magic. Will you both go see Jamsun in town? He is dealing with the rations of our supplies. There is plenty for you to do."

They both bowed again. "Yes, your majesty."

As soon as they both took off, Coor went over to help the people shoveling the snow into barrels while Darha lit her hands up with her fire magic. She was about to start melting the barrels of snow when she caught movement from the corner of her eye. Turning, she grinned broadly, probably too broadly, when she saw Cas approaching. She was glad her brother couldn't see her face right now.

She extinguished her magic and started walking over to him. Coor continued shoveling snow, but Darha noted his teasing smile as she passed, though he deliberately avoided her eyes, pretending to be concentrating on his task.

"Queen Darha," Cas said as he approached.

Darha felt her cheeks flush crimson once more at the sight of Cas's smile. It was a sweet and gentle smile, but also somehow playful, which always made her grin whenever she saw it.

"I told you," Darha said gently, as they stopped in front of each other. "I'm not your Queen. Darha is fine."

He was so tall that the top of Darha's head only came up under his chin, forcing him to tilt his head down to look at her. That caused his golden blonde bangs to nearly fall into his pretty, pale green eyes. Darha swallowed heavily, trying to keep her emotions in check while she spoke to the handsome southerner.

Cas's smile broadened. "I would not dream of denying you your rightful title."

Darha's grin spread across her face before she could stop it, and she bowed her head bashfully. It was quiet a moment before Darha looked back up at him. She noticed for the first time that Cas only had four Frost Nation soldiers with him when he usually had at least a dozen.

Her brows drew together in concern. "Is everything all right?"

Cas nodded. "As all right as things can be."

Darha nodded in understanding. Cas's eyes rested on her, and she saw a new light in them that went beyond their usual playful charm. Something deeper there made Darha's heart beat faster.

"I wanted to ask you if you needed anything else from the Frost Nation."

Darha found herself swallowing heavily. "I don't think so. Your Queen has been more than generous. We have everything we need right now."

Cas's smile brightened. "Good." He took a step, bringing him so close to her she could feel the cold of his ice shield waft over her skin. "I came to also inform you that many of the Frost Nation soldiers are evacuating south. Most have already left." He looked at her with such softness Darha could hardly breathe. "I asked to be reassigned to the guard tower closest to Hurra on The Wall. If you should need anything, I am at your disposal."

Darha tried to catch her breath without being ridiculous about it. She swallowed heavily to try to hide it. "Thank you, Cas," she whispered roughly, and then awkwardly cleared her throat. "Thank you, Cas," she said more strongly. "I'm"—she met his eyes— "I'm glad to know you will be close by."

Cas smiled. "As am I."

Darha grinned in return. Cas bowed slightly at the waist, and with a final smile, he and the other Frost Nation soldiers started south toward The Wall. She watched him go for a moment, and as he departed, her heart seemed to reach out for him.

"Cas!" she called before she could stop herself.

Cas paused and turned to her again as she approached. She was Queen, the most powerful fire wielder in the Fire Nation. She could do things with heat no one else could, so she concentrated on the heat just around her lips. It took a moment, but when she eventually felt it push away from her skin, she lifted herself onto her tippy toes to quickly kiss Cas's cheek without burning him. His ice-cold skin briefly turned her lips to stone, which stung, but it was worth it for that brief exchange. He had bent forward slightly so she could reach, and when she stood flat on her feet again, he was surprisingly close to her.

"Thank you," she said, glancing up at him awkwardly.

She caught him smiling broadly, with slight amazement in his eyes, before she turned and hurried back to her task. Nearing her brother, who still pretended to be concentrating, Darha saw his lips were pressed together firmly with the corners up.

191

"Oh, shut up," Darha muttered as she passed him. This elicited the exact opposite response, as Coor roared with laughter.

Darha smiled although her back was to him. She bit her lip as she began to melt the barrels of snow, with Cas steadfast on her mind. Excuses to summon him from his post, or to go see him, ran through her head for hours as she worked. She hoped it wouldn't be long before she saw him again—or thought up an excuse to ensure she did.

Frost: Chapter Thirty-Three

————————— o —————————

The cold beat against Aradel's cheeks, and the wind pushed her dress against her legs and whipped her hair around. She looked up at the snowy peaks of the Lonely Mountains. As glorious as it was here, she feared that her people would soon be sleeping amongst these very peaks—lost in the drifts of snow and buried in its comfort, abed in this winter wonderland to escape the harshness of the heat in the north.

She was buried up to her knees in the snow as she walked on, ignoring the seductive pull of the snow's frigid lullaby. She was half tempted to clear her path, but there was something exhilarating about being so close with naturally occurring snow. She was constantly torn between moving it and rolling around in it. Unfortunately, time would not allow her to enjoy it.

As she crested the hill she'd been climbing, she could see the bridge below that led to the ice cavern covered in snow. She didn't know what to expect inside that cavern. She had come this far south only once before and she had not been allowed entry. Only Queen Vesna, the possessor of the moon pearls, had gone on.

Aradel reached the snow-covered bridge and frowned at the fact that it had no railings. She took a tentative step onto it, but her foot slipped slightly. Drawing back, she glanced over the side as the snow she had disturbed fell to the rocky gorge below. It may have been covered with snow, but not enough to grant her any comfort if she fell. Only her powers would save her, but it would waste valuable time. She'd have to clear the bridge.

She lifted her hand and swept it out in front of her. Snow cascaded over the sides of the stone bridge and into the rocks below. Crystals of ice sprung into the air, and swirled around her. Miniscule flakes joined the dance, almost like a mist, and she began to cross the bridge. Reaching the other side, she only glanced back for a moment. When she left, she would have to replace the snow so no one could follow her path to this place.

She walked into the cave and stopped abruptly. It was so dark. As soon as she wished for some light, the moon pearls began to glow, illuminating just far enough into the darkness so she could see where she was going. Across the cave, a soft, pale blue glow met her eyes, mingling with the light from the pearls.

Rounding the corner to where the new light shone, she found a great wall of ice before her, extending from wall to wall, floor to ceiling, blocking any further access into the mountain. Her mouth dropped open a little and she softly gasped as she looked up at it. It was solid, and seemly impenetrable. She took a tentative step forward.

Queen Vesna had told all the candidates once, that when they were Queen, they would know what to do if they ever had to retrieve the Ancient Ice Crystal. But Aradel wasn't sure what to do. She studied the wall with a critical eye. Was she supposed to break it?

She reached out to touch it, testing its depth to see if she could, and Aradel's hand went through it as if it were made of water. She pulled her hand back in surprise and inspected it. A triumphant smile spread across her face as she pushed her hand through again. Then she took a deep breath, and stepped in. The magical barrier passed over her body with a little bit of resistance, until the pressure eventually lifted.

When she opened her eyes again she was in another cavern. Ice decorated the walls which shimmered blue even in the limited light. There was a hole in the ceiling that allowed some light, and some snow to fall through. She wondered what the point of the magical wall was if there was a hole in the ceiling, but decided she wasn't one to judge. This cavern hadn't been accidentally discovered in all the years it had been hidden there. If it had, the queen would have known about it.

On a short stone pedestal in the center of the room, was a single floating, shining blue gem the size of her fist. It was smooth on the sides but oddly shaped. Like the wall she had passed through, the gem reminded her of water. Her boots gently tapped against the stone, sending the sound echoing around the cavern. She smoothed her dress, and tucked a cluster of hairs behind her ear, trying to soothe her nerves as she approached.

While watching, the seemingly solid gem suddenly liquefied. It dropped onto the stone pedestal as though it were splashing water. Before escaping over the sides, the water floated up again, joined together in the center of the platform, and returned to its original solid form.

Aradel pulled back at the movement. She had never seen anything like it. Gathering her courage, she stepped up onto the circular staircase surrounding the pedestal; testing the stone briefly to be sure it remained solid beneath her feet, and reached for the gem.

As soon as her fingers touched it, it turned to water again, and quickly slithered up her hand like it had a life of its own. She reflexively pulled back and gasped in surprise, holding her arm away from herself as the liquid circled her wrist, and suddenly became a bracelet of stone.

When she lifted her wrist, it sat like an unhampered bangle, resembling nothing like the power responsible for The Wall.

"Clever," she said aloud, her voice echoing around the room.

Turning from the pedestal, she walked back toward the wall of ice water with purpose. She needed to take it back to The Wall now before the heat got worse. They had tried everything else, but everything had failed. Every day another village close to the fracture was abandoned, and every day they made no advance on fixing it. She prayed to the goddess that this would be enough.

The ice shield pressed closely against her skin as the heat of the world beyond The Wall raged against it. Behind her, the candidates gathered at the crack so they could combine their strength into a single force.

Aradel had feared they would not accept her. But she should have known better. They accepted the decision of the moon pearls. The pearls had never chosen wrong, and the candidates would support whomever the pearls deemed worthy, no matter who the wearer might be.

"It has gotten so bad," one of the girls gasped as she looked up at The Wall.

The only thing that remained was the original ice of The Wall with no magic left in it—The Wall that had been brought forth by the ancients who had used the same Ancient Ice Crystal that now resided on Aradel's wrist. She only prayed it would be enough to repair the damage that was done. She dared not think of the implications of the future damage that would occur if they could not keep the heat at bay.

"Have faith," Aradel said to the women behind her. "The Moon Goddess is with us."

"May the Goddess lead us on our path," one woman said, and many agreed.

The once-frozen grass was wet, and mud stuck to their boots. Aradel was happy she hadn't wasted a moment to change out of them. She had ridden the elk back to the camp closest to the fracture where the candidates were waiting for her. They had walked a short distance, knowing that the camp would have to be moved as the heat continued to spread like a festering wound.

She was Queen, the most powerful user of frost magic, and she had her moon pearls. Even with the crystal, she dared not risk the endeavor alone because she knew she would need all the help she could get. She knew that infusing the crystal with their magic would begin the process of full repair to The Wall. She knew it like she had never known anything before.

"Together," she said as she raised her arms.

A spiral of snow and ice shot forth from her hands and touched the base of The Wall. After a moment, the candidates joined their power to hers. She could feel the force of that much power as it crackled through the air around her. Their magic reached the entire length of the structure, from the west coast all the way to the east. Never since The Wall had been first constructed had such powers been needed at once. She prayed that the Goddess would watch over them and that they'd never have to do this again.

It was a slow process. Hours went by. Soon a full day. By the time the moon came up, a thick layer of ice was added to the already existing structure. The addition was the full length of the wall, and reached the top. The magical fabric that kept their nation cold and safe was repaired.

Under the full glow of the moon, Aradel dropped her arms, and the candidates followed suit. She gazed at it. "It's done," she whispered.

A hand touch hers as one of the candidates came to stand next to her. Aradel glanced over at Rena, who smiled. She was one of the younger candidates and had only recently joined before the disasters started. Her pale blue eyes met Aradel's lively blue ones. Aradel smiled in return, thankful for the company.

One by one, the candidates joined her until they were all in a row, bound together by joined hands. They stood as the cold from her pearls washed over them all, unyielding against the constant assault of heat. They stood in silence as one united entity and prayed together.

"It isn't melting," Rena whispered.

Aradel felt the energy of the candidates rising joyfully with every passing moment.

It suddenly began to rain as though the Goddess herself was weeping from joy. Aradel turned her face up to it and let it hit her skin. The drops left trails of ice down her cheeks, but she didn't care. She had succeeded. No matter the time it took, it was done. Her fingers tightened around the hands holding hers, and her lips curled into a smile. Relief finally flooded in and she tried not to cry.

One of the girls started laughing and began to dance playfully in the rain. Rena soon rushed out to join her. Soon, all the women were pulled into the fun. Aradel lifted her arms, and with a tiny gesture, the rain turned into hail. The women all gasped in wonder and started laughing hysterically as they danced in the falling ice.

Rena returned to Aradel breathlessly and took her hands. "Come on."

With an excited laugh, Aradel let herself be drawn into the fray of dancing women. Their feet squished and splashed in the mud as the hail bounced off their skin. No one else noticed as they celebrated this massive victory. Aradel would make an announcement later. Right now, she watched the women in their bliss. She didn't have the heart to stop them with all the tragedy they had seen recently.

She eventually found herself closer to The Wall, and placed her hands on the ice as the girls shouted and laughed behind her. She rested her forehead against it briefly before looking up at the impassive construct. "You're back to your former glory," and for a moment, she could swear it felt happy.

Fire: Chapter Thirty-Four

"Who are you?" Thea asked, trying to sound brave, but the tremble was clear in her voice. What the young woman was, or seemed to be, was absolutely impossible!

"Oh, how impolite of me not to introduce myself," she said with a wicked smile. "My name is Freya, and I'm the one who is destroying your entire world."

Thea's eyes narrowed. "What? What do you mean?"

Freya indicated the interior of the volcano with a gentle gesture of her hands. "I'm sure the massive natural disasters you have been experiencing didn't escape your notice. They weren't meant to be subtle."

Thea's eyes went wide, and she glanced up at Kirill, who met her eyes at the same time. She looked back at the woman. "*You're* doing this?"

"Of course I am," she said casually.

Thea couldn't even form a coherent thought. "How? W—why?" She couldn't believe what she was hearing or seeing. The world had suddenly become very surreal.

"The how is easy," the woman responded with a smile. "I take a massive, dormant volcano with enough power to destroy your planet, and I heat it up until it does."

"*You're* heating this volcano?"

The woman rolled her eyes. "This is going to be a very long conversation if you have to repeat everything I say." Thea swallowed heavily, stunned. "The 'why' is a little more complex. Would you really like to know?"

Thea's concern for Kirill weighed heavily on her heart. He needed to get out of here or he was dead, and Thea wouldn't allow that. But if there was one thing Thea knew for sure—and Kirill, as a fellow soldier, would know it, too—it was that she needed to hear as much about this young woman as she was willing to reveal. 'Always know your enemy' was the first thing everyone learned as a recruit. This woman was an enemy, an anomaly, an unknown. And Thea knew that couldn't remain so.

"Of course I do!" Thea cried. "I want to hear what pitiful, self-absorbed reason you have to kill hundreds of thousands of innocent people!"

"Innocent!?" the woman shrieked. She cackled a moment before her expression and tone became severe. "No one on this planet is innocent."

Thea took a fearful step back until she could hear Fitzu breathing in her ear. "Kirill's got to get out of here," he said softly.

"I know," Thea replied quietly in return.

She glanced up at him on the iceberg again and saw him start to blink rapidly, likely suffering from the exhaustion of trying to keep his ice shield intact in here. Thea didn't know how much water he had left, if any, to keep cold.

"Not doing so well, are you Sir Knight?" the woman asked, drawing Thea's attention back down to her. She was gazing up at Kirill with a menacing smirk on her face. Thea's heart jumped into her throat. If nothing else, Kirill had to stay on that iceberg for as long as the thing could possibly last in this heat. It would help him stay cool.

"You can wield both fire and frost?" Thea asked quickly, appealing to the narcissistic tendencies that this woman displayed. She had to get the woman's attention off Kirill. It worked. Freya's strange orange and blue glowing eyes rested on her again.

"My, you are quick witted," she said sarcastically.

Thea licked her lips, being careful not to look up at Kirill again lest she draw Freya's attention back to him. "How?"

Freya smiled and started walking to her right. Thea turned with her, not daring to take her eyes away from her face. Fitzu stayed right beside Thea, turning with her. "My mother was a Frost Nation whore who my Fire Nation father bought and bedded," the woman began.

Thea tried to keep her eyes from going wide at that, and failed. She knew black market deals could go down between the two nations—she'd disrupted a few exchanges herself—but she didn't know any involved purchasing people. The thought of people being traded like cattle made her stomach turn over.

"My mother wrote to my father when she was dying. Oddly enough, my father wanted me. So after she died in childbirth," the woman continued, "he brought me home to the Fire Nation. Everything seemed normal until I was eight and started using my frost-wielding abilities. Soon after that, he cast me out with just the clothes on my back and without a coin to my name. I was now his enemy and not worth the effort."

That hit a nerve deep in Thea's heart, and she impulsively wanted to apologize. She knew what that felt like. Both her parents had abandoned her at that age. Thea felt a longing to deal with Freya's father herself for doing that to his daughter, but she knew if she said such a thing, her words would be empty to this woman.

"I escaped to the Frost Nation after that, thinking I could find my mother's family and they would take me in. What a fool I was! None of the Frost Nation soldiers would even let me through The Wall to see Queen Vesna. They could see what I was, and I fled before they could capture me or worse. So, I came back north and went to Queen Berselis, begging for shelter and guidance, but she saw only the frost half of me, and I was exiled from there as well. I finally realized that no one wanted me, that I belonged nowhere."

Thea pressed her lips together. Her adopted mother, Berselis, was a kind, sweet, and gracious woman. She was a good Queen to the Fire Nation, but she had no love for the Frost Nation and wasn't shy about that fact. Neither did Thea's adopted father, Leehin, Coor and Darha's dad, though he was more laid back about it. As much as it pained Thea to think about it now, she knew Berselis could do that to this young woman. It felt even worse to admit this to herself since she had become so close with Kirill.

"So, I made my way back through the Fire Nation, far north, to this volcano where nobody else lived and nobody would dare to come. Here, I perfected both of my magic abilities and became incredibly powerful," she said with a purring sound of self-satisfaction. She met Thea's eyes severely and paused her walking. "Since I don't belong anywhere in this world, I'm going to make a new one—one where even I will belong." She wrinkled her nose. "Punishing you all is just letting me have my cake and eat it too."

Thea swiped her hand over her mouth in nervousness. Freya's words were just words to her; her concern at the moment was Kirill's life. She had to get him out of there. Her family also needed to know about Freya and what she was doing. The Fire and Frost nations needed to be warned.

"I must admit," the woman went on, "it's rather odd seeing a Fire Nation soldier and a Frost Knight working together like this." Her eyes traveled back to Kirill, and Thea's heart started to pound from the gaze she was casting up at him. "I didn't think even a planetary level extermination would be able to unite you two. It's actually quite upsetting." One of her brows went up. "Which is why neither of you will leave this place." With a simple flick of her finger, a large section of the iceberg that was right under Kirill's feet collapsed.

"Kirill!" Thea screamed as he plummeted to the rocks.

He tried to land on his feet, but his knees completely buckled under him. He ended up on his side not moving even as large chunks of ice showered around him. Thea ran to him, completely disregarding the woman and the falling ice, and threw her body over his as best she could to shield him from the hazards that thankfully missed them both.

"What am I witnessing?" Freya said softly in disbelief.

Ignoring her, Thea gently rolled Kirill onto his back. He was burning up. "Kirill," she said, turning his face toward her. His eyes were closed.

Getting a good look at him, Thea gasped softly. Blue cracks in his skin were spider-webbing up his neck from under his collar. Thea's heart clenched and she gritted her teeth.

"Fitzu!" she screamed. "Get Kirill out of here!"

From her knees, Thea spun toward the woman and lifted a stream of lava nearby. With one quick gesture, she tightly wrapped it once around the woman's waist, pinning her arms to her sides so she couldn't maneuver any elements. The woman screamed in rage, and some of the lava pools erupted with the sound of it.

Time. Time. Time. Thea just needed to buy Fitzu time to get Kirill to safety.

The woman struggled to escape, but Thea's arms were stretched out far to her sides, holding the lava stream as tightly as she'd ever held her magic. She pressed her arms outward so forcefully that they trembled with the effort. She imagined the lava stream cutting the woman in half at the waist, which allowed her to keep such a firm hold.

From the corner of her eye, she saw an orange ring of fire start to burn in the stone around Kirill. As soon as Fitzu stepped into it, he crouched down, pressing his palm to Kirill's body. A narrow stream of lava erupted from under the stone, forcing the slab they were both on to rise all the way toward the rim of the volcano. Finally, Fitzu's magic vanished from sight, and she knew they were both safe.

With a final scream, the woman managed to touch a fingertip the stream of lava, which gave her instant control over it. She unraveled the lava current and arced it back behind her for a strike. Thea stood quickly and took up a battle stance, lighting up both her hands with fire magic, and waited.

The woman glared at her. "You're going to pay for that," she growled.

Thea didn't doubt that for one instant. "Well, come on."

201

———————— o ————————

Feeling dazed and exhausted, Kirill opened his eyes. The world was too bright, until a shadow leaned over him. When the sunlight stopped burning his eyes, everything came into focus and he could see Aradel's smiling face.

"Wake up sleepyhead," she said with that same playful smile she used to have as a child.

"I'm tired," he said, his tongue feeling heavy. The room looked vaguely like his bedroom at their home outside of Axion. He hadn't been there since his father died. The memories had been too painful, so he had stayed away.

"You've slept long enough," she insisted, tilting her head. "Nearly the whole day through."

He tried to stare directly at her, but the light around her was too bright. He tried to put his hand up to block it, but it didn't seem to help. The light was everywhere, and seemed to be getting brighter.

"What happened?" he asked. Aradel's hair seemed to shimmer. He didn't remember it being so silvery, but nothing seemed exactly right. It was like he was grasping at smoke trying to recollect the world.

"You've fallen asleep, and now it is time for you to get up," she insisted. She leaned closer to him. "Kirill, you need to get up."

Suddenly it wasn't Aradel's voice speaking. It was a male, and Kirill shrunk away from it. Aradel's eyes were suddenly very stern and harsh as she took hold of his hands. He tried to pull away, but she held fast. He stared down at their hands and watched hers shrivel and turn old in his grip. Looking up again, he saw Queen Vesna's face.

"Wake up," she said before giving him a sweet smile. "It isn't your time."

Water splashed on his face. Kirill woke up, gasping, and immediately groaned. Every inch of his body hurt and burned. Yet it was the parts he *couldn't* feel that worried him more. Fitzu helped him sit up, and had to hold him up when Kirill tried to lie back down. Fitzu barely burned him. Kirill immediately knew his body temperature had to be dangerously warm for that to occur.

"We need to go," Fitzu said as he thrust the water canteen in his hands. "Drink."

For once he didn't argue, and guzzled the water until every drop was consumed, and the canteen left empty. Shaking his head to get the last of the water off his hair, Kirill rested his arms on his knees. He focused on letting the water within his body expand and heal the wounds that had been caused by the steam.

When he had absorbed all the water he could, Kirill glanced around, trying to reorient himself, and saw the rim of the volcano behind him. Not trusting his legs yet, he crawled over to it and looked down. Thea was far below dodging and ducking around the strange woman's powerful magic.

Fitzu crouched beside Kirill and shook his head. "She commanded we leave."

A yell brought Kirill's attention to back down below. A blast of ice hit Thea in the shoulder and sent her sprawling. She was barely able to lift a wall of lava in front of her to melt another assault from the woman's ice magic. Clenching his teeth, Kirill began to stand. His legs wobbled a bit, but they held. It wouldn't be long before the water he drank would reinforce him.

Kirill rolled his shoulders and cracked his neck before looking Fitzu straight in the eye. "Go tell our Queens what happened. Warn them," he said, and pushed his damp hair back from his face to better gain his bearings.

Fitzu shook his head again and took a step forward. "She told me to take you with me."

Kirill put his ice shield back up around him. Thea was holding her own now, but Kirill knew that she was no match for both fire and ice. She needed him.

"Get to the boats," Kirill insisted more firmly. "I'm not leaving her alone." He put his hand out. A circular shield-shaped piece of ice formed in his palm, and he jumped over the side, dropping back down into the tremendous heat of the volcano.

Fitzu yelled his name, but Kirill ignored him and placed the under his feet to control his flight. The smoke and steam hissed against his shield, but he barely noticed. He felt stronger now.

Focused on their battle, the two women didn't notice as he descended. Everything was happening so quickly he could hardly process it. Thea spun out of the way of a ball of snow, while raising another wall of lava in front of her, to protect herself from a second ball of snow that Freya shot in her direction.

Kirill's eyes widened when Freya suddenly formed a wicked spear like icicle. Just as Thea dropped her wall of lava to make another attack, the woman shot it at her.

Kirill watched, as if in slow motion, as the spear impaled Thea's left side. The impact lifted her right off her feet and pinned her to the wall of the volcano with a loud crunch of rock and bone. Kirill stared in wide-eyed horror. Sound and sight seemed to fade from his senses at once, like a tunnel was closing in around him. All he could hear, was Thea's sharp inhale that, to Kirill, seemed to echo around the entire volcano. All he could see, was the look of shock on her face, followed by one of agony as her eyes closed. She slowly reached up and took hold of the icicle, which was painful in itself as her skin turned to stone.

Everything snapped back to normal, and Kirill looked back at Freya. She was smiling, watching Thea struggle helplessly against the wall. The curl of the woman's lips could have frozen fire.

As he neared the bottom, the disk beneath his feet began to break apart from the heat. He let it disintegrate and hit the ground, landing on one knee among the rocks. He hardly gave himself time to recover before he focused on the remains of the iceberg that still survived in this burning heat. Freya lifted her hands to attack Thea again, but before she could get a shot off, Kirill's hands swept down at an angle, loosening a large section of the iceberg, and he buried her under a massive amount of snow and ice. She gave a startled cry and fell to the ground, but it was quickly muffled by the avalanche that accumulated on top of her. She wasn't the only one who could control the iceberg.

He formed a second outer ice shield as he rushed to Thea. Her movements were already weak as she tried to pull herself free, the area around her wound was stone already. Kirill became concerned right away at the lack of blood on the ice piercing her.

"Kirill," she gasped.

Reaching her, he saw blood begin to trickle down her chin. He was no healer, but every soldier knew that usually meant her lung had been pierced and was filling with blood. Fear clutched at his chest as he touched the edge of the spear turning it to water. When it splashed away, she crumpled to the ground. Kirill dropped his outer shield and thinned out the inner shield around his skin so he didn't burn her. Grabbing her clothes in his fist, keeping his cold away from her as much as he could, Kirill lifted her and sat her up against the wall. He tugged at her collar to get a better look at her injury.

"I ordered you to go," she panted.

Kirill could hear the thick liquid gurgling deep in her lungs. Getting impatient, he finally ripped a hole in her clothes to see the sizeable wound in her chest. It had turned to stone and it was staying stone.

He forced a playful, toothy grin on his face. "When have I ever listened to your orders?"

It appeared she was going to cry, but she laughed slightly instead. "Never."

He gently tilted her forward to see the hole in her back that was bleeding just slightly. He knew then that he had heard right. The lack of blood from either wound meant it was all seeping into her lung. Kirill gently sat her back against the wall.

"It's bad, isn't it?" She wheezed, then tried to take a deep breath, but failed.

Kirill's heart sank. "Put pressure here," he said, letting a little bit of his affection for her seep into his expression as he lifted her hand to her injury. "I'm going to get you out of here."

Suddenly Kirill heard an angry yell from behind him. He turned to find Freya pushing herself out of the mount of snow. She crawled out and looked over at him just an instant before the snow exploded off her in every direction, and then disappeared into little puffs of steam before they could hit the ground again.

"You are really starting to annoy me."

Her hair was now pushed back severely away from her face. Kirill stood as both fire and ice began to crackle around her. She reminded him of a cat with an arched back, one about to hiss at him. Worse, she seemed somehow familiar to him. He couldn't place how, but he recognized her for some reason.

"You don't have to do this," Kirill said, and she paused.

"Fight you?" Freya asked. Her face hardened suddenly, "Oh trust me, I want to."

"I meant, you don't have to destroy the world," Kirill said.

"You want me to stop?" Freya asked, astonished. "Why would I stop?"

"You've proven your point," Kirill said. She lifted her hand and fire danced in her fingers. "We are no longer fighting. The Fire Nation and the Frost Nation are no longer divided. You've succeeded."

Surprise flickered in her eyes and she hesitated. But then she lifted her other hand and a ball of ice formed in it. She glanced down at each as though she couldn't decide which one to attack him with.

Normally Kirill wouldn't have tried to reason with such an enemy. But something in his gut was compelling him to try to help this young woman, to save her somehow.

"I don't think I've proven anything." Freya's voice was hard and bitter. "Until I've brought this entire world to its knees, I won't stop. I want hope to die in every person's heart, so they can know what it is like. So everyone knows what true hopelessness feels like."

Kirill put his hand up and cried out desperately, "Give Queen Vesna the chance you only gave to Queen Berselis all those years ago!" The woman paused again. "Let her accept you as she accepted the Fire Nation," he said more gently.

"All Queens are the same," she hissed, but it sounded more angry then sure.

Abruptly Kirill realized she was holding on to her bitterness. That she was blinded by it. No matter what Kirill said or did, she wouldn't listen, and that meant there was only one way out of this.

He shifted his body into a fighting stance, with his shield out in front of him, and he formed a sharp ice sword in his other hand.

A smirk touched Freya's lips as her fire and frost magic started to swirl together, in and around her hands, never touching, just twisting together in a blue and orange dance.

"Finally!" she exclaimed and then shot her hands out, sending the tornado of ice and fire toward him.

Fire: Chapter Thirty-Six

———————— o ————————

With all her heart, Thea wanted to run and fight by Kirill's side, but she couldn't move. She couldn't breathe. She closed her eyes and then opened them, trying to focus. She inhaled as deeply as she thought she could, but her lungs never fully filled with the air she so desperately needed, and thick blood came out when she exhaled. She was dying, and now Kirill was about to die with her. Which meant everyone was going to die. Well, at least she wouldn't have to wait long to see her family again.

But no. That wasn't right. Giving up? She never gave up!

Thea forced air into her lungs and brought her body forward onto her elbows. She then forced her legs to shift and move, until those, too, were underneath her so she could crawl.

She wouldn't give up. She was still alive. She crawled with nothing but desperation driving her toward Kirill and the woman.

Thea watched as the blue and orange tornado rushed toward him. Lifting both hands, Kirill suddenly took control of the blue ice of the storm, and it overwhelmed the orange, sucking it into a vortex of blue. The fire of Freya's attack was extinguished. Kirill then charged her with his shield up and his ice sword in hand. The woman lifted a wall of lava, but his sword cut right through it, forcing Freya to duck. Thea nearly grinned when he pulled it out and it was still fully intact.

She just had to get to Kirill. He couldn't face both elements alone. He was going to need her. She didn't know how yet, but he was going to need her. She knew it with every ounce of her being. It would be her last act in this life, saving her friend, and she was fine with that.

Crawl. Just a little further. Her arms trembled and blood drops fell steadily from her chin, lightly plinking down onto the rocks. One lung was not functioning she quickly realized. She coughed, and blood exploded from her mouth, splattering the stone in front of her.

Crawl! she commanded herself.

Gritting her teeth and gasping for air, she continued to crawl, though the edges of her vision were starting to go dark.

The woman shot fireballs at him in rapid sequence. It was so fast that Kirill was forced behind his ice shield. The constant drumming sounded like vibrations, and Thea couldn't help but be impressed. That was very difficult magic to master. Shifting her eyes back to Kirill, she saw his outer shield start to melt.

Thea's teeth clenched and she started panting, her shoulders moving up and down heavily with every breath. "Kirill!" she screamed as strongly as if both of her lungs were working.

From behind the shield, he met her eyes. A communication passed between them that didn't require words. All they did was see each other's eyes. Soldier to soldier, and friend to friend, they shared an idea without speaking a word.

Thea pushed herself onto her knees, despite every part of her body protesting, and fixed her determined glare on the scattered lava canals throughout the crater of the volcano. She concentrated on them, feeling their swirling heat as if each one was a part of her own body, like extra limbs. Panting, she began to raise her arms. It seemed like nothing happened for a moment, until the low roar of rushing liquid could be heard in the distance. Thea waited, watched.

Freya noticed the rumbling, which caused her to stop her assault on Kirill and look around, wondering where the disturbance was coming from. "What the..." Her voice trailed off when she spotted Thea. "You!" Thea's eyes shifted toward her. "I thought I killed you already!"

Thea knew she shouldn't try to talk—she knew she only had one lung—but she couldn't resist. "Not yet."

Suddenly the cavern started to brighten, forcing the woman to look behind her. There, she saw a half-mile-high tidal wave of lava moving toward her. The woman's jaw dropped. It wasn't moving as fast as an actual tidal wave because Thea was in complete control of its movement.

The woman looked at Thea hatefully. "I'm fireproof, you moron!" she said.

"I know," Thea murmured, too softly for her to hear.

The lava crashed down on top of the woman, drowning her in an ocean of molten rock. She screamed in frustration and thrashed, moving the lava with her own magic as she tried to wade her way through, back to Thea. Thea kept rolling the lava in her path until she was completely consumed by it. That's when the sound of a rushing wind filled the volcano. Thea's skin stiffened from the freezing cold of Kirill's magic as he turned the entire lava ocean into a solid gray stone prison with Freya deep inside. He used so much magic that frost and icicles started to form over the rock, though they gave off steam in the extreme heat.

As soon as Thea ceased using her powers, the whole area started to spin, and she was falling to the stone. She felt her arms hit first but hardly noticed when the rest followed. It was done. She was done. It was time to go now.

"Thea!" she heard Kirill shout.

She couldn't move. It was over. Kirill was alive and safe. He could go home. She could sleep.

She felt Kirill start to pick her up in his arms. She didn't even feel his cold burning her as he cradled her to his chest. She vaguely wondered what he was doing. A sound came to her ears. She wasn't sure what it was, so she listened. It was soft at first, but eventually she recognized it as Kirill's voice. He was talking to her.

"Hold on, Thea. Hold on. Just hold on."

Thea's eyes started to close. It was time to rest.

"Hold on. Hold on."

The next thing she was aware of was a rapid wind tearing at her. Her curiosity forced her to open her eyes and glance around. Her vision blurred intermittently so she couldn't process much, only flashes of information. She was still in Kirill's arms. She thought she detected them trembling. He had to be exhausted, too. The rock walls of the crater were speeding past her. He was lifting her out. Looking down, she saw an ice platform under his feet, and the bottom of the crater got farther and farther away. Her head lulled back, hitting his shoulder, and her eyes closed again. When she opened them next, she was gazing into the volcano once more, and noticed that the stone prison she and Kirill had created was now glowing orange. Freya was burning her way out.

Before she could see much else, they both erupted out the top of the volcano. The wind made her shiver and she could feel herself floating.

"Hold on," she heard him say again.

Then the wind shifted direction and she realized they were rushing downward. Looking down again, she saw the sprawl of the ocean far below her. The surface of the water sparkled and twinkled in the sunlight, giving her a magnificent light show from that height. She smiled a little. She was heading straight for it, but it felt too fast.

Thea weakly shifted her eyes up to Kirill. His head was bowed, he was panting, and he was definitely trembling. She felt it. He was going to crash. He had run out of water and thus run out of magic. She looked back down at the ocean as it came faster toward her. Well, at least she was going to die among a pretty, twinkling light show.

They hit, and everything vanished from awareness.

○

The water was less forgiving then Kirill thought it would be. It slammed into him, jarring him to his bones, leaving his body feeling tingly all over. For a moment, he forgot everything and just floated, forgetting how he had come to be floating in the water in the first place.

He quickly came back to awareness when his lungs needed air. Breaking the surface, he took in a deep breath, and immediately started looking for Thea.

"Thea!" he called hoarsely.

She wasn't floating on the surface. He dove back into the water, and there was just enough light from the fading day to see her form below, sinking slowly into the inky black depths. His arms burned, and his body protested, but he clawed and kicked at the sea to reach her. She wasn't conscious, and didn't fight or help him when his arm wrapped around her waist. Holding her tightly to his side, he fought his way back to the surface. Breaking the water again, he shook his head to keep his long hair out of his face, and pushed Thea's hair back as well. She didn't burn him, and he thought he might be too late. But then she weakly coughed up a terrifying mix of blood and water. Still, relief flooded through him.

"Kirill!" he suddenly heard Fitzu yell.

Kirill looked and was relieved to see a boat coming toward him. Fitzu was waving, and men rushed to the side to gaze at them. Kirill started toward it; he needed to get them out of the water. Who knew what lurked in those foul depths? Worse, Thea was bleeding, so if they attracted something, it wouldn't be something nice.

"Help me get her out," he called as the boat came within range.

Fitzu was shaking his head. "You're both crazy."

Fitzu got hold of one of Thea's arms, while another man grabbed the other, and they hoisted her out. Two other men helped Kirill out. Kirill knew he was too warm, but he would survive. His gazed flicked down to Thea; he wasn't so sure about her.

Kirill dropped to his knees as some blankets were put over her, and Fitzu began examining her wounds. Someone handed Kirill a canteen of water, and he hardly managed a thank you before gulping down half of it. Thankfully it didn't take long to spread.

Fitzu was feeling around the wound in Thea's chest with his hand glowing orange, trying to mend some damage, but Kirill knew his healing abilities were limited. Fitzu was trying, Kirill could see that, but his grim expression said it all.

When Fitzu glanced at him and started shaking his head, Kirill fell back against the side of the boat. After staring at him in disbelief for a moment, Kirill ran his fingers through is hair and looked down at Thea. She was so pale and lifeless he hardly recognized her.

Suddenly Fitzu froze, his expression shifting into one of panic. "No," he whispered.

Kirill looked up as Fitzu frantically started feeling around her abdomen. "What is it?" he demanded.

"She's..." his voice trailed off.

Kirill lunged forward and took the front of Fitzu's shirt in a fist. "Spit it out!"

Fitzu's eyes were wide. "She's pregnant."

Kirill looked down at Thea as she lay nearly dead between them. He slowly let go of Fitzu's shirt and took her hand. It didn't even react to his cold touch anymore. She was nearly as cold as he was and would turn to stone any minute.

"Are you sure?"

"I felt the small fire in her womb," he replied, "but it's fading with her."

Kirill hung his head a moment and squeezed Thea's hand. He sighed despite himself and closed his eyes. What he was about to do could never be undone. He quickly grabbed the water canteen and drank the last of it before tossing it to the side and reached for Thea.

Fitzu immediately moved in her defense. "What are you doing?" he asked, trying to block Kirill.

"Saving her life," Kirill told him harshly. The words had to force themselves past his lips, because in a way he was saving her, and in another way condemning her.

"Stop," Fitzu insisted, trying to keep Kirill's hands away without actually touching him. "I know what you're thinking. She would be damaged forever."

"But not the baby," Kirill insisted, staring him down. "She could carry the child to term. Tell me that isn't worth it."

He didn't answer and they simply stared at each other. Fitzu finally took in a breath and moved his hands out of the way.

211

Kirill lifted Thea's upper body, resting her in the crook of one of his arms, and touched her wound with his fingertips. Slowly he began filling it with his ice. He was careful, and precise, moving the ice intricately to form stone bridges and tubes for vital veins that had been severed by the ice spear, allowing blood flow to her heart again. But the stone would damage the muscle and tissue inside her permanently, disrupting full function of her left arm and her lung. Only time would tell if she would survive at all.

He stared down at her face intently as if willing her to live. "You have to fight," Kirill whispered to her. The irony of those words was not lost on him, though, because the damage from his magic would likely prevent her from fighting again. He wasn't sure how she would react to that, but her life was worth more to him than her forgiveness.

Fitzu was working on her other injuries, trying his best to advance her healing, as the boat hurried toward the Fire Nation's shore. "It's working," Fitzu said. "She and the baby are warming up."

When Kirill's stonework was done, he gently laid her back down on the deck, and fell against the side of the ship still clutching her hand. He let his head lull back, and gazed up at the sky, allowing himself a break to let everything that had happened sink in. They had to hurry and get to the Frost Nation, warn the queens about Freya, and prepare for battle.

Day was fading into evening when they reached the mainland. Fitzu was speaking with the men as Kirill sat with Thea. He couldn't look at her face, knowing what he would have to tell her when she eventually woke up, but he couldn't release her hand either.

"Kirill," Fitzu said, crouching by them. "One of the men lived close to here. He had two carriages and a horse corral. Some horses may have stuck close to familiar territory. We're going to try to retrieve them. I have ten more men going to their own homes to see if any of their horses stayed close by as well. We can use them to get back to the Frost Nation."

"Let's move her to shore," Kirill said, "for when they come back."

Fitzu nodded as the boat ran aground. Men jumped out and pulled it further onto the sand. A handful of other men fanned out in every direction to find horses. Looking back at the sparse company left on the boat, Kirill realized then how few Fire Nation soldiers remained.

"How many did you lose?" he asked Fitzu.

Grief was etched into every line of his face. "The piece of the iceberg she tossed out of the volcano crushed every soldier camped at its base," Fitzu bowed his head. "Kimbro included." He tuned his pained gaze to Thea, "Which is really lousy since he would have come in handy right about now."

"I am sorry," Kirill said.

Fitzu gathered Thea into his arms and picked her up. "Only the few that stayed with the boats are left," he added as Kirill jumped over the side.

The water splashed and rushed into his boots, but he hardly noticed as he reached for Thea, and Fitzu passed her into his waiting arms. Kirill held her close, feeling her growing heat through his clothes, and waded through the water toward the shore. Fitzu splashed into the water behind him.

"Mhmm?" Thea muttered, and Kirill stopped on the beach.

He carefully knelt and set her bottom down as Fitzu hurried to join them. "Thea?" Fitzu asked, leaning over Kirill.

"Hmm?" She asked and then blinked. She seemed drowsy, almost drunk.

Fitzu hurried around to kneel by her side. His hands lit up with his orange magic, and he instantly started to infuse more heat into her to warm her up.

She was having trouble breathing as expected, but she was coming around. Her eyes blinked again, but they started to focus. She glanced between the both of them, confused, and then tried to sit up.

That's when the horror filled her face.

Her wide eyes went down to her virtually useless left arm, then up to Fitzu as she struggled to sit up again. Fitzu held her down. She looked like a terrified animal that suddenly realized it was in trouble, constantly trying to lift her arm and breathe. Kirill forced himself to stare at her, even though he wanted to close his eyes, knowing he'd caused her this panic and agony.

"What's wrong with me?" she demanded, her voice trembling from shock. "Why can't I move? Why can't I—" She squeezed her eyes shut and stretched her chest upward before her eyes flew wide. "Why can't I breathe right?" She started to hyperventilate as she fought Fitzu to try and sit up. She was too weak to be much of a problem, but seeing her so frightened, punched Kirill in the gut. "What did you do?" she asked him.

Kirill braced himself. He opened his mouth to tell her, but stopped when the tears started dripping down her face. She began to weakly beat her right fist against his shoulder.

"It was an honorable death!" she wheezed.

"Thea," Fitzu tried to begin, but Thea cut him off.

"No!" She cried as her fist curled around Kirill's clothes, pulling on the fabric as she began to sob. "I know what you did! I can feel it! I'll never fight again! I'll never be what I was!"

Kirill wrapped his hand around her wrist and met her eyes. "You'll be a mother."

Thea took in a sharp gasp and went completely still as a single tear fell into her hair. "What?" She looked up at Fitzu.

"It's true," Fitzu said with a nod. "You're with child."

Her face scrunched, and this time she covered her eyes with her hand, as sobs racked her body. Kirill didn't know what to do. He just watched her as she realized that, while one life may be over, another could begin.

"Forgive me," Kirill whispered. "I could not let you or the child die when I could prevent it."

She shook her head, and Kirill was sure that meant she could not forgive him. He allowed the agony of that to spread through his heart, and it felt wretched. He was torn between going and staying. He wasn't sure where he belonged right now. He didn't want to leave her, but perhaps she wanted him to go.

"I understand," she said at last, and lowered her hand to meet his eyes. "And, yes, I forgive you." She smiled at him with tears still in her eyes.

Despite himself, he felt the edge of tears threaten. He relaxed his shoulders and let his apprehension fade away.

"Thank you," Thea whispered. "For saving my child's life, Kirill."

Kirill smiled at her, which nearly allowed a tear to escape from the corner of his eye. He quickly rubbed them though, looking as if he were just exhausted, which wasn't very far from the truth.

"You're welcome," he said gently, meeting her eyes again. "Rest now. We have a long journey back to the Frost Nation."

Thea nodded. Her eyes seemed to grow heavy instantly, and she closed them.

The battle wasn't done, but he considered her life a victory. Soon they would be back in the Frost Nation and he could warn Queen Vesna about what was coming. She would know what to do.

He glanced once more down at Thea, who was already asleep—or unconscious. Her hands rested tenderly over her abdomen, as if she were protecting her baby, even as she slept. He could see her breathing was still troubled, but it would get better with a Fire Nation healer and some time. He only prayed the Moon Goddess would see them safely home.

Darha leaned heavily over her desk as she scribbled across the parchment with financial declarations of what the Fire Nation's emergency resources had cost the Frost Nation. Luckily, the town of Hurra had been evacuated and her nation was mostly using the resources that had been abandoned. That saved a lot of currency.

She didn't know how or when she would be able to pay Queen Aradel back, but she was determined to keep track. She didn't want the Frost Nation to suffer later because she couldn't keep accurate records, and she wouldn't risk a future squabble over funds with this new tenuous peace at such an early, tender stage. This debt would be squared if it took Darha her entire royal reign. She owed the Frost Nation at least that much.

Darha had refused to take a house in Hurra. She couldn't conceive of taking up a whole house for herself when many were holding two or more families each. Right now, she resided in her royal tent from home. It reminded her of home and smelled like home, so she didn't mind at all. It was more peaceful and comfortable to work here.

"Queen Darha," Jamsun said. Darha looked up as he pushed the flap of her royal tent aside and poked his head in. "Queen Aradel has requested an audience with you, if you are willing."

Darha grinned broadly at the confused expression on Jamsun's face when he recited that last part. Queen Aradel was polite like that, adding "if you are willing" at the end of just about every request, except in emergency situations. Citizens of the Frost Nation were nothing if not polite.

"Thank you, Jamsun." Darha stood. "Please see her in," she said, and then bent over the parchment again, hoping to get a few more numbers down before she forgot them.

Darha continued writing until she heard the flap of her tent move aside again. She found Queen Aradel standing before her, and Cas right next to her, smiling.

Her cheeks immediately flushed red and she straightened up quickly in surprise. "Cas," she said, her eyes going wide. She hadn't seen him for a few days.

He grinned in that usual playful manner. "It's good to see you, Queen Darha," he said lightheartedly.

"You…you as well," she stammered. She glanced at Queen Aradel who was gazing between her and Cas with her brows drawn in confusion. Darha had to get it together. She cleared her throat uncomfortably and stepped around her desk, approaching the two tall Frost Nation natives. "Forgive me, Queen Aradel. It's good to see you as well. I heard your trip south was a success."

Aradel focused on Cas with a single raised brow before regarding Darha. "It was. Thank you." She glanced back at her escort. "Commander Cas, please wait outside."

Cas bowed to them both, but his eyes came up to Darha's, still dancing with sweet playfulness. Darha blushed harder. "As you command." Then he straightened and left the tent.

Darha watched him go, exhaling heavily when he disappeared. She realized too late, that it might have been a little too loud. Her body stiffened, and she shifted her eyes uncomfortably to Aradel.

The beautiful, regal Queen stepped forward. "Queen Darha, do you need me to reassign Cas elsewhere?" she asked, concern etched across her young face.

Darha's heart jumped up into her throat with panic. "No, no. That isn't necessary," she replied, trying to keep the conversation as professional as possible.

"Are you certain? Your cheeks were very red and you looked incredibly uncomfortable with him nearby."

"No, not at all. He doesn't bother me a bit."

Aradel's expression shifted to an almost pleading expression for the truth. "Please don't stand on the pretense of politeness. You can tell me if one of my soldiers upsets you, and I will assign another to your liking."

Darha swallowed heavily, examining the young Queen. Darha wondered briefly if she could talk to Aradel about such trivial personal matters, or if it was improper. Thea was the one she always went to for this kind of thing. Right now, she missed her sister and her heart longed for her. But gazing at the lovely Frost Nation Queen, Darha decided if they were going to be friends, she might as well open up to her.

Darha wrung her hands nervously and bit her bottom lip. "There are other reasons a man would make a woman blush."

Aradel's face brightened, and she looked suddenly like a young child again. "You like him?" she asked, surprised.

Darha exhaled heavily and deflated. "Yes. Maybe. I don't know." Aradel laughed gently, which made Darha smile and relax deeply.

217

"Please," she said, indicating a cushiony meeting area to the left of her tent. Aradel nodded and both of them made their way to the two plush red couches, where they sat down across from each other.

"I'm so sorry," Darha said, folding her hands in her lap. "It's probably inappropriate for me to bring up such a ridiculous matter."

Aradel was still grinning as she crossed one leg over the other comfortably. "I don't think it is."

That made Darha grin and she sat back in her seat, thankful that the Frost Nation Queen was so gracious and understanding. "Well, this is hardly the time to indulge romantic interests. I feel ridiculous."

Aradel tipped her head in consideration. Her foot bobbed up and down, and she smiled brightly. "Cas is handsome."

"Yes, but..." Darha shrugged helplessly. "We could never take it anywhere. We'd burn each other every time we touched. We can't hold hands, or kiss." Darha's face burned more at the mention of kissing.

Aradel nodded. "True. But not being able to touch doesn't mean you can't be attracted to each other."

Darha grinned at that. "Also true. But," she sighed, "that makes the attraction harder, knowing nothing could actually ever really happen."

Aradel's face turned sympathetic. "I'm sorry. I had not considered that."

Darha thought about Cas for one more moment before pushing his pretty green eyes and playful smile from her thoughts and focused on Aradel. "Do you have anyone?" That made Aradel blush instantly as her foot stopped moving. Darha couldn't help laughing. "I'll take those red cheeks of yours as a yes."

Aradel chuckled a little and bowed her head to gaze at the floor before she met Darha's eyes once more. "I'm not completely sure. All I know is"—she shifted her gaze to the side, and Darha could see some thoughts pass through her eyes before she looked back at her— "he makes me feel safe, and comfortable, and powerful, and...complete."

That word made Darha smile broadly. "Does it feel like a piece of you is missing when he's not near you?"

Aradel sighed and looked at Darha gratefully. "Yes. I miss him and I barely know him at all."

Darha nodded and sat back comfortably on her couch, crossing her legs. "I've never been in love before. The only reason I even know what you're talking about is because of my brother and his wife's relationship." Tears erupted into Darha's eyes thinking about Thea. She glanced away on impulse to hide them from Aradel, but decided not to. The Frost Nation

Queen could see them. It was okay. So, she met Aradel's eyes again and let her tears fall. "You've never seen soulmates like my brother and sister."

Aradel's expression shifted to deep concern as she uncrossed her legs and sat forward closer to Darha in the only gesture of comfort she could offer without touching her. "Your sister is Thea, correct? The one that took the journey with Kirill on the iceberg?" Darha nodded. Instantly Aradel's expression dropped into one deep pain and longing which made Darha curious. "Kirill is basically my brother," Aradel said, swallowing heavily. Darha's brows dropped in concern and she sat forward as well, closer to Aradel. "We were raised together in his mother's home after my parents sold my sister."

Darha's eyes went wide. "They sold your sister?"

Aradel nodded. "I ran away after that, and Kirill"—she sighed and bowed her head— "is all I have left of family. He and his mother, but his mother is slowly slipping away from us both. Soon, he is all I will have and—" she glanced to the side as a tear freely fell down her cheek, "—I fear this journey may take him away from me as well."

Darha shook her head sympathetically. Concentrating on the heat in her hand, she pushed it away from her skin, and took Aradel's hand in hers. Aradel jumped a little from the unexpected touch. Darha's skin burned and became stone stiff, but she hated seeing the woman so distraught. Aradel's gaze shifted down to their hands, and Darha felt the cold push away from Aradel's skin as well. The sting faded, and both women held on to each other without pain.

Darha smiled softly. "Thea is a fine warrior, the smartest and best of any in my nation. The few times I met Kirill, he seemed to be the same. They will return. I don't believe anything could stop either of them from doing something they set their hearts and minds to. And two stubborn warriors together are twice as good as one. They *will* come home."

Aradel squeezed Darha's hand gratefully before they released each other. After a moment of quiet gratefulness and support from each other, both women sat back on the couches, wiping tears from their cheeks.

"Thank you," Aradel said unexpectedly. "It has been a while since I have been able to speak so candidly with someone. Not since Kirill left on this journey."

Darha grinned, crossing her legs again. "I know how it goes. The calm, cool, regal composure you have to always assume as Queen."

"It's exhausting!" Aradel said abruptly.

219

The unexpected burst of exasperation from the usually reserved Queen shocked Darha at first, and then both women started laughing, each one knowing how true that sentiment was. When the merriment died down, Aradel sighed and looked at Darha with some deeper affection then she had upon entering her tent.

"At any rate," Aradel said shifting the subject. "I came here for a purpose. Everyone is running low on food, the Frost Nation included. The Gulf of Gora is nearby, and my council claims it is likely the area least affected by these disasters. I came hoping you would send a few people fishing for food. My people can no longer survive outside The Wall in this heat except for a few powerful magic users. But the drinking water it would take to sustain their magic for an extended fishing expedition is not a resource we have in abundance either."

Darha nodded her head once. "Of course. I will call for volunteers right away."

Aradel smiled and nodded before she stood from the couch. Darha stood as well. "Thank you, Queen Darha."

Darha grinned. "My pleasure, Queen Aradel."

Aradel had just taken one step toward the exit of the tent when the flap was suddenly thrown open and both Coor and Cas poured in with wide, eager eyes. Her brother was nearly panting. Darha and Aradel stopped in their tracks, and Darha's heart jumped into her throat.

"What is it?" both Queens asked at the same time.

Coor swallowed hard. "There's a rowboat crossing the river."

Darha's brows dropped. "More refugees?"

Coor shook his head.

Cas's eyes jumped between both women. "The guard tower says it might be Commander Kirill and Lady Thea."

———————— o ————————

The paddle dipped lazily into the water as they rowed slowly across the River Gora. The river had risen significantly since he left, and Kirill didn't know how long it would be before they would reach the shore. The thick fog that hovered around did nothing to help them see how far or near they could be.

Kirill glanced at Thea's sleeping face on the floor of the boat, and feared what they would find there. Traveling through the disaster that was once the Fire Nation, had made Kirill's heart clench during the entire journey. There was almost nothing left. He feared seeing the condition of his own nation, and selfishly prayed that it wasn't as decimated.

Despite the events of the last few days and their urgency to go home, the rowing motion was lulling him into a state of tranquility. Something about rowing home eased his burdened heart.

"The shore!" one of the soldiers called, which brought Kirill out of his thoughts.

Thea snuggled further into the pile of blankets as Kirill looked behind him toward shore. His eyes scanned the bank as the fog thinned, and they could see many gathering at the water's edge. There on the shore, was an out-of-breath Prince Coor. Kirill couldn't help but smile at the sight.

"Thea," he said softly as they drew closer.

"Hmm?" she muttered. She opened her eyes and blinked up at him sleepily.

"Your husband is waiting for you," he said, nodding toward the shore.

Her eyes shot open and she instantly began to sit up, her fingers desperately gripping the railing of the boat. Still in a weakened state, Fitzu had to abandon his post to help her. Hope filled her face, which made Kirill's heart flutter to life as he got to his feet and gazed toward shore. He was almost home, too.

When Thea's eyes rested on her husband, she gasped and called out, "Coor!"

Fitzu helped her to her knees at the side of the boat as Prince Coor shouted in return, "Thea!"

Thea leaned halfway out of the boat, prompting Kirill to quickly reach down and rest his hand on her back so she didn't fall into the river. Thea reached for her husband, and a moment later Coor was wading into the water toward them. As soon as Prince Coor's arms were thrown around his wife, Thea pushed herself over the side into his arms and into the river.

Kirill and Fitzu didn't try to stop her—there was no preventing them. There was no stopping the love that existed between them; Kirill was certain of that. He watched as they clung to each other, and heard them whispering and murmuring greetings and affection.

Watching them both, Kirill's concern for Thea and her injuries prompted him to speak up. "Get out of the water!" he called, doing his best to sound annoyed, yet the grin gave away his true feelings. They both turned to him, startled, but Kirill gave her a tender look that reminded her that he cared about her, and that she was an idiot for jumping into the water in her condition. "Get to a healer," he said more gently.

Thea threw him a grateful look and nodded before turning back to her husband. Her laughter rung out across the shore as Coor reached into the water and picked her up like he was carrying a princess across the threshold. In each other's arms now, they kissed, and Kirill averted his eyes to give them a measure of privacy.

Soldiers jumped into the water and started pulling the boat the rest of the way ashore. Kirill joined them. His boots filled with water, but he hardly noticed as Aradel and Queen Darha came running toward them. Kirill stopped in his tracks when he saw her. She seemed thinner, and all the youthfulness of her face had been lost. She had a regal and almost severe air. Her face was a little sharper, more mature, and for a moment he didn't recognize her.

"Kirill?" she said breathlessly, so quietly he almost hadn't heard. It was Aradel.

He abandoned the boat and strode through the water as quickly as he could. He hardly noticed anything happening around him except for the expression on her face. He knew he must look as strange to her as she did to him. This journey had changed him, but something about Aradel had changed as well.

When he was out of the water, he could see tears forming in her blue eyes. He could see she was fighting them, but they glistened anyway. When he came up to her, he stopped short of hugging her. They hesitated only a moment, inches apart, before he engulfed her in his arms. Kirill buried his face in her neck and hair as he breathed in her familiar scent. She smelled like home.

"You came back," she whispered. He could hear the astonishment and the tears, mingled with relief and love.

"I came back," he agreed.

He could feel her crying against him and shifted his head closer to her neck to hold her tighter. Something cold and powerful brushed against his chin. Startled, Kirill pulled back. He glanced down at her and noticed the pearls around her neck for the first time. They glowed softly as Aradel sniffled.

"The moon pearls." he said, blinking at them. Then his eyes shifted to hers. "Queen Vesna?"

Aradel shook her head. "I am Queen now."

His heart ached for their lost queen—he would miss Queen Vesna—but it raced with joy at being home and seeing the pearls on Aradel's neck. "Should I bow to you?" he asked playfully.

"No," she said, laughing a little despite the tears. "Never."

"Kirill?" Fitzu's voice called, breaking the moment, as he waited by the boat.

Kirill turned, bringing Aradel with him as he went toward Fitzu. He wasn't prepared to let her go, his family. He had not realized how much he'd missed her until he had seen her face. He hadn't realized how much she mattered to him, and now she was Queen. His Queen.

"What?" he asked, trying to keep the annoyance from his voice.

Fitzu spoke only one word, but it was enough. "Freya."

Kirill was snapped out of his emotional homecoming and back into his duty as a Knight of the Frost Nation. He turned to face Aradel. "We need to gather an army," he told her and saw surprise flash over her face. "There was a woman at the volcano. She was the cause of all of this."

"A woman?" Aradel asked, bewildered.

"She was heating the volcano, causing these disasters," Thea called out of the blue.

Kirill spun to the sound of her voice, and his heart jumped into his throat when he saw Prince Coor still holding her in his arms on the shore. "I told you to get to a healer," he said firmly, his concern for her bringing out his Commander-of-the-Guard voice.

"A healer is on the way," Queen Darha called back to him as she directed Fire Nation magic users to melt some stone and rise a healing hut right on the shore.

"My my," a voice broke in. He turned to see Freya over the river. "Look at this happy scene." His eyes went wide. "Fire and Frost united."

She wore the same clothes, as well as the same expression of hate. She walked on the water that froze under her feet with each step. Pausing, she put a hand on her hip, and her eyes wandered over them. "All the heroes have returned. It is so sweet that it makes me want to vomit."

Aradel suddenly gasped. "Mera?"

Kirill's brows furrowed together as Aradel's hands came up to her face, and she tried to step toward the woman. His arms quickly wrapped around her waist, barring her movements, as Freya's eyes shot over to them both. Aradel reached down to try to push his arm aside but he refused to let her go, holding her tightly against him.

A menacing smile slowly spread across Freya's face, and Kirill realized she was gazing at Aradel's throat. She pointed as she spoke, "I know what those are. Tell me young Queen, will you trade your powerful pearls for the lives of your people? If I have them, I might just go back to my volcano and leave you alive." She paused, as if pondering. "I met a Queen once. I wonder if you are all the same."

"No," Kirill all but growled, but Aradel rested a hand on his arm around her stomach as if to calm him.

"Freya?" Aradel asked compassionately. "Is that your name?"

"Yes," Freya responded suspiciously.

Kirill had often seen concern and fear in Aradel's eyes for the well-being of her people, and it was the same expression of compassion and fear he saw now on her face. His brows dropped in confusion. Compassion and fear for the well-being of this vile woman? He couldn't understand it.

"Freya, will you give me a day to consider?" Aradel asked hopefully.

When Kirill opened his mouth to protest, Aradel glanced at him over her shoulder with a fierce look that made him bite his tongue. Although Kirill didn't like it, Aradel was queen, and he wouldn't disobey her. Even if it was a nonverbal command.

Thea didn't let him down though.

"No way," she called from Coor's arms. Freya's attention turned to his friend who, though still terribly injured, could conjure a fierce look of defiance. "Kirill and I might not have been able to take you on our own, but there is no way you can take both of our armies!"

"What's left of them," Freya added with a smirk.

Thea's teeth clenched, and Kirill couldn't help but silently cheer her on. "Woman, I will absolutely—"

"Lady Thea!" Aradel suddenly called with a level of force Kirill didn't expect from her, silencing Thea immediately. It wasn't anger compelling Aradel to speak so, he noted. It was concealed desperation. "This is not a matter for you to consider," she said a little more gently.

Kirill saw the pleading look in Aradel's eyes and realized that Thea did, too. Thea nodded graciously.

Aradel turned back to Freya. "Will you allow me the time to consider it?"

Freya glanced around the shoreline at all the faces. "Very well," she finally said. "You have one day. But when you make your decision, you meet me back on the river, alone."

"Agreed," Aradel responded, and then Freya turned and was swallowed by the mist.

"Aradel?" Kirill asked as she turned toward him. There was confusion and agony on her face as she stared blankly at his chest, seeming dazed. "Aradel, what is it?"

Her eyes slowly turned up to meet his. Seeming to suddenly focus, though clearly still feeling unsettled, Aradel tucked some loose strands of her hair behind her ear and pushed all emotions off her face, hiding them from him. "She just reminds me of someone," Aradel responded with a forced smile. Kirill eyed her suspiciously, letting her know silently that he wasn't buying it. She put an arm around his back and propelled him toward a Frost Nation healer. "Come. Let's get you tended to."

Fire: Chapter Forty

Soon after the wench was swallowed by mist, the Fire Nation magic users finished the healing hut for Thea, and Meyer had arrived from Hurra. Her assistant had taken Thea from Coor's arms and brought her inside. Meyer had kept him from entering. He begrudgingly obliged, though it took every ounce of his willpower not to pace outside the door.

With his wife returned, he felt whole again, but it looked bad. He could tell Thea's wounds were debilitating. Coor prayed to the Sun God, the Moon Goddess, and whatever other gods that existed for her to remained intact. He needed her to survive, no matter how that occurred. He couldn't exist in a world without Thea.

"Coor," Darha said.

He felt her gently take his hand and interlace her fingers with his. Coor squeezed, but didn't wavier from the entrance of the hut.

"Let Meyer do her job," Darha said calmly.

Coor sighed and let Darha guide him away from the hut to where the Frost Knight was being tended to with Queen Aradel. The two of them were talking, though Coor couldn't hear what was being said. It probably had something to do with the compassion Coor had noticed in Queen Aradel's eyes when dealing with the woman that was responsible for the destruction and devastation of his nation. Coor had a very hard time right now not glaring at the Frost Nation Queen. If that Freya woman was responsible for the decimation of his homeland, and the Frost Nation Queen was kind toward her, Aradel would swiftly find herself his enemy.

As they approached, the Frost Knight quickly glanced toward them. Coor noticed him regard Darha with a new, interesting light, a softness that Coor hardly recognized from the Knight he had first met on the Frost Nation shore. Thea had softened him in their time together, had changed him. She had to be the reason. Before Coor could contemplate it further, Kirill suddenly stood and approached Darha with purpose, leaving his healer behind him.

Noticing him, Darha paused in her steps and stared, confused.

"Queen Darha," he said when he was in front of her. He bowed at the waist and then straightened. "Traveling through your nation, I have seen the devastation." He sighed as his expression became sympathetic. "I see what you have lost, and I am truly sorry."

Coor saw Darha swallow heavily before she nodded in acknowledgement. "Thank you for such kind condolences, Sir Knight." She smiled at him then, though it was a little forced. "I'm glad you have returned safely."

Coor caught the concern on Kirill's face as he looked past them toward the hut Thea was in. "I wish we both could have returned safely."

Coor realized suddenly that Kirill cared about Thea. He cared very much about her, and he was blaming himself for the damage done, whatever the extent of it might turn out to be. The concept seemed impossible mere months ago, but it was undeniably clear on Kirill's face.

"Thank you," Coor said before he realized he even wanted to say anything. His voice cracked with emotion, but he hardly cared as he held his hand out to Kirill. "Thank you for bringing my wife back home to me."

Kirill glanced down at his hand before meeting his eyes with slight surprise. He then took a step forward and firmly grasped Coor's hand. "We got each other back home."

Coor nodded once, even as his heart continued to strain against the walls of his chest, trying to reach out for Thea. He wanted to hold her and kiss her, forever if possible, but he had to be content that she was home for right now.

Aradel stepped up beside Kirill to join them and Coor resisted glaring at her. "What are you going to do?" he asked a little more harshly than he intended.

"Coor," Darha said in gentle astonishment.

Coor didn't take his eyes from Aradel though. She turned her head away from him slightly under his intense stare. "I don't know."

"What do you mean you don't know?" Coor demanded. "She wants your moon pearls. Your heritage. Your power!"

"Coor!" Darha cried in a tone that would usually silence him, but he was too emotional to yield.

"You can't seriously be considering handing them over to her!"

"Of course not!" Aradel cried with sudden conviction. "I would rather die first!"

Coor pressed his lips together and let out a breath before bowing his head, partly in shame for speaking so callously and out of turn, but also in relief that she wasn't considering turning the pearls over. "I'm sorry, Queen Aradel," he said gently. "I just…" He glanced back at the hut Thea was in before looking back at the ground in front of him. "I'm not in my right mind at the moment. Please forgive me."

227

Coor shifted his eyes up to her and saw her face soften. "Of course, Prince Coor," she said with just as much conviction as she did compassion.

"Aradel," Kirill said gently. "Freya can wield both fire and frost."

Every eye in the group snapped to Kirill's face in astonishment.

"What?" Darha breathed.

"How is that possible?" Coor asked.

Kirill just shook his head. "I don't know, but Thea and I together couldn't take her. We only managed to escape by a hairsbreadth. She is undefeatable, resistant to *both* our nation's magic, as well as incredibly powerful at wielding the two." Kirill met Aradel's eyes and shook his head. "You can't take her alone."

Queen Aradel shook her head as well. "I can't let her have the moon pearls."

"Aradel, no," Kirill argued. "You need to trust me. She is too powerful for you, and you know I have never doubted your power before."

"Then why are you doubting it now?" Aradel countered.

"Thea is right," Coor said. "She can't take both our armies."

Kirill nodded at Aradel. "Thea and Coor are right."

"We've lost too many people," Aradel exclaimed unexpectedly, silencing everyone. "I'll not let her take another person from either of our nations!" she said passionately. Coor couldn't help admiring that kind of courage; it was his wife's kind of courage. "I believe I can resolve this," Aradel said more softly. "I have the moon pearls, and they have never failed us before."

"Listen," Darha said, resting her hand on Coor's chest as she looked at Aradel. "We have a day to consider what we should do. We can take some time to rest and reunite with our loved ones. Time I think all of us need."

Kirill and Queen Aradel glanced at each other before looking back at her and Coor. "Agreed," Aradel conceded. She gazed compassionately into Darha's eyes. "Please give Thea my best wishes."

Darha nodded as Coor's heart started to pound at the notion of getting back to his wife.

"Kirill and I will come tomorrow so we can continue to discuss these matters further," Queen Aradel added.

Darha nodded. "Very well." She met Kirill's eyes. "I wish you a peaceful rest, Sir Knight."

Kirill nodded. "You as well, Queen Darha."

Coor met Kirill's eyes, and the two of them simply nodded at each other. Then Coor and Darha headed for the stone hut, while Aradel and Kirill headed for the guard tower north of The Wall. Everyone else in the vicinity dispersed.

Both Coor and Darha waited outside only a few moments before Meyer came out. Coor pounced on her immediately. "How is she?" he asked urgently.

Meyer met his eyes as she wiped her hands on a clean cloth. "The length of time her wound and lung were kept stone saved her life, but she will be damaged forever." Coor swallowed heavily. "The damaged muscles in her left arm will render it almost completely useless, and she'll likely have rapid breathing attacks every time she overexerts herself."

Coor swallowed heavily. "But she'll live?"

Meyer smiled brightly, Coor thought a little *too* brightly for such condemning news. "Yes, she will live." She gazed over his shoulder at Darha. "However, she can no longer be a scout or a soldier. She can't even lift a bow anymore with that left arm, and any excessive output in battle or heavy patrol will induce the breathing attacks."

"Thank you, Meyer," Darha said.

"Can I see her?" Coor asked, trying to keep the desperation from his voice.

"Of course," she replied and stepped aside.

Coor glanced back at Darha who smiled. "Go ahead. I'll wait my turn." Flashing a brief smile of appreciation, Coor ducked into the hut.

Thea was lying on the bed with a beaming smile. "Hey," she said as a tear slid across the bridge of her nose and dropped into her loose hair that fanned out against the pillow.

Coor quickly moved to the bed and crouched beside her, gathering one of her hands into both of his. "Hey yourself," he said softly. He gazed into her light gray eyes for a long moment, savoring the sight of them. Then he swallowed heavily and glanced down at her left shoulder before meeting her eyes again. "Did Meyer tell you?"

Thea nodded. "My career as a badass is done," she said.

As shocking as her acceptance was to Coor, the statement still caused them both to crack up quietly together. When the laughter died down, Thea gazed up at him with her eyes filled with the most light and adoration for him he'd ever seen—and Thea had never been shy when it came to looking at him with affection. Something was different, and Coor wondered if something was wrong.

229

He brought her hand up to his lips and kissed it several times. "How can you be so accepting of this? You have to leave the scouts—the soldiers, your men, Fitzu."

Thea took in a breath, and slowly lowered his hand to rest on her stomach. Coor's brows dropped in confusion, as another tear slid into her hair. "Because you're going to be a father."

Coor felt his heart squeeze, and then his wife's smile registered, and his heart exploded. Hardly able to believe what he was hearing, he leaned down and gathered her in his arms. He couldn't speak; he could only try to breathe as Thea chuckled gently over his shoulder.

He pulled away and looked down at her, stammering, "We...we're...you're...?"

Thea nodded. Coor looked down at her stomach, and then gently pressed his face into it. Thea laughed a little harder, though it was still weak. Coor thought about his child, right there, growing, living, forming. His baby. Thea's baby. Their baby. He kissed her stomach a couple times before hovering over her again.

"I love you," Coor said.

Thea smiled. "I know. I love you, too."

Coor kissed his wife deeply. He was never letting her go again— not her, and not their child.

Frost: Chapter Forty-One

——————— o ———————

The morning light breeched the treetops as Aradel braided her hair, fingers over strands of slivery blond, again and again until the end. Her eyes were unfocused as her deft hands worked. At the end of the braid, she tied a pale blue ribbon into a bow.

Freya. She was the one thing on Aradel's mind, the thing that had kept her tossing throughout the night. Sleep had been far off and unaccommodating. Her mind had raced as she considered all the angles, all the choices, and in the end, she knew she needed to go alone. Darha wouldn't understand, and Aradel wasn't ready to explain; so Aradel also made the decision not to tell her. Worse still was Kirill. He might understand, but he would stop her. He wouldn't think her life was worth the risk—especially not now that she was Queen.

She wouldn't risk either of them after they had been through so much already. The Fire Nation needed their Queen, and Kirill had already done enough for the Frost Nation. The numerous light blue scars on his skin would never disappear. They would always remind him of the journey he'd taken, and what he had endured. How could she look at him and those scars and ask him to face Freya again?

Her fingers absentmindedly played with the moon pearls at her throat. They would protect her if Aradel had misjudged her own memories. If Kirill was right, and Freya was too far gone, or wasn't who Aradel suspected she was, then they would find a new queen if she failed.

Abruptly she stood with a fire in her eyes and went to the door. When she opened it, Cas turned to her with a startled expression. She froze instantly, and then smiled easily at him, hoping she could keep the strain from her expression.

"Commander Cas," Aradel said, and he bowed his head respectfully. "How fortuitous that you should be here."

"I was assigned for your protection," Cas informed her and kept his head bowed. Likely to keep the smile hidden, but she could see it nonetheless.

"Kirill," Aradel said, unable to keep the amused smile from her own lips. He had been home less than a day and was already protecting her. He must have been unnerved by their conversation the day before and

231

decided she needed protection from herself. Perhaps he was right, but her mind was made up.

"Yes, Queen Aradel," Cas confirmed before straightening, the soft smile still touching his lips.

"I need you to bear a message," Aradel said, and his smile faded. She saw he was instantly suspicious.

"I cannot leave my post," Cas insisted, though with some hesitation.

"I command you to bring Queen Darha here," Aradel informed him and saw his jaw set at her words. He knew she was up to something but wouldn't dare speak it aloud. She didn't like to issue orders, but this time it was necessary. "I have urgent matters to discuss with her."

"Your majesty, please," Cas said clearly torn. "Kirill will not like this. Allow me get another guard to carry your message."

Her face hardened as she replied carefully, "I am your Queen. Go and do as I command."

He bowed again, this time from the waist, before hurrying down the hall. She watched him go, and let her eyes fall downcast. She was thoughtful a moment, wondering if Darha would understand why she had sent Cas to her. Would her newfound friend know that she wanted her to be happy, and that love always found a way?

With that thought, she closed the door to her chambers and rushed down the hall in the other direction. She lifted her skirts, hurrying down the steps of the guard tower. She knew exactly what Kirill had ordered Cas to do—guard her and make sure she didn't do anything stupid. Yet here she was, hurrying to the temporary makeshift stables near Hurra.

It was early, and there were very few people around. The few who saw her bowed and called her "Queen Aradel" or "My Queen." She smiled to them all and bid them a solemn good morning, but her feet never paused. Not until she entered the stables where some elk were kept with the Fire Nation's horses.

At the far end, Tallus stood with his back to her as he brushed one of the elks. Her eyebrows furrowed together before she could help it, and a frown touched her lips. She hadn't expected that seeing him would cause her resolve to waver. She walked carefully across the ground toward him. He glanced over his shoulder, and his face instantly lit up at seeing her. He set the brush on the edge of the stable before meeting her halfway.

"Good morning, Queen Aradel," he told her with a smile that was as bright as the sun rise behind him.

"Good morning, Tallus," Aradel replied. "I thought we agreed you'd call me Aradel?"

"Good morning, Aradel," he corrected as the corners of his eyes crinkled. "Where are you on your way to this morning?"

"I came to see you," Aradel said, and his smile faltered in surprise.

Silence fell between them as his eyes searched her face. She could all but see the wheels working in his mind, and she let them go without encouragement. Instead, she stood completely still and waited.

Finally, a grin returned to his face and he said softly, "I'm glad."

Aradel took a single stride forward. Her chest ached from the look on his face, and she knew the feeling in his eyes mirrored her own. She knew he would never take a step forward, not just because he wouldn't rush her, but because of what she was—Queen. So, she took another step and closed the distance between them.

When she lifted her face, she could feel the heat from his breath on her forehead. She could feel the gentle rise and fall of his chest as he continued to stare at her, smoldering her with the heat of his gaze.

She averted her eyes before carefully lifting her right hand. Uncurling her fingers, she rested her palm on his chest. Tallus brought his hand up across her fingers, and wrapped them around hers, holding her hand. Lifting her eyes to his again, partly in hope, partly in agony, the breath she had been holding was suddenly released. She tipped her head back, and he bent his down. Closing her eyes, she felt his lips press against hers. It was tender and sweet, exactly how he was. She would forever treasure that feeling upon her lips and the way her heart raced.

Aradel slowly dropped back to her heels and opened her eyes. "I wondered if it would be that perfect," she whispered.

His lips curved into a half smile. "You are a constant surprise, Aradel," he told her, and her stomach flip-flopped at the way he uttered her name.

She averted her eyes a moment and swallowed. When she looked back, her expression was apologetic. "I have to go."

He nodded understandingly. "The constant demands of being Queen."

He let her hand go, and she reluctantly retracted it before walking around him to the elk he had been tending to, and climbed onto its back. Tallus seemed a little surprised at her abrupt departure. She knew it would seem strange for her leave the safety of the guard tower without at least one member of her personal guard in attendance.

Just before she reached the end of the stable, she paused and looked back at him. "Tallus?"

"Yes?" he asked. He must have sensed something was off because he appeared to be a little worried, but he asked her nothing, for which she was thankful.

"I'm happy we met," she told him before turning the elk and riding it hard toward the River Gora.

Tallus didn't know about Freya or her demands. He was the part of her life she wanted to keep safe. She hoped he would know her like Kirill did one day, but for now, she would leave him safely in the dark.

The trees pressed in around her, enveloping her in shadows. The light of the early morning hadn't penetrated there yet, and the dew on the grass was kicked up by the elk. Her skirts flapped in the wind, and her braided hair bounced against her back with the movement of the elk.

Traveling up river a ways, she urged the elk to stop when she came to a large frozen section that stretched far into the mist; something that would be impossible in this heat without magic.

"Freya?" she called across the ice.

The elk shied a little, dancing from side to side as it sensed what was coming. Suddenly the fog over the river began to lift. Tendrils of heat wafted against her face, and Aradel wrapped herself in a thicker ice shield.

When the fog had completely dissipated, Freya could be seen walking across the ice toward her. Aradel patted the side of the elk to calm him before dismounting. It hesitated only a moment before returning to the safety of the trees.

"Well, I can't say I expected this." Freya called.

"Who is your mother?" Aradel asked abruptly as she stepped onto the ice.

Freya looked both annoyed and curious. "What does that matter?" she snapped as a fireball formed in her hand. "I'm not here to talk, give me the moon pearls or everyone dies."

"Mera," Aradel said softly as she neared the young woman. Shock flickered across Freya's features. "Her name was Mera wasn't it?"

"How do you know that?" she demanded, the fire in her hand shrinking slightly.

Aradel pressed her lips together and bowed her head in relief, and joy, and some fear before meeting Freya's eyes again. Her eyes washed over her face, and hair, and body, and her heart ached knowing who she was, knowing that a piece of Mera not only lived, but was standing a few feet in front of her. Aradel's own flesh and blood, which she'd thought was lost to her so many years ago.

"Mera was my sister," Aradel told her. The fireball in Freya's hand vanished all together with a weak puff of smoke left in its wake. "You look exactly like her," Aradel said with tears in her eyes.

Freya considered her words in astonishment for a moment. Aradel hoped that this gamble paid off, and she would have a niece that she could get to know and love. A part of her sister could live on in this world, and this time, Aradel could protect her.

"I don't believe you," Freya finally said, pointing at her as a hateful smirk spread across her face. "You're trying to trick me to spare your nation. Bad news," her voice dropped to a mocking whisper, "it's not going to work."

"It isn't a trick," Aradel insisted, taking a step forward. "I can still see my sister's face the day she left, the day my parents sold her. That face, her face, my sister's face still haunts all my dreams to this day!" Aradel bowed her head and took in a desperate breath to control herself before turning her gaze back up to Freya. "Stop this, stop everything, and come home with me. You are my family." Aradel held out a hand to her. "Take my hand and come back with me. I will take care of you."

Freya sneered. "Well done. You almost had me." Her eyes remained severe, and the fire that had been extinguished, suddenly ignited in Freya's hand again.

"Stop!" Aradel cried, though she already knew she had lost her. "You are my family!"

"I'll never stop," she replied casually, as though she were commenting on the weather. "Not until every last person is dead." Her eyes narrowed on Aradel. "I think I'll start by killing you."

———————— o ————————

Darha awoke to the sound of arguing outside her tent. Two men were sharing heated words and, though she was groggy, it sounded like a struggle was ensuing. Coming a little more awake, she propped herself on her elbows and tried to listen to the exchange.

One voice stuck out the most. "I must speak with Darha now!"

Darha's eyes flew wide. It was Cas. He sounded upset, and a little desperate. She kicked herself out of her covers and ran to the entrance of her tent without bothering to grab a robe. Throwing the flap aside, she stepped out and saw Jamsun and Rhett both holding Cas back and trying to push him away.

"What is the meaning of this?" Darha asked, addressing her soldiers.

"Darha!" Cas said urgently. Then at the glares of Jamsun and Rhett, he cleared his throat and added, "Queen Darha, I must speak with you."

Jamsun stepped forward. "Forgive us, your majesty. We knew you were asleep. He insisted on seeing you and nearly barged into your tent."

"Rhett, release him!" Darha commanded. Rhett shoved Cas away from the tent and the two men untangled. Darha glared at Jamsun. "How is it not clear to you that Commander Cas has an emergency?"

"I—I'm sorry, majesty. I didn't –"

"Cas is not a threat to me," Darha said firmly. She met Cas's eyes as a gentle smile pulled at the corners of his lips. "He will never be a threat to me," she said more softly.

Cas shook his head. "Never."

Darha smiled and nodded. "Come in."

Cas ducked into her tent first as Darha addressed Jamsun once more. "Don't ever keep Cas from seeing me again, is that clear?"

"Yes majesty," he confirmed with a bow.

Darha ducked into her tent and immediately approached Cas. "What's wrong?" she asked, already a little self-conscious now that they were alone.

Cas politely averted his eyes, though the corners of his mouth turned up in an adorable soft smile. "Would you prefer to get decent first?" he asked, avoiding looking at her in the small black silk nightgown she was wearing.

Darha couldn't help but grin. "If I thought I had time to get decent, I wouldn't have run outside my tent like this," she said, gesturing to herself.

Cas turned his eyes to her and unashamedly glanced briefly down her appearance. "I don't mind. I just don't want you to be uncomfortable."

Darha smiled. "You don't scare me."

Cas gazed at her in the most breathtaking way; with the playfulness gone, and just a very real longing. Her heart raced. She would have given anything for a moment with him to maybe, hopefully kiss his lips. But clearly something of urgency had brought him here.

Darha shifted from romantic mode into Queen of the Fire Nation mode. "What's wrong, Cas?"

Darha saw him shift into soldier-of-the-Frost-Nation mode as well. "It's Queen Aradel."

Darha's brows dropped. "Is she well?"

"She is well, but she sent me to summon you to her chambers. I'm fairly certain, though, that it was just a distraction to get me to leave my guard of her."

Darha eyes flew wide. She ran to her closet, grabbed the first long red gown within reach, and threw it over her head. She hadn't worn her gowns in months, but it was the fastest thing she could throw on—though it wasn't really that fast. She had a length of buttons up her side to fasten.

"Jamsun!" she cried, and he poked his head in. "Get me a horse quickly!" Jamsun vanished from sight.

Darha knew exactly what Aradel was doing. Darha knew, because if she had been in Aradel's situation, Darha would have done the exact same thing. She was going to meet that Freya woman alone. Darha should have known! She should have stayed with Aradel, or guarded her herself or something, or anything! Now she was in danger.

As Darha struggled with the buttons of her gown, Cas appeared on a knee beside her, and started fastening them himself. She gazed down at him and tried to catch her breath as his deft fingers quickly worked up the line of buttons. Her heart ached so badly to touch him that she could hardly stand it; so, she wouldn't stand it.

When he finished and his eyes came up to meet hers, Darha pushed the heat away from her lips and palms. Gently taking his face in her hands, she leaned down and pressed her lips to his. Cas's shoulders went limp when they touched, and he clutched the waist of her gown, taking a fistful

237

of the material in each hand so he didn't burn her, but could still hold her in some fashion. Cas must have been practicing to press the cold away from his own lips because hers didn't turn to stone. It was just her soft flesh on his, and Darha could hardly breathe from the feel of it.

After pulling away, she smiled down at him. "You've been expecting me to kiss you like this, I see."

"No," he said softly and smiled. "Just hoping."

Darha grinned and gazed back into Cas's eyes for a moment longer before going to her closet again. She had to flex her fingers to get the stone stiffness out of them from his freezing skin. She put on a quick, but impractical pair of gold slip-on shoes, and carefully took her gold circlet from its pillow and rested it on her brow.

"Come," she said and hurried to the exit of her tent. Throwing open the flap, they both stepped out. "I need you to inform Sir Kirill of what's happened with Queen Aradel," Darha said to Cas, and headed for the horse Jamsun was bringing to her.

"What will you do?"

"That dreadful Freya woman told Aradel to meet her on the river, so I'm going to ride the shore until I find her. She can't be far. Tell Sir Kirill to watch for my signal of fire when I locate her, and to bring everyone he can muster."

Cas bowed at the waist and headed for his elk in a hurry. Reaching her horse, Darha threw her leg over it and was ready to race off when Cas called her name. She looked over her shoulder and saw him staring longingly after her from the back of his own majestic beast.

"Please be careful."

Darha smiled and nodded, then gripped the reins in her fists, and faced forward. "Ya!" she called and kicked her horse into a fast gallop.

The trees were a gray blur in the morning light as she headed for the river. Reaching the water's edge, she turned her horse west, and opened the stallion up to run even faster. Darha's hair flew out behind her and the wind burned her cheeks from the speed at which she rode. Her gaze constantly traversed the river, searching for any sign of either woman.

A mile up the shore, Darha picked up on a trail of cloven hooves in the dirt alongside which she was galloping. Elk hooves. Aradel had to have come this way. Darha spurred her horse faster, ducking down behind its neck to diminish the sting of the wind.

It wasn't long before she saw the river was white along the horizon. Ice. One section of the River Gora up ahead had been turned to ice, and it was definitely too hot outside for that not to be powerful frost magic. Another half a mile, Darha could make out two struggling silhouettes. Blasts of orange and blue lit up the distance they were both shrouded in.

"Come on," Darha said through clenched teeth to her horse, though she knew it was absolutely pushing its limits to go as fast as it was already.

When Darha could finally see the blue of Aradel's gown and the black of Freya's, she yanked on the reins of her horse, stopping it so fast it reared up on its hind legs and gave a loud cry of complaint before settling. Looking up at the overcast sky, Darha shot a blast of her fire magic high above the treetops into the clouds, signaling to Kirill where his Queen was. Darha dismounted and, pushing the heat away from her feet and ankles, headed over the ice to the two struggling women. Neither was aware of her presence yet—or didn't care—and continued to struggle with each other.

As Darha neared, Aradel was suddenly thrown onto her back by a blast of ice. She hadn't even finished sliding backwards before Freya lit up another blast in her hands and shot it toward her. With a yell, Darha threw an arm out and sent her own blast of fire magic, blocking and melting Freya's attack into water that rained down harmlessly between the two women.

Aradel spun to look over her shoulder as Freya's astonished eyes came up. Not taking her narrowed gaze off Freya's face, Darha pushed her heat away from her hand, and reached for Aradel. Aradel took it, and Darha pulled the Frost Nation Queen to her feet.

Freya's astonished expression melted into a snarl. "This must be my lucky day. Now I get to take out *both* queens!"

With that, Freya's hands went out to her sides. From the depth of the river she brought up pinnacles of ice that rose over fifty feet high on one side. On the other, lava bubbled up from the surface of the water, reaching the same heights.

Darha was oddly undaunted, and both she and Aradel lit up their hands with their magic. Darha was no warrior, but she loved her nation and her people more than herself, and this woman threatened them all. The Fire Nation had already been destroyed; she would not allow such devastation to come to the Frost Nation as well.

Freya shot the lava at Aradel and the ice at Darha.

Darha deflected by moving her fire magic in a fast, horizontal figure-eight, quickly melting it as it flew toward her. Her flimsy shoes were soaked instantly and her feet became stone stiff. She couldn't blaze her core to warm them, though, lest the frozen river melt under her.

Aradel created a spinning tornado of snow that sucked up the lava that threatened her. The hot orange substance slowly dulled and cooled in the vortex, until Aradel was spinning chunks of stone, which she then cast into the river.

Clenching her teeth, Freya shot rapid orbs of fire at Aradel, from which Aradel protected herself by lifting a thick wall of ice. Darha went on the offensive while Freya was distracted with Aradel. She reached to the river depths, melting the bedrock, and pulled it rapidly to the surface. A stream of molten stone exploded from the water, and Darha split it into a thousand tiny pieces, causing a fire storm to rain down over the despicable woman's head. Freya was just barely able to conceal herself in a shield of ice five feet thick as the fire barraged her. With a loud hissing sound, and a cloud of steam, Darha's attack reduced the ice shield to almost nothing, but left the woman unharmed.

While Freya's shield was thin, Darha expected Aradel to attack, but the other woman hesitated, looking horrified. Aradel only expanded her wall of ice out in front of Darha to protect her as well. Observing Aradel, Darha realized there was a conflict of emotions on her face. She realized Aradel hadn't attacked Freya once yet. She had been on the defensive only.

Darha's attention was drawn to the ice wall when it began to warp and waver. Suddenly it exploded toward both women. Darha threw her arms up, igniting a powerful shield of fire around her as shards of ice flew at her face. Every splinter from the obliterated wall melted against her magic, but Darha was thrown back fifteen feet. Aradel called out something that Darha couldn't hear, but it sounded like some sort of plea to Freya.

Picking herself up, Darha contemplated the scene and shook her head. This was ridiculous! They were too evenly matched and this battle was getting them nowhere. Neither one had an edge over the other. All of it was made worse by Aradel's apparent unwillingness to attack the woman.

Aradel pulled a massive amount of water from the river. It splashed over the side of the ice and rushed toward Freya. Freya's gestures indicated she tried to stop it, but it was too much. The moon pearls glowed brightly as it surrounded her completely, encasing her in a bubble that hardened into thick ice.

That's when Darha felt something strange from somewhere unexpected. She narrowed her eyes on the frost magic that danced over Aradel's hands, and realized she could feel *heat* there. Heat? In ice? There wasn't much, only a minute trace of it, but it was there. Curious, Darha held her hands up toward the magic.

"What are you doing?" Aradel cried over her shoulder. Already Freya was heating her way out of her temporary cage.

Darha didn't answer; she couldn't answer, because she wasn't sure herself. Feeling the small levels of heat in Aradel's ice magic, Darha pulled on them, trying to bring them toward herself. Nothing happened at first, so Darha pulled harder.

"Darha!" Aradel called as Freya stepped casually out of her icy enclosure.

Freya was preparing to attack again, so with every particle of power and energy Darha had inside of her, she pulled on the heat in Aradel's ice magic, forcing it toward her.

As soon as it budged, as soon as she felt the heat draw toward her, something incredible happened. The blue light of Aradel's ice magic changed, as did the heat that Darha was drawing to herself. Darha's eyes went wide as blue flames engulfed Aradel's hands, making her jump and hold them away from her body. The same blue fire was also what was coming toward Darha. When it touched her hands, she realized this fire wasn't actual fire, because it burned cold instead of hot, yet Darha's skin was not burned. Out of nowhere, a soft sigh of wind seemed to sweep over them as the blue flames danced on Darha's and Aradel's fingers.

Panting in shock, they met each other's eyes, and stared in horror and wonder at each other. "Cold fire?" Aradel breathed. Darha couldn't even speak.

Both Queens looked back at Freya, who was consumed with such utter horror that Darha nearly smiled. Her expression soon melted into hatred again. "I WILL KILL YOU ALL!" she screamed, and summoned another blast of frost and fire magic in her palms.

Darha and Aradel both moved forward and, side by side, shot a stream of the blue flame Cold Fire magic at the young woman. Freya didn't even have time to scream before she was frozen solid. It was a different kind of frozen, one that didn't encase her in ice like the Frost Nation could normally do. This magic penetrated her skin and froze her blood, and she instantly turned into blue gray stone.

Darha and Aradel stared at Freya in astonishment, and then down at the cold blue flames in their hands. Darha was awestruck by them. She

241

was a proficient magic user, and she'd never conjured such a thing. And to have the Frost Nation Queen summon the same substance was something she doubted anyone had ever even heard of.

A loud crack drew Darha's attention back up to Freya. The ice under her frozen form had broken apart, weakened by the battle, and she splashed down into the water like a rock. Aradel ran. Stunned, Darha ran after her. Grabbing her elbow, Darha stopped her at the edge of the broken ice, and both beheld the depths of the river. The young woman's form was only a sinking shadow.

It was eerily quiet. The only sound Darha could hear was the wind softly whistling past her ears. "We did it," she said gently. She regarded Aradel and saw the pain etched in her expression. Aradel then fell to her knees by the hole and gazed down into it in disbelief. "What's wrong, Aradel?"

Aradel looked up at Darha as a single, involuntary tear slipped down her pale cheek. "I just killed my niece."

Darha's eyes went wide. "Oh no." Aradel didn't respond as she gazed back into the hole. "That's why you looked so conflicted when she first appeared yesterday."

Aradel nodded. "I thought I could save her." Aradel swallowed when her voice almost broke. "She was all I had left of my sister."

Having no words of comfort, Darha knelt beside her and drew her into a warm embrace. Aradel gladly received the comfort and rested her head on Darha's shoulder.

A few moments passed before they realized what was happening. They sharply drew away from each other. "What in the..." Darha breathed, looking at her hand resting on Aradel's shoulder blade.

Aradel in turn gazed at her own hand on Darha's arm. They met each other's eyes, round as dinner plates. "That doesn't burn you?" Aradel asked.

Darha shook her head. "I'm not burning you?"

"No," Aradel responded in a breath.

Both women experimented by touching each other's arms, neck and hands repeatedly, and were shocked each time the other's touch didn't hurt, or fracture skin, or turn to stone. A smile slowly crept over Darha's face. She wondered if this new phenomenon was just between her and Aradel or if it could possibly be nationwide. If it was nationwide...

"Please tell me you have some idea what is going on," Darha said with a smile.

Aradel grinned. "It must be the will of the gods!"

Getting to their feet, both Queens raced over the ice toward the shore. They'd just touched the dirt when Kirill, Cas, and Coor all rode up with half an army of Fire and Frost Nation soldiers and magic users. Neither Coor nor Kirill looked pleased with them at all, but Darha couldn't even bring herself to care when her eyes rested on Cas.

"Aradel!" Kirill bellowed as he dismounted his elk. "I knew you would—"

"Wait, wait," Aradel interrupted him. Darha looked at Aradel, only to find Aradel already staring at her with tears in her eyes. She rested a hand on Kirill's chest when he approached, and shifted her eyes to Cas. "Commander Cas," Aradel said. "Please come here."

Cas glanced at Kirill. Kirill's brow went up curiously before he nodded. Cas dismounted and approached both Queens, bowing at the waist. Darha's heart was racing as she looked at him. What if he could touch her without burning her? What if she could touch him?

"Would you please take Queen Darha's hand?" Aradel said.

Cas's brows furrowed with worry. "Queen Aradel?" he asked, unsure.

"Please," Aradel insisted, her face set in a hopefully expression.

Cas looked back at Darha and bit his bottom lip regretfully. Finally, he reached his hand out and hesitantly took Darha's. Darha gasped, and Cas's eyes went wide when there was no pain. Before Darha could even take a breath, Cas closed the distance between them, and his hands were on her cheeks as he stared at her face in shock. No words were necessary; Darha wasn't sure any were even possible. Cas leaned down and pressed his lips to Darha's, and his kiss said it all. It was Darha's first lengthy kiss, and she never wanted it to stop. Being kissed by a man she loved was indescribable, a feeling she could never repeat.

"Hey, easy," Coor said, feigning irritation. "That's my baby sister."

Chuckling, Cas and Darha pulled away from each other, but Cas didn't break eye contact with her. "I am in love with you," he said as he caressed her cheeks. "I have been in love with you since I saw you crying on the river during our supply run to you."

Darha gazed into his pretty eyes. "I'm in love with you, too."

Cas smiled and kissed her one more time. Darha then melted into his chest and he enveloped her his arms. She took in a deep breath through her nose, taking his warm clean smell deeply into her senses before exhaling again. So, this was the man she was meant to love. She'd always

243

wondered what he would look like, what he would be like. Now she didn't have to wonder. He was here.

Darha's eyes rested on Aradel and Kirill, and Kirill looked at Aradel with unconcealed astonishment. "What happened?"

"It's over with," Aradel told him. "We've won."

"Freya?" Kirill asked.

"Dead," Aradel whispered, and Darha's heart went out to her.

"That doesn't explain," Kirill started, before pointing back and forth between Darha and Cas as they touched each other unhindered.

Aradel laughed lightly and shook her head. "We don't know what happened." She took Kirill's hand and pulled him toward his elk. "Perhaps there is something at the temple. I need to speak with High Priestess Kerin," she said as she mounted. The long train of her dress spread out over the back of the elk.

"The High Priestess? What would she know?" Kirill asked as he mounted in front of her.

"All of the historical books that might explain this were stored under the temple long ago for safekeeping. Cas," Aradel called, "escort Queen Darha and the Fire Nation back to Hurra." Aradel held onto Kirill as she looked at Darha. "I will speak to the High Priestess in Axion and return with any news." Darha nodded as Kirill took up the reins and turned his elk south.

Cas took Darha's hand and guided her toward his own mount before facing her. "Have you ever ridden an elk?"

Darha laughed. "No, I can't say I have."

Cas's grin widened as he took her waist and helped her onto its back. It felt very similar to riding a horse, only an elk had different hair, and a massive set of antlers on its head. Cas mounted in front of her and she wrapped her arms around his waist, her heart still racing over the fact she could touch him so casually all the sudden.

"Hold on," Cas said.

Darha found herself smiling. "Don't worry. I'm not letting go."

Frost: Chapter Forty-Three

———————— o ————————

Kirill frowned at the musty books that surrounded him and crossed his bulky arms to keep from knocking anything over. In a rush to preserve their culture and history when the last war had ended half a millennium ago, many of the most ancient books came here to the temple basement. Aradel was on the floor, her skirts spread out around her, as she turned the page of the hundredth one she'd looked at. Under her was an oversized cushion, and around her were stacks of more unread books.

"Why exactly am I here?" Kirill asked.

"You want to keep an eye on me," she said, turning a page and tipping her head in the process, "and I want to keep an eye on you."

He grumbled a little and shifted his feet. He'd lost the grime but had kept the beard, mostly because his mother had loved it and recognized him. Thea had made fun of him when he went to check on her, as he expected she would, by saying, "Wow, you clean up nice, frost flake. I barely recognize you." But her smile and friendly caress of his face made it clear she liked it as well, so it stayed.

"I'm not worried you'll do anything stupid," he grumbled. "There's nothing stupid left to do."

"Perhaps I'm simply giving Thea a break," Aradel said, and he saw her fighting a smile as she turned another page.

Kirill rolled his eyes. "She's bored and stuck on bedrest," Kirill reminded her. "I'm doing her a favor."

"You're annoying her husband," she pointed out, glancing up at him before turning another page.

His gaze narrowed. After Freya had been defeated, and the Fire Nation was no longer in danger of cold temperatures, they'd invited Thea and Coor to stay at Axion. At first Thea had protested, but when her healers told her it would be better for the baby to lie in a comfortable bed rather than the makeshift cot she'd been on, she reluctantly agreed. Apparently, her motherly instinct trumped her smart mouth.

"He is worse than I am," Kirill said with a frown.

Aradel laughed and put her thumb in the book to hold her spot before resting it in her lap. She gave him a brilliant smile, the type that made him involuntarily smile in return. He inspected her face and saw a strange glow of happiness he didn't remember seeing there before.

She put a hand out, "Help me up."

When he reached over, his hip caught a pile of books and they cascaded down toward her. She gave a surprised cry and pulled her dress out of the way. He managed to catch most of them, but despite their efforts, some still landed on the edge of her skirt.

"You're like a bull in a glass shop," Aradel laughed as she reached for the books pinning her skirt.

Kirill pushed the rebellious books back up onto the table as Aradel stood, hugging the fallen ones to her chest. After placing them on the pile, one seemed to catch her eye. She hesitantly took it, and Kirill peered at it as she turned its spine up.

"What is it?" he asked.

Aradel carefully opened it. The spine protested. It was so old that Kirill could hear it crinkling. When she read the first line, she brought a hand to her mouth, then glanced up at Kirill. "This is it. This is the first queen's diary. High Priestess Kerin was right. It was down here."

"Are you sure?" Kirill asked, leaning over her slightly.

She put her finger on the page and started reading. "'My husband marches to the battlefront, and as he kissed me goodbye this morning, I had this sense of foreboding that I would never see him again. I fear on this day I shall have kissed him for the last time. This time he faces the king of the Fire Nation, and I fear it will end in both their deaths. I am powerful, but Queen. My duty is to my people, safe behind our wall, as my husband marches to certain death...' It is marked for a few days before the end of the war."

Kirill looked at her. "Let's go and tell the others."

Aradel passed him and all but sprinted up the stairs with Kirill close behind. When they reached the upper parts of the temple, it was dark. The torchlight cast shadows across the floor as they hurried out to the street. Some people called to Aradel as their queen. She gave them a moment's regard, but they could tell she was in a hurry. Sometimes Kirill forgot she was queen. For so long she had been Aradel, but she had become more than that to everyone else. She moved with ease through the world now. Finally, she had found her place.

The Queen's sleigh was always ready and waiting as it was now. Kirill couldn't help but smile as she climbed in and immediately sat down to open the book. She had it pressed firmly in her lap as the sleigh took off toward the palace. Kirill leaned back and let the wind wash over him, taking in the fresh air that had been deprived him in the dank makeshift library.

When they reached the palace, workers were returning home so the streets were busy. Some called to Aradel and shook her from her fervent reading. She waved and thanked them as she stepped down from the sleigh. Kirill followed close on her heels. She continued to read as she walked, and Kirill was careful to keep her from running into anything.

"Aradel," he censured when he took hold of her arm so she didn't trip over some stone cutting tools.

"Hmm?" she asked, gazing up at him questioningly.

He put a hand on the book, covering the pages. "We should wait until we're all together."

She looked down at the diary longingly before carefully closing it, and nodded. "Thea will be in the new great room in the western wing. I'll get Darha from her suite and meet you there." Not waiting for a reply, she hurried off.

Kirill shook his head after her before turning toward the northern half of the newly constructed western wing. The new section had been added during the reconstruction to accommodate fires. Just because cold no longer affected the Fire Nation in such a terrible manner, didn't mean its citizens liked heat any less. So, they'd added a new stone wing to the palace to accommodate their needs, while leaving the eastern wing exactly as it had been. Here, stone and wood kept everything together instead of ice.

When he opened the door, heat poured out of the room and against his face. Two heads turned to him as he entered—those of a hopeful Thea and her husband, who stood next to her chair by the fire.

Thea sighed. "No success again today?"

Kirill kept his face carefully neutral as he closed the door behind him, and came over to crouch on the other side of Thea's chair. She glowed with the early traces of pregnancy and happiness. She might not have liked being bedridden, but she had adjusted easily to the idea of being a mother.

"Aradel found something," Kirill informed her and smiled.

Thea's surprise turn to playful annoyance and she punched his leg. "You did that on purpose," she said, and Kirill found himself laughing.

"It isn't nice to jest with a restless pregnant woman," Coor pointed out.

Coor and Kirill had come to an easy accord where Thea was concerned. They weren't really friends, but they both loved the spunky woman between them. It had been enough to ease tensions, and they had come to an understanding of sorts.

247

"I'll show you an *angry* pregnant woman if you don't tell me what she found," she snapped, but her words held no real fire as her smile softened the edges of her voice.

The door opened and a blushing Aradel, flushed Darha, and preoccupied Cas all entered. They each seemed engrossed with different parts of the room, and Kirill surmised quickly what had happened. Apparently Aradel had interrupted something between Cas and Darha. Kirill thought about clapping Cas on the back when they joined them, but one glance at Coor and Kirill decided against it.

"She found the first queen's diary," Kirill informed Thea, which brought the new trio back to reality.

Aradel held the book up with excitement. "I read some on the way over. Apparently after both nations' kings died in the last war, their surviving queens met. That was when the Fire Nation Queen suggested an ancient curse that the Derser Recs had unearthed, and had been protecting for thousands of years."

"A curse?" Darha asked, coming around to stand next to Aradel. "What kind of curse?"

"I don't know. I didn't get that far," Aradel said.

"Well, keep reading!" Thea demanded.

Aradel nodded and scanned a few lines before continuing. "It starts with the two queens meeting in secret. Here it is. 'It was with a heavy heart that I listened to the queen of the Fire Nation. The death of my husband nearly broke me, but what she suggests is far worse. Cursed. We would curse ourselves, and our people, so that we might live. I can see grief on her face, etched into every line. The fight has gone out of her like it has gone out of me. I know this war has claimed family and friends alike, and I am ready to end it. I agreed with Queen Ria, though it made me a little sick. Were it not for the possibility of reversal, I would have denied her suggestion outright. Instead, I took her hands into mine, and we read the curse, infusing it with the power of the moon pearls. In a flurry of fire and ice, we did what was best to end the devastation of this war, and made the cold fire, praying it would be enough. Our nations would be forever separated because of our intolerance for the climate and temperature of the other. The more powerful the magic user, the more they are affected by the opposite temperature source. This will keep them apart, stop them from fighting. I know that it is best, but I wonder how many people will die from an early spring or late winter because of our choice. Only if two queens like ourselves create the blue flame can the curse be undone. We shall say it is in the will of the gods, and build bridges to remember, and hope. And we shall let our terrible deed be lost to time.'"

Aradel's voice drifted off, and the room was filled with silence. Kirill finally spoke after a moment. "Two queens to make the curse, and two queens to break it."

"It must have been so terrible for them," Darha said, shaking her head.

"A terrible burden," Aradel agreed.

"A mistake," Thea interrupted sharply with a hard look on her face. "A mistake we will not repeat."

It was a sentiment that everyone in the room could agree with.

———————— o ————————

Darha's head rested heavily on her hand that was propped up on the arm of the chair she sat in. An easy and gentle smile was on her face as she watched Thea, Coor, and Kirill discuss baby names for her niece or nephew.

"You are not naming your child that!" Kirill cried.

Thea was laughing so hard that her arms were clutched around her stomach and she was almost doubled over.

"Coor!" Kirill cried. "Tell her she's not naming your child that!"

Cas came over to Darha and handed her a mug some sort of Frost Nation native drink that was delicious and warm. She wrapped her hands around the mug and tried to take it, only Cas didn't yield it to her. She looked up at him and he smiled before leaning down to kiss her lips. Darha grinned and took the mug as he sat down on the free arm of her chair.

Coor stiffly shrugged his shoulders with a playful smile at Kirill. "I don't know. Kitzu has a nice ring to it for a boy."

"No," Kirill protested with a groan.

Darha was chuckling as she shifted her position, resting her elbow across Cas's lap, and watched the ensuing hilarity.

"And I do like Firill for a girl," Coor added.

"Darha," Kirill said facing her. "Help me out."

Darha held her hand out helplessly. "I agree with them."

Kirill sighed heavily and rolled his eyes. "You're all insane."

"Kirill, Kirill," Thea said, resting a hand on his knee. "I'm naming our child after you and Fitzu in some shape or form." Her smile was one of deep fondness and tender affection. "My baby wouldn't exist if it weren't for you two."

That did it. Kirill took in a deep breath, then leaned down and kissed the top of Thea's head. "Fine. Condemn your child to a lifetime of bullying. See if I care." He started out of the room, pausing at the door and looked back at Coor and Thea. "But if Kitzu or Firill come to me complaining about bullies, I won't be responsible for my actions after that."

Everyone in the room laughed. "Of course, Uncle Kirill," Thea said.

Kirill had nearly made it out of the room, but stopped in his tracks, and looked back at her with wide eyes. "Oh no. That's not happening."

"Uncle Kirill," Coor said, grasping his chin and pondering as he looked up at the ceiling. "I like that."

Kirill huffed loudly in annoyance before leaving the room, and everyone remaining burst into laughter again. After it quieted down, and Thea and Coor started talking about names again, another Frost Nation soldier came to the open door and knocked.

"Queen Darha?"

Everyone's attention went to the door. "Yes?"

"Captain Idok, majesty," he said with a bow. "Queen Aradel requests your presence in the royal conference room."

Darha's brows dropped. "I'm scheduled to meet her there in two hours. Is everything all right?"

"Yes, majesty. The business to be conducted has unexpectedly been able to be moved forward. I'm here to escort you."

Darha's brows jumped up. She took a long drink from her mug before standing.

"Business?" Thea asked.

Darha nodded and placed the mug on a nearby table. "We're signing the peace treaty." She leaned down to kiss Cas's lips and then went toward the door, smiling back at her brother and sister. "I'll be back. Don't decide on any names without me." Thea and Coor chuckled together as Darha left the room.

Idok was quiet as he escorted her down the halls of stone and wood until they gradually became halls of ice and stone. The cold was still uncomfortable, and Darha shivered as she gazed at the magnificent halls of ice, but at least it wasn't painful. She did pause, however, when she saw a group of Fire and Frost Nation children being escorted by a teacher, who was instructing them on history. She grinned seeing the unruly, red hair of Emma. Her heart warmed. This was a thing she never thought she'd see in her lifetime. Fire and Frost coexisting side by side.

When the children were gone from sight, Darha was guided through the throne room, which was still under construction. Frost magic users milled about, and most nodded politely at her as she passed. She heard a few whispers that mentioned her and their Commander Cas, which made her blush. A few conversations broke out about her using the Wild Fire that took out more than half the enemy army, to which Darha blushed even more. She hadn't meant to summon it. She hadn't even known she could; it had just happened.

Finally, Darha was led behind the throne to a set of open double doors. Idok stepped into the large office area and bowed. "Queen Aradel. Queen Darha has arrived."

"Thank you, Idok." Aradel said.

Idok stepped out and the doors were closed. Crossing her arms over her chest to try to keep warm, Darha made her way over to the wide desk behind which Aradel stood. "Your officials drafted the peace treaty quickly."

Aradel smiled before she went to a nearby closet. Reaching in, she pulled out a heavy wool and velvet cloak of a stunning deep purple color, and handed it to Darha.

"Oh, thank you," she said, wrapping it around her shoulders quickly.

"There was no need to draft it," Aradel went back to her desk with Darha close behind, and pulled open the top left hand drawer. "I had just begun to sort through Queen Vesna's things and found this."

Aradel pulled out a document and rested it on top of the desk. Leaning over slightly, Darha peered at the parchment and scanned it quickly. It was a peace treaty already drafted.

"Look at the date," Aradel said.

Examining the top right hand corner, Darha saw it was dated just one day after the very first meeting between the Fire Nation and the Frost Nation.

Darha's jaw went slack, then she looked up at Aradel. "Queen Vesna knew."

Aradel nodded. "She always seemed to know." She dipped a feather into an inkwell and handed it to Darha with a smile. "Shall we?"

Darha grinned, took the feather from her, and signed her name. She handed it back to Aradel who did the same. Both women took a deep breath and sighed heavily at the same time which made them laugh.

"This was long overdue," Darha said.

Aradel nodded. "It was."

Darha smiled and went to the window of the office that overlooked the Frost Nation's land toward the north, toward home. Aradel joined her.

"Did Kirill agree to head up one of the teams to rebuild the bridges?" Darha asked.

"He did. He claims he's just doing his job as a Frost Nation commander, but I think he wants an excuse to visit Thea and your future nephew or niece after Vlid is rebuilt."

Darha threw her head back and laughed. "That makes sense. Coor also agreed to head up a team."

Aradel's eyes got wide. "Those two working together? Without Thea to keep them in line? This should be interesting!" Both women laughed. After it settled, Aradel said, "Oh, before I forget…" She returned to her desk, pulled out another piece of paper, and handed it to Darha.

Darha's eyes got wide. "It's a permission document for Cas's leave," she whispered in astonishment.

Aradel smiled. "You can't very well cultivate love and a relationship if he stays here while you return home." Tears filled Darha's eyes. "If he wants it, he may take it and return with you to the Fire Nation. He will always remain a solider of the Frost Nation, but the Fire Nation will be his home."

Darha nodded once and wiped her eyes. "Thank you, Aradel."

Aradel rested a hand on Darha's shoulder. "Of course, Darha." A knock on the door commanded both of their attention. "Come in," Aradel called.

Idok entered and bowed. "Tallus, son of Yorten, has arrived, my Queen."

Aradel smiled down at Darha. "See him in please."

Darha smiled a little mischievously when a handsome, curly-haired southerner, with sky blue eyes and dark brown hair walked into the office and bowed. "You summoned me, Queen Aradel."

Darha instantly saw the shift in her fellow Queen to one of deep softness and love as she gazed upon him. This was clearly the man she was speaking about when meeting in her tent a few weeks back. Darha could tell from his posture that he was a humble person. Yet he wasn't mousy in his movements. He had a subtle confidence, and a soft smile.

"Indeed. Tallus, this is Queen Darha of the Fire Nation."

Tallus bowed at the waist again. "A pleasure to make your acquaintance, majesty."

"The pleasure is mine, Tallus." Darha responded with a nod.

"Tallus, if you could wait in the hall, I'll be just another moment."

"Of course." He smiled at Aradel once more before leaving the room.

Darha met Aradel's eyes and saw her smiling in a way only love could provoke. "After years of strife between our people, I believe it's time we made ourselves a different future." Aradel started toward the door with a brilliant smile. "Tell Cas to take the leave and not come back."

Darha chuckled. "I'll pass the message along."

253

Aradel nodded. "Good. I shall see you at dinner."

She disappeared out the door and Darha was left gazing north toward her homeland. So much work needed to be done. But with this new peace, and this new man by her side, she was looking forward to it. There was nothing the Frost Nation and the Fire Nation could not do together as allies, as friends, as lovers, as partners. Everything appeared hopeful and bright, and Darha could not wait for their new, shared future to begin.

Notes from the Authors

————————— o —————————

Readers,

Welcome to the end of yet another adventure! The reason this was unique?
We live on the other side of the country from each other. That's right, we
wrote this amazing adventure together thousands of m iles apart. Which is
amazing if you consider it but not impossible in the world of technology
and unfailing determination. We combined our individual writing
strengths, world-building to action scenes, to bring you the action packed
fantasy adventure you just finished. Don't want the adventure to end?
Take a moment to do a review, send us an email of encouragement, or tell
all your friends about. If it becomes popular enough, who knows what
could happen!

Thanks for reading,

Nichelle Rae and K.T. Munson

Contact Information

○

K.T. Munson

Email: k.t.munson1@gmail.com
Twitter: http://twitter.com/ ktmunson
Facebook: https://www.facebook.com/K.T.Munson
Pinterest: https://www.pinterest.com/authorkt/
Subscribe to my blog: http://creatingworldswithwords.wordpress.com
Favorite me at Smashwords:
https://www.smashwords.com/profile/view/KTMunson
Amazon Author Central: http://www.amazon.com/K.T.-
Munson/e/B00YHQFF2G/ref=ntt_dp_epwbk_1

Nichelle Rae

Email: Nichelle_Rae@yahoo.com
Twitter: @Nichelle_Writes
Facebook: www.facebook.com/NichelleRaeAuthor